PILOT ERROR

Tosh McIntosh

Austin, Texas

PUBLISHER'S NOTICE

This is a work of fiction, which began with the author pondering the meaning of the universe and asking himself a very simple question: *What if?* Names, characters, places, events, and incidents are either products of the author's imagination or used fictitiously. Any resemblance to actual persons, living or dead, is purely coincidental.

Therefore, Dear Reader, if you think you recognize yourself within these pages, it's not my fault.

ACKNOWLEDGMENTS

To those familiar with the publishing industry, this page is considered part of the "front matter" that often includes the author's humble attempt to recognize the contributions of those who provided invaluable assistance along the seemingly never-ending journey from concept to reality.

As well we should, for it is my steadfast belief that few writers, if any, can in isolation bring into existence a story that works from the first word to the last without being forced by others to exit the creative fog required to complete it. The tired cliché ". . . can't see the forest for the trees" is more than apropos.

But if I were to attempt to do that here, the front matter would require far too many pages, and I would undoubtedly fail to include everyone who so unselfishly gave of their time and expertise. To avoid such a *revoltin' development* (and for that term I offer acknowledgement to William Bendix in *The Life of Riley* for borrowing one of the most famous catch phrases of the 1950s), I'll make this simple.

Ann Katherine McIntosh, light of my life, you have my everlasting gratitude for your unfailing support through years of struggle to realize this dream. And to my fellow writers who read and critiqued countless pages of false starts and detours, thanks a million times over to all y'all. (For those of you who don't know, that's talkin' Texan!)

DEDICATION

To my father, may he rest in peace, who wrote short stories and kept the carbon copies in loose-leaf binders on the bookshelves in my childhood home in Dallas, Texas. I never saw the originals. They disappeared into envelopes addressed to many of the popular magazines of the day. To the best of my knowledge, none of his stories made it into print to be read by the public.

And that matters not, because I have never forgotten the experience of turning those flimsy pages and reading the words my father wrote. As for so many other things, I owe him a lifelong debt for unlocking my imagination and instilling in me a passionate love of storytelling.

CHAPTER ONE

Wilson didn't *want* to kill the guard and leave a mess behind. Someone might get curious, nose around, ask questions. No, the job tonight required stealth. He loved that word. And the synonyms, like furtiveness. That just sounded right, especially when whispered. It slid off the tongue. He'd prolong the "s" and think of himself as a viper in the night, coiled like a spring, silent and deadly.

From his hiding place near the edge of the dark, woody greenbelt, he peered through the airport perimeter chain-link fence at the hangar thirty yards away. Raindrops slapped on the hood of his parka and the blanket of leaves around him. Cold wind rustled the branches above his head. He preferred working with nature's white noise as an ally, but tonight it favored the guard, all the more reason for caution.

Wilson had initially accepted this assignment on contingency because he'd never tried to penetrate the secure area of an airport. Especially after 9/11, it seemed far too risky. But his concern proved to be groundless. Of the 19,000 airports in the US, only a small percentage received the security upgrades designed to prevent aircraft from being used as weapons of terror, and for good reason. To fly the largest airplane based here into a skyscraper would be like a suicidal bug smashing into the windshield of a Mack truck.

Earlier that day, he had masqueraded as a salesman for an alarm company and offered the owner of the hangar a security survey. The man laughed him out of the office. Said he couldn't afford it, especially to prevent something that had never happened. Besides, the airport authority paid for a night watchman. Didn't cost him a penny. Now, Wilson understood why.

The guard, a typical rent-a-cop "door rattler," sang country music while walking his rounds. The fool announced he was coming. And he never varied his routine. Every half-hour since midnight, he'd taken a smoke break, protected from the steady drizzle by the awning over a door on the back side of the hangar. Atomic-clock predictable.

Wilson peeled back the cuff of his parka and glanced at his watch: 2:47. The guard was taking his nicotine hit fifteen minutes early. Wilson needed less than ten minutes and could still do this without bloodshed unless the idiot started chain-smoking.

He pulled the pistol from his waistband through an opening in the outer pocket liner of his parka and screwed the silencer into the barrel. Then he checked for a round in the chamber and a full magazine, and slipped the weapon in his parka's belt. Eyes on the guard, he waited.

Two minutes later, the guard dropped the butt on the ramp, ground it out with his boot and began walking toward the far end of the hangar. Wilson stepped up to the fence, reached above his head and shoved his fingers through the links. Lucky for him, it had no topping of razor wire and served primarily to keep deer off the runway. Just like his airport at home. He'd seen what colliding with a full-grown Bambi could do to an airplane on takeoff or landing, and it wasn't pretty.

As the guard turned the corner, Wilson climbed over the fence, ran across the ramp, unlocked the door with a battery-powered pick gun and stepped inside. A row of ceiling lights bathed the cavernous interior in ghostly white. Airplanes, portable worktables, and wheeled tool boxes were jammed together like a jigsaw puzzle. Faint odors of aviation maintenance lingered: fuel, oil, paint, heavy-duty cleaning chemicals. Comforting, in a way. Reminded him of his hangar.

Weaving through the maze, he made his way to a cabinet mounted on the opposite wall. Aircraft tail numbers identified the open, partitioned sections in the cabinet as distribution boxes for each of the airplanes based at Schiller Aviation. The section labeled N924DP held two tattered cardboard containers sitting side by side on a shelf.

He removed the one marked IN, knelt, and placed it on the concrete floor. In the beam of a small flashlight held in a nylon pouch sewn on his watch cap, he thumbed through the contents: two eight-by-ten-inch envelopes imprinted with the logo of a navigation chart provider and addressed to Larchmont Enterprises, LLC, one business envelope from the Golden Aircraft Company, and a small electrical part in a plastic baggie with a green SERVICEABLE tag. The innocuous, everyday items of aviation on their way to an airplane.

And inside his parka, an addition. He lifted out a padded mailing envelope and took one final look at the postage, address, and return labels. No one would ever guess it hadn't gone through the US mail. He placed the mailer in the container, returned it to the shelf and retraced his route across the hangar.

With his face close to the glass, he peered through the small window set into the door. No sign of the guard. Wilson eased the door open and looked to his left where the guard had always appeared from around the corner of the hangar, then to the right. Nothing. He took one step outside and froze.

Embedded within the sounds of rain and wind, something foreign drifted on the gusts. He closed his eyes and tuned out the background. After a few seconds, he retreated into the hangar and let the door close gently. Way early, the karaoke guard had suddenly turned even more unpredictable. Wilson pulled out the pistol, heavy in his hand, comforting. Like an addiction. The anticipation ratcheted up his heart rate just enough to heighten his senses and add another layer of *alert*. He sidestepped left past the hinge edge of the door.

After a moment the guard appeared in the window and stopped under the awning, two feet from the door and facing the forest. Wilson leaned to his right, took a quick peek down, noted the guard's duty belt with a radio and a flashlight carrier. No weapon. He relaxed a bit. All he had to do was wait a few minutes, watch the door handle for any movement to warn him—*damn it!* The door rested against the latch bolt and hadn't closed all the way. If the guy turned around and saw that . . .

Wilson flattened himself against the hangar wall, raised the pistol to the level of the guard's head and took up the tiny bit of slack in the double-action trigger. One step inside, he'd have to put the guy down. So much for an easy in and out.

After a few seconds, barely audible over the wind and rain, a click, a rasping snap, pause, another click. A Zippo lighter. Cigarette smoke drifted through the slim crack between the door and jamb. Wilson eased his pressure on the trigger and took a deep breath. The smoke awakened a familiar hunger that had never really left him.

He had quit over twenty years ago. For his health, although fear of cancer had nothing to do with it. On that night, two steps from the mark, Wilson's knife poised to strike home, the guy had ducked, swiveled, come in low, hard, and fast. Wilson had almost died, and the man's last words remained with him still: *I smelled you.*

He enjoyed a second-hand smoke until a boot wet-grated on concrete, stubbing out the cigarette. The guard began singing a recent country hit, something about being unlucky in love. Not bad, actually. He ought to turn in his flashlight for a microphone. The voice faded away as the guard continued his rounds.

Wilson lowered the pistol, breathed in deep, held it and let his pulse calm down a bit.

Over the years, in spite of all the planning and preparation for countless jobs, it so often came down to something as simple as this. One small coincidence either passes into history as a freebie or changes the complexion of future events. Tonight, he gladly accepted the gift.

Wilson opened the door and checked both ways. He slipped the pistol in a jacket pocket, stepped out, closed the door, and sprinted for the fence. Ten minutes in the greenbelt at a fast walk put him at the edge of the woods along a deserted street. On the other side in a motel parking lot sat his rental car, inconspicuous among many. Just the way he liked it. He closed his eyes to listen and zone in on the night. Nothing. He strode to the car and climbed in.

With the heater on high, he poured a cup of coffee from a thermos, wrapped his hands around the cup, and after a moment drained it in a few swallows. He shook the empty thermos, wishing for more. It felt like he'd never warm up. *Getting too old for this field stuff.*

He yanked off his gloves and blew into his hands, then took a small piece of notepaper from an outer pocket on his cargo pants and set it between his legs on the seat. He removed the flashlight from the pouch on his watch cap, held it close to the paper to shield it and focused the beam.

Holding his cell phone in the other hand, he entered the ten-digit sequence with his thumb, pausing after each number to concentrate before pressing the next one. When the complete phone number was displayed, he carefully compared each digit on the paper with the screen before he pressed TALK. After three rings and a beep, he said to the silence, "Operator Forty-One, activate, one hour," and turned off the phone.

So much for the groundwork. The time had come to watch and wait, to be there just in case. The anonymous voice would soon begin calling on the secure line, pestering Wilson about when it would happen. He would ignore the inquiries as he always did. Contact with clients occurred at his convenience. The next time they spoke, the topic would be money. Lots of it. Enough to call it quits.

And he was so ready. Ready to abandon the double life. Ready to live in the light. And maybe one day he'd be able to stop looking over his shoulder. No more nightmares with the eyes of the dead staring at him. Put his head on a pillow and leave it all behind for longer than a few hours.

A check in the rearview, both side mirrors, and all around the parking lot found nothing but dark rooms, sleeping cars, wet asphalt, and pale shafts of rain under yellow streetlights. He pulled the pistol out of his jacket and laid it in the seat by his leg, then eased the car out of the lot and accelerated into the night toward a rendezvous with someone else's death.

CHAPTER TWO

Miles Larchmont stared into the early morning gloom through the rain-streaked, bulletproof left rear window of the Lincoln Town Car. He yawned, stretched and glanced at his watch. A long day awaited and he was already tired.

The dreary weather reminded him of that moment earlier in the year when he'd been partying for hours and the usual rabble of unrelenting paparazzi ambushed him coming out of a nightclub. Microphones jabbed at his face, bright camera lights blinded him, and a rapid-fire barrage of questions assaulted his eardrums. As his drinking buddies escorted him toward the car, two shouted queries cut through the fog of alcohol.

"What will you say to the American people?"

"Who do you think you are—?"

"A patriot, goddamn it!" His answer stilled the group in a freeze-frame of anticipation. Raindrops pattered on a forest of umbrellas. "Just what this country needs more than ever."

A companion gripped Larchmont's arm and turned him away.

Then, the life-altering question: "How about a real statement for a change?"

Yanking his arm free, he swiveled to face the bastards. "Tell them I won't be going down alone."

Two friends hustled him to the waiting limousine. He slumped in the rear seat along with the bitter knowledge that his loud mouth had done it once again. He'd give almost anything to rewind the tape and—

"We're here, Mr. Larchmont," said the driver.

Larchmont shook his head, sighed, and glanced out the windshield. A sign with the Schiller Aviation logo appeared in the headlight beams. The bodyguard riding shotgun lifted an assault rifle off the floor and nestled it in his lap as the driver pulled into a parking spot by the front entrance.

Larchmont opened his own door, climbed out onto the wet asphalt and looked up. Ragged clouds of the first autumn cold front skimmed overhead, glowing red from the hazard beacon atop the water tower adjacent to the hangar. Depressing. A perfect match to his mood. He faced the two men. "Take a close look at the jet. You got the dog coming?"

"Yes, sir," said the bodyguard. "That's the K-nine unit."

A dark van with no markings careened into the lot and skidded to a stop. A man in black fatigues hopped out and opened the sliding side door. Eager to sniff something, or maybe bite it, a German shepherd lurched against a heavy leash tied to a seat support.

Larchmont stayed behind the open door of the Town Car until the handler had the dog under control, then slammed the door and walked toward the main entrance. To the driver, he said, "Get to it. I'm in a hurry." He hadn't gone three steps when behind him, the rumble of a massive V8 announced the arrival of P. J. Knowles, Larchmont's personal mechanic.

Larchmont glanced over his shoulder. A black 1971 Pontiac GTO turned into the lot. Beads of rain covered the muscle car in glistening droplets on countless layers of wax, vivid evidence of the meticulous attention P.J. paid both to his car and to Larchmont's twin-engine jet.

P.J. revved the engine. Racing slicks spun on the asphalt in a spray of water. Larchmont waved hello, shook his head and continued toward the entrance. With 500 horsepower at his command, P.J. had a reputation as a wild child, especially on the open road. Larchmont shared the common opinion that the hot-rodder was living on borrowed time.

"Mr. Larchmont?"

Larchmont paused at the door and turned. "Morning, P.J."

P.J. trotted up, opened the door and motioned Larchmont through. "Are you flying today, sir? I didn't know."

"Not to worry. The jet's always ready to go, right?"

P.J.'s face registered instant displeasure at such an insulting question. "Absolutely, sir."

Larchmont always enjoyed needling his mechanic. Not a lot, his life was in the guy's hands, but just enough to keep him on his toes, paying attention. He stepped through the door and said, "Then let's pull her out."

With a cup of tasteless coffee from the communal pot, he went to the pilot's flight planning cubicle. After logging on to his favorite aviation website, he checked the weather and filed only the first flight plan of the day to ensure his complete itinerary wouldn't be stored on Air Traffic Control computers. Too many prying eyes out there, and such precautions had unfortunately become a way of life.

Current weather observations and twelve-hour forecasts indicated low clouds and rain for departure and similar conditions in Colorado that evening. Clear weather prevailed over the rest of his route. Good. At least he wouldn't be flying in the murk all day.

He grabbed a copy of the three major newspapers delivered

to Schiller every weekday morning and sank down in a soiled armchair in the pilot's lounge. Two articles about the war on terror appeared in the national and world news sections. Neither mentioned his name or the pending investigation, but one followed up yesterday's announcement of a successful attack on the base camp of a recently discovered terrorist "super-cell."

Then the bomb-damage-assessment photos caught his attention. He snatched his reading glasses out of his shirt pocket, slipped them on, and held the page closer to the lamp beside his chair. His heart thudded in his chest. The room seemed to have lost all its oxygen.

He knew that camp. Or what was left of it. Bomb craters the size of small lakes had replaced most of the buildings, but the unique relationship of the river and the road in a figure eight left no doubt. The bastards were shutting the operation down in the only way they knew how.

With trembling hands he folded the papers and set them on the coffee table. The inside of his left wrist began to itch. He rubbed the red, circular patch of fresh skin, took a deep breath and glanced at the muted TV hanging from the ceiling. Behind an immaculately coiffed blonde, film footage from a smart bomb showed the final seconds of a building Larchmont knew only too well.

He vaulted out of the chair, frantically searched the lounge for the remote, gave up, peered at the base of the TV and pressed the volume control. A sliding green bar advanced across the screen in sync with the loudness of the blonde's words, ". . . and this just in, photos from the special forces team on a mop-up operation confirmed the deaths of all twelve terrorists that intelligence reports indicated were operating out of this base camp. We caution you that the following contains graphic images."

Larchmont's knees tried to buckle as he stared at the photos. Bits and pieces of human beings didn't tell him much, but the face of one relatively whole corpse substantiated his worst nightmare. If this guy had died along with eleven others, Larchmont was the single remaining eyewitness to an undertaking best consigned to the shadows. He had just become the clean-up team's next target.

He rushed into the hangar. A jet undergoing inspection dominated more than half of the enormous building. Mechanics had removed instruments, the refreshment center, overhead and side panels, seats, carpet, and floorboards. In addition to the insurance considerations, this display of apparent chaos was the main reason Schiller never allowed customers into maintenance areas. But as an owner-pilot and substantial contributor to Schiller's bottom line, he could ignore NO ADMITTANCE signs with impunity.

Avoiding the clutter around the dismantled jet, he hurried through the hangar to the parking ramp. The main cabin door on his airplane was closed, P.J.'s head visible through the cockpit left side window. Larchmont always flew solo, but the mechanic on his own initiative had taken over many of the preflight duties normally performed by a copilot. He was probably updating navigation charts.

One of the bodyguards approached with Larchmont's roll-aboard suitcase. "All done, Mr. Larchmont. Would you like us to go with you?"

Unfortunately, what he would like and what he had to do were like oil and water. "That won't be necessary. I'll let you know my return date and time in the usual way."

The man saluted with a casual wave and departed. Larchmont stowed his luggage in the aft baggage compartment and opened the main cabin door. He climbed in, turned left toward the cockpit and squeezed his 200-plus pounds between the refreshment center and the single aft-facing passenger seat.

P.J. sat on the captain's side with a brown leather binder in his lap. Loose, outdated navigation chart pages lay scattered on the copilot's seat. He slipped an en route map into a plastic sleeve and snapped the binder closed. "There. You're all current. Anything else?"

"No, and I'm in a bit of a hurry." Larchmont backed into the cabin.

P.J. nodded and laid the binder in the copilot's seat. He crumpled the outdated chart pages into a ball, hauled himself out of the cockpit, and paused. One foot on the top step, he looked at Larchmont. "When can I expect—?"

"I'm *really* in a hurry."

"Yes, sir." P.J. stepped onto the ramp and strolled toward the hangar. Larchmont closed and secured the cabin door, checked all six locked-pin indicators, and entered the cockpit. He eased into the left seat and picked up the chart binder to put it on the floor between his seat and the center console. A brown padded mailing envelope lay in the copilot's seat.

Larchmont turned to his left toward the pilot's "foul weather" window. A holdover from earlier days of aviation, the window could be opened from inside the cockpit, even while in flight. He couldn't imagine doing that, but on the ground, it was a convenient feature. He rotated the latch, opened the window and peered out. P.J. stood talking with another mechanic. "Hey, P.J.!"

"Yes, sir?"

"You forgot this." Larchmont held the envelope out the window.

P.J. trotted over and took it. "Sorry, Mr. Larchmont."

"No problem." After performing his usual abbreviated

flight preparations, he started the engines, listened to the current weather, received his clearance, taxied to the active runway and launched into the gray overcast on the first leg of a getaway trip.

LATER THAT EVENING AFTER two stops, one in Chicago to visit a safe-deposit box, Larchmont filed a flight plan to Denver Centennial Airport. He had no intention of landing there, but the head fake would keep them guessing. To determine his current position, all they needed was his aircraft tail number, and they could monitor his progress on flight tracking websites. Avoiding predictable routines had become a necessity, like water.

About thirty minutes from Denver, he changed his destination to Cedar Valley, Colorado, where his ranch offered a level of security and protection he could not maintain anywhere else. A large staff and a steady stream of guests meant safety in numbers. The watchers would consider this just another of his frequent visits and never suspect that from there he was about to disappear into the sunset. He couldn't wait to bid the bastards farewell.

He glanced around the dim cockpit. His gaze settled for a moment on the right seat, occupied only by his briefcase. More than one person had told him he was crazy to fly single pilot. They said he didn't have the necessary experience and skills, but their doubts and criticisms only made cockpit solitude that much sweeter.

"Golden Nine Two Four Delta Papa, Denver Center, how do you read?"

Why did the controller sound so pissed? Larchmont keyed the microphone. "Four Delta Papa reads you loud and clear."

"That's the third call, Four Delta Papa. Expedite descent to and maintain flight level three two zero."

Damn it. This was no time to let his mind wander. He acknowledged the instruction, selected the new flight level in the altitude alerter, programmed the autopilot controller for a 2000-foot-per-minute descent, and eased the throttles back. Denver Center soon cleared him to lower altitude. Passing 28,000 feet, he selected the secondary radio and listened to the automated weather report at Cedar Valley Municipal Airport: winds out of the north at ten knots gusting to fifteen, visibility two miles, with light rain and mist, ceiling 800 feet overcast, temperature six degrees centigrade, dew point four, altimeter 29.75. Typical late fall conditions. Not to be taken lightly, but he'd seen a lot worse.

Cedar Valley Airport had no tower control or terminal radar services. Denver Center would position him for an instrument approach, and once he descended into the valley, he'd lose radio contact. Talk about being on your own. With darkness, mountainous terrain, and poor weather, the time had arrived for some of that precise flying no one else believed he could do.

Shortly after Larchmont leveled the GoldenJet at 9,000 feet, the controller turned him to a heading for intercepting the final course and issued the approach clearance: "Golden Nine Two Four Delta Papa, I show you slightly right of final approach. Maintain niner thousand until established, cleared for the GPS Runway Three Five approach at Cedar Valley. Radar service terminated. Switch to traffic advisory approved. Cancel your flight plan via land line after landing. Good evening."

Although he'd often thought of these moments as cutting the umbilical cord from "Mother Denver," Larchmont had heard these instructions so many times it was almost soothing. He acknowledged, changed the radio to the Cedar Valley frequency, and announced his presence and intentions to any other pilots foolish enough to be flying in this crap. He scanned the cockpit: fuel quantity—good, fuel balance—within limits, fuel cross feed—off, landing V-speeds—calculated and set, cabin pressure—checked and set, recognition lights—on—no, that's way too bright in these clouds, altimeter—29.75, defogger— on high, anti-ice—damn it. What was the temperature at the airport?

He flipped the secondary radio selector switch on to check the weather again and confirmed it was above freezing at the surface. The outside air temperature gauge in the cockpit read one degree below freezing. His airplane had cold-soaked for two hours at 38,000 feet. These were perfect conditions for structural icing, and he hadn't prepared the airplane for it.

His breathing increased as he peered out the side window at the left wing. Couldn't see anything. Turn on the wing inspection light, fool. The light flooded the upper surface of the wing with a brilliant glow, stark white against the blackness. His heart pulsed like an internal exclamation point. Ice coated the leading edge, adding weight and disturbing the airflow over the wing. Even his long-dead grandmother knew that equaled big trouble, and here he was letting it happen.

He had to get that crap off: engine anti-ice switches—on, wing and tail de-ice boots—automatic, windshield heat and defog fan—on. Fan noise and warm air on his face confirmed operation of the defog system. White de-ice boot advisory lights on the annunciator panel lit up to indicate proper cycling, but two sets of amber caution lights told him the engine and wing anti-ice systems weren't working. Why the hell not?

He stared at the lights. Ever since initial training on the GoldenJet, he'd thought the ice-protection systems must have been designed by Rube Goldberg. Lights on meant this, when they went out you knew this, but sometimes they blinked and then you had to guess. Why didn't they work like a toaster? Flip the damn switches on and forget about them?

At this moment, they should have been—hold it—maybe that was normal. Or was it? He struggled to recall the systems diagrams, all those valves opening and closing in the right sequence, and finally remembered that turning the switches on sent hot engine bleed air and electrical power to the surfaces, but the lights wouldn't go out until everything heated up. They'd cycle after that. Okay. Ignore them and fly the jet.

His instrument crosscheck settled into a scan of the attitude and horizontal situation indicators, airspeed, altitude, and descent rate, then after a moment came to an abrupt halt. Something didn't correlate. He concentrated on the moving-map navigation display.

The controller had said he was offset to the right of the final approach course. A correction to intercept the desired track to the runway required a heading to the left of the desired course. The GPS had steered him on a heading in the wrong direction. What the hell was going on?

He keyed the microphone and asked the controller to verify his position. No response. Confusion, then the realization that he'd changed frequencies. A glance at the altimeter—too low for radio contact. Climb and start over? No. He was tired and had probably misheard the controller. Back to business.

One glance at the annunciator panel to check on the ice protection dried up his throat. The amber caution lights still glowed bright in the darkened cockpit. The damned things were mocking him, laughing, gloating because the wings and engine intakes weren't being kept free of ice. Why not? He stared at the engine turbine speed indicators. *Damn it, Miles.*

At the lower power settings for the approach, the valves

diverting hot bleed air to the anti-ice system remained closed Get them open. He lowered the flaps to the approach setting and extended the speed brakes to increase drag, then advanced the throttles to maintain his desired approach speed and get the hot air flowing.

Left hand resting on the yoke and right hand on the throttles, he monitored the autopilot. When it captured the final approach course, he rolled the vertical speed control into a descent and checked the altitude alerter for the next level off at 7,900 feet, the minimum altitude specified until reaching eight miles from the airport.

In his peripheral vision, the amber anti-ice lights flickered, went out. Finally. The tension in his shoulders eased. As he waited for the autopilot to capture the new altitude, he glanced at the approach chart clipped to the yoke to confirm his next altitude restriction and acknowledged the special note:

MOUNTAINOUS TERRAIN ALL QUADRANTS.
USE EXTREME CAUTION DURING PERIODS OF
LOW CEILING AND RESTRICTED VISIBILITY. NIGHT
OPERATIONS NOT RECOMMENDED.

Larchmont appreciated the dangers involved, but he'd flown into Cedar Valley too many times for a little bad weather to shoo him away.

After passing the next navigation fix on the approach, he could descend to 6,400 feet and hold that altitude until three miles from the runway. Only then would it be safe to descend to the minimum altitude authorized, pick up the approach lights and complete the landing.

Then he'd drive to the ranch, take that first sip of River Rock Pale Ale, and sink into his favorite chair with his feet propped on the ottoman in front of a crackling fire. His personal haven. He often fell asleep there and woke up the next morning without a care in the world. At least for a while.

He glanced over his shoulder at the left wing and the fear climbed the back of his neck to the top of his skull. Highlighted against the black night in the pale glow of the inspection light, horizontal streams of water droplets sped by at 130 mph. A thick layer of glistening ice still coated the leading edge. The pneumatic de-ice boots had failed to crack the ice so the slipstream could carry it off the wing. That was probably true of the tail as well, but he had no way of checking it.

How much ice was there? The thickness guide on the leading edge was completely covered up. He'd never seen that much. What next? Abandon the approach and climb through the icing to safety on top of the clouds? How far was it to clear air? After a few seconds he realized it didn't matter. The runway was the closest haven, and with the extra weight of the ice, he could descend easier than he could climb. He hadn't been to church in fifty years, but he muttered a little prayer for divine intervention just in case it might make a difference.

At five miles from the airport, he keyed the microphone button seven times to illuminate the runway lighting system and lowered the landing gear. Four miles from touchdown, he keyed the microphone again and reported his position to no one because every other pilot within radio range had his head on a pillow.

He selected full flaps at three miles, retracted the speed brakes and eased the throttles back to begin his final descent.

The nose pitched up.

He disengaged the autopilot and shoved the yoke forward. The airplane fought him, airspeed decreasing, the nose trying to pitch up higher. Bewildered, he pushed the throttles forward and with both hands on the yoke tried to regain control.

Suddenly he remembered a cold-weather operations warning not to use full flaps after flying more than ten minutes in continuous icing conditions. He flicked the flap switch to the approach detent. Pressure on the yoke decreased. But the airplane had climbed. He was too high on the descent profile. He yanked the throttles to idle and lowered the nose.

Through the left quarter panel in the glow of the landing lights he caught a brief glimpse of trees . . . where they shouldn't be.

He slammed the throttles forward and hauled back on the yoke. The jet sagged under him, shuddered, clawed for altitude. Stinging beads of sweat fell from his brow into his eyes.

He blinked. The vertical speed indicator became his world, the needle his salvation.

"Climb, you son of a bitch!"

The needle twitched and began to rise just as the jet pitched down and threw Larchmont into the instrument panel and windscreen.

CHAPTER THREE

Nick Phillips wiped the last bit of white haze off the fender of his Porsche Carrera and stepped back to admire the perfect results. If only he had a place to drive it. Bumper-to-bumper creeping in Washington, D.C., was like riding a thoroughbred in a Fourth-of-July parade. He'd probably spent more hours waxing the beast than he had enjoying the feel of it: alive, eager, its headlights peering ahead in vain for some open road. And truth be told, this Saturday morning's love-fest of elbow grease and Carnauba had only been an outlet for nervous energy.

He glanced at his watch and tapped the crystal. As if that would make the hands move any faster, or encourage his wife and daughter to hurry the hell up, go shopping for that *perfect* homecoming dress, and give Nick a little privacy. Laurie wasn't the problem, she knew all about the project from the beginning. Stephanie wouldn't intentionally spoil the surprise, even for her *totally* obnoxious younger brother, but she came into this world curious, missed nothing, and couldn't keep a secret if her life depended on it.

In the back of the garage three boxes lay hidden from prying eyes, filled with hard-to-find special parts for a 1968 Mustang GT 390 Fastback that Nick was restoring as a surprise for Brad's sixteenth birthday. A buddy of Nick's owned a body shop and had agreed to help finish the remaining few items, which were proving the adage that the last 5% of the work on any project worth doing takes 95% of the time.

The kitchen door slammed. Nick looked over his shoulder. Laurie climbed into her new Suburban, parked in the driveway because the two-car garage was dedicated to a workshop and, of course, the Porsche. He glanced at the clearance between his car and the edge of the driveway, mentally fit the Suburban in, decided no way. Not without a safety observer. Less than a month old, Laurie's "tank," as Nick often referred to it, already had a rear-bumper ding, evidence of her touchy-feely method of backing up.

He walked over to the driver's door and tapped on it.

Laurie looked up from programming an address into the navigation system and lowered the window. "Good morning, sweetheart. You were up early."

Nick leaned in. "Couldn't sleep with that human foghorn beside me. How's the tank been working out so far?"

Laurie shrugged. "That foghorn was caught in *your* throat. As for my *vehicle,* I've been thinking I need something even bigger."

"You're joking."

"Not at all. A real tank. The cannon would be really helpful in beltway traffic."

Nick shook his head. He'd best give up. Laurie could banter him to death with his own words. "When is Brad due home?"

"Haven't you learned that he totally rejects the concept of being *due* anywhere?"

"My mistake. When do you expect he will next grace us with his exalted presence?"

"Aha. Something car-sneaky going on?" When Nick

nodded, she said, "You probably have until Sunday night."

"Roger that."

Laurie laid her hand on Nick's shoulder. "How are you feeling about this?"

The tear dams in Nick's eyes threatened to break. He coughed, swallowed hard, and looked away. His father had wanted to rebuild a classic car with Nick for his sixteenth birthday. Death in a plane crash robbed them both of the experience. Although a generation late, this father-son dream would finally be realized in just over two weeks. "I wish Dad could be here to see this."

Laurie took Nick's chin gently in her hand and turned his head to face her. "I know you don't believe it, but I think he will be."

The kitchen door slammed again. Stephanie ran up to the car, climbed in the front passenger's seat, and immediately began texting on her smart phone.

Nick looked at Laurie, shook his head, said to Stephanie, "What is it about greeting family members in the morning that you do not understand?"

Her thumbs continued tap-dancing on the screen. "Hi, Dad. Can we go, Mom?"

Nick shrugged. "Yeah, you better rush out there before all the really nice dresses are gone. But don't worry. I hear they have some new burlap fashions over at the Bargain Barn."

Stephanie's thumbs froze above her phone as she fixed Nick with a stare that she had inherited, learned, or otherwise acquired from her mother. "Oooh. Cool. I could do a B-movie cave-woman thing. Low cut, slit way up the side, lots of thigh. Get all those young studs fighting for my favors."

Get out of this while you can, Phillips. When he tried to establish restrictions on the amount of cleavage the real dress would reveal, Laurie set him straight.

"That's my department. All you have to do is make sure the—uh . . . that you take care of that leaking faucet."

Nick smiled. "You drive carefully, dear." He stepped between the Suburban and the Porsche. Laurie managed to back up without running over his toes. Nick waved goodbye and went into the kitchen for a cup of coffee before inspecting the parts. A glance at the muted TV in the breakfast nook stopped him in his tracks. The CNN crawler read: Miles Larchmont killed in the crash of his private jet.

Nick's heart did a double thump. He snatched the digital wired-to-the-world device from the holder clipped to his belt. Ringer volume at maximum. No blinking red light. He was the on-call Investigator-In-Charge of the Aviation "Go" Team. The National Transportation Safety Board Command Center should have notified him immediately. What the hell was going on?

He watched a Headline News report. The accident happened last night. If someone had screwed up the notifications, the team was well on its way without a leader. Twenty years' personal experience dealing with government bungling had taught Nick to expect almost anything, but not this. Pick up the phone and scramble the Go Team. How hard can that be?

Nick muted the TV and stared out the kitchen window. Maybe there was a simple explanation. His vacation began in two weeks and covered Brad's birthday and Stephanie's homecoming. Vulnerability for call-out lasted right up to midnight of his final calendar day on duty. To avoid being scrambled on an investigation that would extend into his vacation, he'd arranged for a backup IIC. What if they had done him a favor and replaced him with another lead investigator? Yeah, right.

The NTSB wasn't into favors. No one would automatically make the switch. Scheduling procedures protected both sides of the employment aisle by establishing duty obligations and off-time privileges. There had to be another reason, and for the duty officer to ignore Nick's number-one on-call status meant that someone way above his pay grade had interfered. The question was, why?

He poured a cup of coffee while he dialed the NTSB Command Center. As the phone began ringing, he paced around the center island. Nervous energy usually flowed out through his feet. After the duty officer spouted his standard greeting, Nick said, "Why didn't you scramble me on the Larchmont accident?"

"Hello, Nick."

"Has the team been activated?"

"Good morning to you, too."

"Sorry. I'm just in a hurry. What's going on?"

"We got the team scrambling. Looks like it's going to be a big one."

Nick felt as if his feet had just stepped in floor mastic. "What the hell are you talking about? I'm the duty IIC."

"Uh . . . well . . . that may be, but when I'm told to do something, I usually don't argue."

Nick resisted the urge to bite the man's head off. He was only doing his job. "I apologize for barking at you. What happened, please?"

"Director Nordstrom said he'd pick the team leader."

Of course. Nick ended the call and tapped the handset repeatedly into his other palm. The kitchen felt like it was shrinking, collapsing around him, and he wondered if his being replaced might have something to do with the victim.

Like every other American, Nick had been following the

controversy for months. Miles Larchmont, veteran of the most successful covert operation in CIA history, had allegedly been recruited to mastermind a secret anti-terrorist campaign. Under his direction, a unit of assassins had roamed around the Middle East, snatched bad boys out of their lairs, and filmed the executions.

The operation remained in the shadows until the beheading of a man later found to be innocent. The video contained inconclusive evidence, but enough to implicate Larchmont, and it left him standing alone above the radar. Justice Department indictments loomed. His public statements threatened to reveal links to the White House, and from there all the way to the Oval Office.

Nick didn't care much for conspiracy theorists who blamed any event they didn't like on government dirty dealing. On the other hand, the arrogance of absolute power frightened him, and his trust of politicians wouldn't fill a thimble. He had regularly visited a new website, larchmontwatch.com, to check up on the latest news, rumor, and fabrication regarding the most notorious name in America. In addition to all the mainstream media attention, the website's core assertion touched a raw nerve:

The government asked Larchmont to help keep us safe from the abomination of global terror. He responded brilliantly, but ultimately allowed patriotism to cloud his judgment and jeopardize the operation. Politically disadvantageous, he became a liability. Rather than own up to what they've done, cowards in the White House abandoned him with denial, and they are content to let him pay the price for their violation of national and international law.

And as of this morning, Larchmont was dead. How

convenient. For whom? Who stands to gain the most? That's not a difficult question to answer. The possibility that Larchmont had been eliminated by the very hands that previously patted his back and fed him made Nick's blood run hot.

So, what should he do about it? He could just stay home. Turn off his phone, or like a commercial some years ago about kicking back with a bottle of wine, throw the damn thing as far as he could into a lake. Finish up the Mustang, plan out how he would introduce Brad to his new ride, and get emotionally ready to watch Stephanie be crowned homecoming queen. His little girl. He almost couldn't believe it happened so fast.

But how would turning his back on an unjust world feel as he sat on the sidelines? He pondered that for a few minutes, then hustled upstairs into the study to check the latest on larchmontwatch.com. The site and associated forums looked like they were filling so fast with content they might explode. One article discussed the effect of bombs in airplanes and predicted the investigation would ultimately prove sabotage killed Larchmont. Nick could sit there all day reading and not begin to keep up, but that wouldn't help solve his dilemma. He pushed away from his desk and went back downstairs.

Unsure of his next move, he paced around the kitchen, which felt like a cage. He opened the refrigerator, realized he wasn't hungry, shut the door and stared at the phone. After a few moments he decided to see what his asshole boss had to say.

The infuriating automated phone system at the office put Nick on hold, but his resolve hadn't ebbed one bit by the time he reached Lars Nordstrom, king of the career-obsessed bureaucrats. "What's going on Lars?"

"Uh . . . I'm sitting at my desk and—"

"This isn't a social call, damn it."

"Whoa, Phillips. Last time I checked, you work for me."

Nick almost threw his coffee cup through the kitchen window. He took a deep breath, set the cup down on the counter and shoved his free hand in a jean pocket. "I'm painfully aware of that. I also know the duty IIC gets the first call."

"Don't lecture me on procedure. I wrote the damned book."

A comic book, maybe, titled *Mr. Bumfuck Goes to Washington.* "That's doubtful, but at least we agree on what it says. Why did you replace me?"

Nordstrom sighed, and the earpiece hissed with frustration and impatience. "I didn't. You arranged for a backup."

So that was it. Nordstrom had been snooping around. He probably sent Dickson out to gather intelligence, an oxymoron for sure. "That's between my backup and me."

"Okay. I'll tell the Command Center to call you. Then *you* get the replacement. What I do after that is none of your concern."

"I heard they didn't call me out because you told them not to."

Nordstrom coughed. Nick had worked with him long enough to recognize the signal, a precursor to a well-developed talent for manipulation. The pen-pusher's silky voice oozed out of the earpiece. "I assumed that's what you'd want."

Nick stayed silent, often the best tactic in dealing with Nordstrom. Let him have the floor. The man had a habit of sawing a hole under his feet.

Another cough. "And I want Dickson to get more experience as IIC."

James Dickson was Nordstrom's protégé, even better described as a clone. Political animals both, they'd align themselves with the prevailing winds and never think twice about selling their souls. Nick made his decision as easily as breathing. "Sorry to upset your plans, but I'm taking the investigation. You don't want to fight me on this."

Nordstrom laughed. "And why not, pray tell?"

"Because I'll make a phone call, and an official complaint regarding your blatant favoritism toward Dickson will put the tit of your career in a wringer." Nick held his breath. Gambling wasn't his strong suit, but he was pretty sure Nordstrom had never held a deck of cards, much less played games of chance. *Especially* with his precious career.

After a silent moment, Nordstrom exhaled deeply into the phone. "Okay. Fine. Have it your way."

Nick breathed out as well, hung up and stared out the window above the sink. The garage and the Porsche faded into a haze as his eyes de-focused in thought.

He'd taken a chance, but only a tiny one. Nordstrom's plans to advance to an appointed seat on the Board needed smooth sailing, and supervisors were expected to prevent any turmoil from rising above the surface of bureaucratic tranquility.

And even if his boss had stood his ground, the risk to Nick's career was worth it. No way could he ignore the case being built in the media and on larchmontwatch.com for a high-level government conspiracy of silence. And a Nordstrom-Dickson coalition would be the perfect puppet act for the White House. What better way to arrange a cover-up?

Enlist a couple of government minions eager to please. The investigation would be like dial-a-finding. You want weather to be a factor? Check here. What about pilot error? Fill in this blank. A quick investigation? No problem.

But that was not going to happen on Nick's watch. And to make certain it didn't, he would play two roles during this investigation.

One, official and on the surface, didn't include paying the

slightest heed to political controversy. He would investigate this accident in keeping with the single purpose of the NTSB, to determine cause in the name of safety and accident prevention. Period. And if, in the normal course of the inquiry, he discovered any indication that sabotage had played a role in Larchmont's death, he would hand over lead status to the FBI. Then he'd take directions from the Special Agent In Charge. Just like the book said.

In the meantime, unofficially and behind the scenes, he'd examine every piece of that jet with a microscope if that's what it took. And short of falsifying evidence, he was going to prove what he felt in his gut was true. Somebody messed with that airplane to shut Larchmont's mouth for good.

Nick stood up very straight, as if his backbone had just been fused to a steel rod. *They have no idea who they're dealing with.*

He poured his cold coffee into the sink and scrambled upstairs. From his closet he hauled out a large duffel bag pre-packed with the basic essentials and spent no more than five minutes shoving clothing into it. After consulting his mental packing list, he grabbed his wool-lined flight jacket off a hanger and dragged the bag to the top of the stairs.

He paused and looked down the hall, an essential part of the departure ritual developed over many years of being on call, never knowing when he'd be ripped away from his family or how long he'd be gone. It was as if he had to absorb as much of *home* as he could before he walked out the door. The connection always leached out of him during investigations no matter how hard he tried to resist it. The search for answers, the importance of the job, and its very personal relationship to Nick's past shoved everything else in life aside.

Light from his son's empty room spilled into the hallway.

Nick stepped inside to turn off the reading lamp. A book on muscle cars lay open on the desk, evidence of Brad's fascination with powerful engines and gleaming paint. Nick smiled. He couldn't wait to see his son's face when the cover came off the Mustang.

He glanced at the watch strapped to his left wrist. An old Bulova. His father had been wearing it when he died piloting his airplane. The second hand seemed to be ticking in sync with the beat of Nick's heart. He turned off the lamp and closed Brad's door.

The door to Stephanie's room opened to reveal the environmental disaster his daughter preferred for living space. Along with total rejection of her parents' preference for a neat and tidy house, she had embraced the independence of young adulthood since the age of five.

He took a deep breath. It was as if everything she touched smelled like flowers. As far as he could remember, even changing her diapers—well, that might be going a bit too far. He closed the door and once again stood at the top of the stairs. *I'll miss you guys.* He carried his bags to the garage, called his wife on her cell phone and told her about the trip.

Laurie's voice took on the knife-edged quality she used when she was *not* pleased. "You have got to be kidding me."

Nick swallowed, tried to find moisture for his dry throat. He'd rather walk on bona fide thin ice than do so with Laurie. Whenever she said, *You're on thin ice, Buster,* she meant it, and her tone now carried the message loud and clear. He swallowed again, as ineffectively as the last time. "Listen, I—"

"It's your turn to listen. I was *really* looking forward to this vacation, Nick. I thought you were as well. I guess I was mistaken."

"If you will just let me finish, please?" After a moment

of silence, Nick continued, "It's not an either-or deal. The investigation will slow down by Brad's birthday. I'm taking the airplane, so I can make a quick trip back for that. We'll be done before homecoming. You can trust me. I'm going to be here for the kids. Or for me, which is probably more accurate."

"It doesn't matter who you want to be here for. May I remind you of the term *you* love to haul out of your convenient excuses bag? OBE. You remember that one, don't you?"

Sure he did. Overcome by events. It came with the territory, but he wasn't about to say that. He cradled the phone against his shoulder and began cramming the duffels into the Porsche. The ten-pounds-in-a-five-pound-bag saying came to mind. "Look, I'm not making excuses, but I can do a small private jet in my sleep."

"So can that backup investigator you arranged. Let him catnap through this one."

"I . . . I can't do that."

"Why not?"

Nick wanted to recruit Laurie's support for his decision, but he couldn't involve her in the details. How would he do that? Something like: *I'm going out there to conduct a murder investigation, darling. I know that's not my job, but gee, it will be so much more exciting!* Not hardly.

"I'll have to explain later. It'll work out, Laurie, I promise."

"Sorry, but I'm all full up with your promises. Mark my words, Nick. If any of this crap you peddle about the importance of family means anything, you'll plant your ass at home. Since I don't expect to see you this evening, I guess that settles it. See you . . . whenever."

Nick listened to the dead phone for a moment, stuck it in his belt clip and took a deep breath. His mind struggled with the ever-present dilemma: family first; career first; both first, but in sequence.

Ah, yes. That last one, his own special brand of compromise. He'd balanced the tradeoff for years. He could do that again. Couldn't he?

He glanced at the boxes full of Mustang parts. The mechanic could finish it, but—damn. He'd have to come by for the parts. Maybe this afternoon. Or Monday. That would give him enough time. Pay him a nice bonus. Nick called his friend and arranged it.

Ten minutes later, he eased the Porsche out of the driveway for the drive to a small, outlying airport serving the needs of general aviation. Virginia to Colorado, he could be there . . . about noon tomorrow with a stop for the night just before dark and an early launch in the morning. It felt corny to think it, and he couldn't even imagine saying it out loud, but all these years of picking through piles of wreckage for tiny clues couldn't possibly compare with one week of hunting for evidence of murder.

IN A ROOM FRAGRANT with the aroma of leather and lemon-polished wood, Lars Nordstrom propped his feet on his massive mahogany desk and sipped a very dry martini. He didn't much care for gin, but many powerful people he knew drank it. And he needed some heavy-duty fortification to help control his temper. He was so mad at Nick Phillips he could barely stand it.

James Dickson lounged in an overstuffed chair on the other side of the desk. He set his Jack Daniel's on a coaster and leaned forward. "I should get going."

Lars glanced at his watch. "You've got time to finish your drink."

Dickson settled back in the chair, which appeared ready to swallow him. "I still don't think Phillips would have filed a complaint. He's got as much to lose as you do."

"You can afford to think whatever you want, but you might remember that it's my coat tails you're hanging onto."

Dickson raised his eyebrows. "How could I forget?"

Lars frowned. What the hell was this? National Day For Underling Rebellion? He felt like slapping the starch out of Dickson but resisted the urge and took another sip of the martini. "I really thought it was going to be easy. He arranged for a backup IIC, so why would he care if you took it?"

"Jesus, Lars. That's a no-brainer. He hates my guts. By the way, how the hell did you find out about his vacation?"

"I'm his boss, in case you've forgotten. The dates are in his personnel records. And I keep this," he held up his fist, forefinger extended, "on the subterranean pulse of the Division. He's restoring a car for his son's birthday, and he's committed to being in town."

Dickson shook his head. "Charging off on an investigation is a strange way to show it."

"You got that right." Lars stared out the window overlooking the greenbelt behind his house and thought about this speed bump in his plans. Phillips was a top-notch investigator, but he wasn't going to be the next Director of the Aviation Division. Dickson, malleable, easy to control, had a lock on the position because Lars had given him the key. This investigation would be perfect for showcasing what the NTSB did for the American public: lights, camera, and action with Dickson at the podium, doing and saying exactly what Lars told him to. But with loose-cannon Phillips grabbing all the publicity, no telling what would happen. The guy had no concept of how to manage perception. He acted like he didn't give a damn, and he probably didn't.

Dickson sipped his bourbon and chased it with Perrier. "Okay, we lost this one. What can go wrong?"

"Plenty. This is aviation." Lars drained his glass and poured another dose of power from a stainless steel mixing cup. From the ice-cold gin he retrieved two olives speared on a yellow cocktail toothpick, pulled off one with his teeth and chewed. He pointed at Dickson with the toothpick and remaining soused olive. "I just got an idea."

Dickson grinned. "Quick. Call the Public Affairs Office."

Lars glared at his favorite gofer, who was very close to being shown the door. "I'm in no mood for any of your crap, James. Stuff a rag in it." When Dickson appeared to sink into the chair with his patented subservient expression and lowered eyes, Lars leaned back, gobbled up the last olive and said, "Here's what I want you to do."

CHAPTER FOUR

"Experimental Eight Five November Delta, Denver Center, over."

Nick jerked. Had he been daydreaming? "Denver, Five November Delta, did you call?"

"For the third and hopefully last time," the controller barked, "Cedar Valley is at your twelve o'clock, seventeen miles."

Little sleep and diverting around thunderstorms had dulled Nick's senses. He mentally slapped himself alert and stared through the propeller arc, sunlight glinting on the blades. "Airport in sight, sir. Cancel my IFR." He didn't really see the airfield, but he knew where it was, and with clear skies he didn't need an instrument flight clearance for the landing.

"Cancellation received, Five November Delta. Radar service terminated. Squawk VFR, frequency change approved. Good day."

Nick switched his transponder to the code used for visual flight rules and changed the radio to the local Cedar Valley frequency. He scanned the engine instruments to confirm all the readings were normal and switched to the wing tank with the most fuel. At fifteen miles to go, he eased the throttle back, increased the fuel mixture, and began a descent.

His "ride," an experimental two-seater low-wing monoplane with a 250-horsepower engine, gained airspeed with elegant grace. Fully aerobatic, it also had good cross-country performance and fulfilled his every need as a part-time aviator, who flew partly for convenience but mostly for the pure fun of it.

Cedar Valley Municipal Airport nestled against the opposite side of the ridge, barely visible through the haze. With no control tower to provide safe separation, "see-and-be-seen" rules required pilots to coordinate among themselves. Whenever approaching an unfamiliar airfield, Nick put himself into "head on a swivel" mode to avoid playing "air tag."

Position reports from other pilots alerted him to three aircraft, two performing touch-and-go landings and one on a practice instrument approach. As he neared the ridge and gained line-of-sight to the airport, he banked left to enter a spiraling descent. The maneuver helped control airspeed, avoided shock-cooling the engine with a large power reduction, and lowered a wing to provide a better view of the topography.

Landing at mountain airports presented many challenges, but he'd seen a lot worse. Here, the difference in elevation from the closest peaks to the valley floor didn't exceed a few thousand feet. Foothills blended smoothly with grass-covered meadows. Oriented on a north-south axis, the runway hugged the narrower, northern end of the valley. The approach path centered on the wider portion to the south, which he estimated to be about ten miles from side to side.

A ridge extended westward into the valley floor from the higher rim to the east. Preliminary information indicated that Larchmont's GoldenJet had crashed while attempting to land at night in lousy weather conditions. The purpose of any instrument approach was to provide safe separation between airplanes and unforgiving terra firma. Something had gone terribly wrong here, and Nick wanted to study the terrain before he examined the physical evidence.

With the airport on his left, he leveled his wings and got a good view of the impact ridge through the windscreen. From his altitude, in a shallow descent passing 9000 feet, the obstacle didn't look like much. He banked into a gentle left turn, held the spiral for three circles, and rolled out on a heading to put the ridge in view off his right wing.

A dark scar against the green background of vegetation on the southern slope of the ridge marked the impact point of Larchmont's jet. Nick stared at the all-too-familiar signature of violent death and couldn't avoid the photographic image of another crash site flashing before his eyes: his father's airplane, splattered against a background of charred earth. It always happened like this, a swift attack from ambush by a predatory memory hiding in the darkness. It never failed to strike him directly in the heart.

He'd just turned seven when the crash took his hero and favorite companion. Nick never accepted the NTSB conclusion that his father had made a lethal mistake. Determined to avoid becoming another family statistic, he'd approached flight training dedicated to achieving perfection in academics, procedures, and basic flying skills. Yet underneath all that effort lay the certain knowledge that one crucial misstep could mean death. The specter of pilot error rode with him every time he took the controls. An uninvited passenger perhaps, but one that helped keep him safe through constant vigilance.

Except when he daydreamed. Like today when the controller had to call him three times. Unfortunately, vigilance didn't equate to perfection.

A radio call filled Nick's headset with the voice of James

Dickson. "Experimental Eight Five November Delta, this is Team One, do you copy?"

Nick shook his head. He should have predicted that Nordstrom would send his protégé along to do clone-like things, which generally meant being a royal pain in the ass. After a pause to let his irritation recede, he replied, "Read you loud and clear, Team One."

"Thought I heard you circling. Switch to team common."

Nick acknowledged with a curt, "Roger that," and dialed in the radio frequency reserved for investigations. Dickson cleared him to enter the restricted area surrounding the crash site. Nick descended to an altitude well above any obstacles, set up an orbit, and peered over the left wing.

The highest point of the ridge was about a mile to the right of the course the GoldenJet should have been flying. The small peak appeared to be at about the same altitude specified as the minimum for that point on the approach. The aircraft had hit a few hundred feet below the top, on a gently sloping rise terminating in a steep rock face. The debris trail and length of the smear leading up to the northern edge of the site indicated a shallow impact angle.

Nick had assumed, for no logical reason he could think of, that Larchmont's jet had slammed into a more vertical obstruction. But this looked more like a skip hit. Violent, certainly, though not necessarily fatal. He made a mental note to consider that during his ground inspection.

Easily visible from the air, the distinctive blackened appearance of metal and earth seared by burning jet fuel marked the final resting place of the left and right wings, each of which had sheared off soon after the jet hit the ground. The tail section lay by itself. He couldn't see the forward fuselage well for the trees, but it appeared to be resting against, or very close to, the rock face.

Nick spent a few more minutes orbiting to study the overall site, then signed off with Dickson, switched back to the common traffic advisory frequency and set up for a practice approach. Once established on the published ground track, he noted his position in relation to the ridge and the crash site: plenty of room for error to his left, but much less to the right.

With the landing gear down and locked and flaps extended, he began the final descent. The crash site moved from his one o'clock position steadily farther to his right and aft. He tried to imagine what might have caused Larchmont's GoldenJet to drift off course and hit the ridge. At night and in the clouds, he wouldn't have been able to see anything out the windscreen to warn him of the danger. The thought sent a shudder racing from Nick's toes to the top of his head.

After confirming that another aircraft in the traffic pattern would follow him, Nick chose his touchdown spot a hundred feet down the runway from the approach end, throttled back to reduce airspeed, and raised the nose to landing attitude. As the airplane settled into "the groove," a scratchy radio transmission filled his headset. "Anybody in the pattern at Cedar Valley, mayday, mayday, mayday!"

The shouted international distress call fired every nerve ending in Nick's body all at once. He shoved the throttle forward and selected the landing gear and flaps up.

Simultaneous transmissions from the other three pilots in the pattern turned the frequency into a squealing, garbled mess. Nick timed his next radio call to fit into a silent gap.

"Experimental Eight Five November Delta is on the go, all other aircraft in the pattern at Cedar Valley please maintain radio silence. Break. Will the mayday aircraft only respond and state your position and the nature of your emergency?"

"Can anybody read me?" came through weak, but readable.

Nick kept the throttle full forward and the nose pointed skyward to gain altitude and improve radio reception. The troubled aircraft was probably on the other side of nearby high terrain. "This is Five November Delta. I read you three by three," he said, noting signal strength and clarity on the standard scale of one through five. "What is your position and nature of the emergency?"

Much louder and clearer this time, "I'm in the top of a tree with a bear clawing at my ass. Standby for a position."

A guy crashed and pissed off a bear? That would be a first. Nick half believed it might be some kind of sick joke, but he had no choice except to treat it like the real deal. At least for the moment.

The excited voice spouted geographic coordinates. Nick entered them into his GPS and selected direct-to navigation—286 degrees at seventeen nautical miles—west of the Cedar Valley Airport and five minutes away at 200 mph. He banked, pulled the nose around and rolled out on the heading. The next ridge to the west was barely visible on the horizon.

The voice pleaded, "Can you help me?"

Nick had no idea how, but he'd think of something. "Five November Delta is headed your way. What is your call sign?"

"What?"

"What is your tail number?"

"Don't have one. I was hiking. I'm lucky it's been a good summer and fall. He's so fat he's having trouble climbing up here."

Oh, bullshit. "Okay, look. Time to fess up. This is a prank, right?"

"Not from my viewpoint. I'm staring at a *really big* bear."

"You expect me to believe you carry an aviation hand-held

radio when you hike?"

"If it's okay with you, let's discuss my choice of survival gear another time. Are you going to help me, or not?"

Nick thought about that for a moment and decided no one could fake the concern in this guy's voice. "What's the terrain like around you?"

"I'm in Lone Pine Meadow."

"Are you in the only tree close by?"

"Why the hell you think I picked it?"

Nick liked this guy. "You a pilot?"

"No, but I'd sure like to sprout some wings of my own."

Nick laughed, remembering a Henny Youngman one-liner, something like: "I just flew into town and my arms are really tired." He glanced at the time-to-go readout on the GPS. "I'll be there in three minutes. What's the ground like? Rough, rocky, tall grass, bushes?"

"It's got all that. Maybe you'd prefer the road?"

This might be everyone's lucky day. "Does it have about five-hundred fairly straight feet? I can't land on rocks. Gravel's okay, but it has to be pretty smooth."

After a pause, the hiker said, "At the west edge. Forest Service grades it every year."

"Hang on." Nick began a descent and passed a few hundred feet over the top of the ridge that blocked his view of Lone Pine Meadow. He banked hard left to check it out.

The only tree within a couple of miles sat in the middle of a large grassy area. The road snaked down the western side of the meadow near a line of trees that marked the beginning of a rising slope. Nick circled the solitary pine in a descending spiral. A spot of bright yellow flashed halfway up the tree and a dark shape appeared at the base, might be a boulder—no— boulders don't move on their own. A bear ambled out from under the lowest branches, appeared to gaze at the sky, kind of like, *What's that noise?* After a moment, it disappeared beneath the foliage. The tree began shaking.

Holy crap. That thing could eat airplanes for a snack.

The hiker, really excited, "This guy's getting frustrated. You've got to do something."

Nick had seen airborne videos of bears running from Forest Service helicopters on tagging missions. Would that work? Only one way to find out. He rolled out of his spiraling turn and flew toward the north end of the meadow.

"Where are you *going?*" implored the hiker.

"Hold on, damn it." He didn't have time to explain about how futile it was trying to fly in close proximity to anything inside the airplane's tightest possible turn radius. He needed distance to get lined up properly.

When the rising terrain at the meadow's northern boundary loomed in his windscreen, he pulled back on the stick to pitch the airplane nose up in a sixty-degree climb, neutralized the stick, waited a few seconds, then snap-rolled inverted and hauled back on the stick, grunting against the weight of four g's trying to shove him into the seat. As the nose reached level flight on a southerly heading back down the valley, he relaxed pressure on the stick and brought the tree into the windscreen just to the left of the prop spinner.

Ten feet off the deck, the ground below him blurred into a carpet of green as the airspeed increased. He passed the meadow's namesake close aboard at 230 mph, caught a glimpse of black among the lower branches.

"Wow!" drilled his ears through the headset. "Fantastic, dude! He fell like a sack of boulders."

Nick flew to the southern end of the valley and repeated the classic "split-S" maneuver to reverse his heading. When he leveled out northbound, he smiled. A massive dark shape lumbered toward the surrounding forest. Nick was wearing a noise-canceling headset. The bear wasn't. He made another pass right over the top of the bear, who disappeared into the trees.

When the hiker's cheers over the radio finally stopped, Nick suggested he ought to stay put. With night approaching, a ground recovery would be a much better plan than trying to land on the road. He called an airplane in the traffic pattern at Cedar Valley for a message relay to a Forest Ranger and requested a pickup for one stranded hiker at Lone Pine Meadow.

Nick glanced at his fuel gauges. All that running around at full power had put him close to his personal minimum. For maximum endurance, he slowed to best "loiter" speed to minimize fuel flow and flew in gentle circles over the meadow. After a half-hour, a dust cloud on the road signaled the arrival of rescuers. Nick flew one more low pass, waggled his wings in farewell, and turned toward Cedar Valley.

Fifteen minutes later, the soft bump and chirp of wheels touching pavement washed away the tension from a long, hard day. Nick cleared the runway and followed the signs to transient parking. A crowd of people stood near the entrance to a large hangar. Some were waving, others appeared to be clapping. Word traveled fast in Colorado. Maybe because of the thinner air.

He turned into a parking spot and shut down the engine. The swarm of onlookers crossed the ramp en masse and surrounded his airplane. He opened the canopy. Cheers and applause greeted him as he eased his tired, stiff body out of the seat, onto the wing, and hopped down to the ramp.

Everybody wanted to shake his hand, congratulate him on saving one of their own from the jaws of a rogue male bear that had claimed the area around Lone Pine Meadow as his personal territory. He'd trashed a couple of cars getting to food stashed in the trunks. The Forest Service had relocated him once, but he apparently didn't like his new digs.

Nick overheard a conversation between two men, one of whom thought it had to be a grizzly. No way said the other. There ain't no grizzlies in Colorado. Tell that to Harvey, the first man replied. He may disagree with you.

When the throng finally dispersed, Dickson sauntered up and stood by the left wingtip. "A hero's welcome for the NTSB."

Nick reached in the cockpit for his flight kit. "Glad you liked it."

"Nordstrom assigned me as your number two. That going to be a problem?"

"Not unless he sent you to take over."

Dickson shook his head. "That's ridiculous. It may look like putting me in charge was done behind your back, but he just forgot to tell you."

"Oh. Well, I guess that explains it." Nick placed his flight bag inside a larger duffel and zipped it closed. He picked up the two duffel bags and faced Dickson. "You can do whatever it is you were sent to do, James. I'd prefer that meant staying out of my way, but—"

"No way. I'm here to assist."

Nick almost asked, assist who? But he knew better. Leave it be and make the best of it. "Okay, then. We'll see how that goes. In the meantime, I need to get settled in for a long day tomorrow. Let's meet in the morning about eight o'clock. We'll catch up and get to work."

Dickson almost smiled. "Looking forward to it."

CHAPTER FIVE

The morning after his arrival in Cedar Valley, Nick leaned against the sink and watched the motel-room coffee maker drip light brown swill into a chipped glass pot with no lid. When sugar and grade-A arterial coating disguised as dairy creamer failed to make the stuff palatable, he dumped it in the sink and brushed his teeth.

A muffled ringing brought him out of the bathroom. He traced the sound to an outer pocket of his flight jacket. Fred Anderson's number appeared on the screen. Nick greeted the mechanic with, "You got my son's Mustang ready yet?"

"Last time I checked, this was a two-man project. Where the hell are you?"

"Colorado. You may have heard about the airplane crash out here?"

"How would I? Never get to leave the shop. Got my hands full doing *all* the work on this car."

"How easily you forget all my contributions. Need something?"

"Big bag filled with small, unmarked bills. I found those wheels you wanted, but they aren't cheap."

Nick closed his eyes and tried in vain not to think about how much this project had cost him so far. A bottomless money pit. "You sure they're the same?"

"I rented *Bullitt* and looked at the chase scene. Steve McQueen himself couldn't tell the difference."

"Of course not. He croaked years ago."

Fred snarled into the phone. "Okay, smart ass. I'm tossing this project in the dumpster."

"Bullshit. That car means more to you than it does to me. Can you finish it in time without my help?"

"It'll cost you, but yeah. No problem."

Nick agreed to pay an exorbitant sum for the wheels, confirmed that Fred had picked up the boxed parts, thanked him and sank down on the bed to tie his shoes

Keeping the car a secret had been a challenge since the first day. Nick had sneaked back and forth to Fred's shop, hidden parts in the garage, and made sure Brad didn't overhear any of the phone conversations dealing with problem after problem.

But the most difficult task had been maintaining the charade. The big lie. *Your mom and I have decided we want you to wait a while for your own car.* Listening to Brad complain, you'd have thought the world had come to an end. Some might call it child abuse—Nick knew better. When Brad first laid eyes on that car, the boy would know how much love and affection had been poured into every detail.

Nick stood, grabbed his briefcase and jacket, and left the motel room. The sun had not yet topped the ridge. Shadowed, crisp high-country air condensed his breath into clouds of vapor as he walked to the rented four-wheel-drive Jeep Grand Cherokee assigned to him by the admin crew. Waiting for the defogger to clear the windshield, he decided to stop at a strip mall on the highway near the motel. It might have a real coffee shop.

Ten minutes later, with a large cup of high-octane caffeine

cradled in one hand, he avoided a minefield of potholes in the crumbled asphalt parking lot and eased the Jeep onto the highway. Carved from a hillside covered with evergreens, the road wound its way through shafts of early morning light slanting through the trees. He downshifted to control his speed through descending curves and regretted he didn't have the Porsche. His baby would no-shit come alive on this road. *Let's go for a ride, darlin'.*

A carved wooden sign attached to poles set in concrete pillars marked the entrance to the Cedar Valley Municipal Airport. He turned off the highway through an open security gate. A cluster of media vehicles filled the parking lot of the small terminal building. Out of sight behind the team's temporary headquarters in a large hangar, he locked the Jeep and hurried toward a personnel entry door.

A figure appeared around a corner of the hangar, waved, and jogged toward him. Nick ignored the greeting and prepared to give his standard "no-comment-at-this-time" reply to questions.

A man with the face of the Marine on the recruiting posters aged about ten years in combat approached and extended his hand. "You're Nick Phillips, right? The IIC on this crash?"

Nick shook hands, grimaced as his fingers felt like they'd been crushed in a vise, and read the man's media pass: Harvey Sweet, *Cedar Valley Gazette*. "That's right, Mr. Sweet. Do you offer medical attention with handshakes?"

"Sorry. That was some flying yesterday, Mr. Phillips."

Nick stared at Sweet. "That was you?"

"Still is, thanks to you."

"Glad I could help. If you'll excuse me, I have a busy day ahead." Nick turned away and began walking.

Sweet kept pace. "You headed to the hangar?"

"Yes."

"Mind if I tag along?"

Nick stopped and faced the reporter. "What is it you want, Mr. Sweet?"

"I'll be covering the story for the local paper."

"Good for you. What does—?"

"This is a small town. Nothing much ever happens. The crash is big news, and I've never covered anything like it. How does the investigation *work?*"

Nick motioned for Sweet to follow, turned and walked toward the hangar. "The procedure for liaison with the media is very simple. We disseminate information only during press briefings. Once a day, usually, but that can vary. All you have to do is attend."

Sweet flipped open a small notepad. It looked brand new. "My editor wants to focus on local interest, but I'm more interested in the national implications."

Nick halted and faced the reporter again. "Then you wasted your money buying that notepad, and there's no need for you to talk to me. Or come to press briefings."

"But—"

"You won't hear anything about political controversy from me or anyone else on this team. And for the record, I don't speculate as to cause. When I have releasable information, you'll get it." He turned on a heel and marched toward the hangar. It felt disingenuous to jump on the guy like that, but Nick's private agenda had to remain completely separate from his public image.

"Mr. Phillips?"

Nick turned to Sweet for what he hoped would be the last time. "Yes?"

"You can't avoid it, you know. Celebrity status. Here's my

headline: 'Hot-shot investigator/pilot saves local hiker from killer bear.' You like it?"

Nick smiled. "Was that a grizzly?"

"I'm damned glad it wasn't. I'd be reduced to bear scat."

"We wouldn't want that. Tell me something. I've heard that bears usually tolerate the presence of humans. Why was this encounter different?"

Sweet folded his arms. "Bears are territorial. It's much more common with grizzlies, but especially in the fall when they're putting on weight for the winter, a bear will stake out a food source, like a berry patch. Any animal, human, whatever, they think might compete for food is in danger."

"You seem to know a lot about it."

Sweet smiled. "I'm a woodsy kinda guy. And by the way, if you ever go hiking in bear country, wear one of those wristbands with a little bell on it and carry pepper spray."

Nick nodded. "Let me guess. To warn the bear I'm coming, right? So it can avoid me. And the pepper spray is just in case I encounter a deaf bear."

"Not bad for a city slicker. One other thing, though. You need to be able to tell the difference between black bear and grizzly scat. Just so you know what you might be dealing with."

Nick thought Sweet might be setting him up, but he couldn't resist. "And how does one go about doing that?"

"Grizzly scat will have little bells and cans of pepper spray in it."

Nick clamped his jaw tight and fought back a laugh. "Okay, then. Be seeing you." He turned and walked into the hangar, his official home for the next week. After picking up his identification badge issued for this investigation and getting directions to the crash site, he hurried to the Jeep.

Fifteen minutes later, at an access point off the main

highway, he presented his ID to a county sheriff. Orange tape marked the route through the woods. He parked next to a group of vehicles huddled near the single entry into the secured area.

Detailed examination of the site was well under way. Investigators in dark blue windbreakers with a yellow "NTSB" imprinted on the back dotted the hillside. Stakes and more orange tape marked the perimeter, patrolled by guards.

Nick signed the roster and climbed toward the first point of impact. A familiar but unwelcome voice called out. "Hey, Nick!"

He turned around. Dickson was climbing out of his own rented Jeep. Nick waited, resigned to treating the guy as a team member until he had reason not to. They walked together to the southernmost edge of the impact scar.

Nick asked, "You walked the site?"

"A couple times."

"What's it tell you?"

Dickson pointed along the blackened path. "The airplane hit at a relatively shallow angle. Not sure if it was descending, because the rising terrain would have created the same effect."

Nick surveyed the scene as Dickson talked, studying the image of destruction and picturing the sequence of events. The jet had stayed in one piece until the left wing hit a tree and sheared off. The impact swerved the plane, but it probably hadn't slowed down much. Then the right wing clipped another tree. The scrape veered hard right from that point on.

"The landing gear was down?" asked Nick.

"Yeah. You can see three skid marks just before the heavier scarring. I figure the nose gear hit first and broke off immediately. Then the mains hit and collapsed. Pieces of the gear are strewn around here. The fuselage continued up the slope and stopped against that rock face."

Nick looked behind him down the slope. "Any evidence of breakup prior to impact?"

"Not yet. We have to map the site and inventory the pieces."

They stopped at the left wing. Post-crash fire, fed by fuel from the GoldenJet's punctured wing tanks, had extensively damaged this part of the wreckage. Odors of petroleum, burned wood and grass permeated the area. The right wing lay farther up the increasingly steep slope toward the northern edge of the crash site. The last two major pieces of wreckage rested alone.

Nick could inspect wings and landing gear with an investigator's detachment, but this fuselage had carried a man to his death. He gazed at patches of brilliant azure sky visible through the evergreen canopy. A brisk wind rustled the branches. He took a deep breath. The clean forest scent here was unspoiled by the stench of destruction.

Dickson touched Nick's shoulder. "Anything wrong?"

"Nah. Let's go on up."

They trudged to the fuselage. The aft section with the engines attached had broken free. Scorched metal attested to the presence of fire, but only the ground immediately adjacent to the engines had been charred. That meant they were running at impact.

Flames had not damaged the cockpit and cabin portions of the forward fuselage, which rested against a rock outcropping where the slope of the ridge rose sharply. Nick approached the left side of the wreckage. "Is the body still inside?"

"No. Medical Examiner's doing the autopsy now."

"Were you here when they removed him?"

"Yeah. Looked like his head was barely attached."

That brought Nick to a halt. He turned to Dickson. "What?"

"It was all *floppy*. I asked the ME about it. Broken neck, probably. He said Larchmont hadn't fastened his shoulder harness."

Nick stood very still. He remembered viewing the crash site from the air and thinking that the impact angle might have been shallow enough to be survivable. For a properly restrained occupant, that is. He continued to the fuselage and stopped at the open main cabin door. Rescue personnel would have entered, then backed off when they found no survivors. Avoiding the mud below the door jam, Nick bent over and looked into the main cabin.

"Any passengers?" he asked over his shoulder.

"Not according to the flight plan. If there were any, they crawled out and walked to their destination."

Nick ignored Dickson's comment because he knew well the tendency of investigators to use whatever techniques they needed to distance themselves from the horror of violent death. He bent over and looked to his right. Based on the condition of the cabin, passengers could have survived, assuming they were belted in with shoulder harnesses connected.

To his left, Coke and Sprite cans lay in the center aisle below the remains of the refreshment center, along with packets of sugar, coffee creamer, and red plastic stir sticks. He peered into the cockpit, crumpled inward by impact with boulders visible through the splintered windscreen. Brownish-red stains coated the left seat, console and instrument panel. The odors of blood, feces, and urine caused his stomach to churn.

He backed out and took a few deep breaths before looking through the shattered side cockpit window to evaluate the amount of "living space" it offered. The outer skin of any airplane deforms more during a crash than is obvious after the fact because it partially "bounces back." Even so, Nick couldn't imagine that this cockpit had collapsed to lethal volume. Such a simple precaution—fasten a shoulder harness and live. Larchmont got careless, and he'd been sitting in a death chamber of his own making.

Nick retreated from the wreckage and sank down on a boulder to drink some water. Dry mouth came with the territory. He splashed the last bit on his face. "Who was first on-scene?"

Dickson climbed toward Nick and sat down beside him. "County Sheriff. The weather was crummy, no local traffic. A mechanic working late had a radio tuned to the airport frequency and heard the pilot's calls on the approach. When the airplane didn't land, he got curious, stepped out of the hangar, spotted a glow against clouds to the south and called nine-one-one. Why are you sweating?"

Nick shook his head. "It's only water."

"You look like hell."

"No sleep. Has the Sheriff been interviewed?"

"Not for the record. Fire and rescue had come and gone when I arrived, but local law was guarding the site and I talked with them for a while."

"What's the Sheriff's name?"

"Barry Thornton."

"Okay." Nick stood up. "You staying?"

"Unless you need me down below."

Nick shook his head and zigzagged his way down the hill and across the crash site to see for himself whatever clues there might be before the wreckage was removed. He stopped at the three grooved skid marks made by the nose and main landing gear.

The impressions began as slight depressions in the grass, like vehicle tire tracks. They deepened and became narrower gouges into the dirt at the point where the gear collapsed. He touched the edge of a scar and found it unyielding. The impact had scraped furrows in wet, softened earth, now dried hard. He knelt between the main gear tracks and focused his attention on the mangled evidence strewn up the hillside.

Although speculation that sabotage had caused the death of Larchmont could play no official role in this investigation while the NTSB was in charge, Nick knew that standard forensic analysis would find no evidence of explosives. The extended debris trail indicated the airplane was under control and in a normal approach condition when it impacted the ground. All the pieces would be found at this site, inconsistent with in-flight breakup. So much for that part of the conspiracy theory.

Wind whished in the trees, the only sound except for muffled conversations drifting down the slope. Nick watched investigators going about the business of photographing, tagging and gathering evidence, the physical act of documenting the aftermath of metal meeting earth. In a week or so, they'd probably leave with a draft report and a conclusion that none of the Larchmont watchers would ever believe. Nick couldn't deny a tiny bit of disappointment, almost as if he wanted a different outcome. But it was what it was, or wasn't in this case, and he knew better than to think otherwise.

He scrambled down to the security exit point, signed out and drove to the command post in the hangar. Staff workers had placed portable screens in a rear corner to create a "private" office for the IIC, consisting of a dilapidated surplus government metal desk and two equally well-used chairs. He didn't need much more, but he might scrounge around for a filing cabinet.

He pushed the best of the chairs behind the desk. It must have been used by a gnome. Nick was adjusting the height of a swivel chair when the murmur of voices began filling the makeshift briefing area nearby. Time for the first press briefing? He glanced at his father's watch and silently mouthed, *Rest in peace, Dad.*

At the podium he faced a sea of reporters. Following the set agenda for initial briefings, he summarized the known facts, laid out the current status of the investigation and opened it up for questions. He received nothing but routine queries until Harvey Sweet spoke up.

"According to several sources, Mr. Larchmont was not a highly rated aviator. Could you comment about whether pilot error might be involved?"

Nick stared at Sweet. The man had gone from novice to expert in about two hours. "Any comment on that subject would be speculative at this point. But I can discuss the contribution of pilot error to accidents in general." He explained that aircraft mishaps usually resulted from a culmination of events, linked together like a chain. More frequently than not, removal of any one link might have prevented the disaster.

In cases where pilot error was causal, it might have been the only factor, like flying a perfectly good airplane into the ground. Or after an engine problem, the crew's failure to follow the emergency checklist could have made a situation worse and contributed to the final outcome. "Unfortunately, a large percentage of accidents have some component of human error in the event sequence."

When Nick paused for a drink of water, Sweet followed up. "How do you determine the presence of pilot error?"

"The human factors group begins with the autopsy. Evidence of drugs or alcohol can point to physical impairment. The cockpit voice recorder might have documented a significant departure from standard procedures or a risky decision to push the limits established by fuel reserves or weather. If pilot error occurred, we can usually find what we need to prove it."

"But he was alone. How can the voice recorder tell you anything?"

Nick decided that newbie-reporter Sweet was no babe in the woods. A real head-fake artist, this one. "We'll have to wait and see, won't we?"

Sweet began another follow up, but Nick spoke over him. "I think that's enough for today. We appreciate your interest, and I'll brief you again tomorrow."

Five minutes later, Dickson walked into Nick's office and plopped down across from him with all the energy of a rag doll. He wiped his brow with a handkerchief. "Nice office."

Right. IICs get all the perks. "I'll be glad to share the name of my decorator."

"When I get digs of my own, I'll take you up on it. Did I overhear something about pilot error in the press briefing?"

"I thought you were staying at the crash site."

"Changed my mind. I ask because of your well-known opinion that investigations are generally too quick to conclude it."

Dickson was baiting him. Everyone in the division knew that after graduating with a degree in aviation safety, Nick had spent six months analyzing the final report on his father's accident. He visited the site, interviewed witnesses and investigators alike, and had never accepted the finding that his father made a mistake. After a calming pause, Nick said, "My personal reservations are not a subject for press briefings."

"Okay, but I'm asking you in the privacy of your spiffy office. A lot of people considered Larchmont a lousy pilot."

Dickson had been doing some extra-curricular investigating. Nick furrowed his brow. "Like who?"

"His instructors, and their opinion should count for

something. He flew the GoldenJet single pilot, which requires yearly training to maintain the waiver."

"We'll get to that in the normal course of the investigation."

"And if it turns out to be pilot error?"

The effect of the calming pause was wearing out. "If you have something to say, James, why not say it?"

Dickson frowned. "Everybody knows—"

"Hold it." Nick raised his hand, first finger extended. "If we find something that proves Larchmont screwed up, fine. But if I think you or anybody else is trying to railroad the conclusions, this investigation will grind to a halt while we sort it out."

"Why would anyone want to do that?"

Nick felt like strangling Dickson. The prick was playing with him, bringing up pilot error because he knew why the subject touched Nick so personally. Instead, he gripped the arms of his chair and waited until he could speak without shouting. "Because this situation is a bit different."

Dickson nodded. "Of course it is."

CHAPTER SIX

Wilson peered through the leafy canopy at a pale Virginia sky dotted with scattered clouds tinged a pre-dawn pink. It promised to be a beautiful morning. Just right for taking care of business, even without the white noise of rain and wind. Today he wouldn't need any.

The ex-GoldenJet mechanic usually arrived for work about six o'clock. He had a reputation for punctuality. His routine never varied, including a full-throttle acceleration for one-quarter mile on the only straight stretch of deserted back-country road between Schiller Aviation and his home.

In Wilson's line of work, routines had to be both avoided and exploited. He seldom did anything the same way twice, but his targets usually moved through their lives with a predictable certainty that made his job so much easier. Tethered-goat simple.

Concealed in the tall grass and weeds bordering the shoulder, he listened for the distinctive sound of the GTO's highly modified engine. Eyes closed, he mentally silenced the gentle rustling of grass and wind in the trees. After a moment he heard it. Wouldn't be long. He eased up into a kneeling position.

The black muscle car announced its impending arrival

with a distant thunder, rapidly increasing as it appeared in view and rounded the far curve with tires squealing in protest. The mechanic usually played a game of chicken with himself on this straightaway, waiting until the last second to brake for the curve just past Wilson's hiding place. What an unfortunate daily practice.

He glanced down at the remote. A press of the ARM button illuminated a red light. Thumb on DETONATE, he waited, picturing the sequence he had built into the modifications on the mechanic's muscle car: a squib would fire, drive a plunger into the throttle linkage and pour high-octane fuel into the engine. Deadly torque would reach the rear wheels. After that, physics would rule.

The GTO had to be doing at least 120 mph when the driver came off the gas and hit the brakes. Wilson pressed the second button. The roar of 500 horsepower accelerating out of control ripped through the morning stillness. Enormous racing slicks overpowered the rear brakes and sent the car into a skid. Sideways to the road, it flipped, slammed to the ground upside down, went airborne again. Three rollovers later, the mangled heap came to rest against the trunk of a huge elm.

Wilson stared at the scene and wondered if maybe he should delay his retirement. He was getting really good at this. He checked the road in each direction and trotted to the wreckage. The GTO lay on its back, rear wheels still rotating. Thin wisps of smoke rose from the engine compartment. He bent over and peered through the driver's open window. Crumpled against the crushed roof, the mechanic's battered body evidenced enough blood and trauma to guarantee death.

The hood had been ripped off. Wilson pulled out his flashlight, lay down beside a front fender, and trained the beam on the carburetor. Although he'd intended to retrieve the added components, the destruction under the hood made that unnecessary.

He stood up. No small-town cop would give this accident a second thought, much less examine the wreckage closely. He turned toward the woods. A shift in the wind brought the sharp odor of fuel to his nostrils. He paused.

Flames hide lots of secrets. Never without a lighter when he was a smoker, he could use his trusty Zippo. He considered searching the interior of the GTO, but abandoned the idea when he heard a vehicle approaching. He ran deep into the woods to hide and wait.

The car slowed and stopped. A door slammed shut. Wilson eased up. The rotating flash of a police cruiser's light bar filtered through the trees. He slid backward on his stomach into the shadowy forest.

As IIC, NICK'S PRIMARY role involved far more supervision and coordination than probing into details. But he had a different view. If he organized and delegated all the tasks so the team ran itself, he could afford the time to personally shine a flashlight or focus a microscope on anything of interest.

Draft reports were a case in point. All of aviation seemed bound by the saying: *Do not attempt takeoff until the weight of the paperwork equals the weight of the airplane.* For an investigator, a similar rule applied: *The work is never done until the draft report folders are filled to overflowing.*

Only a couple of days on the job, and already a hefty collection of documents lay in front of him. Open to the METEOROLOGY tab, the report included a sequence of automated weather observations. Indications of frontal passage an hour before the crash, with abundant moisture and decreasing temperatures, suggested the possibility of icing.

A thick stack of photos lay on a corner of the desk. Nick thumbed through them to find a view of the cockpit instrument panel with the ice-protection switches. With the GoldenJet flight manual for reference, he was concentrating on each switch one at a time to understand its purpose when he paused, stared at the stack, and picked up the previous photo showing the center console and throttle quadrant

The throttles were positioned full forward. On the approach, whether descending or in level flight, Larchmont would have had the throttles no more than halfway between the "flight idle" position and the forward stop. Nick pushed away from the desk and leaned back in his chair.

Multi-engine jet airplanes have an excess of thrust. Even on takeoff, normal procedures don't call for maximum power because it isn't needed, and reduced power lessens wear and tear. But whenever safe separation from the ground is in question, the first pilot action is to shove the throttles forward as far as they'll go and sort it out later.

From the photo, it appeared that Larchmont might have abandoned the approach and tried to climb out of danger. Maybe he loaded up with ice, or caught a glimpse of the terrain ahead. Or both.

Nick stood and stepped out of his office. Slanting rays of late-afternoon sun streamed through the open hangar door. Nine-to-five workdays on-site were as rare as an honest politician, and this day promised to be typical.

The recovered wreckage had been arranged with the fuselage as the centerpiece and the remaining pieces placed around it to show their correct relationship to each other. He scanned the hangar for Clyde Morrow, an engineer for the Golden Aircraft Company, which had been given "party status" for the investigation. Go Teams usually included specialists from outside organizations to provide expertise not available within NTSB employee ranks.

Clyde had to be six-five in his stocking feet, but Nick didn't see him. He zeroed in on the only chunk of wreckage large enough to hide the man and made his way past clusters of investigators to the fuselage. As he approached the main cabin door, two enormous shoes, toes down, appeared at the lower jamb, followed by a very long pair of legs. A commercial for a big-and-tall men's clothing store came to mind as Morrow backed out of the aluminum tube and stood up.

Nick held out his hand. "How did you get in there?"

Morrow shook hands. "In's the easy part. I can see where I'm going. What can I do for you, Mr. Phillips?"

"Help me understand the ice protection systems on the GoldenJet."

"My pleasure."

And Nick knew it was. Like any representative of a company who manufactured airplanes or major components for them, Clyde's first obligation was to his employer. That didn't mean he would try to hide anything, but neither would he allow investigators to draw conclusions unsupported by facts or specific systems knowledge.

Nick crossed his arms, leaned against the fuselage and told Clyde that about the time of the accident, Denver Center had received a report from a pilot within thirty miles of Cedar Valley indicating the tops of the overcast were at twenty-thousand feet. Combined with a forecasted freezing level at twelve thousand and a near-freezing surface temperature, the conditions were ideal for structural icing.

Morrow leaned against the fuselage beside Nick. "You a pilot?"

"I own a single-engine experimental airplane, but it isn't equipped for flight in icing conditions."

"Have you ever had an *inadvertent* encounter with ice?"

Nick recognized Morrow's get-out-of-jail-free emphasis. A pilot-in-command of an airplane not equipped for flight in known icing conditions should never *intentionally* fly into them. "Only once. I tried to skirt the edge of a cold front. It permanently altered my attitude about the combination of water and cold air."

"Then you know how fast ice buildup on an airframe can add weight and degrade the ability of a wing to produce lift."

Did he ever. Nightmares still paid occasional visits, forced him to relive his surprise at how fast the airplane had loaded up. The feeling of helplessness. Of being along for the ride on a lead sled. By the time he found clear air, he could barely maintain enough airspeed to avoid stalling.

He'd had no choice but to descend. The damned ice refused to budge. Talk about pucker factor. With no more than a thousand feet of altitude under him, the first chunk broke away. Then another, and another, a clattering sound so horrible he wanted to cry and so sweet he felt like laughing. Which he did, uncontrollably, when he managed to level off and finally climb away from the unforgiving earth.

Personal experience aside, Nick's limited knowledge of the GoldenJet left a hole in his understanding of what Larchmont had to deal with. He questioned Morrow about how to combat ice in the GoldenJet.

The flight manual instructed pilots to turn on the protection systems anytime they detected ice, which seemed like pointing out the absurdly obvious, but also when flying in visible moisture with the temperature ten degrees above freezing or lower. And further, to anticipate the possibility of icing by warming up the systems. If Larchmont had been paying attention, he would have had the anti-ice on well above twenty-thousand feet.

Most modern business jets used only anti-ice systems. Hot engine bleed air and electrical heating elements prevented ice buildup on all critical portions of the airplane. But Larchmont's 1991 model GoldenJet used a combination of anti-ice and de-ice. The wings and tail had pneumatic "boots" that removed the ice *after* it had formed, which seemed to Nick like letting a wild beast clamp its jaws around your leg just so you could more easily club it to death.

Morrow stepped over to the left wing, supported on stands to position it relative to where it used to be attached to the fuselage. A shiny section of the wing leading edge extended outboard about three feet from the wing root. Black rubber coated the remainder. Morrow pointed aft along the fuselage at the left engine, still fastened to the detached rear fuselage and tail section. "Airflow over the wing root lines up with the engine intake. Ice buildup can shed off and be drawn into the engine, so we keep this shiny part ice-free whenever the engine anti-ice system is turned on."

Then he explained that because ice farther out on the wing can't enter the engine, the pilot could let it form and periodically de-ice it. The rubber "boot" on the leading edge swelled with engine bleed air to destroy the structural integrity of the ice layer. "The boots are divided into top and a bottom chambers, which expand and retract alternately to create asymmetric stress on the ice coating."

Nick knelt in front of the wing at the inner end of the boot. A wedge-shaped protrusion, visible to the pilot and illuminated by the wing inspection light, served as a depth guide. He peered down the length of the wing and thought about how much ice it would take to cover the guide.

It gave him a serious case of goose bumps. He couldn't imagine sitting alone in the cockpit at night, in bad weather, approaching a mountain airport, and waiting until the wing became loaded with that much ice before doing anything about it.

He stood and looked at Morrow. "This system isn't very pilot-friendly."

Morrow responded with a slight nod that seemed to say, *I agree.* All outside representatives had to walk a tightrope between personal opinion and representing their employers. Then he voiced what was probably the company line. "The manual mode does require a bit more attention."

Nick had read the ice protection chapter in the GoldenJet flight manual, but that didn't help him very much at the moment. "I thought you said cycling of the air is automatic."

Morrow shrugged, as if to say, *I didn't design the damned system.* "It is, and it isn't. The de-ice switch has three positions: off, manual, and automatic. In manual, the sequence of alternately filling the chambers is automatic, but each activation of the switch only schedules one complete cycle."

Nick frowned. This seemed ridiculous. "Then why wouldn't a pilot use automatic all the time?"

"Because in heavy icing, continuous cycling can allow an inner layer of ice to form around an expanded boot and leave a void. Subsequent buildup can thicken the layer until the boots can't crack it. The flight manual recommends using the manual mode in heavy icing conditions."

Nick could only shake his head. Like many pilots, he felt that every engineer working in aviation companies should be required to fly in the airplanes they design and use the systems themselves before offering them for sale. How could any sane person advise pilots to ignore an automatic mode and use a procedure that increased workload? Especially in the worst conditions. It had to be someone who sat in the safety of an office and never faced what Larchmont did. As in the television commercial for a rotisserie, he should have been able to set it and forget it.

Nick glanced at Morrow, who appeared to be sympathetically reading his thoughts. "Okay. Cockpit photos indicate that Larchmont had turned on all the ice protection systems. Did your physical examination confirm that?"

"Yes, but it's perishable data. A switch could have been moved during the impact sequence as a result of inertia, or flailing about of pilot extremities, or even post-impact by careless investigators."

"My guys aren't careless. The de-ice switch was found in automatic, which might not have been the best choice. And what's really frustrating is that the switch is spring-loaded from manual to the off position. If the pilot had followed the recommended procedure, we couldn't tell the difference between that and failure to use the system altogether."

"Unfortunately, that's true."

Nick sighed, frustrated beyond measure. Flying single pilot, and being less than a stellar aviator, Larchmont would have been busy enough without having to look over his shoulder at the wing every couple of minutes. So he selected automatic mode, which might have allowed a layer of ice to compromise aircraft performance. It wouldn't be a primary cause, necessarily, but it could have reduced the margin for error if something else had happened. Like getting off course, especially hazardous in the mountains, and trying to climb out of danger.

And that raised the next question. Did the engines suffer any damage from ice ingestion? Nick asked Morrow what he had learned from examination of the valves that controlled the flow of hot air to the wing root and engine intakes.

Morrow had just sucked a mouthful of brown liquid from a bottle. The stuff looked like gutter water after a hard rain. Little bits of mystery debris floated around in it. He nodded, his narrow face bobbing atop an elongated neck with a prominent Adam's apple. Then he shook his head. Ichabod Crane in a button-down shirt. He placed the bottle on top of the wing and explained how a dizzying array of valves moved back and forth, which ones were electrically controlled and actuated, and they had springs to drive this one open and that one shut with the loss of electrical power.

Although Nick's eyes had almost crossed from all the detail, he realized the importance of this safety feature, which prevented uncontrolled engine bleed air from overheating aircraft components. But as an investigator, he had to deal with the resulting data loss. Examination of the engines could determine only the *current* position of the valves, not their position at the time of the crash.

At that moment, he made up his mind to be reincarnated as an engineer. He'd dedicate himself to designing aircraft systems that helped pilots rather than hindered them. And his systems wouldn't hide from investigators what they needed to know. He realized it wasn't that simple, but this was ridiculous. He might as well toss a coin.

Nick pointed to the horizontal stabilizer, which had the same kind of pneumatic ice boots that covered the leading edge of the wings. "You said each cycle of the de-ice system expands those as well?"

Morrow drank some more of the mystery liquid and nodded. "It's more critical than keeping the wings clear. Ice on the tail can affect pitch control. The nose pitches up, the aircraft stalls, recovery is problematic at best."

Nick thanked Morrow and returned to his office. They'd never know for sure, but in his gut he felt it. Alone in that cockpit, at night and in bad weather, Larchmont had become overloaded. When it really mattered, events cascaded beyond his ability to control the outcome.

What a waste. Nick looked at his father's watch, rubbed the face of it with his thumb and wondered if such tragic events were simply preordained. The doubt nagged at him often, but as on every other occasion, he shook it off.

His only other choice was to give up, an option he refused to acknowledge.

CHAPTER SEVEN

Back in Colorado again, hopefully for the last time, Wilson moved through the dark, quiet forest, placing each foot on the ground and slowly transferring his weight for the next step. He had no reason to be this cautious, other than to test himself. Practice. Training. Discipline. The watchwords of his profession. Take every opportunity to use all the techniques for silent movement.

The almost-dead rent-a-cop at Schiller Aviation knew nothing about that. Wilson could teach the idiot a lot, like how not to let caterwauling about lost loves and deceased hunting dogs announce his presence. On the other hand, that twangy shit had saved the guy's life. Country music to the rescue. Maybe a top-ten hit could be found in that idea. Yeah, right.

Another useful maxim for a hired gun was, *Don't be stupid.* Wilson ignored that one on occasion. What the hell was he doing out here in the pre-dawn stillness freezing his ass off when he didn't have to?

And the answer was simple. To revisit the scene. To revel in the thrill of success. To relive a moment when all the best feelings combined into one with a synergistic effect like no other.

He knew all about the really bad boys lurking in the

shadows. The serial predators who so often returned to the scene of their conquests. Those bastards described it as the ultimate fantasy, to prolong the ecstasy of power, the thrill of exerting domination and control over another human being for the pure enjoyment of it. Freaks, all of them. They had nothing in common with Wilson, except maybe this. To remember a very special night and smile.

A week ago, less than twenty-four hours after making the activate call from the rental car, he'd entered this same Colorado forest for the first time with no expectation that it would happen that soon. But then he received the alert. The mark was headed his way. He remembered the pleasant surprise and the glow of satisfaction at how well the plan was coming together. The final pieces of the puzzle were in his hands. An old saying came to mind: *I'd rather be lucky than good.* Of course he was already very good, the luck nothing more than a bonus.

On that night, he'd scaled the airport perimeter fence and crept through tall grass to a cluster of small buildings with electrical components for the airfield lighting system. He picked a lock, pulled a circuit breaker to kill the approach lights, and retraced his steps. With the guidance of a handheld GPS receiver, he navigated over a ridge in thick, pitch-black woodlands. When the distance to go measured about a half-mile, he stopped and faced south. All around him, the trunks of large evergreens poked up from the forest floor and rose no more than fifty feet before disappearing in low-hanging clouds. Perfect weather for a plane crash.

And now, standing in a patch of wounded earth, the odors of jet fuel and burned vegetation sharp in his nostrils, images appeared before him in the darkness. Vivid. Thrilling. Each moment crisp. He closed his eyes and allowed the memory of that night of all nights to consume him.

LEANING AGAINST THE TRUNK of a tree, he glances at his watch. Based on the last word about the mark's progress, he figures no more than a half-hour before—*What is that?* He peers into the gloom and notices a faint, pulsating glow, rapidly growing brighter. Airplane landing lights.

He knows better than to let emotion interfere when on the job, but he can't prevent a flush of excitement as the lights pass overhead, along with the flashing red glow of an anti-collision beacon and the whine of jet engines at low power.

Clouds swallow the lights.

The sound fades, then suddenly increases to a ripping howl for a few seconds before going silent again, followed by the shriek of torn metal, cracking wood, and the muffled whump of an explosion. An intense flare lights up the clouds, goes out.

He stands motionless, his feet frozen in place. *Holy everloving—*

Another explosion rips through the stillness. A bright glow appears behind the top of the ridge.

Heart pounding, he runs across a shallow ravine and up the rocky slope. Heat on his face stops him at the base of an evergreen, its top sheared off, splinters glowing white against the black forest canopy. Fire shimmers, backlighting the trees between him and the crash site, a scene out of nightmares. An airplane lies scattered in pieces amid pockets of flame. He circles the fires and passes the tail section resting alone in a blackening circle of glowing, charred earth. An undulating dance of yellow light reflects off the registration number: N924DP.

Ignoring the desire to pause and savor it, he hurries to the last chunk of wreckage. The fuselage rests nose-first against the rocky face of a cliff. He peers through a shattered window on the left side of the cockpit. His target slumps forward, motionless, chin on his chest.

Wilson smiles. He's done it. His most complicated operation ever. All that preparation, hours of—

Larchmont moans, shudders. His head rises slightly, turns. Beseeching eyes stare.

Wilson stares back and shakes his head.

To his right, the main cabin door. He's practiced opening one on a mockup GoldenJet fuselage, but it wasn't lying on its belly in the Colorado mud. He rotates the handle. The latches snap free. He pulls. The lower edge of the door jams against the ground. He lets go of the handle, grips the aft edge of the door in both hands, sets his feet and yanks as hard as he can. The door opens about halfway.

He pulls out the steps, lays them on the ground, bends over and low-crawls forward to the cockpit. With both gloved hands on the back of Larchmont's head, a quick downward shove. He feels the crunch of bone and hears a crisp snap.

Backing out of the cockpit, he notices a silver briefcase in the empty copilot seat. He pauses, tries the latches. Locked. Why did Larchmont put it up here and not in the baggage compartment or in the cabin? Wilson considers whether he should take it. What if someone other than Larchmont knows the briefcase is here and it comes up missing? But there might be something inside that—

In his peripheral vision, through the side cockpit window, a flash of light against the black forest. He grabs the briefcase and backs out of the airplane. Empty darkness, invaded only by glowing flames, surrounds him. He steps away from the fuselage, eyes darting left and right.

Nothing. He stands motionless, a vague uneasiness doing battle with a sense of solitude, until a blinking light appears in the trees on the other side of the wreckage.

He crouches down, scrambles back to the fuselage, sticks his head inside the cabin and stares through the emergency exit door window on the opposite side. A beam of white, barely visible, dances among the trees, coming closer. Someone walking with a flashlight.

A local, out for a nightly walk and stumbling on a plane crash? Or maybe the law?

He bolts into the forest with the fuselage between him and the unwelcome visitor. Lying thirty yards away behind low bushes, he aims his pistol at the fuselage door.

Soon a uniformed man emerges from the forest at the back end of a flashlight beam. The cop reaches the fuselage, bends over, and shines his light inside the cabin through a window.

Wilson lowers his forehead to the ground and considers his next move. One task remains, but it isn't worth killing a cop. Better to leave it for later. Or leave it alone. They'll probably never notice it. He retreats from cover and slips away into the night.

STANDING IN THE MIDDLE of the crash site a week later wasn't the smartest move, but Wilson relished the memory of the toughest challenge of his career. *No other operator will ever top this.*

For a moment he considered another sentimental visit, to the site of the mechanic's death. But that had been child's play in comparison. And, he'd thought a lot about the single remaining task here in Colorado. Nothing essential, just the cherry on the vanilla malt that epitomized his attention to detail. The hallmark of his services. Leave nothing to chance, slim though it may be.

No loose ends. Not even tiny ones.

CHAPTER EIGHT

On the gray, overcast early morning of his fifth day in Colorado, Nick entered the hangar pursued by a gust of cold mountain air. He'd been arriving before dawn to make the most of each day and avoid the attentions of reporters who wouldn't let go of the hiker rescue story. He tossed his coffee cup in the trash, trudged to his office and sank into his chair, a squeaky military-surplus torture device apparently designed to inflict permanent spinal damage. The thing probably had a sticker on the bottom of the seat: MARQUIS DE SADE INDUSTRIES.

In spite of the extra personal attention he'd paid to visual examination of physical evidence, none of the typical bomb markers had turned up. Subsequent scientific laboratory analysis would find nothing to refute what he tentatively concluded the first day: the GoldenJet had not been brought down by an explosive device.

In over twenty years of investigating, Nick couldn't remember a single instance of being disappointed by lack of evidence. And yet he felt cheated. Or maybe tricked. Like someone out there was laughing at him, mocking, like a kid: *You'll never find it! You'll never find it!*

"You in there, Nick?"

"Yo."

Dickson stepped through the doorway and took his customary seat across the desk. In spite of the underlying tension, they'd been working well together. "I think you may look worse than I do."

Nick shook his head. "If I'd seen your face in my mirror I'd have dropped dead on the spot."

"Maybe I can arrange that. You read the draft final report?"

"Last night. Why don't you start?"

Dickson nodded and opened the report folder. Two minds reviewing the findings were always better than one. The process often included playing devil's advocate by challenging each other to justify a conclusion.

They alternated between reading aloud and listening through all the major investigative areas: operations, structures, power plants, systems (including instruments, navigation, fuel, hydraulic, electrical, pneumatic, and flight controls), meteorology, air traffic control, survival factors, facilities, and, finally, human performance. It was the investigator's to-do list, and they had no choice but to check off every item.

A few facts received extra attention. The runway lights were inoperative at the time of the crash due to tripped circuit breakers in the power supply. The failure could not have contributed to the accident, because the impact ridge would have blocked Larchmont's view of the runway even if it had been lit. Night and bad weather played a contributory role. Unable to see the ground, he had no way to determine that he was off course. And with the ridge obscured by clouds, he had no warning of the danger prior to impact. Air Traffic Control records indicated Denver Centennial Airport had been Larchmont's original destination. They found nothing to explain why he had changed course en route and attempted to land at Cedar Valley.

Dickson finished the meteorology tab and tossed the folder on the desk. "I'd bet my last dollar he iced up."

Nick thought so too, but he wanted to hear Dickson's analysis. "What makes you say that?"

"Perfect icing conditions. He descends from high altitude with a cold-soaked airplane. It's clear above the clouds, no moon, if I remember correctly, so he may not notice the cloud layer until he's into it. It's below freezing, but not too much. Super-cooled water droplets are just waiting for a frozen wing to come along."

"But he had all the switches on."

"Yeah, but maybe he turned them on late. And if he didn't anticipate using ice protection, he might have planned to descend at idle power. The engine valves don't close right away and it takes too long to heat the components up. He gets rushed, decides to press on, flying an airplane coated with ice. Maybe it causes him to lose control, or it compromises aircraft performance, whatever. The ice melts before anyone notices and we end up taking a best guess."

Nick yawned, the fatigue of poor rest and long days getting to him, along with trying to analyze a possible sequence of events. His conversation with Morrow fit Dickson's scenario perfectly. Larchmont had been completely overloaded, and in more ways than one.

When they got to the subject of radar and audio tapes, Dickson noted that the controller's final transmission indicated the airplane was slightly right of course. But just before Denver's radar lost contact, the target plot showed a *right* turn as Larchmont acknowledged clearance for the approach and changed radio frequencies.

Nick stared at the metal ceiling high above his cubicle and

formed a mental picture of the radar track. "He was on a good heading to intercept the final approach course, then turned away from it."

"Well, there you have it. A right turn explains why he was off course to the east. Maybe he got confused. Accident reports are full of such things."

"But it says nothing about *why* he made the turn."

"So we make an educated guess. Night, bad weather, and fatigue combine to put him behind the airplane and what's happening. He's single pilot, with no one to provide crew coordination and catch his mistake."

"Okay, but that's one hell of an error. He would have had to ignore data from multiple sources."

Dickson leaned back and crossed his arms. "Let's say he dials in the reciprocal of the final approach course. The deviation indicator would display reverse sensing. He turns toward what he thinks is the proper course displayed on the screen, but it begins moving farther away. He's confused. He hesitates. He questions what he's seeing. Before he can figure it out, *badaboom*. He does a face plant on the instrument panel."

Nick got a bottle of water from his cooler and took a long drink. Dickson had a good point. One of the classic mistakes when flying on instruments was to set the course needle 180 degrees off. But Dickson wasn't a pilot, and specific systems knowledge wouldn't be second nature to him. Nick nodded. "I could buy that possibility except for one thing."

"Which is?"

"The only instrument approach at Cedar Valley is the GPS to runway three five. When you select GPS as the navigation source and choose that approach from the database, it automatically drives the deviation indicator to the correct course. It can't be manually set."

Dickson looked up, thoughtful, with the appearance of searching for an elusive fact catalogued in dusty stacks of brain matter. "Unless . . . he selected the OBS mode."

Whoa. Impressive. Dickson had been doing some reading. The term referred to the ability to dial in a desired course on an omni-bearing selector when on *other* types of approaches. Larchmont would have had to command the OBS mode to override the GPS automatic course feature. Nick nodded. "He could have done that, but it wouldn't be the correct procedure for flying this approach."

"So he made another mistake. Or it could have malfunctioned. Did the instrument capture the final course?"

Nick picked up a pile of photos. He thumbed through them to a view of the instrument panel and the face of the GPS navigation receiver, made by the same manufacturer of the one in his airplane. He stared at the photo. The receiver was a newer model than his, but he recognized all the controls.

A small pushbutton selected the OBS mode and turned on a green light. Filament analysis could determine whether the OBS annunciation was illuminated at impact, and standard investigative procedure called for examining each cockpit instrument. An indicator needle might be found jammed in place and thus record readings at the moment of impact.

Unfortunately, Larchmont had upgraded the avionics in his GoldenJet and replaced the original analog instruments with digital flat-panel displays. Pilots loved them. Nick was no exception, but as an investigator, he had to live with the downside: loss of electrical power left no recoverable history.

He passed the photo to Dickson, who studied it, set it on the table and made eye contact with Nick. It felt as if unspoken agreement flowed between them: in the absence of hard facts relating to mechanical failure, this airplane had suffered controlled flight into terrain. Investigators even had an acronym for it: CFIT, shorthand for an event common enough to need one. The question of *why* had to address the human part of the equation.

As it all too often did. Nick had dedicated his professional life to reducing the contribution of pilot error to aircraft mishaps. At times like this, he felt like stuffing his head in the sand, or sticking his fingers in his ears and babbling like a kid who doesn't want to hear something.

Dickson picked up the draft report folder and continued his review. Larchmont's pilot's license indicated he was qualified to operate the GoldenJet as pilot in command. His flight log documented less-than-average experience for piloting a jet, but he had completed an approved training course three months earlier, including the special requirements to operate under the single-pilot waiver.

As for currency, the aircraft flight log recorded over 250 hours in the last twelve months, rather high for this type of privately owned light jet. Larchmont had a current medical certificate with a waiver requiring glasses for near vision. Medical personnel found a pair of readers hanging from a cord around his neck.

About five years ago, Larchmont's legendary problems with drug and alcohol abuse had ended after a very public rehabilitation. As evidenced by more than one recent drunken outburst on video, his sobriety had ended just as openly. Autopsy results would determine whether he was under the influence at the time of his death. He wasn't currently under a doctor's care or taking prescription meds. No one knew anything about his sleep-wake cycle for the twenty-four hours preceding the flight, because he lived alone. The accident occurred after a relatively long duty day of about thirteen hours. Fatigue could have played a role, but they would never know to what extent.

The cockpit voice recorder preserved only the last thirty minutes of activity. For most accident situations that was sufficient to examine anything of significance. In this case, the tape told them zilch. With no copilot on the intercom, there had been nothing to say.

The most telling evidence relating to human cause involved Larchmont's competence. Interviews with his simulator and flight instructors documented that although he had the basic flying skills, the finer points of operating the jet remained outside his usual crosscheck. Simulated emergencies frequently caught him napping. He muddled through procedures, and all the instructors agreed he barely met minimum standards. This information focused attention directly on him.

Nick leaned back in his chair and closed his eyes. No one in aviation was infallible. Mechanics, air traffic controllers, and pilots all made mistakes. At every level of involvement, the tactic for dealing with less-than-perfection relied upon multiple layers of defense against small missteps becoming big ones.

In a two-pilot cockpit, standard procedures defined the duties of a "pilot flying" and a "pilot not flying." Larchmont's decision to operate his GoldenJet single pilot in an environment devoid of air traffic control meant that he had to catch all his own blunders. And yet even with that isolation, he had a system on board his aircraft that should have been "covering his six o'clock," as the military pilots put it.

Nick looked at Dickson. "Some years ago, the FAA mandated that all transport-category airplanes be equipped with terrain awareness warning systems."

Dickson nodded. "TAWS-B as a minimum. Larchmont installed TAWS-A when he upgraded the avionics."

"Why didn't the very best system available alert him to the danger?"

"Maybe he activated the terrain-inhibit feature."

Nick thought about that. Pilots flying TAWS-equipped aircraft sometimes selected terrain inhibit to avoid nuisance warnings. In some locations, flying the approach exactly as published could still result in terrain alerts. Computer-generated warnings of, "PULL UP! PULL UP!" could get old in a hurry, not to mention the effect on passengers.

"Did we look into whether he selected terrain inhibit?"

Dickson grabbed the draft report off the desk and thumbed through it. After a moment, he tapped the folder with the back of his hand. "We did, and he didn't. It's activated with a push-switch that turns on a caution light. Technicians confirmed that the bulb was not lit at impact." Dickson tossed the report on the desk. "Maybe the situation developed too rapidly."

Nick nodded. Depending on how steep the obstacle was and the speed of the airplane, the TAWS warning might not give the pilot enough reaction time. But Nick had gotten a good look at the crash site from the air, and the initial slope of the ridge appeared relatively gentle. He thought about other possibilities, then said, "Or maybe the TAWS didn't know where it was."

"Come again?"

"Terrain warning systems don't look ahead and *see* the terrain, right? They're GPS-based. They only know where the airplane is in relation to terrain features in the database. If the combination of distance from an obstacle and altitude of the airplane doesn't penetrate the computer-calculated danger area, no audible caution or warning is provided."

Dickson tossed the folder on the desk. "It could have malfunctioned, but the GPS satellite signals were sufficient for accurate positioning at the time of the accident. And the bottom line is that Larchmont wouldn't have had to trust his life to *any* system if he'd turned left instead of right."

Nick shook his head. "I guess we'll never know." He stood and walked to the door. The wreckage covered the hangar floor with a puzzle of a thousand pieces. To himself, to Dickson, and to the memory of his father, Nick muttered, "Goddamn it. Aviation is dangerous enough without pilots killing themselves."

LATER THAT AFTERNOON, NICK stepped out of his office and stretched his aching back. The Marquis de Sade *must* have designed his chair. Retreating sunlight angled through the open hangar door and another late evening of work awaited. He hated this part of the job and the stacks of paper required to document everything. Maybe take a walk around the airport to clear the cobwebs? No. Procrastination only delayed the inevitable. As he walked into his office, his cell phone rang.

After preliminaries, Laurie said, "Brad's been acting like a real jerk. This car thing has become a big deal, and I may end up killing him before he gets it."

"Let's avoid that. Can you put him off a little longer?"

"Not sure. When are you coming home?"

"I'll know better in a day or so."

"Okay, but I'm regretting that I went along with this deception. If you just told him about the Mustang, or at least let him know he'll get a car for his birthday, he'd be an angel."

"Okay, I'll—"

"And he wouldn't care how long the investigation takes. You could stay out there without worrying about keeping a promise to him."

She was right. Brad probably didn't give a damn about

anything but getting a car. The quintessential teenage rite of passage into the world of transportation freedom. "Okay. I'll tell him." Nick ended the call and stared at the surface of his desk, or what little he could see of it between the stacks of investigative paperwork.

The car saga had begun with a simple misdirection. Nick wanted to heighten the impact of the surprise gift by leading Brad to think that he wouldn't be getting his own car right away. You'd have thought the world had come to an end. That his parents might as well just kill him and get it over with. They'd deflected Brad's complaints well enough so far, but Nick had left an angry wife at home to deal with the endgame, which apparently had intensified to the point of teenage mutiny. To prevent Laurie, or Brad, or both from open rebellion, the time had come to insert a red herring.

Nick reached Brad on his cell phone. Following a short and typically vague report on school happenings, Brad switched to his favorite subject. "About this car thing, Dad. All my friends are getting them. It's not fair to make me wait."

"I agree."

After a moment of silence, Brad said, "You do?"

"We'll go shopping for one as soon as I get back."

"When are you coming home?"

"As soon as I can. I was thinking about one of those hybrids. It'll be economical, serve you well for a long time."

"You're kidding."

"Not at all. I figure a young man operating a car on a limited budget would appreciate not having to empty his wallet to fill it up every week."

"If I drive one of those to school they'll laugh me off campus."

"What kind of car do you want?"

"How about a BMW?"

"Now who's kidding?"

"What's wrong with a Beemer?"

"Other than way too expensive and totally outrageous for a teenager, nothing."

"You drive a Porsche."

"Yes, and I'm an adult. My first car was a—"

"We could buy a used one."

"Tell you what, Brad. Why don't you look in the classifieds and find out what used BMWs go for. Contact a dealership and get the scoop on maintenance costs. I'll look the information over with you when I get home."

"Cool. When *will* you be home?"

"I told you, as soon as possible. In the meantime, relax. And be extra nice to your mother so she doesn't have to terminate your breathing."

"I can handle Mom."

At least somebody thought he could handle something. Nick signed off and wondered if he could find some excuse to put off the paperwork a bit longer. He'd just given up when the distinctive voice of a temporary reprieve drifted into his office. He stood and walked into the hangar.

The ice-protection systems on Larchmont's airplane had been designed by a collaborative effort between Golden Aircraft and the Wellborn Company, who supplied the engines. Nick's conversation with Morrow had covered only half of the question about the possible contribution of icing to the accident.

Doug Zachary, a Wellborn tech rep, stood talking with another NTSB investigator. Zachary's vocal cords must have been made from eighty-grit sandpaper. He spoke softly, but from twenty yards away, his words caused Nick's eardrums to retreat. The word *raspy* didn't begin to describe it. Nick waited for their conversation to end before he approached and posed his questions.

Zachary led Nick to the one of the stand-mounted engines. "The condition of the other engine is similar to this. Both received only minor damage from impact, so it's much easier than if we had a crumpled mass. We started by examining the casings for evidence of gross failure, indicated by holes punched or burned through from the inside. There were none, so we can rule out catastrophic malfunction in flight." He bent over slightly, because the intake lip was lower than it would be when mounted on the airplane, and pointed the beam of a flashlight at a notch in a fan blade. "We have a lot of minor damage like this. The impact kicked up plenty of debris, and the engines vacuumed up all kinds of stuff. We can trace the path of objects through the engine and determine their origin."

Nick wasn't a jet pilot, but he knew that internal engine damage could be caused by a "foreign" object, i.e., from outside the engine, or from a "domestic" component breaking loose within. He asked Zachary about that.

Zachary nodded. "We've examined individual blades with a borescope and determined whether the damage came from a rock, or rivet, for example. These engines ate some of both."

"How about ice?"

Zachary turned off the flashlight, leaned against the engine and crossed his legs. "I read a novel once about a killer who used a bullet made of ice. It melted and left no evidence that could be traced back to the weapon. Totally impractical, of course, but ice damage to engines is like that."

Nick then asked about engine power setting at impact, a crucial piece of evidence for analyzing the sequence of events.

Zachary explained that his team had examined the fuel control units, bleed air valves, fuel flow indicators and transmitters, and cockpit instruments. None of these components provided anything useful, but other methods could be used to estimate power setting. "Depending on the severity of impact, the rotor shaft may have shifted. Interference between the compressor and turbine sections and the casing would then grind the blade tips down. The degree of rotational scoring on the inside of the case varies with power setting, although this indicator can lead to false assumptions."

Nick paid close attention. He had flown only piston-engine airplanes, and his knowledge of jet engines was purely academic. No investigator could stay current in all areas of expertise required for investigating accidents on every type, make, and model of airplane. He asked Zachary why this technical analysis could mislead them.

"Because the relationship between thrust and RPM isn't linear. This engine running at eighty-percent RPM produces only about fifty-percent thrust. Worst case, with the engine shut down and producing nothing but drag, it will still be windmilling at about twenty-five to thirty-five percent. That can create a lot of rotational damage, but is still zero thrust."

Zachary then described how an analysis of foreign-object damage could provide a more reliable indication of power setting. If a rock passed through the first stage and took a small chunk out of one blade, both objects entered second stage. This multiplier effect often created increasing damage farther into the guts of the engine. The distance the debris traveled could be used as an indicator of RPM.

"And in this case?"

"We figure about eighty-five percent on the fan speed. That's a bit high for the GoldenJet on approach."

Nick remembered the photo of the throttle quadrant. He walked over to the fuselage, peered through the shattered left side cockpit window and confirmed the throttles were positioned at full power. "It looks like he initiated a go-around."

"Maybe not. Inertia can throw a pilot's hand forward and take the throttles with it. I've seen that happen in cases where the engines were at idle thrust at impact. Did the autopsy find any fractures to the pilot's right hand or wrist?"

"No, but that's not definitive. Let's come at this from another angle. Jet pilots don't have to worry about rapid throttle advance exceeding temperature limits or causing compressor stalls, right? For a go-around, especially at night in bad weather, Larchmont would have shoved the throttles full forward. But the engines never reached one-hundred percent."

Zachary nodded. "Because jet-engine acceleration isn't linear. The time delay from throttle movement to max power depends on the starting condition. What if he had pulled the power to idle before he decided to go around? It still wouldn't take very long to reach maximum thrust, but a split second could make all the difference. Especially at low altitude."

Nick sighed. "And even more especially if he had structural icing. Did you confirm position of the valves in the ice protection system?"

"With loss of electrical power they failed to their proper positions, and we found nothing to indicate they wouldn't have performed as designed in flight."

Nick thanked Zachary, returned to his office, and collapsed into his torture chair. For all practical purposes, this investigation had run its course and reached the all-too-common conclusion that it could have been prevented.

He stared at the wall and reflected on too many years of investigating accidents resulting from gross negligence, minor mistakes compounding into disaster, bad luck, and the very rare maintenance error. And in all that time, never once had he encountered a situation preordained to cause death.

But this one had that aura about it, beginning with a guy who probably approached life with supreme confidence in his ability to handle anything. Nick had seen the tragic effects of the expert syndrome far too many times. Why would anyone think that aviation would be any less demanding if you had a lot of money? Or if you lived a charmed life filled with one success after another? Or if you had been born with nothing and in spite of the odds succeeded through hard work and determination?

Gravity didn't care. Hard earth didn't care.

Captain A. G. Lamplugh had nailed it in the early 1930s: "Aviation in itself is not inherently dangerous. But to an even greater extent than the sea, it is terribly unforgiving of any carelessness, incapacity, or neglect."

Nick stood and got a bottle of water out of the cooler by his desk. He drank half, leaned over, poured the rest over his head, rubbed it on his face and through his hair, and wiped his hands on his cargo pants. The transcript of Deputy Sheriff Barry Thornton's statement lay on the desk and beckoned, *Review me.* Nick glanced at his watch, sighed, sat down and began reading.

On the second page, he read that the GoldenJet's main cabin door had been open when Thornton arrived at the crash site. It was as if someone pressed his pause button. Nick read the statement again. How had he missed that before? He rummaged around on the desk and found photos of the wreckage. He flipped through the stack to a close-up of the main cabin door.

When Nick and Dickson had done their walk-through, the door had been open about halfway, with the steps pulled out and lying on the ground. At the time, Nick assumed rescue personnel had opened it. He stared at the photo for a minute, examined the next few showing the entryway carpet, laid them aside and searched for a listing of key personnel.

NICK HAD BEEN STUDYING the GoldenJet flight-manual description of the main cabin door mechanism for no more than ten minutes when he sensed that someone, or some*thing,* had filled the doorway to his office.

"Howdy," the big man said. He leaned over Nick's desk and extended a hand that looked like it was covered in leather. The nametag above his right breast pocket introduced him.

Nick shook hands. "Care for some coffee, Deputy Thornton?"

"Ah, yes. Another all-day coffee drinker. It any better than mine?"

"Probably not."

"I'll take some."

When they were seated with their coffee, Nick sipped his and said, "Thanks for responding so fast."

"Always looking for an excuse to put my boot into the carburetor. What can I do for you?"

"I've been reviewing your statement."

"I need a lawyer?"

Nick thought Thornton was serious until he caught the hint of a smile. "Do you?"

"Hold on a minute." Thornton reached into the breast pocket of his shirt and produced a Snickers bar. He held it out to Nick. "Wanna share my *last* one? When Nick declined, Thornton tore open the wrapper and bit off a big chunk. Through a mouthful of chocolate, caramel, and peanuts, he said, "If I have to be sharp, might as well keep my blood sugar up." He gobbled the Snickers in two more bites and swallowed the candy so fast it reminded Nick of a cormorant gulping down a perch. Thornton tossed the wrapper in the wastebasket, chased the snack with two sips of coffee, removed his Stetson and wiped his brow with a huge red bandana. Perspiration dampened his shirt. "I'm ready."

Nick almost said, *It's about time,* but a little voice in his head urged restraint. "I understand you were the first person to reach the crash scene."

"That's right."

"Would you mind repeating your account for me?"

"Not at all. Emergency dispatch got a call from a mechanic. Said there might have been a plane crash. I scrambled fire and rescue and drove out there. Flames were visible from the highway. I radioed for the fire boys to come in from the other direction, by way of the airport perimeter road. Figured they could get closer and maybe make it all the way to the site. I went in on foot. Took me about ten minutes.

"The fire had pretty much died down. Looked like the fuel had burned itself out, and the ground was still wet from the rain. I walked right up to the fuselage. It was pretty dark with the cloud cover, so I used my light to look inside. Found a body up front."

"Did you check to see if he was still alive?"

"Been a cop for more than fifteen years, Mr. Phillips. Seen enough torn-up bodies to know what death looks like. That guy died on impact."

"How long before fire and rescue showed up?"

"About fifteen minutes. I searched the area to make sure no passengers had wandered off. People in shock will do that, you know."

"Good idea. Just to clarify something, what made you

think someone might have gotten out?"

"I figured they could have exited through the door."

"So this part of your statement is correct? The main cabin door was open?"

"Yeah, but I didn't see it at first because I was on the other side of the fuselage. I checked the emergency access door over the right wing, then went around to the rear, thought I might be able to see into the cabin. The aft bulkhead blocked my view. Then I shined my light in the left side windows to check each row of passenger seating and the aisle. That's when I noticed the door."

"Why do you think the door was open? I mean, if there were no survivors?"

"I assumed it came open during the crash."

Nick knew how unlikely that was, but he didn't need to mention that to Thornton. "Did you look inside through the main cabin door?"

"No. As soon as I confirmed the passenger compartment was empty, I checked the cockpit. Used my light, shined it through the broken side window."

"Okay. How about later? Could one of the firefighters have opened the door?"

Thornton's eyebrows lowered as he tugged at his uniform belt and shifted in the chair. "What's this all about?"

Nick shrugged. "It's my job, Deputy Thornton, to consider all the facts. Especially the insignificant ones."

"Well, you're in the wrong business. I haven't been grilled this hard testifying at a murder trial." He sipped his coffee and grimaced. "You're right about this java. Did a firefighter open the door? Don't think so. I told them about the body as soon as they showed up. An EMS tech confirmed the pilot was dead, and the firefighters spent most of their time back down the hill working the burn sites. I don't remember any of them coming up to the fuselage."

"As far as you know, only the tech went inside the cabin?"

Thornton thought about that a moment. "Come to think of it, I didn't see whether he did or not. He could have checked through that shattered side window."

"How about other law officers?"

"No. All the county boys know to stay out of a scene we don't control. The Cedar Valley cops do, too."

Nick glanced at the stack of photos on his desk, remembered the mud. "You said it was wet up there that night?"

Thornton patted both breast pockets on his shirt. "You happen to have a Snickers?"

"Uh . . . no. I think there's a machine—"

"That's okay, thanks." He patted his belly. "I should join Snickers Anonymous and try to wean myself from those things. It rained all day prior to the crash. I was soaked from my knees down after I trudged in and out of there."

"What about later that day?"

"Cleared up."

"Would that dry things up pretty fast?"

Thornton nodded. "Mountain air and sunshine, it doesn't take long."

Nick pictured the deep, hard gouges in the earth where the landing gear had plowed three parallel tracks. "One more question before I let you go. Did you notice any ice buildup on the airplane?"

"Hell fire, Mr. Phillips. The whole thing could have been covered with it as dark as it was. Even in the daylight I probably wouldn't have paid attention to a detail like that."

"Okay, Deputy Thornton. I really appreciate your time."

Thornton drained his cup. "No problem." He picked up

his hat, smoothed the brim, and stood. "I like the quiet around here, don't get me wrong. Worked big counties with bad boys looking to do mischief and worse. Had enough of that. But this place gets a little boring. Call me if you need anything, and tell dispatch you want me to hurry. I can light her up."

Nick laughed and shook Thornton's hand. "You got a deal." He escorted the deputy out of the secure area and returned to his office. Under other circumstances, without all the controversy and media speculation, he would have been tempted to push the possibility of a mysterious visitor quietly into the Highly Unlikely file.

But the atmosphere of inevitability surrounding this crash lingered—or hovered—like a hologram. Wherever he looked. Based on the evidence, he had no logical reason to doubt that a combination of poor aviating and bad weather had killed Larchmont. Except for the open door, it should be a done deal. To keep the investigation officially alive would require handing it over to the FBI, and he had nothing to warrant trying to do that. They'd laugh him out of the room.

So, what next? Wrap it up in Cedar Valley, return home to celebrate a birthday and a homecoming. That's what he should do. Forget all this crap for a while. Or forever. Just turn it over to Dickson. Might as well.

He began straightening the papers and folders on his desk, filled with the myriad facts of an investigation into an event that took the life of a human being. All that effort to prove, Yeah, just like everyone thought he would, Larchmont Flew that GoldenJet into a ridge. You can't turn the wrong way on an instrument approach in the mountains and get away with it.

Nick stared at the desk, neat and tidy. The way he liked it. He started to get up, sank back into the chair.

Who opened that goddamned door?

CHAPTER NINE

wo hours after Deputy Thornton had left, Nick sat at his desk with his head feeling like it was attached to one of those rear-window toys in cars. A voice from out of nowhere barely saved his chin from another bounce off his chest. He swiveled around in his chair.

Dickson stood in the office doorway. "May I come in?"

Nick had to stare at him for a second to realize what looked different. Dickson had an air about him, kind of like . . . satisfied. Feeling good. All's right with the world. But it wasn't, and the time had come for Nick to scratch the itch that had been bugging him. He motioned to the chair on the other side of his desk. "You read Thornton's statement?"

Dickson pulled the chair out, sat down and propped his feet on the edge of the desk. "Skimmed it. Pretty straightforward."

"He said he was first on scene. How long was that after the crash?"

"Why are we talking about this?"

Nick hadn't thought about it enough to know why. To gauge Dickson's reaction, maybe? "Humor me."

Dickson paused. "The mechanic called nine-one-one immediately. Thornton was cruising up north on the interstate. We could check the tapes for when he responded to the call from dispatch and then reported leaving his car, if he called it in."

"I've already done that. He told me it took about ten minutes from the time he left the highway until he arrived at the site. Put all that together, I come up with less than a half-hour delay between the crash and the first person on the scene."

"Sounds about right. So what?"

Nick slipped the close-up of the forward fuselage out of the stack of pictures and handed it to Dickson. "Did the main cabin door look like that when you arrived?"

"Is this a trick question?" Dickson looked at the photograph. "Yeah, I guess so."

"You think the door was open at that same angle to the fuselage?"

"I didn't notice. Fire and rescue were already there. They would have opened it and pulled it out far enough to do what they had to."

"That's a valid assumption, but guess what?"

Dickson shook his head. "I don't have to, because you're about to tell me."

"Thornton told me the door was open when he showed up." Nick held up a fist to count off the points on his fingers. "If he was the first one there, and if Larchmont was killed on impact, and if there were no passengers in the main cabin, then who opened the door?"

Dickson's eyebrows furrowed, then he shrugged. "Maybe it popped open."

"Impact *could* cause that, but check it out." Nick pointed to the photograph lying in front of Dickson on the desk. It showed the main cabin door about halfway open. The bottom edge of the door was jammed against the ground. Nick used his pen to indicate one of three pins that extended from the edge of the door into the jamb to hold it closed. "These pins are retracted, which is what happens when the door is opened normally. If the door had ripped opened as a result of the crash, the pins would have broken off." Nick put another picture in front of Dickson, a closer shot of the door jamb.

Dickson stared at the photo. "There's no major damage to the jamb."

"Someone must have opened the door from the outside before the Sheriff arrived."

Dickson yawned and leaned back in his chair. "A Good Samaritan, maybe."

"That's possible, but they'd have to know how to open it."

"The instructions are written on the damn door, Nick."

"But at night?"

Dickson sighed. "He had a flashlight. Saw the crash, grabbed it out of his car, went there to check it out. That's reasonable."

"But why would he leave the scene? If you were there to help, wouldn't you stay around? You'd probably call nine-one-one. The mechanic was the only one who reported it."

"Maybe this mysterious visitor didn't have a cell phone."

"You know anybody who doesn't?"

Dickson rolled his eyes. "Maybe he didn't have it *with* him. I don't see what difference it makes. This is all conjecture."

"I agree. I wouldn't have thought much about it until I examined these photos and talked with Thornton. As far as we can tell, only one *official* person would have approached the door that night, and we're not sure he did. If that's true, then I asked myself, who else was up there, and why?" Nick laid in front of Dickson the series of photos showing the interior detail.

Dickson stared at them. "What am I supposed to be

looking at?"

Nick used his pen again. "That's a lot of mud on that carpet. Who do you suppose tracked it in there?"

"Lots of people. It was a crash scene. Firefighters, EMS, and you."

"I never stepped inside the cabin."

"But a whole bunch of other people might have."

"I talked to Thornton about it. He can think of only one official person who even came close."

"Bullshit. How could you, Thornton, or anyone else know that? And what difference does it make?"

"Maybe nothing. But if—"

Dickson slapped the desk twice with his hands. "Okay, okay. Tell me about this phantom."

"He planted a foot when he opened the door, maybe leaned forward with his weight on it as he checked inside the cabin, something like that. His boot picked up mud from the wet ground and he tracked it inside."

"Maybe Larchmont did that during the day."

"It's possible, I guess, but he was known to keep the airplane spotless. I doubt he was tramping around in the mud before he left home or on either of his stops earlier in the day." Nick picked up one of the photos. It showed the carpet from the main cabin door forward to the cockpit. He laid it in front of Dickson. "And Larchmont's business attire didn't include boots with cleated soles."

Dickson stared at the photo, which showed a muddy footprint on the light beige carpet. "And Deputy Thornton never saw anyone?" When Nick shook his head, Dickson picked up one of the photos. "The date-time stamps show these were taken the morning of the day after the crash. Even if nobody official did this the previous night, they could have done it the next day. Like when they were taking the body out."

"Except for two small details."

"Such as?"

Nick reached across the desk, picked up a photo deeper in the stack with a view into the cockpit, and laid it in front of Dickson.

"These photos were taken before the body was removed. And when we were up there that morning, the ground below the door jamb was hard as a rock."

ON THE WAY TO the motel that evening Nick stopped at Maudie's, a diner advertising the "best chicken-fried steak within a hundred yards." He stepped inside. The place greeted him with the aroma of coffee, freshly baked yeast rolls, and cinnamon. A stainless-steel-and-Formica counter with round stools stretched the length of the building. A break about halfway down led to a pair of scarred swinging doors. Booths with red vinyl cushions lined the opposite wall, where two customers sat talking quietly. At the counter, a third read a tabloid newspaper.

Nick nodded as he passed one of the men and sat down in the last booth. Tattered menus rested vertically against the wall behind a chromed holder with salt and pepper shakers and sugar packets. He reached for a menu.

A female voice said, "Don't bother."

Nick looked up at a middle-aged woman standing beside the booth, holding a coffeepot and a large white mug. Her deep green eyes reminded Nick of emeralds. Reading glasses perched in her short, brown hair with silver highlights. A pencil poked out from above an ear. Her almost-perfect smile revealed a slightly displaced canine tooth that only added to her attractiveness. Nick tried to speak, but his tongue got in the way.

She didn't appear to notice. "I'm Maudie. You're making a big mistake if you don't get the special."

"Listen to her, son," said the man at the counter. "She ain't lying."

Nick recovered control of his tongue and held up his hands. "Who am I to ignore unanimous advice? I'll have a cup of that, too."

Thirty minutes later, as he scraped the last of the gravy off his plate with a roll, he had to agree they'd both been right. He signaled Maudie for another cup of coffee and ordered a piece of apple pie, warm, with vanilla ice cream. He was taking the first bite when a voice behind him said, "Well lookie here. A real, live *investigator*."

Nick's least-favorite reporter, the bear-challenged Harvey Sweet, stood a few feet away. "May I join you? There's no more seats left."

Nick resisted the urge to look around the virtually empty diner. "Help yourself."

Sweet nodded at Maudie and slid into the booth. "I see you've discovered the apple pie. Nobody makes it better."

Nick savored the flavor of apples, a heavy dose of spices, and rich butter crust. "I'd have to agree."

Maudie handed Sweet a cup of steaming coffee. "Good evening, Hotel. The usual?"

"No thanks, Maudie." To Nick he said, "How's the investigation going?"

"What did she just call you?"

"It's just a nickname my friends use."

Nick took a sip of coffee and wiped his mouth with a napkin. "Since you've been at all the press briefings, you know as much as I can tell you."

"How long before the final report is made public?"

"Hard to predict. Not for months, even best case."

"What will it say?"

"You know I can't talk about that."

"Sure you can. Off the record works."

"Really?"

Sweet sipped his coffee. "For both sides. Reporters need a place to begin digging. They can do that without compromising sources. Happens all the time."

"Sorry, but you'll have to use your own shovel."

Sweet peered at Nick, eyebrows narrowed. "Then I better get going. Wouldn't want to be late for the church social and bingo night over at the Methodist."

Nick took the last bite of pie and ice cream, followed it with coffee, and gazed out the window. Darkness had settled into the valley, broken only by the twin headlight shafts of cars on the highway. The dinner crowd was arriving, the hum of conversations punctuated by laughter and the loud voices of an elderly couple, both with hearing aids, repeating themselves.

He pushed the plate to the edge of the table. "Assuming I'm the least bit interested in helping your career, what do you expect me to do?"

"For the moment, just listen." Sweet moved deeper into the booth, with his back against the wall and his feet stretched out on the seat. He sounded like a lecturer as he related how in the 1980s, the most successful covert operation in CIA history provided assistance to the Freedom Fighters in their struggle to eject the Soviet Army from Afghanistan. Defeat proved to be the final nail in the coffin for the Soviet Union. It precipitated the end of the Cold War, along with an unintended consequence: out of the ashes rose a rejuvenated militant Islam. America's involvement effectively traded one global threat for another. Sweet held up one finger for emphasis and said, "To this day it's still like a fairy tale most people don't have a clue about. People like you, for example."

Nick knew the history, but watching Sweet in action was too much fun. "That's quite a story."

Sweet sipped his coffee and nodded. "And I'm just speculating, along with a bunch of other people, that twenty years later the government decides to run a clandestine war on global terror. No longer are we hesitant to recruit baddies from the Arab world. Hit squads infiltrate the network with sniper teams, roadside bombs, and a brand-new tactic: filmed executions of terrorist leaders. Make them public with false attribution to one terrorist group or another. The struggle for supremacy within the militant Islamic movement intensifies. It's a cancer, eating them up from within. Terrorist attacks are down, it's working great. Then rumors surface about the beheading of an innocent man. Mistaken identity. The incident jeopardizes the entire operation."

Nick disguised his knowledge of the events with a look of outrage. "I should think so. We're the good guys. But rumors aren't proof. Why not ignore them?"

"Because a video won't let us." Sweet paused to sip his coffee.

Nick ignored Sweet's attempt to elicit a question. He scooted deeper into the booth and mirrored the reporter's position.

After a moment, Sweet said, "I can tell you're just dying to know, so I'll ease your pain. The video has a clue about the guy wielding the sword."

"Ah," said Nick. "You mean something other than being dressed in black from head to toe?"

Sweet nodded and leaned forward. "You've been preoccupied recently and probably don't know this. Some guy analyzed it with enhancement software. Found a tattoo. On the executioner's inside left wrist. One frame, the sleeve of his robe open just enough."

"Must be a distinctive example of body art."

"I'd say. Supposedly belonging to a small group, less than a dozen veterans from the Afghan campaign."

"The guy was Mujahideen?"

"Hell no. Born-and-bred white Anglo-Saxon Christian who helped the Freedom Fighters kick the Soviet Army's ass back to where they came from. Member of a very small fraternity that helped reshape the world."

"Good for him. How does this connect current events to the past?"

"Guess who was intimately involved with America's support of the Mujahideen."

Nick was loving this. Playing dumb and playing Sweet at the same time. "You have *got* to be shitting me."

Sweet shook his head. "Nothing hypothetical about it."

"But something has to tie Larchmont directly to our phantom war."

"And we're back to supposition. Maybe the government recruited his experience in shadow ops by exploiting his legendary patriotism with a simple question: 'How'd you like to eliminate the plague you helped create?'"

Nick drank some coffee gone cold, and motioned to Maudie. With two fresh cups on the table, he leaned forward and whispered, "So he jumps at the chance. But that doesn't put him at the execution."

Sweet pointed to Nick's briefcase. "Is the draft report in there?"

"Yes, but I can't—"

"You performed an autopsy, right?"

"Of course."

"Notice anything of particular interest?"

"Like what?"

"A fresh scar."

Cold night air had chilled the window behind Nick and fogged it up. A warmth built inside him, climbed his spine and met the layer of coolness that caressed his bare neck above his shirt collar. He'd read the autopsy report and noted Larchmont's cause of death: blunt-force trauma and a broken neck consistent with excessive g-forces on the upper body unrestrained by a shoulder harness. No evidence of foul play.

But Sweet was on to something. He had to be.

Nick's briefcase sat on the floor, under the table next to the wall. He lifted it and set it between them. The snap of the latches sounded especially loud, as if his hearing had narrowed along with all his senses to concentrate on the details of this moment.

Sweet's face disappeared behind the lid as Nick opened the briefcase. Without removing the report, he found the tab labeled AUTOPSY PROTOCOL. Under the section marked IDENTIFYING SCARS/TATTOOS he read: four wound scars, two from bullets, one shrapnel, and one stabbing; and a final notation in figurative bold letters, evidence of a recent non-expert surgical procedure to the inside left wrist—probably tattoo removal.

Son of a bitch. What the hell have we here?

He shuffled some papers around, delaying for time to wipe the excitement off his face. Then he closed the briefcase and looked at Sweet. Casually, like, *This is no big deal.* "I've got a hypothetical for *you*."

Sweet rubbed his hands together in exaggerated glee. "I *love* fiction."

"Good, because that's all this is. Let's say that during an investigation into a fatal aircraft accident with the only occupant killed, you found that the main cabin door had been opened post-crash but before the first responder arrived on scene."

Sweet cocked his head to one side. "That might get my attention."

"Right." Nick related the details, plainly identified as supposition, of the emergency response timeline, open door, and muddy footprint on the carpet.

Sweet's eyebrows climbed about an inch. "That may not be so hypothetical." He recounted a series of unexplained facts surrounding the death of a prominent public official in a suspicious crash of a military jetliner some years prior in Europe, including a .45 caliber bullet hole in the victim's head. "I'm surprised you've never seen the accident report."

Nick shook his head. "The NTSB doesn't investigate crashes of military aircraft, and the reports are closed to outside agencies. You're saying somebody on the airplane shot him?"

"Probably not. It's a risky plan for the assassin to be on the airplane when it crashes."

"Somebody shot him post-crash?"

"A clean-up crew. And they probably had to open a door to do it."

Nick smiled. He knew all about the crash and speculation about political assassination. Great minds think alike.

"Well, how about them apples?"

CHAPTER TEN

Lars Nordstrom, Director of the Aviation Division of the NTSB but feeling as useless as a teat on a wild boar hog, had begun the day by retreating to his study with a carafe of coffee. He loved solitary mornings when his wife was gone on one of her frequent shopping trips, and he resented the intrusion when she remained home.

This morning, she had ripped him out of a dream starring Meryl Streep with incessant harping about how she couldn't find *anything* to wear, as if he knew shit about the fashion industry or gave a damn one way or the other. Then she returned home in record time and wanted him to sit while she modeled six bags of new clothes. By the third outfit, he'd had his fill of the latest in fall styles.

Free at last, he brewed fresh coffee and took refuge in the study. He poured a cup, sank into his custom desk chair, and noticed the red missed-call light on his cell phone reflecting off the mirrored surface of the desk. He turned the phone over. James Dickson's number appeared on the screen, date-time stamped earlier that morning. Lars punched the CALL button and waited.

"Is that you, Lars?"

Lars sighed. The availability of caller ID remained an elusive concept to Dickson. "What's going on?"

Dickson's voice crackled over a bad connection "You are not going to believe what just happened."

"You're right, especially if I never get to hear it. Tell me and forget the buildup before my service provider decides we've talked long enough."

Lars forgot about his coffee as Dickson told him about Phillips obsessing over new evidence involving an open main cabin door and muddy footprints on the carpet, and asking idiotic questions about why anybody would have been roaming around the crash site before first responders showed up. When Dickson finally ran out of breath, Lars said, "Any idea who it could have been?"

"Hell, no. Neither does Phillips. I told him it was nothing, but I don't think he's let it go."

"Has he mentioned anything about taking it to the FBI?"

"No, and I doubt he will. He can buy into this conspiracy crap all he wants, but they'll toss him out on his ear. We haven't found evidence of sabotage, or anything inconsistent with a conclusion of pilot error."

"That figures. Anything else?"

"Oh, yeah. An article appeared on the local rag's website with all this stuff about Larchmont being murdered. It—"

"But you just told me Phillips can't prove any of that crap. And even if he can, it's probably a souvenir hunter looking for a piece of history to put on the mantel. Like with the shuttle."

"If you'd let me finish . . . the article didn't mention the details. It used the catch-all 'sources close to the investigation' to suggest somebody was waiting for Larchmont. Just in case."

"How in hell did a reporter come up with that?

"Guess."

"Can you prove it?"

"I don't have to. It's the only explanation."

Lars sighed. "Damn it. This is *not* good. Anything else?"

"No, but the way it's going, all we have to do is wait a minute."

"If that happens, make sure you don't wait another minute to let me know." Lars signed off and rotated his chair to look out the picture window behind his desk. The greenbelt bordering the rear of the property had turned brown, but the view still helped him zone into periods of reflection.

Crossroads in life's journey showed up in the most unlikely places. Lars wasn't particularly religious, at least not with regard to the trappings of organized worship, but he regularly attended services with his wife. On occasion, he'd get the feeling of being trapped in the pew, which always resulted in fidgeting. She'd reach over and lay a hand on his, kind of like a, "There, there, sweetheart, it'll be over soon" move. Combined with the monotonous droning from the pulpit, her concern usually drove him outside.

On the Sunday after the Larchmont crash, while waiting for the service to end, he had taken shelter from a light drizzle under a garden pergola at the rear of the church. A man soon joined him, nodded, and stood apart, staring into the morning fog.

Lars recognized the countenance of power when he saw it, and he never missed an opportunity to ingratiate himself with someone who might help him get some of his own. Showing interest without prying usually worked to get a person talking. He introduced himself and soon asked, "What do you do, Mr. Osborne?"

"I'm in government."

"How about that? I'm the Director of the Aviation Division of the NTSB."

Osborne nodded. "Your life must have taken a turn for the hectic last Friday, huh?"

"That's an understatement. What do *you* do, exactly?"

Osborne shrugged, as if to imply, *Nothing much,* then added, "Let's say I have Oval access whenever I need it."

Lars felt the delicious tingle of excitement that came with the unexpected convergence of luck and preparation. "That must be exciting."

Osborne gazed into the mist and stuck his hands in his pockets. "It should be, you know. Politics aside, it's a noble undertaking to help shape a nation's destiny. But consider the latest distraction. We're being inundated by ridiculous accusations that we financed a shadow army of assassins. That Miles Larchmont, a true patriot, helped set it up and was murdered because he knew too much. Total fabrication, of course, but it sells newspapers."

"That it does, Mr. Osborne. For what it's worth, I don't believe a word of it."

Osborne nodded. "I wouldn't expect a man in your position to follow the crowd. Our problem is that the election is a little more than a year away. That's tomorrow in politics. The aftermath of this crash, the way it feeds the Internet frenzy, could last long enough to affect America's choice at the polls."

He said our *problem.* "It should be a straightforward investigation. I'd be happy to—"

In a move typical of a man used to wielding power, Osborne had terminated the conversation with a finality befitting a person familiar with the Oval Office. He left Lars alone in the gazebo, hungry for a few more moments of Osborne's time and determined to find the brass ring and grab it. But how?

Nothing he'd done so far had put him in jeopardy. He'd sent Dickson to Colorado as Phillips' assistant just to keep tabs on the bastard, who often butted heads with reporters. Like he enjoyed it. With all the media attention, that wouldn't play well on camera for publicizing the crucial role of the Aviation Division and help advance Lars' career. And after the encounter with Osborne, Lars had only told Dickson to push a little. A nudge here and there to keep things on track. Don't let Phillips be a pimple on the ass of progress.

So what should he do in response to the Phillips/reporter coalition threat to pitch another tent at the Larchmont circus? To sit idle seemed timid. More active personal involvement risked losing everything he'd worked for. Then an apropos bureaucratic saying came to mind: "The key to flexibility is indecision."

Of course. Lars smiled. He really did have a pocket full of keys. All he had to do was find one that fit. He poured himself a fresh cup of coffee and leaned back in his chair, content to wait for events to unlock the door to his future.

WITH HIS BELLY AND mind both still full from last night's dinner at Maudie's and his conversation with Sweet, Nick sat in his office trying to concentrate on the human-factors section of the draft final report.

Mid-morning inside the hangar was quiet, peaceful, deserted. Many of the specialists had departed for home, and those who remained had little reason to show up for work much before lunchtime. But he hadn't slept well, and he kept nodding off. To spare his neck the trauma, he finally gave up.

Nick's discussion with Sweet had replayed in his mind so many times that he knew they were onto something. Any next step could pry open the lid on a box with sabotage inside and justify calling in the FBI. It would also trap Nick in Colorado while the Feebies sorted things out. He'd had enough of paperwork to last him a lifetime, and the draft final report could wait a few days. Not only that, but Sweet had picked up the scent. Nick detected the tenacity of a hound dog in the man and had no reason to hold the reporter's leash.

Why not take a quick flight home? Speed differential notwithstanding, he could make the round trip in his airplane in about the same total travel time as in an airliner. And come to think of it, more reliably. Without being strip-searched, which was always a plus. All he needed was some decent weather. He stared at the forecast. A mild cold front approached, with little moisture expected.

The mental tug-of-war began and ended immediately when he recalled his conversation last evening with Fred Anderson about the Mustang. Almost ready, it rested in the shop on its new wheels and tires, the Highland Green paint gleaming like a mirror. When Nick had asked how the engine sounded, Fred said he had no idea.

"You haven't even *started* it?"

"Why should I?"

"But what if—?"

"There isn't any *what if.* I've rebuilt and installed dozens and never had a problem. Besides, Brad ought to be the first person to turn that key, right?"

Nick smiled as he had then. *Absolutely.*

He retrieved a pre-packed duffel bag from the Jeep and hauled it to the flight line. His airplane sat waiting on the ramp, sleek and sexy. An aviator's winged thoroughbred. Kneeling on the wing, he crammed the duffel into the small baggage compartment behind the back seat and secured the restraint straps.

"Headed home?"

Nick looked over his shoulder. Dickson's normally lackluster face was lit up as if he'd swallowed a light bulb. Nick stepped down off the wing. "It would appear so."

"Fantastic. I'm happy for you. Getting back in time for Brad's birthday and all. He must be excited about the car."

Nick's spine tingled. "I never told you about that."

Dickson shrugged. "Maybe you didn't. Anyway, there's no need for you to come back. The draft report is almost done, and I can finish up. Nice working with you, and have a good flight." They shook hands. Dickson walked away, whistling the opening bars of "Happy Days Are Here Again."

So, a man with whom Nick shared nothing personal knew about Brad's car. From the very beginning, Nick had kept the project under wraps. Watching it come together from two disassembled junkers lying on the floor of Fred's shop, rising from the dead, piece by piece, he had yearned to share his excitement with someone. Ease the pressure before he exploded with the anticipation of seeing Brad's face when the cover came off.

Thinking back, had he ever mentioned it to anyone at work? At the snack bar, maybe? Over coffee? No telling. He'd been living with it for almost three years. Plenty of time to let something slip. Or maybe not, and someone had been paying special attention. To what purpose?

Nick glanced at the clouds and the layer of water droplets on the wing. The outside air-temperature gauge in the cockpit read eight degrees above freezing. He pulled the weather printout from his jacket pocket to confirm the forecast freezing level. Goddamn it. It was below his cruise altitude, and he couldn't fly lower because of the terrain. Where were the cloud tops? He called Flight Service on his cell phone. They had no pilot reports in the vicinity to verify current conditions.

The extended twenty-four-hour forecast called for improving conditions by mid-morning tomorrow.

This was a no-brainer. He removed his bag from the airplane, tipped the line guys for their trouble, and asked for a morning pullout.

CHAPTER ELEVEN

Much later than usual after a long night on deadline, Hotel awoke, alert for anything unusual, not in its proper place. Caution, a habit from a former life, remained like a vestigial thumb as an impediment to normal existence.

Pale early-morning light caressed the blinds. The faint aroma of garlic and onion from last night's Basque Chicken dinner reminded him that he had eaten too much. Maudie's soft, rhythmic breathing and the warmth of her body calmed him, as always.

He rolled onto his side toward her. She had the covers pulled over her head. He reached out to draw the comforter back and give her a good-morning kiss.

"Forget it. I'm not awake yet."

"Good morning to you, too, Grumpy." Hotel slipped out of bed and walked across the cold wood floor to his closet. Dressed in his favorite warm-up pants, sweatshirt, and a pair of thick wool socks, he yanked the covers away from Maudie's head, planted a kiss on her cheek, and ran out of the bedroom.

Old faithful had once again brewed a fresh pot. Steaming mug in hand, he went into the study and plopped down in his favorite chair. Ideas seemed to flow up from the cushion whenever he needed inspiration for an article. When he didn't, a virtual blank piece of paper waited, ready to record his thoughts.

His conversation with Nick Phillips the night before had bolstered Hotel's conviction that Larchmont was murdered as part of a conspiracy of silence. He'd rushed home from Maudie's to write the article, which combined his hypothesis with local controversy: aviation proponents against the complaints of the Cedar Valley Airport Neighborhood Association.

His premise: this was not a safety issue arising from the proximity of residential areas to the runway. The pilot never had a chance against conspiratorial forces arrayed against him, so don't blame him or the airplane he flew. Hotel had filed the report online last night ten minutes after deadline and hit the sheets, exhausted, barely able to sleep with the anticipation of how quickly the story might make the big time.

Soft footsteps on the upstairs wood floors signaled that Maudie would be down soon. Never a morning person and always late for work, she'd fill a travel mug with coffee and charge out the door with a wave over her shoulder. As owner of a diner famous for breakfasts, she fortunately employed a cook who never seemed to sleep and could be trusted to do far more than wield a spatula.

Hotel remained at a safe distance from her normal path. Then he replenished his coffee, returned to his study, and gathered his notes from the previous evening. He found the number and dialed.

After three rings a man's gruff voice answered, "Schiller Maintenance, Ellis Thompson speaking."

"Mr. Thompson, this is Harvey Sweet, *Cedar Valley Gazette*. I'm glad I reached you on a weekend."

"This place has more work than it can handle. We'd need

fourteen-day weeks to get it all done."

"Then I'll state my business, sir, and let you get back to it. I'm investigating the GoldenJet crash out here in Colorado. You know the one?"

"Hell, yes. But you could have saved yourself the call. P.J. was a damn fine mechanic and nobody out here did a thing to cause that crash."

"I believe you, Mr. Thompson. We haven't found anything to suggest anyone at Schiller was at fault. I just have a few questions about . . . P.J., did you say? And he *was* a mechanic?"

"P. J. Knowles. He's dead."

Is that so? Hotel didn't like hearing about death, but he damn sure loved this journalistic trolling. Sometimes when he went fishing for news he got a strike. "I'm sorry to hear that. How did it happen?"

Thompson broke out in a round of coughing with no attempt to cover the mouthpiece. Hotel almost got sick hearing it. His mom coughed like that. The old guy had to be a smoker.

Finally Thompson was able to rasp out a few words. "P.J. had this hot-rod. Only a matter of time. Ran off the road, flipped a bunch of times. Never wore his seat belt. Didn't trust them."

"Do you know if the police conducted an investigation?"

More coughing. "What's there to investigate? Damn fool drove too fast. Everybody knows that."

Hotel scribbled *convenient auto accident?* in his notes. "I need to contact his family, sir. Could you help me?"

Hotel wrote the number down, thanked Thompson in the middle of another coughing spell and dialed the Knowles residence. The phone rang eight times before a shaky female voice answered.

"Hello?"

"Mrs. Knowles?"

"Listen, you piece of garbage. I don't need a burial plot, lawyer, life insurance on my baby, or someone to warm my bed. Take your—"

"Hold on, Mrs. Knowles, please. I'm not calling to sell you anything. My name is Harvey Sweet. I'm an investigative reporter out here in Colorado working with the NTSB."

"The what?"

"The National Transportation Safety Board. They investigate accidents in the transportation industry."

"You're investigating my husband's accident?"

"No, ma'am. Look, Mrs. Knowles, I'm very sorry to hear about your husband. I apologize for bothering you, but I need a bit of information." He waited to give the poor woman a moment to decide whether or not to hang up on him. The way he felt, he wouldn't blame her.

Her voice seemed to lose volume, as if she had pulled her mouth a little farther away from the phone. "What is it you want?"

"Did your husband ever mention being contacted by anyone outside Schiller Aviation to work on Mr. Larchmont's plane?"

"Not that I remember."

"Did he talk to you much about work?"

"We're . . . um . . . we were close, Mr. Sweet. We'd sit down in the evenings to share our day, talk about . . ." The widow broke down in a flood of sobs.

Hotel waited. He had a job to do, but much more of this and he'd hang up his media pass. As the crying receded into sniffles, he said, "Did P.J. happen to mention anything about strange things at work? Unauthorized access to Mr. Larchmont's airplane, evidence of tampering, anything like that?

"No, and he would've told me for sure. He considered that plane his own. Didn't really like turning it over to the pilot, if you know what I mean."

"Yes, ma'am, I do. Good mechanics are like that. Did P.J. recently come into any extra money?"

The woman's voice turned hard. "Are you suggesting my husband would take a *bribe?*"

"No ma'am. The NTSB has no interest other than finding a cause for an accident involving a plane P.J. worked on."

After a pause, and in a softer but reserved tone, Mrs. Knowles said, "There's nothing to find out about P.J. He loved that airplane like he loved that car. He had mechanic in his blood, Mr.—um—what was your name?"

"Sweet, ma'am. Harvey Sweet."

"Anything he did to that plane would've been good for it, Mr. Sweet."

"Yes, ma'am. Just one more thing. Can you tell me who handled the report for your husband's accident?"

After a long pause filled with muffled crying, Mrs. Knowles answered, her voice shaking. "That would be Trooper Mark Littlejohn. I have his number right here."

Hotel cradled the phone between his ear and shoulder as he wrote down the number. "Thank you, Mrs. Knowles. I appreciate your time. I'm really sorry."

The line went dead. Hotel sighed. The sadness in the woman's voice depressed him. If all of investigative reporting was this tough, he might decide to reenlist. In the meantime, he was on a roll. He checked the trooper's number on his pad and made the call.

A man answered immediately. "Corporal Littlejohn speaking. May I help you?" The trooper's words all ran together. *Mayahhepyew?*

Hotel introduced himself without mentioning the paper. "I'm conducting a follow-up investigation into the crash of Mr. Larchmont's airplane. Maybe you've been following the story in the news?"

"Yes, sir. Can't help but hear more than I ever wanted to know. How's that involve a state trooper?"

"It probably doesn't, but I have a few questions if you have the time."

"And who are you with again, Mr. Sweet?"

"I'm investigating—"

"I heard that. You apparently didn't hear me. Who are you *with*, Mr. Sweet."

"Uh . . . the *Cedar Valley Gazette,* sir."

"Nice try, son."

Hotel listened to the dead phone for a few seconds. He'd been two-thirds successful. Even the big boys would probably kill for that ratio. And he had another option right here in Cedar Valley.

Nick finished his breakfast and waved at the cook for a coffee refill.

Maudie charged through the front door of the diner. She snatched the pot out of the cook's hand, motioned him back to the grill and walked to the booth. "Morning, Nick."

"And to you as well, fair maiden."

Maudie peered at him over her reading glasses and waggled the coffee pot. "You might want to resist the temptation to kid around with an armed woman about her appearance this early in the morning."

Nick held up his hands. "Point well taken."

Maudie poured him a cup. "Hotel came to bed really late

last night. You guys tie one on?"

"I never drink when I'm working. Or talking to reporters."

"Darn good idea." She walked behind the counter and shooed the cook away from the grill. This was her place, and she obviously enjoyed personally taking care of her customers.

The door opened with a bang and Dickson stalked in. He looked around, made eye contact with Nick, and marched over to the booth. Fists resting on the table, he leaned close. "I thought you were headed home."

Nick met his angry stare. "I did too."

"Well?"

"Want some coffee, James?"

"No, I do not want any *fucking* coffee. In all the time I've known you, the question of professional ethics has never come up."

Nick gripped his mug with both hands. "And what brought that up?"

"We can't find anything mechanical. A turn in the wrong direction takes Larchmont to his death. You look for a reason buried in the avionics, then insert media conjecture and rumor into the investigation. I don't care one way or the other until you start talking with that reporter. You're a disgrace to our profession."

Nick took a deep breath and exhaled slowly. "Let me remind you that in spite of Nordstrom's plans, you aren't running this investigation. Take your objections and stuff them up your ass."

Dickson shook his head. "That's not where they're going."

Nick uncrossed his legs under the table and pictured his initial moves: throw the hot coffee at Dickson's face, shift his body in the booth, and kick the SOB in the knee. "Let me ask you something, James."

"What?"

"What are you trying to cover up?"

"Fuck you!" Dickson stepped back from the table, his face instantly a crimson mask.

"Hey!" Behind Dickson, Maudie rounded the corner at the break in the counter and marched toward the booth. She gripped a short baseball bat in her hand. The diner had become very quiet.

Nick nodded in her direction and said to Dickson, "You might want to check your six o'clock."

Dickson looked over his shoulder. He turned to face Maudie and held his hands out to his sides. "You don't need that."

Maudie got right in Dickson's face. "Nobody cusses in my place. Leave."

Dickson sidestepped her and strode to the door. Maudie followed close at his heels. As he left the diner, she said, "You aren't welcome here." She returned to the grill, and over her shoulder to the customers, "Y'all can relax."

The diner began to refill with the hum of interrupted conversations. The door opened. Sweet entered, nodded to Maudie and sat down opposite Nick. "Did I just see one of your investigators storm out of here?" When Nick nodded, Sweet said, "I think he's the first person ever who didn't like the food."

"A bad case of indigestion would be my guess. What are you doing here?"

"Finding you. Ready for another story?"

"Sure. I love fiction. Just like everybody else."

"Okay, then. Somebody with a lot of power, and by that I mean *money*, wants to kill a guy who flies his own airplane. The killer is looking for a way to make the death appear accidental. A plane crash would be ideal, but he doesn't know how to set it up. What would you do in his place?"

Nick sipped his coffee, picked up his spoon and tapped it on the table. "Pay an expert a whole bunch of dough to arrange it."

"Good, but it could be better. Try again."

Nick thought about that for a moment. "Double-cross the guy. Keep the money and set him up to take the heat."

"Or better yet?

"Get rid of him."

Sweet nodded and pointed to Nick's coffee cup. "Finish that and let's go."

Nick followed Hotel to his pickup and climbed in the passenger seat. "Why is it so cold in here?"

"Heater doesn't work."

"Then let's go back inside."

"We don't need anyone hearing this. Larchmont's mechanic is dead."

Nick faced Sweet. "I assume this part isn't hypothetical. How did you find out?"

Sweet recounted the details of the two phone calls.

Nick shook his head. "You called the man's *widow?*"

"Yeah, I know. Pretty heartless, and I don't feel very good about it. But I was nice." Sweet produced a piece of notepaper from his jacket pocket. He unfolded it, placed it on the console in front of Nick and tapped it with a finger. "Call him."

Nick stared at the name and number. "A trooper?"

"He investigated the crash that killed the mechanic. My bet is he'll talk to you."

"You have your phone handy?"

"He's already seen my number in caller ID."

"Good point." Nick dug his phone out of his jacket pocket and dialed the number.

After introductions, the trooper said, "You know any reporters out there?"

Nick looked at Hotel and smiled as he said, "I hate those bastards, excuse my French."

Litttlejohn laughed. "My time's yours, Mr. Phillips."

"I appreciate your courtesy. Did you conduct an investigation into the automobile accident that killed P. J. Knowles?"

"Don't know if you'd call it an investigation. I was on duty that morning and rolled up on it. Must have just happened. It was a bad one. I did all the standard accident-scene stuff and wrote a report."

"Anything unusual about the circumstances?"

"Except maybe for the skid marks, no. Everybody who knew P.J. figured he was going to kill himself in that car. He was always tinkering with one thing or another. Had a measured course set up on his way to and from work, looking to shave bits of a second off his best time. Seemed pretty cut and dried to me."

"What about the skid marks?"

"Well, on single-vehicle accidents where a car loses control and alcohol's involved, these old boys will come up on a curve and never try to stop. It's like they're asleep at the wheel, and they probably are most of the time. There won't be any skid marks to speak of.

"But when it's just excessive speed, kids drag racing, it's like they all of a sudden realize they're not going to make it. The brakes come on and stay on until the vehicle stops. Lots of rubber on the road."

"How was this accident different?"

"Well, sir, P.J. drove like a maniac. He had a lot of tickets with my name on them. But I *never* found him driving under the influence. I'm not sure he ever got on the brakes. The skid marks looked to me like tires spinning, not locked up."

"You have any explanation for that?"

"No, sir."

Nick glanced at Sweet, who raised his right hand, first finger extended, his mouth forming a silent question. Nick nodded. "See any signs of mechanical failure?"

"Didn't look. As I said, this accident appeared to be nothing more than destiny. That boy was born to die in a car."

Nick stared out the windshield. How about that? Was it only coincidence that two people connected through an airplane have died in an expected manner? A bit too convenient, perhaps? "Would you be willing to do me a favor?"

"Don't know why not. It's official, right?"

"Of course. But it's part of a confidential investigation. I'd appreciate it if you'd keep this between us."

"Not a problem. What do you need?"

"Examine that car to see if anything appears to have failed prior to the accident, or might have been tampered with."

"Hold on, Mr. Phillips. If we're talking criminal act here, that's my jurisdiction."

"And it will be, Corporal. There's probably nothing to find, but I'm sure you don't mind helping out with an important federal inquiry."

A pause, then, "How do I contact you?" After Nick gave him his cell phone number, the trooper said, "I have something for you."

"What is it?"

"We always inventory personal effects of accident victims. Everything goes to the families unless we find illegal drugs, weapons, that sort of thing. Something in P.J.'s jacket looks like it might be for an airplane. I put it on my desk to take to

Schiller. Before I got around to it, I read an article about that crash out there in Colorado. It had a picture of the site, and damn if the number on the tail of that airplane doesn't match a number hand-printed on this envelope. It's got something hard in it. You know, not just paper. What should I do with it?"

Nick glanced at Sweet and gave him a thumb's up. To Littlejohn he said, "It's probably nothing, but how about sending it to me overnight priority? Here's the address and a shipping account number."

CHAPTER TWELVE

After his conversation with the trooper and getting a delicious punch in the heart from excitement-induced adrenaline, Nick had tried and failed for most of the day to concentrate on the draft report. Bored to tears, he closed the folder, walked out of the hangar and stared up into a darkening sky.

His eagerness to get home couldn't compete with common sense. This morning's low clouds and drizzle had pushed his planned departure into the afternoon. But a stiff north wind and the temperature down about ten degrees in the last hour grounded him with the possibility of icing. The weather gods must be angry. Something he'd done had pissed them off. He zipped his flight jacket and shoved his hands in the pockets.

He'd missed the career of a lifetime by not becoming a meteorologist. What a great job. Get paid for reading instruments that automatically record weather data, report it to the public, and use computer programs to predict future conditions that no one expected to be accurate.

Based on tomorrow's forecast for improving conditions, he went to the line shack and asked for a dawn pullout. Back at the operations hangar, he found lying on his desk a cardboard quick-pack from Trooper Littlejohn. Nick tossed it in his briefcase. He was tired, hungry, and ready for Maudie's special.

An hour later he finished dinner and declined her offer of dessert. He had eaten way too much pie over the past week, and the waistband of his pants reminded him of the consequences every time he took a breath. He got the quick-pack out of his briefcase and opened it. Inside he found a printed note on lined paper:

Mr. Phillips:

I took another look at the wreckage of P.J.'s car. It was pretty well messed up, like I told you, but I did find something that might explain what happened.

P.J. had a carburetor on that GTO looks like it could power a spaceship. I'm no mechanic to speak of, but it appears the throttle was jammed full open. That for sure could explain the spinning tires. The car must have rolled four, maybe five times, so I couldn't tell anything about the condition of the linkage, and there's a lot more stuff on top of that engine than I'm used to seeing. Sorry I can't be of more help.

Remember your promise to let me know if there's any reason I need to consider this accident out here a criminal matter. Good luck with your inquiry.

Mark Littlejohn.

P.S. This is the envelope I mentioned.

Nick removed a brown padded mailer, pre-addressed to the manufacturer of the GPS navigation receiver installed in the GoldenJet. A notice in bold capital letters identified the contents as TIME SENSITIVE NAVIGATION INFORMATION CRITICAL TO FLYING SAFETY. The tail number of the airplane, N924DP, was handwritten on the back. Wondering how many years he could get for tampering with the mail, he slit the envelope open with his pocketknife and removed the contents: a plastic baggie with a datacard Nick recognized as an update for the North American navigation database. The label identified the expiration date at which a new datacard must be installed for the system to remain current: in thirteen days.

Nothing unusual about that. GPS systems accepted installation of the new database before the old one expired and automatically switched to the updated version on the effective date. The manufacturer charged customers for failure to return outdated datacards, and to find this datacard in the mechanic's jacket and ready for mailing probably meant nothing other than he forgot to drop it in the mail.

As Nick tossed the baggie on the table, a blast of frigid air flowed into the diner. Harvey Sweet came through the front door, rubbing his gloved hands together. He wore camouflage outdoor clothing. A motorcycle helmet hung by its chinstrap from the crook of his left arm.

"The usual, Maudie," Sweet called out. When he saw Nick, he added, "I'll take it over here with the out-of-towner." Maudie waved a spatula. Sweet ambled over to the booth and sat down.

Nick pointed at the helmet and thick pair of gloves as Sweet laid them on the seat. "Where'd you get your death wish?"

"Passed down from my daddy, along with a hunting cabin in the mountains. You're welcome to come along."

"No thanks. I can't imagine riding one of those things even in warm weather."

"Your Jeep will make it. It's probably got a heater that works."

"No, thank you again. I'm heading home, remember?"

Sweet nodded as Maudie delivered a plate of bacon and eggs. He wolfed down a biscuit and pointed at the datacard. "What's that?"

"A navigation datacard for the GPS in the GoldenJet."

"From the trooper?" When Nick nodded, Sweet said, "Is it important?"

"I was pondering that when you showed up for a heart attack. The answer is, maybe."

Sweet stopped eating in mid-bite. "You got a lot of nerve. My guess is that plate used to be filled with Maudie's special. What do you mean by maybe?"

"That I'm not sure. Aviation GPS navigation receivers are updated regularly. The system in my airplane and the one in the GoldenJet are made by the same manufacturer, but they're different models."

"So what?"

"I think this datacard was removed from the GoldenJet shortly before the fatal trip and replaced with a revised one. I haven't received an update. Basic navigation data is common to all models and would be revised at the same time."

Sweet wiped his mouth with a paper napkin and started in on his eggs. "So the question is, have you missed an update, or did the GoldenJet get a special one?"

"Exactly." Nick motioned to Maudie for coffee, picked up the datacard and handed it to Sweet. After Maudie poured their refills, Nick cupped his hands around the mug. "It looks exactly like the ones I receive for my GPS. I don't remember when my last update was installed, or when I'm due for another, but something doesn't make sense. Look at the date."

Sweet nodded. "It hasn't expired."

"Which probably means nothing more than the new update was installed early. But when grasping for straws, one needs to think outside the box, right?"

"Absolutely. Have you been doing that, or just getting fat on Maudie's cooking?"

"Both."

"And?"

"There's always the chance of an out-of-sequence revision."

"Why would they do that?"

"To address a serious problem with the data that compromises safety of flight and can't wait until the next revision."

Sweet handed the datacard to Nick. "Is there any way to check that one out?"

Nick dropped the datacard in his briefcase and sipped his coffee. Carefully, because Maudie served it scalding. "Maybe. The GoldenJet logbooks will confirm the model and serial number of the GPS installed. I'll need that information when I call the manufacturer. And unless there are differences in the datacards not externally apparent, we could put this one in my airplane and look at the start-up screen."

"To see if this update was in sequence."

"Right."

Sweet finished his bacon and began cleaning the plate with a piece of toast. "I've got a question."

"Me first. Doesn't Maudie have a dishwasher?" When Sweet glared at him and didn't answer, Nick said, "And the question is?"

Sweet pointed at Nick's briefcase. "If we want to check out whether the removal of that datacard is connected to the accident, why examine the one that wasn't in the airplane when it crashed?"

THE LAST REMAINING DETAIL of Wilson's assignment carried risks well beyond its importance, but he couldn't walk away without trying. It'd be like an itch he could barely reach, much less get to quit bugging the shit out of him.

He'd spent a day watching the Cedar Valley Airport from vantage points in the forest, getting the feel of routines. In disguise, he wandered around the airport like one of those airplane gawkers. The kind who parks his car off the end of a runway, sits in a lawn chair and takes pictures, the dreamer who's never been *in* an airplane, much less flown one, invisible to airport insiders who have outgrown their fascination with planes. Or at least don't display it with their mouths hanging open.

That was *always* a nice touch, hiding in plain sight. Look like a doofus and people feel uncomfortable staring. Somebody asks what a stranger looked like and all they can offer is a description that fits a few million folks.

But tonight, the time for watching had passed. The airport lay below him in the distance. Scattered security fixtures cast pale circles on the wet asphalt ramp. The last sign of human activity had occurred an hour ago, one of the line guys leaving in a battered pickup with a hole in the muffler. The NTSB operations hangar was guarded at night by a rent-a-cop who appeared old enough to have started out protecting biplanes. No way would grandpa be an obstacle.

Wilson descended the slope to the perimeter chain-link fence, knelt in the tall grass and paused to listen and watch. After a few moments of nothing but deserted quiet, he scaled the fence and dashed to the rear wall of a long row of T-hangars. He peered around a corner, then advanced to the next row, and finally the third, from which he could see the larger building in which the remains of the GoldenJet were stored.

A cautious intermission, to close his eyes, zone into the sounds of the night and listen for anything not of the natural world around him. A few minutes passed.

Satisfied, he took a peek and retreated. Nothing but deserted ramp, glistening with a thin film of misty drizzle that threatened to become ice if the temperature dropped even a few degrees.

He checked the pistol, held it close by his right leg and stepped from cover into the open space between the T-hangars and the larger one. He walked with purpose, but without visible urgency, to a point about halfway across the ramp.

A sound brought him to a standstill. A vehicle?

Light flickered through the trees and disappeared. He stared into the darkness.

Headlight beams swung an arc through the murky night between Wilson and the airport entrance gate. He turned on a heel and spotted a dumpster sitting beside the T-hangar wall.

Ten seconds later he crouched behind it, the pistol held in both hands. The cold, black steel of the barrel caressed his face, smelled of Hoppe's 9 solvent and gun oil. Familiar, comforting.

THE DELAY WOULDN'T ADD more than twenty minutes to the trip, but Nick had to endure Sweet's incessant bitching about the brand-new tire on his dirt bike that wouldn't hold air and forced him to rely on Nick for a ride. Sweet was on deadline, damn it, and he didn't appreciate having to make a stop at the airport on the way to his house. He seemed to think that every article he wrote deserved the Pulitzer.

Nick parked the Jeep and turned off the engine. When Sweet reached for the passenger door handle, Nick said, "Hold it. I can't legally take you into a secure area. The guard won't care, but I don't want you with me."

"I was wondering why you parked so far away. What's the problem? You're just borrowing the datacard."

"True, but I'd just as soon keep this low key."

"Why wouldn't that objective be served best by a visit during normal duty hours?"

"I'm headed home tomorrow morning. If the salvage team takes control of the wreckage while I'm gone—"

"Got it." Sweet shrugged and relaxed into the seat. "Hurry up."

Nick picked up a large cup of Maudie's coffee from the console holder, opened his door and got out. He walked fifty yards to the vertical shaft of drizzle under the light above the personnel door into the hangar, stepped inside and waved at the security guard. "Hey, Larry."

"Hello, Mr. Phillips. What's up?"

Nick handed Larry the coffee. "You know how it is. Work's never done."

"Ain't that the truth? Thanks for the java. This'll hit the spot."

Nick asked Larry about his family. They had worked together on a number of investigations over the years, and Nick had helped arrange a job interview for one of Larry's sons.

Larry blew into the cup and took a sip. "I appreciate the visit, but you must've come out here for something more than small talk."

"I just need to check something out. Can you point me to where the aircraft records are stored?"

"Yes, sir. Right over there." Larry nodded toward a stack of boxes. "They're all sealed up and ready for shipment. I'll get a box cutter for that tape."

Oops. That would leave physical evidence of an off-the-record visit. "Hold on, Larry. I can do it after we get home. But I also need to look in the fuselage. It won't take a minute."

"Help yourself. Let me know if I can do anything."

Nick approached the remains of the GoldenJet. The fuselage still rested in the center of the hangar, looking like a large crumpled tin can sheared off on one end. Avoiding the surrounding detached pieces, he walked up to the left side of the fuselage and leaned into the open main cabin door.

In spite of all his experience investigating aircraft accidents, he found it difficult to comprehend the forces that had done this to a pressure vessel strong enough to support human life at 45,000 feet. He knelt down and crawled into the cabin, turned left and stopped between what remained of the refreshment center and the aft-facing passenger seat. Ignoring the signs of violent death, he leaned forward into the cockpit, removed the datacard from the GPS and replaced it with the one from the mailing envelope. Keeping both wasn't an option. Someone might notice the empty slot in the GoldenJet's GPS control panel. He crawled out of the fuselage, waved to Larry and left the hangar.

WILSON LINGERED IN THE shadows, watching. Why did the lone figure go into the hangar this late at night? Why leave his SUV so far away? An NTSB guy would park beside the entrance. *Something's up.*

He ran behind the hangars to the edge of the airfield and knelt where grass had crept onto an unpaved strip between the fence and the asphalt. Daily workouts at sea level didn't help in this thin mountain air. He inhaled deeply to slow his breathing and calm his pounding heart. After a moment, he crawled from behind the cover of the last hangar and lay in the tall grass about twenty feet from the SUV. He freed the pistol from his waistband and eased up onto his knees.

When the guy returned, he'd pass in front of the SUV,

open the driver's door and climb in. An opportunity to spread a little fear, maybe? To the right guy? Or not? No matter. Fear is contagious.

A dark shape appeared from behind the corner of the hangar.

NICK HESITATED A MOMENT when he couldn't see Sweet inside the Jeep. Then he remembered the tinted windows. He approached the driver's door and yanked on the handle. It snapped out and back. He fumbled in his jacket pocket for the keys, dropped them, bent over and snatched them off the wet pavement. It was too dark to see the labels on the remote, so he punched every button in quick succession.

All the Jeep's lights came on, a shrill alarm cut through the silence, and the slumped figure of Sweet jerked awake in the front passenger seat.

Nick peered at the remote in the pulsating glare of the headlights and pressed the panic button. His heart felt like it wanted to go for a run and leave him behind. He took a deep breath and climbed in and shut the door. "Sorry I startled you."

Sweet glared at him. "That's okay, but you might not want to make a habit of it." He pulled his right hand from inside his unzipped jacket, leaned forward, and slipped a black pistol behind his back.

After a silent pause, Nick said, "I didn't know reporters carried concealed handguns."

Sweet nodded. "Some do."

CHAPTER THIRTEEN

Wilson woke up to the chatter of a squirrel perched on a branch above his head. A dove cooed. Water droplets tapped on the thick layer of pine needles covering the forest floor. The aroma of moist earth brought back memories of more innocent times, when phone calls from anonymous voices over secure lines didn't send him out to take care of loose ends.

He yawned and looked around him. A hint of dawn gold tinged the trees on the ridge to the east. He bolted upright and checked his watch. *Damn it, running late.* His stiff body complained as he stumbled down the mountain to a cluster of boulders at the edge of a cliff overlooking the valley.

Scanning the airport with low-light binoculars, he confirmed the same sleepy look of the night before. This morning's lousy flying weather would keep students and casual flyers at home. The two young men who usually opened up the line shack at 5:00 a.m. probably wouldn't be on time. If he hurried, maybe.

He shouldered the rifle and started down, stepping carefully on the steep, rocky terrain. The thin soles of his urban-style boots tended to fill up with mud, and he'd fallen on his ass a couple of times during the night traveling to the rented Explorer and back. After that damned car alarm had sounded and he saw the passenger in the Jeep, he abandoned the plan to spread a little nighttime terror among the locals and changed out of black field clothing into forest camouflage. Better concealment in daylight, and anyone he ran into would consider him just another deer-hunting fool.

At the edge of the woods he checked both ways and crossed the highway to walk facing traffic like a good, safe pedestrian. Friendly waves to a few passing cars helped make him unmemorable. Approaching the front entrance to the airport, he scanned the ramp and hangar areas. Still deserted. He knelt down as if to tie his shoes, lowered the rifle to the ground and concealed it in tall grass.

With hands in his jacket pockets, he strolled through the open front gate. The grip of the pistol tucked inside his pants at the belt line poked through a slit in the pocket lining. Nice feature. Saved his life once. The guy had died with both eyes looking like question marks.

As if he did this every day, Wilson ambled to the personnel door at one end of the NTSB operations hangar. Shading the small window in the door with his hand, he peered in. The guard was sound asleep in a chair, head cocked off to one side, mouth open.

Wilson took a last look around, opened the door, and stepped into the semi-darkness. The door squeaked as it closed. The guard woke up. Wilson walked directly toward him, waving his hand. "Howdy, there, old timer."

The guard stood up. He carried a revolver in a belt-slide holster that left the barrel exposed. A faint sheen of gun oil glinted on the metal. With a quick flick, his thumb released the hammer tab that secured the pistol.

Be careful with this one. Wilson smiled. "Nick Phillips asked me to come by. Is he here?"

The guard appeared to relax a bit. "He normally comes in around seven. You need—"

Wilson extended his right arm as if to shake hands, rushed the guard and chopped upward with a blow to his throat. He gripped the guard's pistol with his left hand, tore the weapon free, lashed out with his leg and swept the guard's legs off the floor. The man hit the concrete with a moist thud and lay still.

Wilson knelt, felt for a pulse—erratic, weak—then stuffed the guard's revolver, watch, and wallet into his jacket pocket and hauled the body out of sight into a corner. He trotted to the wreckage of the airplane, crawled into the cockpit, and removed the GPS navigation datacard. No one would notice the empty slot this late in the investigation, but he still didn't like leaving loose ends. People paid him to take care of things, unlikely or not.

He stepped out of the hangar onto the deserted ramp and sauntered toward the terminal building and front gate. At the road he looked around for prying eyes, retrieved the rifle and entered the woods. It would be tougher going, but less conspicuous than walking along the highway.

A hundred yards into the trees, he found a loose rock and pulled it free from the deep layer of pine needles. He put the guard's weapon and possessions in the hole, replaced the rock and smoothed the pine needles to cover the disturbed earth.

As he climbed the ridge to reach the eastern slope where he had parked the Explorer, the flush of success triggered an element of doubt. He *loved* this part of his work. Could he live without the head rush? Was this really his last assignment?

He paused to catch his breath, removed the datacard from his jacket pocket and stared at it. So much power in such a small package. It didn't weigh more than—*uh oh.*

With a small magnifying glass attached to the Explorer

keys, he examined the label.

THE WEATHER FORECASTER HAD lied to Nick again. Low clouds blanketed Cedar Valley most of the morning. Conditions were supposed to improve by mid-day before deteriorating again by nightfall, so he asked the line guys to leave his airplane out just in case. When he stepped out of Maudie's after a late breakfast, patches of blue sky to the south lured him back to the airport. Approaching the entrance gate, he caught glimpses of the runway, hangars and ramp area through the trees. His airplane still sat by the line shack, ready for preflight and departure.

He parked the Jeep and walked out on the ramp. The line guys waved at him from the shack, where they camped out when the weather turned cold. Directly overhead, the clouds had thinned. By the time he completed the external preflight, opened the canopy and stowed his duffel, more blue sky had appeared above. Typical mountain weather, which could change its mind faster than a woman. Nick smiled. He knew better than to think, much less say, anything like that around Laurie or Stephanie. They'd hand his head to him in a basket.

To be ready for the approaching departure window, he climbed into the cockpit and fastened the seat belt and shoulder harness. While waiting, he decided to check out the GoldenJet's datacard. He removed it from the baggie and turned the power knob on his GPS to OFF. This released the latch holding the datacard in its slot. With a gentle tug on a small tab, he slid the datacard out and compared the labels. They both expired on the same day.

Okay. The dates on all three datacards, his and the two from the GoldenJet, matched. If the one he had removed from the GoldenJet was an official update in normal sequence, the new effective and expiration dates would be noted on the label. They were not. But if an out-of-sequence revision had been issued, there would be something to distinguish it from the old one received from Trooper Littlejohn. There wasn't. Could one or more of the external labels be incorrect?

He reinserted the datacard from his GPS and flipped the aircraft battery on, followed by the avionics master switch. After the self-test program completed, he checked the dates. Same as the label.

Nick was repeating the process with the second datacard when a voice got his attention.

"Mr. Phillips?"

"Yes?"

"Do you want me to pull these chocks?"

Like every pilot who has ever forgotten to remove chocks and didn't want anyone to know, Nick acted as if he had planned to leave them jammed against the tires. He smiled and waved. "That'd be great, thanks." He'd heard stories of pilots who were so embarrassed they actually tried to roll over the chocks after engine start by shoving up the power. That usually just resulted in far worse and well-deserved humiliation.

The line guy bent down out of sight below the engine cowling and reappeared holding two faded yellow chocks by the frayed rope connecting them. Nick gave him a thumbs-up and noticed water droplets on the windshield.

Damn. He peered up at the clouds. Shifting patches of blue sky still drifted past, but the moisture didn't bode well. Caution and reason battled with the urge to get home.

But the overcast wasn't very thick. *Go.*

After a rushed start and taxi, Nick took off and climbed into the soup. He had an instrument clearance to enter the clouds, with departure instructions issued while he was still on the ground talking with air traffic control on a land line. Once high enough to establish radio contact, he checked in on the designated radio frequency and stated his assigned heading and altitude.

The controller answered, "Experimental Eight Five November Delta, Denver Center, squawk ident."

Nick triggered the identification feature of his transponder, which helped the controller distinguish Nick's enhanced radar return from other airplanes on the controller's scope.

After a few seconds, the controller said, "Experimental Eight Five November Delta, radar contact seven miles south of the Cedar Valley Airport. Altimeter two niner seven seven. Climb to and maintain eleven thousand, turn left zero niner zero."

Nick acknowledged the instructions and turned east as he settled into the special world of instrument flying. He'd been taught early in flight training that the human sensory apparatus is poorly equipped to maintain orientation in the three-dimensional world of flight. Without a visible horizon, instruments provided the only reliable method for maintaining pitch and bank of the aircraft within safe parameters. Over the years, he'd developed a personalized crosscheck sequence in which his eyes constantly scanned the panel.

Useful, though less dependable, feedback surrounded him. The sound and feel of the engine, airflow over the canopy, and small sensations of climb, descent, and bank joined in a marriage of the senses and an uneasy truce with gravity.

Passing 8,000 feet, Nick questioned his earlier assessment of a thin overcast. He needed to reach clear air soon. Level at 11,000 feet and still in the clouds, he glanced above the instrument panel at the windshield. His chest expanded with a quick, nervous breath.

The outside air temperature gauge read zero degrees centigrade. He peered over his shoulder at the left wing. Opaque white nuggets of ice coated the leading edge.

"Denver, Eight Five November Delta, I'm picking up ice. Request immediate climb. Do you have a tops report?"

"Experimental Five November Delta, you have traffic in your left ten o'clock for fifteen miles, level at twelve thousand. I'll have a climb for you when clear. I have no tops reports in your vicinity."

"Is that traffic above the clouds, Denver?"

After a pause, the controller replied, "Negative, Five November Delta. He's also reporting ice."

In spite of the cold air flowing through fresh air nozzles into the cockpit, beads of sweat trickled down Nick's forehead and stung his eyes.

With no deicing system, he had two choices: immediately climb into clear air and hope he didn't pick up more ice than the airplane could carry, or descend to warmer temperatures to melt it. He stared at the left wing. The ice layer appeared to be thickening, and fast.

"Denver, Five November Delta, I need an immediate return to Cedar Valley."

As the controller issued new instructions, Nick silently offered the universal pilot's mantra: *Hands, don't fail me now.*

WITH THE FINGERS OF his left hand poised over the keypad on his phone, Wilson struggled to recall the number. As usual, it didn't help. No matter how hard he tried, his brain jumbled numerical sequences into a hopeless mess. Doctors called it "sequential processing deficit." Wilson called it a pain in the ass.

And if he'd only looked at the datacard sooner, he wouldn't have had to deal with returning to the airport. He'd scrambled down the mountain and paused at the forest's edge to catch his breath. A faint wail drifted through the trees. He retreated a few feet into the shadows. The siren grew louder. A sheriff's car blew by him, lights painting the forest with an intermittent bloody glow. He walked in the woods parallel to the highway until he had an unobstructed view of the airport. Emergency vehicles filled the ramp by the hangar. He'd lost the opportunity to put this operation to bed forever. The only good news came when he saw the investigator's airplane roll onto the taxiway and out of sight into the mist. Good riddance.

Time for the phone call. He didn't like carrying a hard copy of information best kept secret, but sometimes convenience demanded it. From a jacket pocket, he removed a small notepad, opened it, stared at the number as he dialed.

While the sound of secure phone connections being established crackled in the earpiece, he knelt, tore the page out and crumpled it. He placed it on a rock, set it alight, and watched the flames consume the link to his current employer.

The voice answered. "Speak."

"I got what I came for."

"You called to share that?"

"And to tell you the investigator has left."

"You sure?"

"Of course. And also to remind you of our agreement. I expect the money within twenty-four hours."

"Tell you what. Why don't we wait a bit, see if you really got it done?"

"I told you—"

The connection went dead. Wilson made a silent promise to himself that someday, he'd find the SOB with that voice and cut out the man's tongue. He slipped the phone in his pocket and trudged up the mountain to leave this miserable valley for the last time, accompanied by the knowledge that this job still had a small hole, with no way to plug it.

NICK REQUESTED A SHORT approach to the runway, and the controller vectored him back toward the airport with a series of close-in turns. The automated weather broadcast reported the ceiling and visibility barely above minimums. Thanks to the weather gods for small favors.

He descended in the clouds, tracking the final approach course inbound. One mile outside the final fix and nine miles from the runway, he leveled at 7,500 feet. Ice continued to build on the wings, coating the leading edges with a heavy, lift-destroying layer. The propeller shed its accumulations every few minutes, the ice clattering against the engine cowling and windshield. Every time it happened, his heart rate kicked up a notch. Or two.

At eight miles, he could descend to 6,400 feet, the minimum safe altitude until he reached three miles. This was the restriction dictated by the obstruction where the GoldenJet had crashed. Tension-induced sweat covered Nick's face, chest and armpits. The airplane felt heavy and sluggish.

Landing gear and flaps?

No. The extra weight of the ice combined with the increase in drag might exceed available power.

He focused on the "T" of six instruments that defined his world and reminded himself not to look up until he broke out of the clouds. Spatial disorientation, a common killer in weather-related accidents, lurked as a consequence of erratic head and eye movements.

But after a moment, the temptation proved irresistible. Just one little peek. He glanced up. A layer of opaque ice coated the center portion of the windscreen. He leaned to the left to look around it, and the movement created false turn indications within his inner ear. *Vertigo.*

He locked his eyes onto the artificial horizon. His wings were level, but the turning sensation would not abate. He knew better than to be fooled by the erroneous signals. His only task: concentrate on the instruments and ignore everything else.

Nausea brought bile to his throat. He tried to swallow, but his mouth was too dry. A water bottle sat on the floor beside the seat, but he couldn't get to it.

What about the autopilot? Too late to try it.

Disorientation gradually subsided, replaced by a renewed and persistent desire to find the runway and get this airplane on the ground.

A fleeting glimpse of the ground appeared in his peripheral vision. Was that the road slightly left and parallel to the final course? He should be able to see it.

Too fast to identify, a dark strip flashed by on his right side and disappeared in the gray murk. Another glimpse a few seconds later. Looked like an irrigation canal.

The urge to abandon the approach swelled within him. He fought it down.

Wait a little longer, you'll see it. A patch of green passed just below the left wing.

Nick shoved the throttle forward and yanked back on the stick.

WILSON HAD REACHED HALFWAY to the top of the ridge when the sound of an airplane passed overhead. He looked up just as ragged clouds covering the ridge swallowed a white fuselage and wings with red and yellow sunburst stripes. The engine powered up and quit abruptly, accompanied by cracking and snapping sounds.

That was the investigator's airplane. Did the fucker just crash? Wilson grabbed his GPS out of his jacket, selected the user database, entered direct-to the GoldenJet crash site and stared at the bearing and distance.

Holy mother of pearl.

The final quarter-million payout might have just been delivered via air mail.

CHAPTER FOURTEEN

Nick regained consciousness to the ticking of metal, like an engine cooling off; wetness on his face; the smell of a copper penny from his own blood; pain and numbness; blurred vision, and fear. A sentence from a basic textbook on accident investigation appeared in his mind's eye: Post-crash fire is the most common cause of fatalities in aircraft mishaps.

You've got to move.

He released the shoulder harness and lap belt and tried to open the canopy. The internal release handle was jammed. He gripped it with both hands and pulled. It didn't budge.

Holding a deep breath, he yanked on the handle with all his strength. It snapped rearward as something sheared inside the carry-through mechanism to the external handle.

He gripped the handholds on the canopy bow, pulled aft over his head, straining, grunting. The canopy didn't move. Exhausted, he slumped into the seat. Visible through the plexiglass, the external handle mocked him. So close, and yet an eternity away.

His focus zoomed out and over the wing to the ground. He stared at grass, rocks, dirt, and remembered one of his flight instructors saying, "After a gear-up landing, from the wing to the ground is the shortest step a pilot will ever take."

He didn't remember lowering the landing gear. A stupid mistake . . . no . . . he chose to delay it . . . why?

Oh, yeah. The ice. Why can't I think?

A soft whump. The odor of burning aviation fuel, oil, and electrical wiring stung his nostrils. *Concentrate, Phillips!*

Pressing his palms against plexiglass above his head, he shoved. It felt as strong as steel. He pounded on it until his arms couldn't take any more.

The first flames rose up in his peripheral vision.

A thought settled in his brain. Could he use the fire extinguisher to fill the cockpit with enough foam to protect himself? But the foam displaced oxygen. He reached for the oxygen mask, stopped when he felt the heat. No time to experiment.

A last chance idea. He glanced at the fire extinguisher fastened to the floor between his legs in front of the seat, snatched it free of the clamp, smashed it into the canopy above the broken release handle. Three blows created a spider web of cracks. A final punch broke out a section of the plexiglass. He reached through the jagged hole and felt a stinging slice across the top of his hand as he jerked the external handle aft.

With a clunk, the sweetest sound he'd ever heard, the latches released. He slid the canopy back, tossed the fire extinguisher onto the ground, climbed out of the seat, over the canopy rail and onto the wing. His legs buckled. He crawled off the wing and onto the ground, rolled over and sat up.

Flames licked skyward from underneath the crushed engine compartment. The fire extinguisher lay a few feet away. He grabbed it. Fighting pain and nausea, he struggled to his feet, his mind replaying a safety training film.

He twisted the plastic safety tab until it snapped, stuck a

finger in the metal ring at the side of the trigger and jerked sideways to remove the pin. With the nozzle aimed at the base of the fire, he squeezed the trigger and fought the flames until the extinguisher hissed and sputtered to a stop.

As he stared at the smoldering remains of his airplane, dots appeared before his eyes. The ground appeared to be moving, rising up to meet his face.

WILSON PAUSED TO CATCH his breath at the observation point he'd used the night of the GoldenJet crash. With the binoculars, he took a closer look. Scarred earth marked where the GoldenJet had skidded to a stop against the rock outcropping. To the left and higher on the ridge, just above the crest, broken limbs dangled from several trees. One appeared to be chopped off near the top. Behind the ridge a column of smoke climbed toward the overcast. Black smoke. Fuel fire.

He surveyed the ridge. The smoke changed to grayish white. Somebody was using a fire extinguisher. Wilson shoved the binoculars into his jacket pocket and began an easy trot down the gentle slope.

NICK REGAINED CONSCIOUSNESS AND rolled onto his back. In spite of the reflected heat from the smoking wreckage, a shivering chill had invaded his body. Cold and shock were his enemies, killers looking for a victim. He had to take control or he'd never get through this. In a minute. He closed his eyes.

Get the fuck to your feet.

But I'm so tired.

Okay. Go to sleep. I'll let your family know you gave up.

Nick's eyes popped open. The faces of Laurie, Stephanie

and Brad drifted by in wisps of smoke against a background of gray sky and evergreens. That did it.

He got to his feet and fell down, crawled over to a tree and hauled himself erect. Three hard slaps across the face made him so mad he wanted to kick himself in the ass. Anger helped him focus on details.

He hadn't closed his flight plan. With no control tower at Cedar Valley, Denver Center would contact the airport manager to see if Nick had landed. The manager would search the airport for the airplane. Hours would pass before Nick was reported overdue. Search and rescue operations wouldn't begin until daylight tomorrow at the earliest. Too late.

Get off this mountain or say hi to the Grim Reaper.

He pushed away from the tree and headed down.

WILSON MAINTAINED A STEADY pace until the GoldenJet crash site appeared through the trees. He hurried across a broad draw, up the side of the impact ridge, and slowly climbed the last fifty feet. With low brush for cover, he peered over the crest. A scan with the binoculars showed no sign of Phillips. The airplane had clipped the tops of trees on the south side of the ridge and barely missed the crest as it fell onto the descending north slope. It lay at the end of a trail of broken tree branches, chunks of metal, and wounded earth. White, foamy residue covered the wreckage.

He maneuvered over the crest from one cover position to the next to gain a small knoll. Using the binoculars, he found no evidence that Phillips had remained at the crash site. With the pistol in his right hand, muzzle-down by his leg, and the rifle hanging from his left shoulder on a sling, he slipped through the quiet forest to find out just how blessed this day might turn out to be.

NICK STUMBLED DOWN THE slope, concentrating on where to put his feet. If he fell down, he probably wouldn't give a damn about getting back up.

He'd never crashed an airplane before. What happened? He'd been trying to land with ice on the airplane. The approach looked good until—

The thought hit Nick like he'd slammed on a foot brake. He reached in his jacket pocket and pulled out the navigation datacard. He stared at it. Was this—?

The world began to spin. Lightheaded, he bent over, vomited, almost fell. Legs spread, he gasped for air, waited until he could stand erect.

What a dumb-ass move.

He gritted his teeth, turned around and began climbing back up the slope. How long had he been walking? He glanced at his father's watch. The smashed crystal and hands frozen in time gave mute testimony to how close he had come to death. Overhead through the forest canopy the light had begun to fade. He did not want to be out here when the sun went down.

Panting hard, he crested a small rise and looked down at the crash site about fifty yards in the distance. He stopped to catch his breath and sucked in a huge lungful as a man dressed in camouflage and carrying a rifle on a sling appeared out of dense forest and walked toward the wreckage. Nick stepped behind a tree and peered around the trunk. A strong scent of pine reminded him of his mom's favorite household cleaner.

The guy looked like a hunter. Maybe he'd heard the crash and decided to investigate. Nick stepped from behind the tree and opened his mouth to call out, but his throat clamped shut.

The man's right arm appeared stiff, unnatural, close and tight against his body. Just like Nick had seen on TV, a plain-clothes cop on a drug bust holding a pistol as he approached a suspect's car.

Nick backed away into deeper cover and scrambled down the rugged slope to lie on the ground behind a waist-high evergreen bush.

WILSON STARED AT THE charred, twisted fuselage. A sharp odor hung in the still air, not the same as where the jet had gone down, but unpleasant nonetheless.

He turned slowly and surveyed the scene. Birds twittered. Wind sighed in the branches. Peace reigned in stark contrast to the shattered evidence of destruction. A fire extinguisher lay on the ground, so Phillips was healthy enough to fight the fire. But he might have collapsed nearby.

Wilson considered looking for him, decided against it. He stepped onto the wing and leaned into the cockpit. Fresh blood stained portions of the gray leather front seat cushion, but not enough to indicate fatal injuries.

Excitement flushed through him as he removed the datacard from the GPS and stood up. He slipped the pistol inside his jacket and got the Explorer keys out of his pocket. Squinting through the attached magnifying glass, he found the tiny mark he had made at one corner of the label.

Halle-fucking-lujah.

NICK CROUCHED BEHIND A bush, heart pounding in his chest. A deer hunter might carry a pistol, but this guy was not looking for venison. Nick watched him slip the weapon into his right jacket pocket and walk into the lengthening shadows among the trees, whistling a country song, one more reason for Nick to dislike songs about cheating hearts.

He waited for a few minutes and limped to the wreckage, saw it. The outline of a boot with a cleated sole stark against the white paint and fire extinguisher residue on top of one wing. The guy couldn't have missed the blood. Then, as if finding a fresh crash site in the woods were a common occurrence, he'd strolled into the sunset.

Talk about cold. The iceman leaveth.

Nick leaned over the canopy rail and reached out to remove the datacard. Arm extended, he stared at the empty slot. Fury surged through him. He backed away. Rage climbed in his throat and filled the silence around him as a coherent picture emerged of a series of events culminating in two plane crashes within a square mile of Colorado mountains.

Fists clenched, he breathed deeply and retreated from the wreckage, eyes locked on the spot where the man had disappeared into the forest. When convinced he wasn't being followed, he trotted down the slope until he had to stop and catch his breath. In a jacket pocket he found his cell phone.

A NO SERVICE message teased him.

Ignoring sore muscles that screamed for relief, he climbed toward the nearest sliver of sky visible through the trees. From the crest, he spotted a bare rock ledge a quarter-mile away. He trotted to the edge of the cliff. The Cedar Valley Airport lay barely visible in the distance through gray mist and ragged bottoms of wispy clouds. He lifted the phone and prayed. The phone god answered with two bars.

The 911 operator answered on the first ring.

"This is Nick Phillips . . . where am I?" *Oh yeah. You're on a cell phone.* "On the outskirts of Cedar Valley, Colorado.

My emergency is that I need to speak to Deputy Sheriff Barry Thornton. He knows me. I don't care if he's on a scene . . . excuse me for interrupting but I don't have time to tell you what kind of emergency. Get him on the phone. This is a matter of national security. The President will be calling shortly and I need information from Deputy Thornton."

The operator put him on hold. Nick had been taught to tell the truth, but he hoped that from their resting places his parents would forgive him for stretching facts this one last time.

"Deputy Thornton."

"Nick Phillips, Deputy. I need your help."

"I'm on a crime scene, Mr. Phillips."

"So am I." Nick explained his suspicions as quickly as he could. Breathless, he waited for a response.

Thornton finally said, "This sounds too weird to be true."

"That's what they want us to think. If we give up, assuming no one could possibly have gone to all this trouble to kill someone, they win."

"What do you want me to do?"

"He's got to have a car parked nearby. Send a cruiser south on the airport road, and another east on the intersecting highway that takes you over the ridge. We have a small time window. Can you do it?"

"I can always come up with probable cause to search a car and driver."

"Perfect. And Deputy?"

"Yeah?"

"Watch out for this guy. He's killed two people I know of, and he's carrying a concealed pistol with a draw through the right jacket pocket."

"Goddamn. You're full of surprises."

"Just being observant. Please hurry."

"I'm on my way. And Mr. Phillips?"

"Yes?"

"It's probably three."

"Three what?"

"Kills. We got one here in the hangar. A security guard. I thought it was robbery, but that doesn't make nearly as much sense as this."

Wilson took his time leaving the forest. Anybody came along, they'd see another hunter after a lousy day, up before the crack of dawn for nothing.

The Explorer waited in a rest area beside the highway parallel to the airport road but on the other side of the ridge. Cops routinely ran tags on parked cars. That far from the airport and with hunters roaming about, they probably wouldn't connect it to the guard's death. Even if they tried, it would come up rented to Harmon Gardner of Cincinnati, Ohio. The real Mr. Gardner would eventually convince them he knew nothing.

Wilson sang the country tune he couldn't get out of his mind, put there by the Schiller security guard: "Unlucky in love/crying for you/heartbroken and sad/what will I do?"

He smiled. Today would make up for a lot of heartbreak.

Deputy Sheriff Barry Thornton sat in his cruiser and watched an Explorer, the third unoccupied vehicle he'd found parked within ten miles of the airport. He'd dispatched a unit to seal off the other end of the airport road. None of the three vehicles would be able to leave without the occupants being questioned.

Figuring that a criminal would stay in the woods and move

in a direct line from Phillips' crash site to his vehicle rather than walk the highway, Thornton chose a position to hide his cruiser from view until the man left cover.

After a half-hour of waiting, a deputy reported contact with a lone hunter who approached the first of the vehicles. Subsequent radio traffic indicated that when the individual became belligerent and refused to identify himself, the deputy took him into custody. The man's driver's license came up fake, and Thornton decided they might have found their suspect. He started the cruiser and reached for the microphone to report leaving his location. Movement in the trees stilled his hand.

A man stepped out from the shadows, dressed in camouflage and carrying a rifle slung over his left shoulder, barrel-down, with his right hand free. The man hadn't noticed the cruiser, and Thornton figured he probably wouldn't until he was almost to the Explorer.

He waited until the man's head snapped to his left, eyes on the cruiser, before he eased forward. The man waved, changed course and walked toward him. Thornton put his hand on his weapon, released the hammer tab, and considered getting the guy at gunpoint. Sort it out later. But they had another person in detention, and this was probably just a hunter at the end of an unsuccessful day.

Thornton left the hammer tab unsnapped and waved back. As he rested his hand on the steering wheel, the man came within about ten feet of the Explorer. Thornton stopped the cruiser, put the gearshift in PARK, and glanced in the left rear-view mirror before he opened the door. As his eyes came back to the man, in a blur of movement the guy's left arm, hand gripping the barrel of the rifle, moved upward in an arc to point the muzzle directly at Thornton's head.

He was reaching for his weapon when the man's right

hand moved across his body and stopped with the first finger extended inside the trigger guard.

WILSON PULLED OUT HIS pistol and approached the cruiser with the front sight on the sheriff's head. Or what was left of it. Rifle rounds did ghastly damage at hundreds of yards, and up this close, it looked like the guy had stuffed a grenade in his mouth and pulled the pin.

Wilson holstered the pistol and trotted into the woods, once again amazed at how gullible cops could be. The idiot allowed a wave to lure his gun hand away from his weapon without a clue that it would be the next to last thing he would ever do.

CHAPTER FIFTEEN

Lars Nordstrom sat in a haze of frustration, feet on his home-office desk, sipping a very dry martini. Dickson had left a message promising to call back at five o'clock with important news. Lars glanced at his watch again. The damned thing seemed to be slowing down. For all he could tell, the outrageously expensive timepiece might have been running backward for the last hour.

His cell phone finally rang. Lars snatched it off the desk and saw Dickson's number displayed. "It's about fucking time."

"You are not going to believe what happened this afternoon." Dickson's voice had a lilt to it, unlike his usual monotone.

"Try me."

"Phillips crashed."

The news sent Lars' feet to the floor and dumped ice-cold gin in his lap. "Jesus Christ! Is he dead?"

"Almost two-thousand years ago."

"James, I will be more than happy to tear out your heart and feed it to my dog."

"You don't have a dog."

"Damn it. I'm getting sick—"

"He's bruised, very sore, and somewhat bloody. His airplane looks like a coffin. I'm surprised he made it out without having to carry some of his body parts in a backpack."

Lars dabbed the gin from his crotch with a handkerchief. "Any idea as to cause?"

"Oh, yeah. The idiot iced up."

Lars refilled his glass, knocked half of it back and felt the power coursing through his bloodstream. "This is perfect. I want you to finish up the GoldenJet investigation. While you're at it, let's tack on Phillips' crash."

"Roger that. And Lars?"

"Yes?"

"Somebody murdered one of our security guards. It looks like a robbery attempt."

"Remind me never to visit the Old West. Need more people?"

"Nah. With Phillips and his never-ending review of the draft report out of the picture, there's not much left to do. A single-engine light-airplane accident will be a cakewalk."

"Okay, but don't let it interfere with getting the Larchmont business done. You hear what I'm saying?"

"Absolutely."

"Get to it."

Lars drained his glass and poured another dose of clout as the glow of anticipation spread through him with a satisfying buzz. He stared at his blurry reflection in the heavily waxed surface of his desk and nodded at the next appointed Board member of the NTSB.

NICK SAT IN A chair while an EMS tech treated him. The head injury wasn't serious, although it had bled enough to soak the front of his clothing, now stiff with dried blood. He had no broken bones, but scrapes and bruises had sprouted over most of him like a bad case of skin rash.

News of the NTSB security guard's death had hit Nick hard. When Thornton mentioned the possibility of another victim and Nick realized it was Larry, the memories came flooding back. He had helped Larry's son avoid becoming another sad example of failed dreams and lost youth. The personal bond of friendship had remained strong for many years, only to be shattered by a murdering son-of-a-bitch assassin with a trail of bodies in his wake.

When the EMS tech finished cleaning and bandaging the head injury, Nick looked around for a cop. He tried to stand but the tech put a hand on his shoulder. "You need to stay seated, sir."

Nick looked at the tech's nametag. "I appreciate your expert attention, Bonden. What's your first name?"

"Most people call me Bondo, sir. You know, after the body filler? It's a 'you-bend-'em, I-fix-'em' kind of thing."

Nick grinned, and it felt like his face wanted to peel off. "I may not be as good as new just yet, but I don't need any more work in the body shop."

"You refusing to go to the hospital?"

"I have things to do that won't wait."

Bondo nodded. After taking care of the paperwork, he gathered his equipment, wished Nick good luck and drove off in the ambulance.

Nick stood and almost fell. The dizziness refused to be denied. After a moment of standing still, he shuffled toward the hangar. No one except Larry and Sweet knew Nick had been in the hangar the previous evening. He needed to check the GoldenJet's GPS receiver to see if the killer had taken the datacard. Nick could use it to support his theory.

Who would take the datacard? Why was it worth killing for?

He desperately wanted to question the man in the forest, or to watch from behind one-way glass. The killer strapped to a chair and a burly deputy doing whatever it took to learn the truth. Protect the bastard's rights? Maybe after.

Yellow crime-scene tape blocked his way. As Nick lifted the tape, a sheriff's car drove up. A deputy stepped out. After introductions, Nick asked if they had heard from Thornton.

"No," said Deputy Logan. "Dispatch called him a little while ago and got no answer. Said Thornton went south on the airport road looking for a car *you* wanted found. Want to tell me about that?"

Nick gave him the details. "Isn't it standard procedure to report in whenever you stop to check out a vehicle?"

"Sure. But we aren't perfect. Guys forget, get lazy, whatever."

"Is Deputy Thornton the lazy or forgetful type?"

Logan stared at Nick for a few seconds. "Get in."

A few minutes later Nick's fingers were digging into the armrest and seat of the cruiser. He loved speed in an airplane, but this was different. Logan had the big V-8 howling and the speedometer pushing ninety plus.

Rounding a sharp curve, they both saw the parked cruiser at the same time. Logan stood on the brakes, tires squealing. He steered to the right as they skidded to a stop on the shoulder in a cloud of dust.

Logan was out and moving before Nick even got his shoulder harness released. The deputy drew his weapon as he yelled, "Thornton! Talk to me, man!"

Nick scrambled out of the passenger seat, gritting his teeth against the pain. He trotted toward Logan, who held up his hand in a "stop" motion. Nick obeyed. As a gentle breeze carried away the dust he tried to comprehend the scene.

Logan had stopped about ten feet from the cruiser. With

his weapon at the ready and his head on a swivel, he advanced a few feet, stopped. Head tilted to his left shoulder, he pressed the mike button with his left hand, said some code numbers, their location, and the words, "Officer down."

Nick followed Logan to the cruiser. The front windshield and rear window had shattered in a spider web of cracks radiating out from holes at the driver's eye level. Thornton's head, or what was left of it, lay against the headrest. Gray matter and blood covered most of the interior.

The words "through and through" came to mind as Nick ran to the edge of the rest-area pavement. For the second time on the worst day of his life, he vomited until there was nothing left to lose.

NICK SAT IN THE lobby of the Sheriff's office waiting to be interviewed. They wanted the full story on why Deputy Thornton had been looking for a man Nick identified as a murder suspect. He lowered his head into his hands, elbows on his knees, and closed his eyes.

Thoughts of a near-fatal accident due to his own pilot error, of the investigation yet to come, and of a career gone forever became almost too much to bear. All he wanted was to go home, immerse himself in family, celebrate two very special days with his children, and forget about this horror for a while.

The front door opened with a gust of frigid air. Nick glanced up. Dickson entered the waiting room and looked around. He strode over, picked up a battered plastic-and-metal chair from the row in front of Nick, turned it around and sat down. "You all right?"

Nick winced with pain as he eased his body erect. "I've been better."

"What the hell happened?"

Nick sighed, weary beyond measure with the whole business, and related the short version. Dickson remained silent, but his expression turned stony, with the chiseled appearance of granite.

By the time Nick finished, Dickson looked like a Mount Rushmore carving. "I can't believe you did it again."

"I crashed before and don't remember it?"

"Figuratively. This time it was a crash and *burn*. But that's not what I meant. While the rest of us did NTSB work, you know, the *official* kind, you ran a private investigation."

"What the hell are you talking about?"

"I was appointed IIC by Nordstrom and you just couldn't stay away. That's your prerogative. We end up working together. But when you found something curious—"

"I told you about that."

"Uh huh. Then you team up with a reporter, develop a theory that Larchmont might have been targeted, and ignore what the book says. Look where it got you."

The back of Nick's neck heated up. He gripped the edges of his chair and struggled to keep his voice down. "And where would that be?"

"Earth to Nick, come in please. You fulfilled the legacy. I'm sorry about your father, but he fucked up and so did you."

Nick launched out of his chair and slammed into Dickson, knocked him backward and sent them both to the floor. Rage fueled his blows to Dickson's face with fury and the red-hot desire to make him take it all back.

The rest of the world didn't exist until hands grabbed the collar of Nick's jacket and hauled him off. He jerked free, turned, took a blind swing and ended up on his back.

Harvey Sweet stood over him.

Nick struggled to rise, shoving at Sweet's hands to push him away.

"Stop it, Nick."

Nick's anger subsided like a deflated balloon. He released his grip on Sweet's arms. "I'm done."

Nick accepted a helping hand from Sweet, stood up, and glared at Dickson. "They killed Larchmont and you've been collaborating with Nordstrom in a cover-up. I swear to Christ I'll—"

Dickson's face reddened. "Larchmont fucked up just like you and your daddy! There is no cover-up!" He moved toward Nick. "Nordstrom is Director of the division. I can work with him all I want without your permission."

Nick's hands clenched into fists. He stepped forward, but Sweet reached out and popped him in the chest with the heel of a hand. "That's enough."

Nick's view of the world around him opened wide as the voice of Deputy Logan cut through the fog of hatred. "I second that."

The deputy faced Dickson. "I saw him attack you. Want to press charges?"

Dickson wiped blood from his split lip. "He's got enough trouble as it is. I'll just stand by and watch. Maybe laugh a little bit."

"Not here you won't," said Logan. "We have business with him. Unless you're here to see us, I'm asking you to leave."

Dickson nodded. "I'm out of here." He stepped closer to Nick.

Logan extended his hand between them.

Dickson leaned forward until his chest barely touched Logan's arm. "Before I go, I want to tell this son of a bitch something. Ever since we were brand-new investigators not knowing dick about this job, you've made it plain what your goal was. You never once considered that I might have wanted the same thing. It was always about you, and how you were going to rise to the top. I've heard enough of that to make me puke, and I want you to know how pleased I am to see you up to your neck in your own shit." Dickson turned on a heel and stalked out of the lobby.

The entire building seemed especially quiet, as if everyone had stopped to listen and watch.

Logan faced Nick. "This is not a good place to assault people. Do that again, and I'll toss your ass in the tank." The deputy turned and disappeared into the bowels of the office.

Nick collapsed into a chair.

Sweet sat down beside him. "Dickson may be right. You look like you've been bathing in a treatment plant. What the hell happened?"

Nick gave him a quick summary. "And the real fun starts when Logan gets through with me. I'll be investigated by the NTSB, probably face federal charges."

Sweet leaned back in his chair. "So what's all this about? I walk in and you're pounding on your friend."

"He's *not* my friend. Just a Nordstrom minion."

Sweet shook his head. "There's more to it than that. If I hadn't pulled you off, you might have killed the guy."

Nick stared at nothing with unfocused eyes. The rest of the lobby faded into blurry images of people, furniture, walls, a water fountain, an officer behind a counter taking a report from a woman insisting that an alien stole her husband. Nick sighed. "It's a long story."

"You going somewhere?"

Nick sighed with the weariness of failure and lost resolve. "My father was killed in a plane crash when I was seven. It was like the glue disappeared from my universe. Nothing stayed together anymore. When I learned the investigators blamed him, I refused to believe it. No way my dad would make a mistake that killed him." Nick paused as the bitter memory choked him. "I've fought against accepting that for over thirty years."

Sweet laid a gentle hand on Nick's back. "What did Dickson say that set you off?"

"It doesn't matter. He and the boss figured I'd screw the investigation up. Go off on my own wild-goose chase. Hah! Little did they know. I bet they're having a long laugh."

"Why should you care? You still have the advantage."

Nick stared at Sweet. "How do you figure that?"

Sweet's eyes sparkled in the dim lighting. "You've got me on your side."

Nick chuckled, winced as pain stabbed his chest. "That's something, I guess."

"How about I give you a ride when you're done here?"

Nick pointed to Sweet's motorcycle helmet. "No way. I came real close to dying once today."

"I'll go by my place and get the truck."

"Then I'll take you up on it. Thanks."

"Call my cell." Sweet donned his helmet and walked into the gathering dusk, pulling on his gloves.

Nick stared after him, the only person within a thousand miles he could count on, and wondered what the future held in store. Even if he had a crystal ball, it would probably be as dark as night.

WILSON SAT IN A bar at the Denver International Airport with a double shot of Jack Black on the rocks and stared out the window. An airliner squatted beside a jetway in the darkness. Caution and hazard lights reflected off the wet tarmac. Figures in yellow rain gear tended to their duties like worker ants around a queen. He glanced at his watch. Boarding had begun, but the red-eye flight was only half full and he had a row all to himself.

As an aviator and owner of a single-engine aircraft, he felt the best "window" seat in any airplane was in the cockpit. Being nervous at the hands of another pilot didn't enter into it. It was simply a matter of confidence in his own abilities. He could fly anything with wings, and he'd much rather be doing that than staring at the back of a seat with somebody's brat kicking the back of his. With the contract filled, he might get the chance to do some aviating of his own. He was looking forward to it.

Although the voice on the phone had tried to play hard ball about the final payment, Wilson knew he'd get his money. Especially after today's success. No one had *ever* cheated him. He'd give the asshole a day to think about it and come to his senses.

This assignment had no ingredient more important than the handling of the GPS datacards. Wilson's reputation reflected his success over the years taking care of such matters. And in spite of one small detail still lingering in the shadows—a thin, empty slot in the GoldenJet's GPS—the Larchmont controversy would die a natural death before any complications crawled into the light.

He drained the last of the bourbon and left the bar. Fingering the two small datacards in the pocket of his slacks, he strolled down the concourse toward the boarding jet.

Chapter Sixteen

On the morning after his accident, Nick woke up wishing he hadn't. The damned sun streamed in, cutting his darkened Cedar Valley motel room in half. His pain medication had worn off, and he felt like one big sore. A monumental hangover added to his misery. Memories of the previous evening nagged at him. He'd waited until well into the bottle to call home. Big mistake. His voice sounded normal to him, but Laurie hadn't thought so.

"Have you been drinking?"

"Not so you'd notice."

"Since when do you mumble half your words?"

"I'm not drunk, Laurie."

"You could've fooled me."

Nick's voice cracked. "I crashed."

"You *what?*"

"My beautiful airplane is—"

"Forget the damned plane. Are you *hurt?* "

"Nothing that won't mend. I was on my way home, and I . . . I really screwed up."

"We can talk about that later. How soon can you leave?"

If only he could. "The situation has turned really complicated."

"Sounds like a good reason to pack your bags. Your son would like that. He's so excited he can barely eat. I know you don't like hearing this, but the NTSB can do without you for a while."

"It's not about the NTSB. Something's come up that I have to take care of."

"What could possibly be that important?"

No way he could tell her about this, any more than he could walk away from it. "I'll explain everything when I get home."

A heavy sigh. "I'm not going to argue with you, Nick. But I'd like to point out one thing."

"What?"

"You've always regretted that the demands of your job exact such a heavy toll on the relationship with your family. We've supported you in spite of our wish that you'd share more of you with us. This seems like a good time to reorient your priorities."

The lightly seared right side of Nick's face heated up. He shifted the phone to his other ear. "I hear you. Let me . . . I'll be home as soon as I can. Okay?"

It wasn't okay, and they both knew it, but they agreed to talk the next afternoon and signed off for the night. Nick lay on the bed and stared at the ceiling, his mind unhinged, out of control, playing a futile game of *What if?* Colossal weariness and alcohol had finally knocked him out cold.

This morning as he rolled over to subdue lingering nausea, the obnoxious sound of a ringing phone drilled into his gray matter. He snatched the handset off the cradle and tried to say, "Hello," but his vocal cords didn't work. Again he tried, but it came out as a grunt.

Sweet said, "I think that's you, Nick. How you doing?"

"Coffee."

"Okay, got that. I'll bring a very large, very hot cup to your room in about fifteen minutes."

Nick mumbled something in gratitude and dropped the handset on the floor. He reached the shower without tossing his stomach contents. After ten minutes of motionless ecstasy under an old-fashioned shower head with no flow restrictor, he opened the soggy curtain to clouds of misty vapor coating the bathroom with condensation.

Wrapped in two towels, he began wiping the mirror with a third when it occurred to him that shaving would be far too dangerous. He rummaged around in his duffel bag for a warm-up suit and had just finished tying his shoes when three authoritative knocks announced a visitor. Nick shuffled painfully to the door and opened it.

Sweet held out a huge paper cup.

Nick took it, yanked off the lid and took a long swallow. It burned going down, but sometimes good things do that. He motioned for Sweet to come in.

Sweet looked around the room, frowned, and pulled out a chair at the small table. "Does this place offer maid service?"

Nick closed and bolted the door. "Yes." His voice sounded like he had a bullfrog in his throat.

"You're getting ripped off."

Nick eased into a chair. "I don't like housekeepers rummaging through my things. They only clean when I ask them to."

"Looks to me like they've had the last few weeks off."

Nick rolled his eyes and almost fell off the chair. His equilibrium was still on holiday. "I'll be giving testimony to the NTSB tomorrow morning. Want an exclusive on what I'm going to tell them?"

Sweet frowned. "But Mr. Straight Arrow By-the-Book can't

do that without violating non-disclosure. What changed?"

"I'm through in the NTSB."

"Your decision or theirs?"

"Both."

"Then wait until they make the report official. You can say whatever you want."

"It doesn't matter because I don't give a damn. Speaking from an official pulpit will gain visibility that might help find the truth and catch these bastards."

Sweet raised his eyebrows. "You sure about this?"

"You want the damn story, or not?"

After a moment, Sweet nodded.

"Okay, then. When I get through telling you what I'm going to say, you'll understand. But first, I need some food."

Sweet stood. "Let's go to Maudie's. She makes the best—"

"Uh-uh. I'm not moving outside this room."

"All right. I'll get something. What do you want?"

"Lots of grease."

EXUDING THE LINGERING AROMA of fries and Maudie's famous mammoth bacon cheeseburgers, the remains of two takeout meals lay on the table. Sweet was transcribing notes from his digital recorder into a laptop. Nick stood by the window, gazing through a gap in the curtain at the parking lot, and pondered the uphill battle facing him.

Sweet's voice interrupted Nick's thoughts. "I don't know about you, but I'm feeling a kindred connection to Woodward and Bernstein. White House involvement in the death of a prominent political figure is a dynamite story."

Nick closed the curtain and turned away from the window. "Don't go thinking Pulitzer just yet. Those two built a case with facts. All I've given you is unsubstantiated suspicion. They don't give out prizes for guesswork."

"Having second thoughts?"

"No way." He sat down opposite Sweet and picked at a few lonely fries in a paper container. "If they don't feel threatened, they'll stay below the radar and nothing changes."

Sweet shook his head. "Don't bet on it. The folks who pulled this off think they can do whatever they want. It's the classic bulletproof syndrome in action."

"Speaking of which, you should get one of those Kevlar vests and practice ducking before you walk into your editor's office with this story. Might come in handy afterward as well."

"I can handle my editor. And what're they going to do? Kill both of us? Doesn't seem consistent with keeping things quiet."

"Maybe not, but this is a dangerous move. They're professionals. We have two suspicious deaths and two murders with no connection we can prove. What if more bodies show up? No one will be able to connect the dots."

Sweet tossed his pen on the table and crossed his arms. "Professionals don't leave dots. They'll make sure the bodies *don't* show up."

They stared at each other for a moment before Nick said, "We're making me nervous. Who the hell are we working for, anyway?"

"Ourselves. And the truth."

"But I'm the only person with first-hand knowledge of a suspicious datacard. So what if the original is missing? Shit happens."

Sweet perked up. "Then you're the only one in danger. I can sleep well tonight."

"Sleep all you want, but file the story first."

WILSON'S HOUSE STILL SMELLED like paint from a kitchen renovation, so he'd decided to take a few days of sorely needed vacation in Key West. With his feet propped on the hotel balcony railing, he sipped a tropical fruit concoction and watched the sun sink into the Gulf of Mexico. He had no idea what was in the drink, and he didn't give a damn. But this was going to be the last one. The little paper umbrellas had been trying their best to put his eyes out, and he needed his peepers to get his money. And to see it once he got it. Then he could close his eyes and *fondle* and *sniff* all those greenbacks owed him by a guy who had no idea who he was dealing with. *Soon.*

Wilson blinked and stared at the first sequence of numbers printed on a small piece of paper. Ten digits, the only link to the most recent in a series of voices that had sent him into the world on another job, always involving death in one form or another. Waiting for the connection, he removed the umbrella from the drink and twirled it between his thumb and first finger.

"Speak," said the familiar voice.

"The money has not been transferred. I assume, in the absence of other explanations, that you have not sent it."

"Actually, I was planning on calling *you*. There's a problem."

Wilson sighed. "Here we go again. Previously, it was either my problem or yours. This time it's just out there, ownership not yet determined. Let me clarify it for you. If I don't have my money by tomorrow noon it will definitely be your problem."

The voice turned flat, a dry whisper. "It might be wise to remember that the world is a small place."

Wilson chuckled, knowing it would piss off the man behind the voice. "And it is for you as well."

A pause. "Then maybe we should both remember that and get on with business."

"That's what I'm doing. Conducting business. The part where I get paid. What about that do you not understand?"

"I understand this. We have a shit storm raging out there in the papers. Your assignment was to take care of certain things quietly. Your performance sucks."

Wilson resisted the urge to scream at the asshole and took a deep breath. "My methods are *my* business. The end result may not be as pretty as you like, but the job is done. Pay me the goddamned money."

Wilson listened to the dead phone for a moment, then hung up. Terms and conditions of the verbal contract specified the objective and payment of fifty percent in advance nonrefundable, the remainder due immediately upon completion. And for the first time in a long career, an employer had complained about his performance.

Anger welled up inside him, the volcano of wrath that usually ended in bloodshed. He fought down the urge to find the man behind the voice and have a come-to-Jesus meeting. That would *feel* really good and solve nothing.

He sipped the drink, fidgeted with the little umbrella, and helped the molten lava of his black rage subside by remembering a line from one of his favorite characters: "All good things to those who wait." *Oh, yes.* Hannibal Lecter knew something about revenge.

CHAPTER SEVENTEEN

Lars Nordstrom almost dropped his phone as he collapsed into his office chair. "He did what?"

"He laid out all the reasons he suspected the crash wasn't an accident. Detailed the proof he found, the mistake he made with the datacard, everything."

"Listen to me carefully, James. I don't care what that son of a bitch is saying. All the evidence proves that Larchmont flew that airplane into the ground. Phillips is doing what he does best—imitating a pit bull. To hell with him. This investigation is going to bed."

"It may appear so to you, but distance has a way of distorting images. The shit could hit the fan real quick. What if somebody asks why I didn't take this story seriously enough to contact the Feebies? At least run it by them. Or what if they show up on their own? They might do that, right? And when I tell them—"

"Be very careful what you say next."

"Damn it, Lars. If you're so sure of yourself, why don't you come on out here and take over?"

Without a second of hesitation, Lars said, "Fine. Haul your ass back home. And send me your resignation. Goodbye." He slammed down the phone. Trembling with a heavy dose of fear, he questioned his previous decision to sit back and wait. He'd never considered that Dickson might turn on him. But his professional relationship with the traitor made him vulnerable. And although the guy might not have the backbone to do anything, Lars' world had suddenly filled with way too many surprises.

He called his assistant. "Empty my schedule for the week, then call my wife and ask her to pack me a bag and send it to the charter company we used for that ski trip a couple of years ago. Have her tell them I need an airplane to Colorado this afternoon. Do it now."

Standing at the window, Lars gazed at the dreary, brown landscape of approaching winter. He could handle this. Phillips was finished, and the FBI had no jurisdiction. He would terminate the on-site Larchmont inquiry, take over the investigation into Phillips' crash, and put this whole mess to bed. Then he'd let the dust settle before calling in the favor owed him by Tanner Osborne, Oval Office gofer.

BACK HOME AND ALMOST used to the lingering odor of latex paint, Wilson took a mug and a carafe of coffee onto the elevated deck off his study. He plopped onto a chaise lounge, poured a steaming cup of the dark, heavy brew, and leaned back to enjoy a little more personal solitude before leaving for one last trip to that wretched Rocky Mountain valley.

His house sat on two wooded acres, offering the privacy he craved while providing the convenience of easy shopping and access to big-city pleasures. Although a loner most of the time, he cultivated an alternate existence far removed from his professional life. Known as a semi-retired businessman with enough money to live well, he traveled a lot, leaving his plants, a dog, and a huge Siamese cat in the care of an elderly housekeeper.

Years ago he'd considered hiring a security service or a live-in watchman, but he rejected the idea as inconsistent with his image as an innocuous middle-aged citizen. Why live in a fortress if all you did was a bit of consulting? Besides, he was already paying for twenty-four-hour security in a gated community. So he let Mrs. Frazier stay in the house whenever he was away, confident that total separation of his two personas best served his purposes.

While "consulting," however, he was far from harmless. He didn't mind hurting people, nor did he enjoy it. He simply did what the job called for. But that was about to change if his money didn't show up pretty damn quick. Under normal circumstances, he'd have no way to seek retribution. But this time, fate had intervened and handed him Larchmont's silver Halliburton briefcase containing all he needed to know.

So, what should he do about it? Killing the man wouldn't be easy. And it wouldn't get him the money, although loss of the unpaid balance wouldn't jeopardize his imminent retirement. But in the larger context, which involved a reputation for excellence and the expectation of prompt payment, his employer's actions were a serious breach of contract and totally unacceptable.

No one had ever complained about his performance, added requirements after the fact, or refused to pay on demand. This was not the time to let it happen. In his line of work, expectations of others and confidence that his word meant something carried a unique brand of power. He didn't plan on needing it ever again, but neither did he plan on retiring without it.

He poured a warm-up and pondered his options. Why not

complete this last assignment in a manner that would leave his distinctive signature for all to see? Carve his legacy in stone, a lasting monument to a career without equal? But first, he needed to collect the remainder of his fee. He'd earned it, and he believed in the Golden Rule of Business: *Never leave money on the table.*

In the meantime, his employer didn't want loose ends and continuing media interest. The more Wilson thought about it, neither did he. Problem was, he had a rabid *accident* investigator, for Christ's sake, foaming at the mouth, his attacks chronicled by some hick-town reporter. Although Wilson was confident those two idiots would never find proof of sabotage, the only way to guarantee that the secret didn't see the light of day was to eliminate the threat.

A fatal accident would take too much time to plan. A series of random crimes might do it: a serial predator stalking Cedar Valley, leaving multiple victims, one of whom happened to be the only person with first-hand knowledge of the datacards. Silence the reporter's source and drive the crash story off the front page. Wilson sipped the coffee and thought about that solution.

He'd never been comfortable with collateral killing, especially since the hit on the mob lawyer who'd skimmed a few million in cash from a contingency fund. The contract included information on the mark's work and vacation schedule. He was supposed to be alone, the rest of his family on a ski trip.

A vivid mind picture remained with Wilson to this day: the kid, couldn't have been more than ten, lying at the head of the basement stairs with his young life's blood flowing onto the hardwood floor. Tough little guy, his daddy's pistol in his hand, defending the homestead. Wilson had reacted on pure instinct, but that didn't erase the memory.

He decided to put the final option on hold and create a diversion. Something to prey on Phillips' well-known family ties and encourage him to rush home to take care of a problem rather than stay in Colorado and be one.

Movement behind Wilson caught his attention. Samson the watch cat strolled out on the deck, surveying his domain with the casual air of complete control. Wilson reached down to scratch the cat's head, only to be rebuffed by his highness, lord of the property.

"You'll be sorry, old fellow. Mrs. Frazier won't take care of you the way I do."

Samson ignored him, as usual, and would until he was ready for some attention. The cat also paid little heed to Delilah, a pit bull who seemed to know better than to compete for supremacy.

Wilson put down his empty coffee cup, picked up the portable handset and pressed the speed-dial number for his housekeeper. After telling her of his pending absence, he pulled his sterile, secure cell phone out of his pocket and paused with it in his hand.

Maybe the time had come to stop using the transportation service. Take his own airplane. He'd be in a better position to activate his retirement should something unforeseen block his view of the next stage in life. He slipped the cell phone back in his pocket, stood, and walked into his study to write the final chapter in the story of Wilson, gunslinger.

A PERSISTENT KNOCKING BROUGHT Nick out of the bathroom. He checked the deadbolt and looked through the peephole. An unlikely visitor waited. Nick opened the door.

Awkward silence, then Dickson said, "May I come in?"

"What do you want?"

"To talk to you. And I'd rather not stand in the cold."

Nick motioned him inside. "Pardon my mess." He offered coffee, which Dickson refused.

Seated at the small table, Dickson cleared his throat and asked how Nick's injuries were coming along.

"Let's not pretend you care one way or the other, or that it matters to me in the slightest. What do you want?"

Dickson tossed his gloves on the table. "I'm headed back. I may resign."

Struggling to keep his face impassive, Nick said, "What does that have to do with me?"

"Nothing directly, I guess. But I thought you might be interested in why Nordstrom tried to replace you."

Nick's heart rate quickened. "I thought he wanted to put you on the fast track."

"That's part of it. But he also knew how much media attention would be focused on the outcome. He didn't want you in the spotlight. Feared you might go off on a crusade again. Stir up trouble."

"This may be the first time he's been right since I've known him. Is he acting on his own?"

Dickson nodded. "As far as I know."

"Then why are you leaving?"

Dickson stood and began pacing the room. He related how Nordstrom refused to call in the FBI, even after Dickson told him about Nick's statement. "That decision is going to backfire."

"Why are you telling me?"

A noticeable change came over Dickson, an emotional shift into a more stable place. "If the things you said in the interview this morning are true, I don't want any part in ignoring them.

Nordstrom's probably on his way out here. Just thought you might want a heads-up."

"What's next for you?"

Dickson shrugged and picked his gloves up off the table. "Who knows? Tomorrow is another day."

Nick followed him to the door. "Is Nordstrom taking over as IIC on both investigations?"

Dickson stepped into the gray, dreary mist, a perfect match to his demeanor. "He'll do it all, just the way he wants it. And the buck will stop there, where it belongs."

Nick nodded. "I have a question."

"What?"

"How did you find out about my rebuilding the car for Brad?"

"Nordstrom."

"How the hell did he learn about it?"

"I have no idea. He knew about your vacation and that you'd arranged for a backup. He was planning on that so you wouldn't fight being replaced. I have to get moving."

Nick looked at a man he had despised for years as being an ass-kissing bureaucrat and decided that Dickson might actually have a few redeeming qualities after all. "Take it easy, James."

Dickson extended his hand. "You too."

They shook hands, and Nick watched Dickson disappear into the fog. He closed the door, sat down at the table and stared at nothing as his mind tried to wrap itself around what had just happened.

It could mean nothing. Or everything. But one thing was for certain. Whatever happened *next*, Nordstrom had just lost the immunity of a buffer between him and the real world, where bureaucracy shielded no one.

Welcome, asshole.

LARS NORDSTROM THANKED THE scheduler at the charter company and disconnected the call. The plane would be standing by.

Tanner Osborne had called about two o'clock that afternoon and wanted to meet. He didn't mention a subject. Lars knew it wouldn't be to congratulate him on his good work, even though he deserved it. He asked for a later meeting time to ensure that Osborne would join *him* at a table. A little power-play move to set the stage.

He called the Pig's Foot Tavern to confirm the address, entered it into his GPS, and followed the instructions. He liked having the electronic map, but he wished they would install a less domineering female voice. Missed turns got her all pissed off. Sometimes he expected a hand to rise up out of the dashboard and slap the living shit out of him. As he spent more time idling than moving in heavy afternoon traffic, he couldn't help but be pleased at how well things were turning out.

The findings would show pilot error had killed Larchmont. All Phillips had done was temporarily roadblock the process with his suspicions. Nothing more to worry about there.

The loss of Dickson didn't mean much. Lackeys were a dime a dozen in government. Way more important, this afternoon's meeting would be a perfect time to mention his career goals. Osborne couldn't ignore him any longer.

Open parking spots were members of an endangered species. Lars circled the block five times before he managed to beat out some fool in a monster Dodge Ram pickup who couldn't make the turn into an open space. As the guy backed up to try again, Lars darted in, locked his environmentally friendly sedan, and scurried around the corner threatened only by the sound of an angry horn.

The Pig's Foot was an iconic local hangout Lars knew about but had never been in because he figured the patrons would be the kind of folks who felt the *need* to be seen there. He waited just inside the door for his eyes to adjust, then walked past the long mahogany bar to an empty booth in the back. A crowd had already gathered, bodies packed together, voices mingled in the banter of men on the prowl and women acting uninterested. Or vice versa. He had no idea how it worked any more. A waitress asked for his order, but he declined. It wouldn't be good politics to serve yourself before a man as powerful as Osborne showed up.

The waitress punished Lars by glaring at him every time she walked by. He ignored her. Peering at his watch, he pressed the light button to check the time, and his carefully devised plan evaporated when a voice from the next booth said, "Nordstrom! Is that you with the spotlight?"

Lars leaned around the partition. "Mr. Osborne?"

"Come on over here."

Lars eased into the booth, trying not to let his embarrassment show. "I didn't see you. Sorry if I'm late. I thought we were meeting at four."

"I always like to be early. Apparently, so do you."

Lars wasn't sure how to take this comment, so he said nothing as Osborne put some papers into a leather folder and pushed it against the wall. He gulped the last of his cocktail and said, "What're you having?"

"Jack Black straight up, water back." Lars didn't like bourbon any more than gin, and except for the occasional martini, seldom drank hard liquor straight. But real men did, and he wanted Osborne to know he was dealing with a player.

Osborne signaled the waitress for another Manhattan and

ordered the bourbon. Lars waited for him to say something. The silence became awkward, until Lars realized that Osborne probably didn't want the waitress to show up while they were talking about important subjects. Private things about favors, and returning favors, and careers. He sat quietly until the waitress brought the drinks. Sipping the bourbon, he decided he might learn to like it.

Osborne drained about half his cocktail in one swallow. "I wanted to meet in person because it's important you understand how unhappy certain people are with your performance."

Lars almost spit the bourbon across the table. His throat dried up and made his voice crack. "What are you talking about? The investi—"

"Let me tell you about the investigation. According to you it was supposed to be straightforward. 'I'll take care of it, Mr. Osborne,' you said. 'I have a man on the scene and he'll make it happen.'

"Then the firestorm rages. Some loose cannon who works for you never climbs on the fire truck. He even throws fuel on the flames with a *ridiculous* notion about unauthorized access to the crash site. He teams up with a local reporter and fans the inferno with a bunch of hot air about how convenient Larchmont's death is to certain people in government. The national media jump all over that. Pure speculation, but it sells newspapers."

"But it all came out okay, Mr. Osborne. The findings will show pilot error. Phillips is in no position after his crash to make trouble for anyone. You got what you wanted."

"I didn't want anything. Your commitment goes a lot higher than that. This lead investigator you can't control is not keeping a low profile, and that was your responsibility. The fact that he's out of the picture doesn't erase the damage."

Too stunned to speak, Lars sipped the bourbon and drank some water. When the silence became unbearable, he leaned forward. "Mr. Osborne, I don't know what more I could have done. And besides, the end result is all that matters."

"Can you afford to think that?"

"What do you mean?"

"You want something from me. It's written all over your face. But there's unfinished business between us, and you need to take care of it. Then maybe we talk about what you want."

Lars had no choice. It wasn't fair, but nothing in life was. "What do you want me to do?"

"The same thing I've always wanted. Since you can't seem to focus, let me clarify it for you. President Kilpatrick was elected at a time of deep division in America. We have a public relations disaster on our hands. Until the NTSB confirms the truth the media will not acknowledge, it can only get worse."

"I voted for him, Mr. Osborne, and I'm doing my best—"

"I don't want your best. I want *results*. Americans have the shortest memories on earth. Give them a reasonable chance at the lifestyle they've grown to expect, cover it with a blanket of security so they can enjoy living without the unrelenting fear of getting blown up, and they'll forget Larchmont faster than you can blink."

"But the President is doing that."

Osborne drained his drink and signaled the waitress for another. "Damn straight he is. But he can't operate effectively with the media breathing down his neck, getting his critics all riled up, accusing him of running a secret war. He's hitting the bastards where it hurts, just like he promised when he took office, and just like the American public said they wanted. But the average guy on the street—"

The waitress arrived with the drinks.

Osborne pulled out a twenty and tossed it on her tray. After she moved away, he leaned heavily on the table and fixed Lars with a cold stare.

"Joe citizen wants the freedom to do as he pleases without interference, especially from a militant religious fanatic trying to ruin his way of life. But he isn't willing to face the hard reality of the sacrifices required. It's like, 'Keep me safe and my tank full of cheap gas but don't tell me how you're doing it.'"

Osborne tapped the table hard with a forefinger. "President Kilpatrick believes that bringing terror to the terrorists gets results. It robs them of sanctuaries, hits their funding, blows them up in the desert far from the glory of dying publicly for a cause, and punches their leaders into the dirt with a fifty-caliber slug in the brain from a thousand yards. So what?"

Lars drank about half of his bourbon. Through a burning throat he said, "I guess—"

"I'm not saying we did any of those things, mind you, but you get the point, right?"

Sounded like typical doublespeak to Lars, but he nodded vigorously. "Yes, sir."

"And you understand that our purpose is not to keep details from Americans, but we have no choice if we want to succeed?"

"Absolutely, Mr. Osborne."

"Excellent!" Osborne slapped the table with his palm. In a lowered voice, he said, "All right then. Get this investigation done and publish the results."

"But the final report won't be ready for weeks."

"Then publish the draft results, or hold a press conference, or get on David Letterman. I don't care. Do *some*thing to publicize the conclusions and put the rumors to bed."

CHAPTER EIGHTEEN

Wilson liked working weekday nights. Especially when the target lived in a nice neighborhood. Residents generally went to bed early, making it easier for him to move about unnoticed. At midnight, after a few hours of sleep on the floor behind the front seats of the rental van, he checked that the interior dome light was off and slipped out of the vehicle into the heavily landscaped border of a small park. A few minutes of cautious maneuvering put him in a narrow greenbelt between the rear property lines of thirty-year-old homes.

He had planned a back-alley route to avoid strolling down a residential street dressed in black combat gear. Cops seldom had time to conduct voluntary patrol outside high-crime areas, but all it took was one insomniac staring out a bedroom window. Aunt Gertie calls 911 and all hell breaks loose.

At the wood-plank-and-stone-pillar fence of the Phillips home, he paused, glanced in each direction, listened. A quiet, peaceful night in suburbia. Dogs were often a problem. He carried drugged snacks, even though an earlier visit had found nothing to indicate family pets.

Gloved hands gripping the top, he pulled himself up and bent over the fence at his waist. His equipment vest cushioned him against the sharp edge. One leg over to straddle, thankful he wore the hard, protective cup, then the other leg, and he dropped to the ground in a crouch behind a row of tall evergreens. Another pause.

Silence. No lights inside the house. The moonless, cloudy sky helped mask his approach to a planter bed of overgrown shrubs. Homeowners were such fools, landscaping their property for the convenience of thieves and other undesirables.

He found the electrical panel and beside it the phone box. He snipped the line. A quick peek into a rear window identified a utility room with washer-dryer, sewing table, and ironing board. Using a glass cutter, he removed a circle of windowpane above each of two latches, slipped both, eased the window up an inch.

Nothing.

Okay. Silent alarm? Probably not. Homeowners want noise to scare an intruder off, wake up the neighborhood, summon help. And besides, the phone line was cut. They might have a separate line dedicated to the alarm, but he'd seen nothing to indicate that level of security. The window wasn't armed or the system was turned off.

What about motion detectors? He raised the window and climbed in. Silence didn't mean much. They probably wouldn't motion-protect a single room. He opened the door, stepped into the kitchen, the dining room, stopped at the entrance to a large family room. They'd put one here. He walked to the center of the room and waved his arms.

All right, then. Wilson one, Phillips home security zip.

He walked into a hallway and stopped at the foot of the stairs in the front foyer. A grandfather clock somewhere on the second floor ticked away the seconds. A faint odor lingered: onion and garlic from an evening meal. Good. Somebody's home.

Careful on the stairs. They often creaked. He placed the toe of a boot on the front edge of the first tread and eased his weight on that leg. Slowly, one step at a time, he reached the top. A long hallway opened into rooms on either side. The clock punctuated his heartbeats, still calm, under control. Staying close to the wall, he stepped to the first closed door on the right, placed his ear against it, and listened. Light snoring.

Gloved hand on the knob, he turned it slowly and eased the door open.

Girl's room. Blonde hair splayed out over a pillow. Size of the bulge under the covers suggested a teenager. He closed the door. The next room on the left was also occupied and all boy. Sports trophies, rock-star posters, and covering one wall a hand-painted scene of a tarpon breaking the surface at the end of a fly line connected to a fisherman in the background.

Then a bathroom, an empty bedroom, and at the end of the hall, another door, slightly ajar. He nudged it open and moved to the edge of the bed.

Woman. She lay in a curled position, hands tucked under her face. Such a private moment to share with a stranger. He leaned over, took a deep breath, savoring her scent, then reached out and touched her hair ever so lightly. Beautiful. Reminded him of a shampoo commercial.

Back to business, he went around the room, rearranging items just enough to make the point: put the clock in alarm mode, lay a family picture flat on the dresser, open a drawer, take out a lacy pair of panties and place them beside the picture. In other rooms he left similar calling cards. He unlocked the back door to leave it open as a final postscript to the message.

Hand on the knob, he paused. The task felt incomplete. Too random, not personal enough. It lacked the kind of threat that sent bottomless fear into hearts and minds. Back in the girl's room, he stood over the bed. She lay on her side, facing away. Perfect. From his equipment vest he removed a patch of gauze and a stoppered vial. He sprinkled chloroform on the gauze and returned the vial to the vest.

He lifted his right leg, bent at the knee, and in one continuous motion drove his shin into the small of her back as he grabbed a handful of blond hair, hauled her head off the pillow and planted the gauze across her mouth and nose.

She was strong, but only for a few seconds. He pulled her limp body to the edge of the bed and knelt. With her body draped over his shoulder, he stood and left the room.

At the end of a hallway off the foyer, he found the door to the cellar. The stairs emptied into a large game room with a pool table, big-screen TV, and entertainment system. At the opposite end of the room, a wet bar, built-in desk and bookshelves. He pulled out the desk chair and propped the girl's body in it.

Wonderful stuff, duct tape. When she was strapped down and gagged, he drenched a dish towel with cold water from the wet bar, pulled her head back and dribbled the water onto her face.

As she began to regain consciousness, he knelt in front of her, eyeball to eyeball. The full face mask as the first thing she saw would do wonders to prepare her for the message. He gripped her chin to support her head and slapped her gently across both cheeks.

"Wake up. Wake up, sweetheart. That's it. Hold your head up so I can talk to you."

He felt the control return to her neck muscles as her head bobbed up and down. Her eyes fluttered, blinked, opened, widened in horror as a muffled scream tried to escape the duct tape. Her whole body fought, jerked, struggled. Looked like the Energizer Bunny with tits.

"Shhhhhh. Stop it," he whispered. "I need you to get control." Another few moments of panic, and she seemed to lose her charge. Energizer would not be pleased.

"You ready to listen?"

Racking sobs, sounds of despair. Tears flowed from eyes clenched shut.

Wilson waited until she seemed to run dry. "Look at me."

She shook her head, didn't open her eyes.

He slapped her, not too hard. Be a sin to mark that face. *"Look at me."*

When her eyes finally opened, she began to shiver.

Wilson got an afghan off the couch and draped it over her shoulders, making sure he covered her breasts.

She appeared to relax just a bit. Ready to listen.

He moved in close, the mask inches from her face. "First, let me say that you are one gorgeous hunk of female delight, and I'd love to taste your honey." When she began sobbing, Wilson whispered, "Shush. You weren't listening, I said I'd *love* to. That means I'm not, okay?" He waited until she regained control. "But in return for my kindness, you have to do something for me. Will you do that?"

After a pause, a hesitant nod.

"Good. I want you always to remember this night. How close you came to being my play toy. But I didn't show you my special games, because that's not what I'm here for." He waited for a moment. "I know what you're thinking. What *is* he here for? Right?"

A nod.

"So I'm going to tell you. Are you listening?"

A double nod.

Wilson leaned forward, with his mouth nuzzling her ear. He

slipped his hand inside the Afghan and slid his fingers between her legs, caressing the soft silk of her nightgown covering her thighs. She tensed, jammed her knees together. He continued upward, stroked her belly, then her breasts, and stopped with his hand at her throat.

In a whisper as soft as the caress, he said, "You will tell your mommy that an intruder brought you down here. You talked him out of raping you. If you mention anything, and I mean *anything,* about this conversation, I will be back. You wouldn't want that, would you?"

She shook her head and whimpered.

"And you'll tell your daddy you're terrified the guy might come back. You need him home. Got it?"

She nodded, tears flowing down smooth, milk-and-honey cheeks.

"Good. Remember this. If you fail, your daddy will die. It's all up to you." He waited a moment. "I'm going to leave. But first, one little taste." He licked her, from jawbone to the top of her ear, and whispered, "Bye bye."

Back at the van, Wilson checked a map for the shortest route to his next destination. He placed the gas cans on the floor in front of the passenger seat and drove into the early morning stillness to send yet another message.

CHAPTER NINETEEN

Nick awoke in his motel room to the *William Tell Overture*. He rolled over, snatched his cell phone off the bedside table, and smiled when he recognized the caller's number. "Good morning, sweetheart."

Laurie's sobs almost stilled his heart. "Oh, N-Nick, I'm so glad I g-got you. We had a break-in last night and . . . Stephanie . . . she—"

"Is she okay?"

"No! Yes! I mean . . . the son of a bitch came through the utility-room window. He took Stephanie d-d-down—"

Nick snatched off the covers and bolted upright up in bed. "He did *what*?"

"He took her down to the basement and . . . and . . ."

Nick's entire body filled with pain for his little girl. "God, no, Laurie, don't tell me . . ."

"She says he didn't rape her. She talked him out of it."

A surge of relief, but tinged with doubt. "You think she's telling the truth?"

"Why would she lie?"

"Shame, denial. Or she's forgotten. Trauma victims sometimes block the memory of horrific events."

"It don't think she's hiding anything, but . . ."

"But what?"

"She's been really tight-lipped. To us and the police. Like she's holding something back."

Nick got out of bed and paced around the room. "You'd expect that after something like this, wouldn't you?"

"How the hell should I know what to expect?"

"You're right, sorry." Nick's brain seemed to have run out of control with a slide show: images of his baby girl in a bassinet, the first steps, a school play, a cheer competition. He stopped pacing, forced his attention back to the present and stared at the wall with wet eyes. "Do we need to get her examined? To preserve any . . . evidence? If there is any, I mean."

Laurie gasped. After a pause, "Her shower this morning emptied the hot water heater. If she's hiding something or suppressed the memory, any physical evidence is gone."

"What about . . . you know . . . other indications?"

"I can't even think about that, much less talk about it. Let's accept what she says. She's been through enough."

"Okay."

"By the way, you know the officer who responded. He worked with you on the Little League project."

"Walter . . . Thorpe, or something like that? A corporal?"

"He's a detective."

"Have his number handy?"

Laurie gave him the number. "Stephanie asked for you, Nick. She wants you home."

Nick's voice cracked when he said, "I'd like to speak with her."

"Later. I gave her something to help her sleep. When can you leave?"

"I'll be out of here as soon as I can."

"Uh huh. That's what you said last time we talked. And just

in case this will help you quit stalling, there's something else."

"What?"

"The bastard was in every room. I found lots of things moved, not much, but enough to notice. Why would he do that?"

The question hung in the earpiece, begging for a logical answer. Nick began pacing again. "I don't know. Ask Stephanie to call me when she wakes up."

"I'll do that. In the meantime, pay attention. You're right on the edge with me. If you don't get your ass home pretty damn quick, I'll have divorce papers in your hands faster than you can spit."

Nick halted in the middle of the room and listened to the silent phone. After a moment, he went to the window and stared into the parking lot. He and Laurie had a good marriage, but not without occasional turmoil. Nothing that ever threatened separation or divorce, at least as far as Nick was concerned. Then again, they'd never faced anything like this. Coming together to get through it was the answer. He couldn't let it create an irreparable rift.

A deep breath didn't help settle his nerves much, so he took few more. He was punching in Thorpe's number when he got an incoming call from the mechanic working on the Mustang.

"Hey, Fred. I need to call you back."

"Won't take long. It's about the car."

"How's it look?"

"Like a smoldering pile of junk. We had a fire here last night."

On a scale of importance, the car meant nothing in relation to the safety of Nick's family. But this news hit him in a different way, deeper in his personal history. He sank into a chair. "How'd it happen?"

"Not sure yet. Got a call from the alarm company about four this morning. By the time I showed up the shop was pretty far gone. Firefighters couldn't do much. The inspector said it looked like an accelerant might have been used."

They discussed filing an insurance claim on the Mustang and agreed to talk when Nick got in town. As he flipped the phone closed, the pain of another loss gripped his chest. A dream for the future had been shattered when his father died, and Nick's plan to realize the fantasy a generation later lay in ashes on a shop floor. Still, it was just a thing.

He was making coffee when he got a call from Detective Walter Thorpe. "It's been a long time, Nick. I wish we were discussing Little League."

"Me too. Could you fill me in on what you found?"

"Cut phone line, footprints in the flower bed, forced entry through a window at the back. Typical scenario, no outdoor lights, overgrown bushes blocking the neighbor's view. You need to take care of that."

"No more procrastination, believe me."

"He cut sections out of the window. Efficient and quiet. We got a couple of muddy footprint impressions on the floor beneath the window. Nothing else of forensic value anywhere in the house. No prints, hair or fiber, at least so far. I'm guessing there won't be."

"Why not?"

"Mostly gut feel. The typical break-and-enter low life wears tennis shoes. This guy had tactical street boots with a distinctive tread pattern used by only one manufacturer. The brand is favored by cops, especially SWAT, and they aren't cheap. A pro would more likely have the bucks to buy them, and he won't make many mistakes."

Nick leaned against the bathroom sink. "Why would a pro

break into a home, terrorize a teenage girl without molesting her, and walk away with nothing of value?"

"If you try to apply normal logic to the actions of criminals, you'll be wasting your time."

"Isn't the combination of B and E and crimes against persons relatively rare?"

"It depends. Future sexual predators often begin with petty crimes and escalate to more significant and violent ones. This guy could be in transition. His entry might have had nothing to do with burglary. Maybe he's practicing for what he is to become."

Nick felt the sudden and almost overwhelming desire to make certain the son of a bitch had no opportunity to become anything but dust. He had to will his clenched jaw into working. "Stephanie says she talked him out of it. Does that sound reasonable?"

"It doesn't have to. These guys don't think like the rest of us. My guess is he wasn't there to rape because he hasn't reached that point yet. It's like evolution in reverse, and it takes time."

"Did you interview Stephanie?"

"A female detective handled that, but your daughter allowed me to be present. She's a strong young woman, Nick."

Nick almost lost it. After a moment, "It's her mother's influence. This . . . this is a really hard question for a father to ask, but do you think Stephanie was telling the truth about what *didn't* happen?"

"I want you to believe me when I say yes. I've interviewed more victims of violence than I care to remember, male and female, and it didn't feel like she was hiding anything. I'll give you the number for the other detective if—"

"That's not necessary, Walter. I have no reason to doubt your assessment."

"Okay. Anything else I can help you with?"

As Nick thought about that, two mental flash cards appeared in quick succession: footprints at the GoldenJet crash site and on the wing of his airplane. His neck began to tingle. The sensation rose to the top of his skull. "Do me a favor, Walter?"

"Sure."

"Take a picture of the best footprint and send it to me." Nick gave him his email address and said, "I don't know if Laurie mentioned this, but it appears the intruder went into every room and rearranged things. Made it obvious."

After a pause, Walter said, "That's interesting. It's not uncommon for them to take souvenirs, but I've never heard of anything like that. Probably another early indicator of an evolving criminal career."

"What about him coming back?"

"I wouldn't rule it out."

"You know any good security types?"

"Oh, yeah. How about an off-duty cop?"

"Perfect."

"I'll take care of it."

Nick thanked Walter and poured a cup of coffee. He called Fred and said, "Got a question for you."

"Shoot."

"Any signs of a break-in at the shop?"

"Uh . . . no, but I'm not sure anyone's looked. It's pretty obvious the fire started inside with the car, so if it wasn't accidental they had to get in somehow."

"How's your security system?"

"Cheap. And I don't have special locks on the doors. I think I'll get some."

"Is the front well lit?"

"Yeah, and traffic on the highway stays heavy most of the night. Somebody wanted to break in, the back is the best place."

This was probably a waste of time, but Nick had to know for sure. "You free to take a look for me?"

"Why not? Everything I was working on is burned the hell up." After a few minutes the mechanic said, "What am I looking for?"

"Any damage to the door? Or the lock?"

"Not so I can tell. But it wouldn't take much to jimmy it."

"Was the rear of the building heavily damaged in the fire?"

"Nope. It started in the front where the Mustang was. Like I said, the fire department got here quick, and it didn't have time to spread much."

Nick closed his eyes and pictured the building. "That back lot is dirt, right?

"Usually. But we had rain yesterday morning, so it's mostly mud. There's a small concrete pad under the door. Why?"

Nick took a long shot. "See anything on that pad looks like a footprint?"

After a pause, "It's a crosshatched pattern, like maybe from a muddy boot."

CHAPTER TWENTY

Lars Nordstrom parked beside the operations hangar at the Cedar Valley Airport and opened the door of his rental car. A cold, wet wind reached inside and pierced his lightweight jacket like it wasn't there. He should never have trusted his wife to pack for him. In her mind, normal people only visited destinations with tropical breezes and temperate climate. She seemed unable to understand that many places around the globe turn cold periodically.

Inside the hangar was warmer, but not by much. He found the excuse for an IIC's office and put his briefcase on the floor. Stacks of paper covered the desk. He had so much to do he didn't know where to begin. Some breakfast might help him figure it out. As he stepped out of the office his cell phone rang.

Tanner Osborne asked, "Where are you?"

"Good morning, Mr. Osborne. Colorado. I thought—"

"Just so you know what we're dealing with, go find a copy of the local rag." The line went dead. No wasted words from this guy.

Lars stepped out of the hangar into the gray mist and looked around for someplace that might have food and a newspaper. Barely visible in the distance, an unlit café sign hung in a window on the first floor of the terminal building. Interior lights cast a welcoming glow onto the glistening asphalt. He trotted over and peered in. A wire rack by the cash register had a sign at the top: *Cedar Valley Gazette*. He shoved through the door to the tinkling of a bell and yanked a paper off the rack. As he scanned the front page, he heard a raspy voice behind him.

"You're plannin' on payin' for that, ain't you, sugar?"

Lars turned around. An elderly woman, dressed in what might at one time have been a waitress's uniform, stood at the door to the kitchen. One hand on her hip, she held a pot of coffee in the other and stared at him over the top of reading glasses with bright red, gold-speckled frames. A faded pink hat perched on top of her rat's-nest hairdo.

He glanced at the paper. "But it's yesterday's."

"It's all you're gettin' this early. You want it, or not?"

Lars approached the counter. "Yes. And you can add a cup of that coffee. Got any doughnuts?"

"Make 'em here myself. You want plain, cinnamon-sugar, or chocolate?"

"One plain, one cinnamon-sugar."

While Loretta, according to her lopsided nametag, poured his coffee and served the doughnuts, Lars found the article. He had read only a few lines when Loretta said, "That boy Hotel has gone and done it again."

Lars took a bite of doughnut and a sip of coffee, which almost singed his lips off. "Who's this Hotel fellow?"

"Harvey Sweet. Local boy. Known him all his life. He really put it to those bastards, 'scuse my language, mister."

Ah, yes. You can always get the real skinny from a local. Lars put the paper down. "What's the article say, Loretta?"

"That Larchmont fellow was murdered."

Choking on a big bite of doughnut, Lars almost spit a

mouthful onto the counter. He used the napkin to cover his face.

"You okay, there, son?"

Lars nodded, but he lied.

THINKING ABOUT EVENTS AT home took Nick's mind off the nagging pain, stiffness, and persistent headache of the past few days as he dealt with keeping the bandages dry during his shower. He gave up on trying to shave. When he finally sat down at the desk and fired up his laptop, an e-mail from Walter Thorpe chimed in.

Nick opened the three attachments: two pictures of the flowerbed in his back yard below the utility-room window and one of the floor inside. Walter must have dusted the footprints with a white powder and illuminated them with side lighting. Nick's anger grew exponentially. The man who wore these boots had invaded the sanctity of Nick's home while his wife and children slept upstairs, terrorized his daughter, and slithered away into the night like a goddamned snake.

He stared at the stack of investigative paperwork in his briefcase. No one had missed it, or Federal Marshals would have paid a visit. He found the photos of the ground below the GoldenJet's lower main cabin door jamb and the muddy footprint on the carpet, compared them to the pictures from Thorpe. All showed lug soles in a distinctive crosshatched pattern.

An image flashed before his eyes: the wing of his airplane and the print of a boot in the white foam. At that moment, he knew the photos from the shop would match as well. This guy was messing with his family.

Bad move, motherfucker.

LARS SAT IN A booth at the terminal café and finished reading Sweet's article for the third time. The unsubstantiated conclusion about a conspiracy of sabotage and murder didn't come across as the ranting of a lunatic. The reporter had done a masterful job of presenting the supposed facts as if he didn't really buy Phillips' hypothesis but considered the allegation fit to print and let readers decide.

Loretta hovered over him, refilling his coffee cup nearly every time he took a sip. Lars had just waved her away when the door to the café opened and a man walked in. Dressed in a conservative dark blue suit, white shirt, regimental-stripe tie and open trench coat, the stranger strolled over to the counter. Lars went back to the article and tried to tune out Loretta taking a coffee order and her probing questions, including comments about the man's slender build and how he needed fattening up.

"Excuse me, Mr. Nordstrom?"

Lars glanced up. The man stood beside the booth. "Yes?"

"Sir, I'm Special Agent Paul Montana, FBI."

Lars drank some water to cure a sudden case of dry mouth and asked what an FBI agent wanted with him.

Montana smiled, two rows of perfect teeth arranged like ivory piano keys. "Nothing much, Mr. Nordstrom, just a few moments of your time. May I sit down?"

Lars motioned to the other side of the booth. If Osborne had involved him in the cover-up of a murder, Lars would spill his guts so fast it would burn up the recorder.

Montana settled into the booth and sipped his coffee. "Wow. That old gal knows how to brew a cup of java."

Lars relaxed a bit. Montana seemed like a nice guy, and Lars hadn't done anything wrong. At least not yet. They were on the same team. The tension in his body eased a bit more. "You should try the doughnuts. Loretta makes them herself."

Montana patted his stomach. "I've got to watch the old waistline. It isn't as easy as it used to be." He took another sip of coffee, put down the cup and reached inside his trench coat. After a glance around the café, which had no other customers, he brought out a folded black leather wallet, flipped it open and handed it to Lars. "My identification."

In all of the years Lars had worked for the NTSB, he'd never met an FBI agent and wouldn't have known an authentic shield from one out of a cereal box. He closed the wallet and handed it back. "Nice picture."

"I had it touched up."

Lars nodded. "Good idea." He immediately regretted the comment. "What I meant was, I need to do that. How did you know who I was and where to find me?"

"The 'who' was easy, sir. I have your picture. The 'where' was pretty simple, too. Went to the hangar and asked the first person I saw. He noticed when you left and in what direction. It's early morning. This is a café. Breakfast is served here. We call it deduction."

A flush of anger turned Lars' face hot. What a sanctimonious prick. "I'm familiar with the concept. How did you know I was out here in Colorado?"

"Child's play for the FBI, Mr. Nordstrom."

Lars sipped his coffee. "What do you want with me?"

"Answers to a few questions."

"Concerning?"

"The Larchmont crash."

"I can't talk with you about that."

"Why not?"

"The report isn't complete. We aren't ready to announce

our findings."

Montana leaned forward with his elbows on the table, forearms steepled, fingers interlaced. "May I suggest that you be careful here, Mr. Nordstrom?"

Lars coughed, suddenly doubtful about getting into a pissing contest with a federal agent. In a softer tone, he said, "Of what, Special Agent Montana?"

"Obstruction of justice, for starters."

Lars set down his coffee cup. "The hell you talking about?"

"Oh, a little item in NTSB operational procedures that requires you to hand over lead status to the Bureau for any investigation in which evidence of criminal wrongdoing is discovered. That sound familiar?"

Uncertainty settled over Lars. How should he play this? After a moment, he decided to push back, but not too much. "Maybe you've been reading too many papers."

"Just enough, actually. Sufficient to connect a series of events that separately might not trigger our involvement. But when viewed in light of the controversy surrounding the victim, we take notice. You are aware of Larchmont's past, are you not?"

Lars cautioned himself not to bend over backwards by making too nice. "I haven't been living on Mars."

"Splendid. May I make another suggestion?"

Lars sipped his coffee and stretched. Make the guy wait a bit. "Please do."

"If this goes much further, and it turns out that you should have called us in and didn't . . . well . . . you *are* the new IIC, correct?"

"I assumed the lead yesterday and arrived this morning. I'm also going to handle the light-aircraft crash that occurred two days ago."

"And that pilot is an investigator?"

Lars glanced at his watch and nodded. "Phillips."

"So he works for you?"

"He may still officially, but he's finished in the NTSB."

"Is he here in Colorado?"

What is this, an inquisition? "I assume so, although I haven't seen him. You still haven't told me why you're here, Special Agent Montana."

Montana lowered his voice. "In case you haven't been paying attention, this article," he tapped an extended first finger on the folded newspaper lying between them, "made it all over the country at the speed of light. It reinforces the common belief that somebody wanted Larchmont dead, and it's the first time a named source has gone on record."

Loretta charged into the dining area waving a pot of coffee. "Fresh mud, gents?"

Lars waved her away and leaned back against the faded red vinyl that covered the back of the booth. The sharp edges of a split in the cushion jabbed him through his thin clothing. He shifted position, picked up a spoon, reached for a sugar packet and stopped. What the hell was he doing? He didn't like sweetened coffee. "Then talking to me is a waste of your time. The Bureau should be taking over whether I call you in or not."

Montana moved closer and lowered his voice another notch. "That's not the way it works. If that reporter and his source had any hard evidence, you think they'd hold back?"

"So, again, why are you *here?*"

In a whisper Montana said, "You may not have noticed, but I'm not wearing my photo tag."

"Your what?"

"The tag that clips to the outside of clothing with my picture and big letters that say F . . . B . . . I."

"You're right. I didn't notice. What's that got to do with my question?"

"Everything. You may also not have noticed that there's only one of me. Special agents normally travel in pairs. That's kind of like I'm not really here. For you, that's a good thing."

When Montana paused to sip his coffee, Lars said, "And I suppose you're going to tell me why?"

Montana put down his cup and wiped his mouth with a paper napkin. "It's called 'let's make a deal.' You show me what the NTSB really has, or doesn't have will probably be more like it, and we'll decide this together. If there's insufficient evidence, I'll be on my anonymous way. But if we find something solid, *you* follow protocol. That way, it'll appear that you just discovered it. The blame for not sounding the alarm will fall on the previous IIC, and you're home free."

"Why do you care?"

"About you? I don't. But hear me well, Mr. Nordstrom. I don't like murderers, and I don't give a damn how high they sit on the throne of power. I especially don't like cop killers. If there's any truth to these allegations, and I can help get this investigation in the hands of law enforcement, I'll risk my career in a heartbeat."

Lars waved to Loretta for more coffee. The flurry of her activity gave him the delay he needed to figure this out. She asked if anyone wanted a doughnut, refused to take no for an answer, and brought two cinnamon-sugar fat pills to the table.

Lars' quick grab of the brass ring offered by Tanner Osborne didn't seem like such a good idea with an FBI agent staring at him. If Larchmont had been murdered, and Osborne had anything to do with it, and Lars got caught up in the scandal of a cover-up, the resulting shit storm would make current events smell like roses.

He leaned forward, in part to reclaim a feeling of authority over the conversation. "Tell you what. *I* can't speak to you about it, but I know someone who can. Would you like to meet him?"

Brilliant white teeth brightened the booth. "How about one of these doughnuts and another cup of mud before we go, gent?"

NICK PRESSED THE END button on his cell phone and sat very still as he stared at the motel-room carpet with wet eyes. His conversation with Stephanie had aroused a strange mixture of emotions. Anger, relief, and pride seemed to be fighting for dominance. He'd promised to get home as soon as he could, the third such commitment in as many days. Question was, how soon would that be? And would he find the locks changed and his clothes piled in a heap by the curb? Part of him said Laurie would understand when she found out why he couldn't walk away without finishing it. Another part recognized the symptoms of wishful thinking.

He called Laurie. "Did you have the alarm on last night?"

After a pause, "No. I've gotten careless again. But what difference would that have made? He cut the phone line."

Nick gritted his teeth in frustration. No matter how hard he tried, he couldn't create in Laurie the same security awareness that was an indelible component of his being. And although this was not the time to press home the point, he could not let it pass. "Remote monitoring is only half the benefit of the system. The local alarm uses house power, has a backup battery, and is completely independent of the phone line. It would have alerted you to the break-in."

"Oh, my God. Of course." Laurie began crying.

Nick waited a moment, then said, "Walter Thorpe will be contacting you. He knows cops who moonlight as security guards. I want one there every night for a while."

Between sobs, Laurie said, "Only until you get home, you mean?"

Nick paused. "I don't want to frighten you more than you already are, but the intruder might not have been a burglar or a less-than-committed rapist."

That stopped the crying. Laurie's voice regained her normal steel. "Then what the hell was he?"

"A messenger. I think the same person may have torched Brad's car, and he knows his way around Cedar Valley."

Her voice regained a little tremor. "Somebody burned the Mustang?"

"Last night."

"What the hell kind of message are we talking about?"

"I'm not positive, but it could be . . . kind of like . . . intimidation. To get me out of here."

"So what happened here, in our home, where our *children* live, is all about your investigation?"

With no way to soften the answer, Nick related the short version of recent events.

"Goddamn it, Nick. You knew we might be in danger and you stayed there?"

"That's not what happened. I had no reason to think they'd try anything like this. And I don't think they'll try again."

"Why not?"

"They'll be a lot more effective coming after me directly."

"Wonderful. My husband's being stalked by a killer."

"I'll be careful. Don't worry."

"Oh, sure. Like that will make me feel better. Why not just walk away?"

"Because I'm going to get these sons of bitches, Laurie. You and the kids are safe. Please understand that I have to see this through."

"I don't understand it and never will. You're an accident investigator. Man-hunting is not part of your job description."

"I'm going after the *evidence.* Law enforcement will take it from there."

"Fine. My lawyer will take it from here. Goodbye."

"Laurie! Wait a minute—damn it!" Nick tossed his cell phone on the bed. She didn't *really* mean that . . . did she? A sharp knock on the door startled him. Sweet's comments about unsolved disappearances came to mind. He went to the peephole and squinted through it.

A blood-red eyeball filled the viewer.

"Who's there?"

"An exhausted reporter. Open up."

Sweet entered the room dressed head-to-toe in camouflage hunting gear. He tossed a helmet and riding gloves on the bed, plopped down in a chair, and yawned. "The *Gazette* has been a zoo. Tried to go home yesterday for some shuteye, never made it. You see the article?"

Nick motioned to a copy of the *Gazette* on the bed. "Nice work. Want some coffee?"

Sweet shook his head. "I've been living on it for a couple days. What do you think the chances are I stirred them up?"

"Damn good, actually." Nick related the incidents at home and his conversation with Dickson.

Sweet stared at him. "These SOBs threatened your family?"

"To get to me. I don't think they'd—"

"You can't remove anything from the table when you're dealing with people like this, Nick. Have you arranged for close protection?"

"Yes."

"Who?"

Nick told him about his past relationship with Thorpe and that he trusted him to take care of security details. "I'm frankly more worried that Laurie was serious about getting a lawyer."

Sweet's eyes shifted around the room for a moment and settled on Nick. "Why don't you go home to your family and let me take it from here?"

"Do us both a favor and don't even think about it. I'm in this to the end."

"Okay. Your marriage is your business, but I think—"

"With due respect, drop it."

Sweet's expression sent the clear message, *Okay, but don't say I didn't try.* He nodded and began scribbling in his notepad. "Could Dickson's visit be the first crack in the conspiratorial armor?"

Nick shook his head. "Nordstrom might be slightly higher on the food chain, but if either of them has anything to do with this, they're both being used and don't know details."

"It appears we're in a wait-and-see mode."

"In the meantime, let's hope that people who read your article will ask the key question: 'Who profited the most and what did they stand to gain by Larchmont's death?'"

Sweet waved his arms with a flourish. "And the answer is, President John Kilpatrick and another four years in the Oval Office."

Nick leaned back in his chair. "But it's going to take a lot more than a bunch of conspiracy theorists. With the degree of congressional oversight in the system, the average American will want to know how anyone can funnel millions of dollars into a black hole filled with counter-terrorists running a secret war."

Sweet looked up from his notepad. "So we use the power of modern media to create enough doubt in enough people. We show them loopholes that always exist in bureaucratic systems. That money flows through a pipe the size of a railroad tunnel. That the President is the only person who can approve funding for covert operations outside of committee. That it occurs behind closed doors in dark rooms with no accountability."

Nick fought back a smile. "Ambitious goals for a rookie reporter at a small town rag. One that has no standards, by the way. Your editor printed the article without corroboration."

Sweet didn't take the bait. "Those of us in the business know that's necessary only for stories based on confidential sources. You were more than willing to be quoted."

"But will that work for subsequent articles?"

"It will if I keep the focus on what happened here. Investigating motive and tracking money around the world is way out of my league. That's a job for—"

Three sharp knocks rattled the door.

"Wow," said Sweet. "That was quick. Is this place bugged?"

Nick got up and checked the peephole. "Well I'll be damned." He opened the door. Nordstrom stood a few feet from the threshold, hands in his pockets and shivering. A man stood a couple of feet behind him. After an awkward moment of silence, Nordstrom said, "We'd like to speak with you."

Nick sensed a presence behind him and glanced over his shoulder. Sweet stood close, concerned. Nick mouthed a silent, "What?" as the stranger's voice drew Nick's attention back to the visitors.

"Mr. Nordstrom and I need to speak with Nick Phillips. May we come inside? It's cold out here."

"Perhaps it would be best if you identify yourself first," said Sweet.

The man nodded. "Tell you what. Why don't we both do that? I'm Special Agent Paul Montana, FBI. Who might you be?"

Nick started to respond, but Sweet's words stopped him. "Have any identification on you?"

"Of course. What's it to you?"

Nick said, "I thought you were cold."

Montana produced his ID wallet, flipped it open, walked past Nordstrom, stopped in front of Nick and extended his right arm toward Sweet with the wallet lying open in his hand. He smiled. "Here you go." He had flawless teeth, and his breath carried the aroma of mint.

Sweet accepted the identification. He inspected it and handed it back. "Thank you, Special Agent Montana. You with the Denver Office?"

"Yes. May we come in?"

Sweet backed into the room. Montana followed Nordstrom inside. Nick closed the door, locked the deadbolt and reached for the security chain.

Sweet said, "Hold up a minute, Nick."

Montana turned to face Sweet. "And you are?"

"Harvey Sweet, *Cedar Valley Gazette.*"

Montana's smile shown bright against his tanned face. "Of course! I enjoyed your article."

"Thanks." To Nordstrom: "How'd *you* like it?"

Nordstrom's expression never changed. "A little short on facts for my taste."

Sweet nodded, his mouth a thin, tight line. "It's hard to please everybody, I guess." He picked up his riding gear. To Nick: "I'm headed up to the cabin. Be back about six for a beer, and I'll buy."

Nick secured the door behind Sweet and faced his guests.

"And to what do I owe the honor of this unannounced visit?"

Nordstrom opened his mouth but Montana beat him to it. "Perhaps we could have a seat and get right to that."

EMPTY BEER BOTTLES LAY about the room. After a short period of mutual suspicion, Nick, Nordstrom and Montana had spent most of the afternoon discussing the lack of hard evidence to support a conspiracy theory and what they could do about it.

Initially, Nordstrom used his position as IIC to justify silence and refused to join in. But he paid close attention while Nick provided Montana with details, and he appeared to become more agitated as the conversation progressed. His eyes darted back and forth. He leaned back in his chair, one thigh bouncing, then stood, paced for a minute, sat and repeated the sequence. A bundle of nerves in Dockers and a lightweight sweater that wouldn't stop a breath of fresh air.

During a lull, Montana paused to write in his notebook. Nick made eye contact with Nordstrom, who immediately looked away. He picked at the label on a beer bottle, peeling it off in wrinkled, damp strips. Then he sighed and in a flood of words admitted that in his eagerness to please a man he believed was connected to the upper levels of the White House, he had agreed to speed up the investigation. He worried about what it would mean to his position that he had failed to remain impartial.

Nick felt like a priest in the confessional. He had always thought of Nordstrom as worthless, but he had to admit that the man might have a few redeeming qualities. Dickson and now Nordstrom. *Who would have ever thought it?*

When Montana asked for the man's name, Nordstrom refused to give it. He said that an FBI agent ought to be able to put the pieces together without his help. No amount of badgering changed his mind. By mid-afternoon, the impasse appeared permanent.

Montana sat at the table studying pages in his notebook. Nordstrom was in the bathroom. Nick dropped an empty beer bottle into the trash can, pulled a fresh one out of a Styrofoam cooler and went to the window. The day hadn't improved, gray and dreary. Nordstrom came out of the bathroom and sat down at the table.

Montana closed the notebook, stood, and began some pacing of his own. "Okay. Nothing we know passes the litmus test for FBI involvement. I can't use public opinion, website speculation, or even the sworn testimony of an on-site investigator to barge in and begin a criminal investigation. Do either of you have any idea how we might put our hands on physical evidence to prove somebody tampered with that jet?"

Since unburdening his conscience, Nordstrom had dropped his reluctance to participate. His conversation with Montana blended into the background as Nick's cell phone rang. Sweet's number appeared in the caller ID.

Nick stepped closer to the window. In a lowered voice, he said, "Hey, there, Hotel. I hope it's all right to call you by a nickname your *friends* use."

"Fine by me. Is Montana still there?"

"Yeah, he and Nordstrom—"

"Don't let on anything about what I'm saying, but I got a funny feeling about him."

"Uh . . . okay." Nick listened as Sweet described his suspicions and suggested that Nick terminate this call with a relaxed, nothing's-wrong goodbye, discontinue the meeting, and send Montana on his way. Nick resisted the urge to glance over his shoulder. "All right, then. We'll see you later."

He slipped the cell phone into an outer leg pocket of his cargo pants, pulled the window curtain open more, sipped his beer and thought about how to do this: *My injuries are hurting. I need to take a pill. It can cause nausea, unpleasant for everyone, and it may knock me flat on my ass. Perhaps we should continue this tomorrow?*

Nick let the curtain fall back into place and turned to face the table. He waited for a lull in the conversation and said, "Excuse me, gentlemen."

Montana was standing beside the table, hands in his pockets. He looked away from Nordstrom and at Nick. Then the agent smiled, but it wasn't a real smile, and not nearly as bright as before. His expression never changed as he pulled both hands out of his pockets.

The scene slowed way down as Nick tried to comprehend what was happening.

In a smooth backhand swing, Montana's left arm thudded a black leather sap against the side of Nordstrom's skull, while his right hand slid inside his suit coat, rear edge of his palm first, moved his coat back and drew a large pistol in a continuous, fluid motion.

Nordstrom collapsed in a heap, hit the edge of the table. Beer bottles hopped, bounced, fell to the floor in a spray of River Rock Pale Ale.

Nick's eyes locked on to Montana's pistol and the long cylindrical extension. His brain finally caught up. FBI agents don't carry suppressed weapons.

Nick took a step back against the curtains as Montana swung the pistol toward him. The wicked, black eye of the suppressor stared him in the face.

"Freeze," Montana growled, "and you might live through this."

"What do you want?"

"Shut up." The words came out in a whisper, a dry, malevolent hiss. "Turn around, very slowly."

Nick complied. His face brushed against the curtains. The dry odor of dust and aged cigarette smoke filled his nostrils. He waited.

"No quick movements. Place your hands on top of your head and interlace your fingers."

Nick obeyed. It felt like it took an hour.

A strong hand grabbed his fingers and crushed them in a vice-like grip.

Movement behind him, then cold steel around his right wrist, click, click, click of the handcuffs, his arm pulled down and behind his back, soon joined by his left.

Montana yanked Nick backward and into a chair. He tried not to look, but he failed. Nordstrom's body lay sprawled in a heap on the worn carpet. Bile rose in Nick's throat.

"Don't you puke on me, you miserable prick."

Nick swallowed it down.

Montana came into view and stood in front of him. "Who was that on the phone?"

Nick hesitated.

Montana drew back his right arm and slapped Nick so hard it knocked him out of the chair onto the floor. Stinging pain seared his cheek. Montana leaned down, his face a few inches from Nick's. In a quick thought totally inconsistent with the dread he felt, Nick decided he didn't like the aroma of mint.

Montana pulled a folding knife from his pocket, flicked it open with his thumb. "I'll ask you one more time. Answer the question, or you'll be begging to tell me everything you've ever known."

Nick's breath left him as he stared at the gleaming blade.

"The reporter! Sweet. He called to cancel his offer of buying the beer tonight."

"Bullshit." Montana stood erect, walked out of sight, returned with a washcloth and stuffed it in Nick's mouth.

Nick lay on his back, heart beating like a jackhammer, and watched Montana go to the window, peer through a gap in the curtains, and leave the room. He glanced toward the overturned table. Nordstrom's body lay very still in a scattering of beer bottles. Nick's stomach revolted again. He closed his eyes, turned his head away, and fought to control the nausea.

After what seemed like hours, the door opened and closed. Movement around him, and the sudden, distinctive sound of ripping duct tape.

CHAPTER TWENTY-ONE

Wilson had hoped it wouldn't come to this. But when Nordstrom spilled his guts and it became obvious that Phillips had no intention of heading home, that he was committed to following his suspicions wherever they led, Wilson's mission had changed. No more playing nice with these assholes.

On the floor by the bed lay Nordstrom and Phillips, looking like mummies wrapped in duct tape. Actually, Nordstrom had passed the first stage of becoming a real mummy by choking to death on his own vomit. Always a hazard with gags.

Wilson had been waiting all afternoon with nothing more to do than watch a diffused sliver of light peek through a gap in the curtains and march across the worn carpet, up the ancient wallpaper, and finally fade away to nothing. He glanced at the bedside clock. A red 6:35 cast a dull glow on the night table. Where was that reporter, anyway? He said he'd return about six o'clock with some beer. It wasn't so much the waiting, but Wilson was running out of time.

Phillips' cell phone had rung about a half-hour ago. A message-waiting beeped in with a local phone number displayed. Wilson retrieved the voicemail with an access code Phillips had traded for the right to keep all his fingers. Some idiot calling himself Hotel wanted Phillips to have dinner with him at Maudie's but couldn't be at Phillips' room until around seven o'clock.

Wilson was very good at his job, but two people showing up about the same time could prove troublesome. Especially when one of them had that look . . . the one Wilson had learned long ago to recognize as indicative of a hunter rather than of prey.

He peered through the thin space between the curtains and watched a truck with four camouflaged hunters leave in the direction of town. Probably for dinner. They'd be gone at least an hour. Only two vehicles plus his Explorer sat in the parking lot, awash in pale yellow radiance from overhead lighting. It probably wouldn't get much better than this, but he decided to wait a little longer, just in case.

Putting this assignment to rest for good with a single move would be so *sweet*.

HOTEL HAD LEFT NICK'S room for his hunting cabin this morning with every intention of returning to Cedar Valley in time for an early dinner. But he'd found a broken water line in the kitchen, and the repair developed a life of its own. A little after noon, he took a lunch break and the concern that had been nagging at him all morning rose to the level of conscious thought.

Was it because Montana had used his right hand to show Hotel his identification? The bulge in Montana's coat at his right hip, combined with the fact that law enforcement officers typically never presented identification to civilians with their strong-side hand, had lit the pilot light of Hotel's suspicion.

Or maybe the absence of a photo tag? Hotel didn't know for sure, but didn't agents wear them when on official business?

Or was it only when in a restricted area, like on a crime scene?

What about the fact that Montana wore gloves and never took them off to shake hands? Hotel had recognized the logo identifying the gloves as lined with Kevlar for puncture protection. An agent might wear them when expecting physical confrontation, but on a visit to the room of an NTSB investigator?

And that tan. Denver had a lot of sun, but you had to be outdoors to get it. FBI agents don't have a lot of free time, and Montana's face looked like he'd been lounging at the beach for days on end.

So after calling Nick with the suggestion to get Montana out of the room, he'd waited an hour and called again. No answer. Two messages left on Nick's cell phone had not been returned. Being available was a religion with him. Where the hell was he?

By the time Hotel had fixed the leak and started down the mountain on the dirt bike, uneasiness invaded his thoughts even more. What if something had prodded the conspirators into action while he'd been playing amateur plumber? He decided to take an off-road shortcut that crossed over two ridges. The route put him on a descending slope above Nick's motel. When the lights of the parking lot became visible through the trees, he coasted to a stop well back from a vague break in the rocky terrain. Mindful of a steep embankment near the lot entrance, he eased forward until he could see the edge.

As he searched for a way to traverse the incline, something moved in the parking lot. He couldn't see enough detail to determine whether it was a person or a vehicle. From his saddle bags he retrieved a souvenir of a past life in the military.

The night-vision binoculars, so useful for checking out bucks feeding around his hunting blind, produced a ghostly image of the lot with a bloom of brightness from a solitary security lamp flooding the left edge. Back-up and brake lights flared on an SUV as it eased up to the motel and stopped. A person got out and entered a room that was either Nick's or close to it. Vague apprehension guided Hotel's thoughts, a leftover from the moment Montana had walked into Nick's room.

Movement by the SUV. Hotel snapped the binoculars to his eyes and watched a fuzzy figure carry a large, cold bundle draped over his shoulder from the room to the vehicle and dump it into the cargo area. He got off his bike to get a better view and braced the binoculars against a tree. The scene repeated, except for one crucial detail: the bundle was human-body warm.

Hotel felt the rush as adrenaline kicked in, the familiar sensation of his whole body becoming more alive. The binoculars seemed to be glued to his face. When the figure climbed into the SUV and the backup lights came on, Hotel forgot all about being a spectator. He turned toward the bike and slipped, landing hard on his butt. The binoculars fell out of his hand, tumbled down the slope and fell to the highway.

He scrambled to the bike and rolled at an angle to traverse the slope. The SUV's headlights came on as it moved away from the building. Hotel stopped, looked over his shoulder as the vehicle entered the highway, and noticed the glow of his brake light painting the forest in a circle of red.

WILSON SET HIS SPEED at five miles an hour under the limit. He didn't expect to see any cops at dinner time on a deserted road to nowhere, but a traffic stop meant another body to dispose of. As he looked up from checking the speedometer, a red light flared in the forest above the road.

He picked up the pistol off the floor and laid it in his lap. Eyes darting from the road to his rearview and outside mirrors, he steered the Explorer around a curve and lost sight of the dark slope.

Hotel released the brake lever and cursed himself. The SUV—an Explorer—accelerated past him toward higher elevations and the lonely expanse of the Lost Cedar Wilderness Area.

Should he check Nick's room or follow the Explorer?

The conversation with Nick replayed in his mind, fast-forwarding to the part about reaction to the article and the potential for retaliation. He had to do *some*thing.

When the rear lights of the Explorer vanished around a curve, he kicked the bike into life, descended to the highway and turned away from the wilderness area. He flicked on the headlight, found the binoculars lying on the gravel shoulder, leaned over and snatched them off the ground. With the strap of the binoculars held between his teeth, he sped across the highway into the parking lot and skidded to a stop in front of Nick's room.

No response to repeated knocks elevated his heart rate even more. He tried the door. Locked. With a flashlight out of the saddle bags he peered through a slender opening in the drapes. A chair lay on its side by the overturned table. Beer bottles rested on the floor.

Mute testimony of recent violence filled Hotel with dread and a single purpose all rolled into one.

Center striping on the asphalt guided Wilson through the forest along the curves of the narrow mountain road. On each straightaway, he checked the rearview. Brief flashes of light in the darkness behind him warned of a tail.

A deer appeared out of nowhere, straddling the center stripe, eyes glowing in the headlight beam. Wilson jerked the wheel. The Explorer swapped ends as the tires lost traction. The rear bumper slammed into the deer and Wilson's head banged against the headrest.

Dazed, he blinked his eyes and waited for his vision to clear, then opened the door and climbed out. The buck lay wedged against the tires, legs kicking in the throes of death. The impact had crumpled the cargo door inward. He tugged on the handle. Secure, probably jammed. He grabbed one of the animal's legs, began dragging it off the highway, paused, thought about it for a moment, and hauled the carcass onto the center stripe.

Back in the Explorer, he turned off the headlights. With the gear shift in low, he jammed the accelerator down, snapped the steering wheel to the right and spun the vehicle around. Just past the next curve he pulled off the road, killed the engine and turned off the overhead light switch. Pistol in hand, he opened the door and trotted toward the carcass.

HOTEL SAT ON THE idling dirt bike with exhaust fumes drifting past his nose. He glanced up. Patches of stars glittered through breaks in the canopy. Little or no moon tonight. Ahead, nothing but an empty road disappearing into the darkness.

He'd been following intermittent glimpses of white and red lights. When headlights flashed through the forest off the road and came to rest shining toward him, he braked hard and steered onto the gravel shoulder. After a moment the headlights went out. He couldn't see anything in the binoculars.

This road dead-ended in the wilderness area. The driver, had to be Montana, could leave the road well enough in the Explorer, but how far could he get? And where would he go to dispose of bodies?

Bury them? Not hardly. Hotel had dug enough post holes up here to know why they're called the Rocky Mountains.

But how about a ready-made hole, really deep, off-limits to everyone, but accessible with four-wheel drive?

Hotel steered the bike onto the center of the black asphalt ribbon to follow his worst fears.

WHEN THE CARCASS APPEARED as a dim bump on the highway, Wilson knelt and looked around for a good spot. Trees lined the road on both sides, no more than ten feet from the narrow gravel shoulder. To his left, no cover. On his right, a lone evergreen bush about three feet high with no foliage on the lower half. He ran to it and lay down to verify his firing lane. Perfect. The bike rider would come into view just before reaching the carcass and not be able to gain cover before Wilson had ample time to take him.

As he checked the pistol, it occurred to him that he didn't need to sacrifice accuracy for noise reduction. He removed the suppressor and slipped it in his jacket pocket. Eyes closed, he concentrated on the quiet stillness and listened for the sound of an approaching engine.

JUST ENOUGH STARLIGHT FILTERED through the trees for Hotel to see the center stripe without the headlight. He wanted to hurry, but the curves in the road limited his sight distance. He hadn't seen any more lights. How far ahead was the Explorer? Did Montana know he was being followed? He's a professional, probably feels it in his bones, and an ambush would be so easy.

Hotel eased back on the handle grip. The bike slowed, coasted to a stop. Then he thought about two bundles, one warm. The last to be killed, or still alive? Fifty-fifty chance it's Nick.

Hotel powered the bike into the night and prayed that he could make it in time.

A SOUND, GROWING LOUDER, filtered through the forest. Dirt bike. Wilson extended the pistol under the bush at arm's length and seated the grip in his off hand. Forearms resting on the ground, he spread his legs with toes pointed out. Three pale dots of reflected light framed the deer, barely visible over the barrel. He regretted not bringing his laser attachment, but the open notch-and-post tritium night sights would do.

Why no headlights? The guy must be riding blacked out. No matter. The son of a bitch would soon be dead meat and complete the second hat trick of Wilson's career.

HOTEL CRANKED THE HANDLE grip and hauled back on the handlebars into a wheelie. The front tire barely missed the carcass. His bent knees absorbed the shock as the rear tire slammed into the deer and vaulted the bike upward. He was concentrating on the landing when a hornet buzzed in front of his nose, something tugged at his left arm, and he felt an impact in the frame of the bike, all timed with a rapid BAM! BAM! BAM!

The bike hit hard on the front tire and rebounded off the

rear. With the highway center stripe curving to his left, he centered the handlebars. The bike landed, stayed down. He steered to miss a tree and barreled into the forest. Branches slapped at his body, trying to jerk him off the bike. He couldn't see a damn thing.

Ignoring the fear that it would backlight him, he flipped on the headlight and ducked. Splinters of bark peppered his face as two more reports of a large-bore handgun ripped through the night. Swerving to avoid trees, shrubs, and rocks, he kept the bike revved up and charged into the darkness behind a horizontal shaft of jittering light.

THE HEADLIGHT CAME ON, silhouetting the rider against vegetation caught in the beam. Wilson jerked to a stop and squeezed off two more rounds as the bike and rider punched into the trees. He sidestepped, tracked the rider with the sights for a follow-up shot, but dark pine boughs swallowed the target.

Goddamn it! He took in deep breaths to counter the adrenaline rush. He'd been sure the guy would lay the bike down or hit the deer and flip. But a wheelie? He took another deep breath, held it, and in the distance heard the retreating sound of the bike's engine suddenly quit.

Did he crash? Wilson trotted to where the bike had entered the forest and pulled out his flashlight. A tire track. Broken branches. A fresh scrape on the trunk of a pine tree. He followed the trail and found the bike lying on its side, handlebars askew. No sign of the rider. In the beam of the flashlight, drops of blood on the gas tank and seat. Not a lot, but the guy was hit, injured in the crash, or both.

Wilson pulled the knife out of his boot, slashed both tires, and ran to the Explorer.

HOTEL WATCHED MONTANA DISAPPEAR into the forest. After a few minutes, he ran to the bike, flicked on the headlight and examined his left upper arm. The bullet had only nicked him. A warm stickiness spread toward his elbow. He pulled a bandanna out of his pocket and with the help of his teeth cinched it around the wound. He hauled the bike up, saw the slashed tires, laid the bike on its other side. Good thing Montana hadn't noticed the scabbard.

The rifle didn't appear to be damaged, but the scope might have been knocked out of alignment. *Need to remember that.* He yanked the backpack off the bike, slipped it on and draped the rifle over his shoulder by the sling.

Montana had to be thinking he was home free, at least for the time being. A man in an Explorer versus one on foot? He'd be thinking, Bye bye, good buddy.

But Hotel had two advantages. He knew exactly where Montana was headed. These mountains had been his to explore since he'd first come up here at the age of five with his dad. The Explorer could make it only by staying on the paved road and then following a four-wheel-drive-only track for the last few miles. Although on foot, Hotel had far less distance to travel.

The backpack *always* contained the ten essential survival tools for outdoorsmen. Hotel pulled out his compass, took a bearing on the most distant landmark he could see, and jogged toward it. He repeated the process until intersecting the paved road for the fourth time, which he figured put him close. But which way should he turn on the road? He peered left, right, saw the outline of a post in the distance. A mile marker. He trotted to it and ran the number through his memory map. It's got to be this way.

After a few minutes of jogging the road, a glimmer of reflective tape atop a brown metal post appeared to his left. He ran to the sign and stopped to catch his breath, which kept trying to abandon him.

OLD DUTCHMAN MINE TRAIL
CLOSED TO VEHICULAR AND
PEDESTRIAN TRAFFIC
DO NOT ENTER

Montana would have to stay on the highway until it dead-ended at the mine entrance. He'd be able to drive around the barriers and enter the main complex, but he had to get there first.

Hotel stepped between two barrier posts and began jogging up the mountain. After ten minutes of barely controlled stumbling over deep ruts, protruding rocks, and dry streambeds, he paused at the crest of a ridge. A thin footpath trailed away in the darkness. Not too much farther. He slipped the rifle sling over his shoulder.

Cold steel chilled his fingers through thin gloves. He eased the bolt to the rear. Dim starlight reflected off the copper-tipped bullet and dull brass of the cartridge waiting at the top of the magazine. A quick forward shove and downward snap of the bolt handle drove the round home in the chamber and locked it. He flicked the safety on, lowered the sling over his head, trotted into the black forest.

CHAPTER TWENTY-TWO

Nick awoke to a foggy nothingness of sight, sound, or feeling. A blindfold, sticky like duct tape, squeezed his head. Something pinned his numb arms behind him. He could bend his knees, but his legs were bound together. A force catapulted him up and slammed him down on a hard surface. Sharp pain cut through his confusion, roused his senses and brought reality into focus.

He lay in the trunk of a car, or the rear of a van or SUV, and the road was getting rougher. One vicious bounce landed him on a softer, rounded bundle. A body. In panic he struggled against his bonds and almost vomited into his gag, a death sentence if he breathed it in rather than swallowed. *Christ! Fight it, Phillips!*

He forced his mind into a better place: deep blue sky, evergreens hugging the rocks down to the water's edge, sun glinting in a million sparkles on a mountain lake. The fly arcs overhead, trailing leader and line, and lands gently on a dark eddy that erupts in a foam of white water. The rainbow trout surges upward, body arcing to the side, and tosses the barbless hook, free to strike another day.

The memory worked until another bounce deposited him on top of the body. The odor of vomit brought bile surging into his throat. He fought it down and concentrated on the memory of a shiny ribbon of cold water cutting through a meadow of pale green grass waving in the breeze. A voice from his childhood spoke to him: "Brookies and browns take a different technique." He pictured his father standing knee deep in the shallows, patiently showing him how to lay a fly against the deep-cut opposite bank and lure a big one from the shadowed lair.

Nausea retreated. With the fog in his brain slowly receding in the rising light of consciousness, he formed a coherent understanding of the events leading to this moment: Montana, or whatever his name was, had engineered the quiet death of the Larchmont conspiracy.

And Nick was going to die along with it, all because he'd let the crusader in him take over. Let it pull him away from home and family on a futile quest to fight the most powerful army in the world. An army that carries no weapons, enters no battlefields, but simply pulls strings from afar in the righteous name of whatever they think is best.

Nick rolled to one side of the small space left to him and tried to shut it all down; to resign himself to his fate, to accept the inevitable he had brought upon himself. Time had no meaning. It could have been a few minutes or several hours before he became aware of the stillness. A door opened, closed. He waited, heart pounding.

The rear cargo hatch opened with the sound of grating metal. Cold air enveloped him. His heart thundered in his chest as the body beside him slid away and landed nearby with a thud. A rustling noise, something being dragged along the ground. Silence. The cracking sound of wood breaking. More silence. A soft splash, very far away.

Then hands grabbed his feet and pulled. Cloaked in terror

that the bastard might bury him alive, Nick prayed for a quick death. He hit the ground hard, breath knocked out of him. The hands hauled him along rough ground and let go. He breathed furiously through his nose, savoring each lungful of mountain air as his last.

FIGHTING PAIN AND EXHAUSTION, Hotel reached deep inside for the strength to maintain the grueling pace. With every step he told himself he still had a chance. The mine had to be Montana's destination. Where else would he go to dispose of bodies with less risk of discovery?

Gasping for breath, he reached the base of a small hill overlooking the Dutchman's main shaft, boarded up and unused for many years. He slipped the sling over his head, and rifle at the ready, waited for his body to stop shaking. He'd need steady hands. He climbed to the top of the hill and peered over the top.

And his heart swelled with the adrenaline rush of a successful hunt.

Two shafts of horizontal stationary light filtered through the forest from behind the entrance to the mine. He scanned the area with the binoculars and found the vague outline of a vehicle with a hot, bright engine and a warm, moving human shape nearby.

A few moments of searching found a closer spot with concealment and a good view of the mineshaft. When the ghostly image of Montana in the binoculars disappeared behind the vehicle, Hotel broke cover and scampered down the rugged slope to a ravine, traversed to his right and paused at the base of a small knoll. A faint glow backlit the top, covered in a mass of low underbrush.

NICK'S BREATHING RETURNED TO normal. He sensed a presence above him, then closer, just above his face. Warm breath caressed his cheek. A slight fragrance of breath mint he'd learned to hate triggered a memory of white teeth and the image of Montana's face behind the black muzzle of the suppressor.

After a moment, Montana said, "I'm glad that unlike your boss, you managed not to choke to death on your own puke. It gives me the opportunity to tell you something. You could have packed up and left, done the right thing for yourself and your family. But no. You had to play Dick Tracy. Snoop around. Cause trouble."

Nick's brain told his mouth to say, I was only doing my job, but it came out a lot different than that.

"Trying to say something?"

A gloved hand shoved Nick's head into the rocky ground. Another picked at the tape around his mouth and yanked it off. Nick's face stung with searing pain. He gasped at the cold, dry air, sucking great drafts into his lungs. Phlegm gagged him. He spit up a ropey mass.

"That's disgusting."

"What are you going to do with me?" Nick didn't recognize the words as his own, raspy and weak.

"First, remove your blindfold. Must be uncomfortable."

Hands grabbed Nick's head.

He struggled. "No, don't."

"Why not? You've already seen my face. There's no reason to die without sight."

Nick knew it had to come to this, but facing it brought a new surge of nausea. He fought it down as hands tore off the tape. His eyelids felt like they'd almost been ripped off. He eased them open. Bright light drilled through dilated pupils and into his brain. He squinted and turned his head to the side. Blinking rapidly, he waited for his eyes to adjust and looked up.

Montana stood over him, bathed in twin horizontal beams of light. "Listen very carefully. You are about to die because what happened here to a fucking stranger was more important to you than what happened at home to your own daughter."

Nick lifted his upper body off the ground, spit more of the junk in his mouth at Montana's face and screamed, "You goddamned *prick*! I swear to Christ I'll cut your nuts off and make you eat them!"

Montana easily dodged the spit. He put his foot on Nick's chest and shoved him back onto the rocky ground. "Empty threats from a hogtied NTSB pussy." He leaned over, his face an inviting target. "Before you die, I need to know something. Who is Hotel?"

Nick wanted to tell this bastard that Hotel's was the last face he'd see from the execution chamber, but that would only put the reporter at greater risk. In a voice barely under control, he said, "Just a guy I know."

Montana raised his hand and smashed it into Nick's face, splitting his lip. Blood seeped into his mouth and down his chin. Montana gripped Nick's hair, hauled his head off the ground and peered into his eyes.

"You don't lie worth a shit."

HOTEL KNEW THAT UNUSED skills often fade, but they can lie dormant until needed, like riding a bicycle. Sniper school had taught him many things he had hoped never to use again. But he delved into lessons from his past as he crawled up the rocky knoll. He picked a short evergreen shrub among the vegetation dotting the crown, maneuvered just below it, and took a peek through the branches.

Thirty yards away, the Explorer sat parked nose to the mine shaft, high beams flooding the scene. A man knelt by a prone figure. Across the ravine drifted a muffled conversation between Nick and Paul Montana, FBI Special Agent, AKA Impostor.

Montana's repeated question hung above Nick like a dark cloud. "He's a reporter. But he doesn't know anything."

"The guy I met in your room? Harvey *Sweet?*" Montana laughed. "Oh, I get it. Suite, like the hotel chain. That's great . . . really great. He writes an article based on what you told him but he doesn't know anything?"

"He never saw any of the evidence. You don't need—"

"Shut the hell up. I know what I need."

"But it's all conjecture. You have the only hard evidence."

Montana grinned. "Thanks for that, by the way. But there's still an empty slot in that GPS panel, thanks to *you.*"

"There's no reason to go after Hotel. He's—"

Montana held up his hand. "Wait a minute. Two of you provide mutual corroboration. Only one has to die. What if I give you the choice?"

The eyes of a professional-killer-turned-psychopath stared down at Nick. Everything Montana had done up to now could be justified with the obscene logic of those who dealt in death, but this spoke of pleasure. He was getting his kicks exerting ultimate power. Tormenting his victims was part of the thrill.

Nick couldn't protect Hotel any more than he could save his own life. He sighed, long and deep, reverberating with despair and lost hope. "After you kill me, you'll do whatever you want anyway."

"No, I mean it. My word is good. You or him?"

CONCEALED BEHIND A SMALL evergreen bush, Hotel lifted the rifle and rested the barrel on a rock. He reached for the scope cover and paused. Was there enough light to use it? Would the Explorer's high beams reflect off the lens and alert Montana?

After a moment, he realized it didn't matter because he didn't have a choice.

He slipped the cover off. The scope wasn't designed for night work, but the Explorer's headlights threw enough light for him to distinguish between background and the image of a kneeling man. He lined up the crosshairs with the center of the man's upper body as his right thumb flicked off the safety with a soft, oily *snick*.

NICK IGNORED MONTANA'S QUESTION. Resigned to his fate, he forced his eyes to stare at the killer and waited for the end.

Montana stood up, his face barely visible in the shadow thrown by the headlights. "Did you hear me? You can save your life. All you have to do is choose your friend for death."

Sudden fury swelled up in Nick. "Fuck you! Kill me and get it over with, you bastard!"

Montana's head tilted back to peals of laughter, swallowed by the dense forest. "So I'm a bastard and you want to have your way with me, huh? I don't think so."

Nick's heart rate spiked as Montana leaned over, grabbed Nick's ankles and began dragging him toward the splintered wood mineshaft cover.

He kicked out with all his strength, but Montana pulled him around in a half circle and stopped with Nick's head resting on the edge of the black hole. Frigid, damp air tinged with the odor of decay rose from the depths to fill his nostrils.

HOTEL SETTLED THE TIP of his index finger against the trigger and took up the tiny bit of slack built into the sear. Montana moved. Hotel relaxed his finger, shifted the crosshairs and reapplied pressure.

Montana's image dropped out of the scope field of view. Hotel tried to reacquire the target, but lost awareness of which way to move the rifle. He lifted his head from the stock and refocused on the scene. Montana held Nick by the ankles with his head toward the black pit.

Hotel shifted his upper body to swing the rifle and get Montana in the crosshairs again. He snapped his head down to the stock, peered through the sight and saw nothing. He looked up. A branch of the shrub had flipped the sight cover closed.

TOO EXHAUSTED TO RESIST, Nick closed his eyes and waited for a horrible death as Montana wrapped his arms around his bound legs and began shoving him backwards. His head bounced off rocks. Dirt packed under the collar of his shirt and slid down his back. His head banged into something above ground level. Wood. The mineshaft cover.

"Montana!" echoed a voice.

Time seemed to cease for Nick as Montana stopped pushing him toward the shaft.

"Let him go!"

Nick opened his eyes. Montana was bent over, looking into the darkness, his shadowed face a mask of surprise.

"Slowly," said the voice, "lower his legs to the ground and back away."

Nick turned his head. Blinded by the glare of the headlights, he saw nothing beyond a few feet. Montana probably couldn't see anything either. He dropped Nick's legs and faced the voice. "Who the hell are you?" he shouted.

"I won't tell you again to back away."

"You going to shoot an unarmed man?"

Nick glanced at Montana. A pistol protruded from his waistband at the small of his back.

The scene spun out of control as Montana crouched down, right hand reaching behind him.

"*Gun!*" yelled Nick. He cocked his legs back against his chest and kicked Montana on the outside of his left knee.

A guttural scream ripped through the night as Montana collapsed. Nick peered past his hiking boots. Montana was on his hands and one knee, his face contorted, favoring the left leg. He raised his head and locked eyes with Nick.

Nick stared back, and he couldn't help it. "Hold that position. I may have my way with you tonight after all."

Montana bared his perfect teeth and bellowed, "Aaaaaarghhhhhhh!" His right hand came off the ground and disappeared behind his back.

Nick dug his heels into the ground and shoved himself backward.

Montana's hand reappeared with the pistol. Nick frantically thrust out with his legs again and again to flee the deadly, dark muzzle. The wood under him began to splinter. He was rotating backwards, headfirst into the depths of the mineshaft, when a sharp crack punctured the night.

THE RIFLE BARKED. The stock punched Hotel's shoulder with the heavy recoil of a magnum bullet. He racked the bolt, searched for Montana with the scope, couldn't find him, shifted the rifle to the right. Nick had disappeared. Back to the left. Vague movement under the Explorer. He settled the crosshairs on the spot and paused.

Rifle against handgun, no contest at this range. But what if Nick was still alive? Hotel couldn't wait for a better shot. Had to keep the pressure on. He concentrated on the thin strip of ground barely visible under the Explorer in the dim glow of the driver's side running light.

Movement? He fired. Dirt kicked up under the Explorer. He cycled the bolt, fired again with the crosshairs centered under the Explorer at ground level. He chambered another round, peered over the scope. Nothing.

Fire and maneuver. Crouching low, he scrambled to his left and found cover with a view of the Explorer's rear cargo door. The dark silhouette of the vehicle against the headlight beams filled the scope. Vague movement just to the left of the crosshairs. He corrected and fired another shot between the rear tires and angled toward the driver's side, worked the bolt and waited, heart pounding.

Silence. No movement in the scope. He moved farther left until he could see the driver's side of the Explorer. No Montana. Was it safe to use the binoculars? He couldn't wear them like the combat version and shoot at the same time. He decided to risk it.

Heat blooms from the vehicle's engine filled the image. No sign of human warmth. Montana could be dead. Or waiting in ambush. Or he might have slipped away in the darkness.

Two of two of those possibilities were acceptable, and the time had come for Hotel to guarantee the third.

WILSON LAY ON HIS stomach about thirty yards from the Explorer. The first bullet had ripped through his side at the waist, felt like he'd been pounded with a club, but he didn't think it had struck bone or vital organs. He tightened the belt on his parka until he could barely breath, and the flow of blood decreased. His knee throbbed. A couple of bumbling amateurs had him scrambling.

He'd rolled away from the vehicle as soon as he hit the ground. The sniper seemed to *know* where he was as follow-up shots had driven him farther into the forest.

What next? If the shooter came after him, Wilson's only advantage was to lie in ambush. But what if the guy had a night vision device?

He eased his head up and scanned the darkness around the sphere of light covering the mineshaft. If the sniper approached the vehicle to check on Phillips, Wilson might get a shot. Or he could just get the hell out of here and—hello, vague movement in the forest. A slight rustle in the foliage, and the soft clink of metal on rock.

New game. The hunter might just become the prey.

HOTEL WORKED HIS WAY around so he could see the passenger side of the Explorer. Quick peeks with the binoculars found no sign of either Nick or Montana. Even if Nick was in the mineshaft, he might not have dropped all the way. Hotel had roamed these mountains for years. In some of the shafts, heavy timbers lay across the openings to keep out adventurous trespassers and snag clumsy tourists before they took the last trip of a lifetime.

He crawled away from the vehicle to circle around below

the knoll and approach the mineshaft from the other side.

WILSON GRITTED HIS TEETH and crawled closer to the Explorer. He'd watched vague, shadowy movement and an occasional shiver of foliage mark the sniper's maneuvering toward the mineshaft. He waited, for the shooter to highlight himself trying to check on the fate of Phillips.

After about ten minutes, a dark shape appeared between the tires on the far side of the Explorer. The passenger door opened, the interior still dark. Wilson had turned the dome light off, a precaution turned against him by the sniper. The Explorer's headlights went out. He inched his body up, pain rippling through him. A slinking black shape moved between the front of the Explorer and the wood cover of the mineshaft.

Wilson couldn't stop trembling. The sights on his pistol wavered, his shooting hand too weak to squeeze the grip and control the muzzle. With his forearm as a prop, he steadied the wrist of his shooting hand and sighted down the barrel.

He took deep breaths to steady his aim at movement above the three sighting dots. The pistol settled down. As he began taking up slack in the trigger, a big piece of mineshaft cover rose vertically, blocking any view of the entrance.

Wilson lowered the pistol. He craved revenge more than anything he had ever wanted. But not tonight.

His side burned with pain and his mind smoldered with rage as he struggled to his feet and retreated into the night.

DAMP, STALE AIR ROSE from the shaft. From behind a large piece of the cover, Hotel peered over the rim into dense blackness. He took his flashlight out of his vest, shielded the lens with his hand, flicked the button on and off.

In a burst of light, his retinas recorded the image of a body wedged between a vertical face of solid rock and an angled support post.

"Nick!" No response. "Can you hear me, Nick?"

A moan, low and weak.

"Stay put. Do *not* move."

Hotel slid backwards into the forest to intercept Montana's most probable escape route.

NICK REGAINED CONSCIOUSNESS IN darkness, pain, and confusion. He lifted his head and opened his eyes. A jagged circle of lighter blackness above him framed the mineshaft opening. He was lying on his back, draped over a large beam and suspended above a vast emptiness ready to swallow him.

He might have heard someone call his name, but he couldn't be sure. "Hotel?" Silence. Again, louder, but no answer. He tried to move, felt a rock dislodge from the wall beside him, held his breath. A soft plop drifted up from the depths as the rock joined Nordstrom in a watery grave.

Time passed. Nick prayed, thought of family, prayed some more. Then, in a rush of determination, he screamed his defiance. "Somebody get me the fuck out of here!"

Echoes below ridiculed his plea and faded to silence.

Okay. Count the seconds in a minute, or maybe ten minutes, then yell again. Give himself something to do. Somebody might—hold it. If Montana had survived, he'd finish the job by covering the mineshaft. But if Hotel had killed him, or driven him off, why isn't he—? What's that? Footsteps? "Who's there?"

The dim silhouette of a head and upper body appeared at the rim. "At least your voice still works," said Hotel.

CHAPTER TWENTY-THREE

Nick woke up on a soft surface and eased his eyes open. Above him, the outline of a person. Gentle hands put something on his face that stung like fire. "Ouch."

"Welcome back."

Soft light from somewhere behind Nick illuminated the hazy face of Hotel. Vague memories of being hauled out of the mineshaft with a tow strap and lying on the rear seat of the Explorer for a harrowing ride down the mountain helped bring the scene into focus.

He lay on a couch in a single-room log cabin. A blazing fire radiated comforting warmth. Something aromatic bubbled in a pot on a camp stove. Hotel wore the same camouflage fatigues as before, and he did not look like a reporter. Nick eased himself up on a cushion. "If I didn't say this before, thanks."

"You're welcome. Thirsty?" When Nick nodded, Hotel said, "Nauseous?"

"A little."

"We're going to go real slow."

After sipping water and keeping it down, Nick tried a cup of broth. Hotel pulled up a chair and sat. "You look like a train wreck."

"I don't doubt it. Want to fill me in?"

Hotel related his concerns over not receiving a reply to Nick's phone messages and described the scene in the parking lot with Montana hauling bundles to the Explorer.

Nick's mind flashed back on the image of Nordstrom collapsing onto the table and lying on the floor. "Any sign of Nordstrom's body?"

Hotel shook his head and described his pursuit, the ambush, taking the shortcut, and what he had seen from the knoll.

Nick stared at him. "How the hell did you do all that?"

"I learned to hunt as a youngster. The military found my skills useful and refined them. And a little luck never hurts."

"What does luck have to do with it?"

"Montana left the headlights on. Not a bad idea as dark as it was around that mineshaft, but it gave me enough light to shoot."

"Is he dead?"

"Probably not. I found a blood trail from the Explorer to where he'd holed up. Good bit on the ground, then a trail leading away."

Nick shuddered. He could still feel the cover giving way under him. A tremor rippled through his fingers. He clenched his fists. "Goddamn."

Hotel nodded. "An abandoned mineshaft deep in a closed-off wilderness area is a perfect place to make problems disappear."

"But the article appeared only a couple days ago. How'd he get out here so fast?"

"His masquerade had to have been planned in advance. I'm more concerned about when he'll be back."

They stared at each other for a moment before Nick said, "If we're smart, we call the cops."

Hotel leaned back in his chair and crossed his arms. "He's had almost eight hours. We'd never get a search up and running in time. And I'd like to hand the cops more than we have. Like maybe a real name and address."

"But what if you're wrong? He could be watching the cabin."

Hotel shook his head. "He'd have to know about this place. And from the mineshaft to here is deeper in the wilderness area, away from medical attention. He's on foot, hurt, and he'd have to walk over thirty miles and cross two ridges if he stayed off the road."

That all made sense, but it didn't offer much comfort. "Find anything in the Explorer?"

"I stopped looking when I saw the tow strap. Had my hands full getting you out of there without dropping your sorry ass. I'm going back as soon as it gets light."

"My sorry ass is going with you."

"Not a good idea. You—"

Nick pointed at Hotel. "Better go get your rifle if you think I'm staying here. My life is in the toilet. I had a big part in that, but it all started with murder. This son of a bitch is the only link we have to whoever set this up."

"Forget about it. Nobody in his line of work is going to carry anything showing who he really is."

"But they've made mistakes. Maybe we'll get lucky for a change."

Hotel shook his head. "I may have used up all my luck at the Dutchman."

"That's okay. I'm overdue, and I have no plans to waste it in Vegas."

THEY LEFT THE CABIN in the Explorer as soon as Nick felt better and regained most of his equilibrium. The last rugged mile of off-road jarring had him wincing with every bump by the time he finally glimpsed the Dutchman's main entrance. The portal to a watery grave. A shudder rippled through him.

Rocks poked out of the ground all around the area, but there was enough dirt to see the pattern of drag marks to the dark gullet of the mineshaft. A blood trail led into the forest. Nick pointed at it. "Should we follow this?"

Hotel walked past carrying his rifle. "Search the interior of the Explorer while I take a look around."

"Is splitting up a good idea?"

Hotel stood at the rim of the shaft and stared into the depths. "He's dead or long gone. If he made it out, he'll need medical attention, and he won't stroll into a local emergency room."

Nick hadn't thought about that. "Where *can* he go?"

"All sorts of shadow surgeons out there. Guys like Montana have a network that includes doctors who've had their licenses pulled, or veterinarians looking for bigger bucks than they get working on animals."

"I had no idea."

"That's the way they like it." Hotel pulled a handgun from inside his jacket. "Know how to use this?"

Nick took the weapon, a full-size semiautomatic, heavy in his hand. "It's been a while, but if I see that bastard I'll remember just fine."

"On the contrary, run like hell if you have the choice. Otherwise, it's ready to rock." Hotel motioned to the Explorer. "Search every inch of it. I'll be back soon."

Nick opened the driver's door. It took about ten minutes to examine the seating and cargo areas. He found a set of keys and a duffel bag. He set the bag on the hood and loosened the compression straps. As he reached for the zipper, a scuffling noise sounded in the shadowy forest behind him.

He swirled around into a crouch. The pistol in his waistband almost fell out. He yanked the weapon free and pointed it at the forest, thought about the safety, looked for one, didn't see it. Hotel said it was ready to rock, but Nick hadn't checked that for himself.

Damn it. I hope this thing works. He scanned the trees, following his gaze with the pistol. A low bush rustled to his right. He sighted on it. A ground squirrel scampered up on a fallen log.

"They're out of season."

Nick's head snapped around toward the voice behind him. Hotel emerged from the forest, walked to the Explorer, and laid the rifle barrel-down between the driver's seat and the console. Embarrassed, Nick slipped the pistol into his waistband.

Hotel got a water bottle out of his backpack and took a long drink. He tossed the bottle to Nick. "I tracked his trail farther than I did last night. He's out of here."

Nick sipped water through split lips and winced as the cold liquid shocked a loose tooth. He glanced at the bottle label: SWEETWATER SPRINGS. He tossed it back to Hotel. "That's the best water I've ever tasted."

"Comes from the spring at the cabin. Dad bought the bottles in bulk and had the labels printed. He'd keep them at the house, hand one to a visiting flatlander and say, 'Have a taste of paradise.' I still do it as a tribute to him."

"Then here's to your father." Nick drank and for a moment reflected on the memory of his dad's face and broad smile. The image comforted him today no less than it had over thirty years ago. "Back to dealing with this mother of all assholes, I'd like to think he's got maggots for company."

"Me too. But we have a body down that mineshaft that needs to be taken care of."

"Can it be recovered?"

"Probably. Is Nordstrom married? Family?"

"A wife, no kids."

"Okay. Before we notify the authorities, what's the plan?"

"Let's go back to the cabin to figure that out. Standing out here makes me nervous."

LATER THAT MORNING, HOTEL discovered that his binoculars were missing and returned to the mineshaft to hunt for them. Nick stayed at the cabin to deal with the foul layer of dried sweat, dirt, and who knew what else that coated every inch of him.

The cabin had been built by Hotel's father a few years after finishing the house on the outskirts of Cedar Valley. Camp lanterns served for most lighting purposes. A tank above the site collected spring water and gravity-fed the plumbing. An abundant supply of firewood heated the small interior. A diesel generator supplied electrical power for limited use, which included three lamps and a flash water heater.

After a "shipboard" shower according to Sweet's cabin rules, Nick changed into some of Hotel's spare clothes. They didn't fit too well, but anything clean was an improvement. He dumped on the dining table the contents of the duffel bag found in the Explorer: some clothes, a cheap leather wallet with two hundred dollars in cash, a credit card and an Ohio driver's license issued to Harmon Gardner, of Cincinnati, a rental agreement made out to that name, a second bi-fold leather case with Montana's FBI identification, and the Explorer keys.

Nick examined the documents. They looked real enough, but they all had to be fake. How would a person get them? Could they be traced back to a source? Maybe with professional help—

The lights flickered as the diesel generator began to surge. Then it quit. Semi-darkness claimed the room.

Nick eased up from the table, his body so stiff and sore he couldn't imagine a time when it didn't hurt to move. He shuffled outside to the small covered porch and leaned over the railing to peer down one side of the cabin. No generator. Ditto on the other side. It had to be in the back. Hotel probably had more fuel stored there. Nick stepped off the porch and paused, aware of his vulnerability.

He returned to the cabin, locked the door and thought about where Hotel might have stashed a weapon. A quick search produced a handgun in a nylon holster attached to the side rail of the lower bunk. He checked that the pistol was loaded and stepped onto the porch. A background of wind in the trees and the twitter of birds implied solitude. He listened for a few minutes. No foreign sound interrupted the atmosphere of peace.

At the rear of the cabin he found the generator mounted on a concrete slab. He removed the fuel cap. Diesel fumes wafted over his face from the black chamber. He couldn't tell for sure if the tank was empty and looked for a fuel dipstick. There wasn't one, or a spare fuel container.

The door to the storage shed was locked. He looked around for a remote auxiliary tank mounted on its own slab but didn't see one. Invigorated by the clean scent of pine in the crisp mountain air, he paused to savor the moment.

The sun hadn't yet topped the ridge to the east. Dense shadows cloaked the cabin and small clearing around it. The scene reminded Nick of early mornings waiting with Brad for the sun to let them legally take that first deer of the season. After what he'd been through, he was more than ready to head home. In the meantime, he needed light.

He went back into the cabin. Where would Hotel keep a flashlight? After a futile search, Nick spotted a mini-flashlight attached to the Explorer keys. He rotated the lens housing. A brilliant halogen beam cut through the dim cabin interior. He returned to the dead generator thinking about the flashlights of his youth, huge D-cell tubes generating a pallid yellow ray even with fresh batteries. Sometimes technology came up with useful innovations.

Ink-black darkness parted with the mini-light trained into the fuel tank. Empty. Maybe Hotel had spare fuel—the sound of tires on gravel intruded on the silence. Nick slipped the pistol from inside his waistband. Muscles tense, he waited.

Movement, barely perceptible in the gloom. He crouched down and brought the pistol up.

Hotel emerged from the forest on a silent trail bike and braked to a stop. "I'm glad you're being careful, but point that thing somewhere else."

Nick lowered the pistol. "Sneaking up on me isn't a good idea."

"Sorry. I usually coast in the last half mile."

Nick inclined his head toward the bike. "You left here in the Explorer."

"That I did. With two bike tires to replace the ones Montana slashed."

"Picked them up from your local wilderness tire shop, did you?"

"Ride in these mountains, you get flats. I always keep spares at the cabin." Hotel nodded at the generator. "Out of fuel?"

"Yeah. You have an auxiliary tank?"

"No. How about some coffee?"

Nick shoved the pistol inside his waistband and returned to the cabin. He was pouring two cups when Hotel walked in, carrying the strap of a duffel bag over his shoulder. He dropped the bag on the table and sat down.

Nick brought him coffee. "Find your binoculars?" When Hotel nodded, Nick pointed to the duffel bag. "Where'd you get that?"

"The Explorer. I thought you were going to check every inch of it."

"Obviously I failed. Where'd you find it?"

"Under the spare tire cover in the cargo area."

"You look in it yet?"

Hotel nodded. "Clothes mostly. And these." He pulled out a pair of black combat boots.

Nick turned one of the boots sole up. He picked up the mini-light and examined the distinctive, all-too-familiar pattern. His jaw tightened so much he could barely speak. "This bastard sneaks into homes like an apparition and is an angel of death around airplanes and cars."

Hotel stood and went to the sink. "We need to figure out where we go from here." He was rinsing his coffee cup when he stopped and turned off the water. "Damn it." He stepped back from the counter, staring at the floor.

"What's the matter?"

"A water leak I thought I'd fixed." He opened the cabinet doors, sat on the floor and eased his head and upper body under the trap. After a moment, "I need a flashlight."

Nick grabbed the Explorer keys off the table and tapped Hotel's arm with them. "Use this."

Hotel pointed the mini-light where the pipes entered the

cabin through the wall and pressed the end with his thumb. Nothing happened.

"Turn the lens housing," said Nick.

"I wonder what the button's for." Hotel turned on the mini-light and pointed it above him. The shaft of halogen-white illumination looked like a searchlight in the dark cube under the sink. After a moment, he said, "Nick?"

"Yeah?"

"You've got to look at this."

"I've seen leaks before."

"Look . . . at . . . this."

Nick bent over and squinted into the brightly lit box. "What the hell am I supposed to see?"

Hotel shined the light on a pipe, a trickle of water plainly visible under a mask of silicone sealer. Then he looked at Nick, wiggled his thumb, and pressed the button at the end of the flashlight.

Within the circle of brilliant light, lines of numbers projected from the mini-light lens snaked along pipes, flexible hoses, supply valves, and the trap.

Ten minutes later, Nick and Hotel sat at the table staring at a piece of notepaper. "These numbers," said Nick, "are ingeniously concealed in a flashlight belonging to a killer who has scattered bodies all over southern Colorado. Why do you suppose he carries them?"

"Not a clue. He must have a damn good reason."

"Apparently." Nick got up for more coffee. "If there's anything useful here, we need to find it."

"The two ten-digit sets of numerals are probably telephone numbers. The third set of more than ten digits is also, but for an international call from the States."

"And in his line of work, you wouldn't have a phone

traceable to you or enter numbers into memory. You have an area-code listing up here?"

"This is a hunting cabin, Nick." Hotel got his cell phone. "Crap. Low battery, and no service. Where's yours?"

"Hell if I know. Did you search that bag?"

"I was waiting for you to think of that." Hotel opened Montana's duffel and spilled the contents onto the table. A cell phone bounced off and landed on the floor.

"That looks like mine," said Nick. He picked it up. The NO SERVICE message mocked him. "You ever make cell phone calls from here?"

"Rarely. I called you yesterday from that bald ridge to the north." Hotel rummaged through the pile of clothing, found another cell phone in a toiletry kit. He powered it up, said, "Hot damn. A satellite phone. Remind me to thank Montana when I see him." He pressed a series of buttons, wrote down a phone number and shook his head. "Nothing in memory or call history. It's time for some outside help."

Hotel called a sergeant in the Cedar Valley Police Department who owed him a favor. After stating that he needed the information as part of research for an article, subject unspecified, he got a reverse-directory search started.

Nick picked up the piece of paper. "The four sets of two-digit numerals could be . . . the combination to a safe? The last string is anybody's guess."

They discussed what kinds of numbers would deserve all the trouble Montana had taken to conceal them. The possibility that they had the combination to a safe led to a discussion of how a hired gun would get paid and whether the last string might be a bank account number.

Montana's satellite phone rang.

Nick looked at Hotel. "His employer?"

"Or Montana wants to say hello." Hotel picked up the phone. "The caller ID is blank."

"Would the cop be calling from a blocked phone?"

"Probably." Hotel opened the flip. "Hello?" He listened for a moment, gave a thumbs-up to Nick, wrote something on the piece of paper and thanked the cop.

"Okay. The first number is for the residence of somebody named Wilson in Florida. The international number is a bank in the Cayman Islands."

"And the last one?"

"No such area code."

"How can that be?"

"Wish I knew."

"Maybe he copied it down wrong."

Hotel nodded and set the phone on the table. "I might agree, except that Montana's phone has the same area code."

After a moment of silence, Nick said, "We need a *really* good next move."

Hotel tapped the piece of paper. "The safe bet is to take this to the cops."

"I don't want to do that yet. Even if we had our hands on some real proof, we'd be turning it over to an arm of government controlled by the same people who conspired to murder Larchmont. The only connection to the sabotage is Montana. If he disappears for good, whoever's behind this is home free. The link between the Wilson residence and Montana is the only lead to something we might be able to use."

"Can't argue with that."

Nick picked up Montana's phone, glanced at the paper, dialed the unlisted area code number and pressed TALK.

The phone rang two times. Nick held his breath. Nothing but faint clicks and hissing noises answered. To Hotel: "This isn't working. All I'm getting is—"

"Speak."

The man's voice seemed so distant that Nick almost didn't understand what he said.

"Is it over?" said the man, "or did someone cut out your goddamned tongue?"

Nick hadn't thought about what he'd say. He blurted, "They're all dead."

"Who the hell is this?"

"Who do you think?"

"Son of a bitch." The line went dead.

Nick stared at Hotel, who leaned forward in his chair, eyes eager. "Who was it?

"Someone who did not like getting a call from a stranger. What if—?"

"So we've just shown our hand?"

"All he knows is that someone has his number. This phone is certainly blocked, so where did the call come from? We used my interview and your article to get the conspirators to *do* something. The plan worked. Maybe this call will accomplish more of the same thing."

Hotel peered at Nick under furrowed eyebrows. "And result in a higher body count?"

"But we'll be ready. Time for the next step." Nick dialed the number for the Wilson residence in Florida.

After seven rings a female voice answered, "Hello?"

"Oh, I'm sorry ma'am, I may have the wrong number. Could you please tell me whom I have reached?"

"This is Mr. Wilson's house."

"And may I ask who you are?"

"I'm Dorothy Frazier."

"May I speak with Mr. Wilson, please?"

"He's not here at the moment."

"Mrs. Frazier, do you know where Mr. Wilson is?"

"He doesn't tell me where he's going."

"Yes, ma'am. Do you have a number where I might reach him?"

"He doesn't accept calls when he's on the road. Says that's one of the reasons he leaves town. To get away from the phone."

"I can understand that. When do you expect him back?"

"I have no idea. But he always calls from the airport. He likes the house to himself when he returns from trips."

An early-warning system just might keep Nick out of trouble. "My name is Nathan Porter, Mrs. Frazier. I'm a business associate of Mr. Wilson's. Maybe he mentioned me?"

"Why on earth would he do that?"

"To inform you of my visit. He said I could wait for him there if I arrived early for a meeting."

"That's news to me, Mr. Porter. Anything to do with his business would be, you know. I'm just the housekeeper."

"Yes, ma'am. Well, if it's all the same to you, I'll just stop by and wait for him."

"Suit yourself."

"And I'm so sorry to be a bother, Mrs. Frazier, but would you confirm Mr. Wilson's address? I have a package to send him and don't have my address book."

Nick copied the address and hung up the phone. "It's worth a trip to check this out."

Hotel nodded. "How much do you know about guns?"

Nick glanced at the handgun lying on table between them. "Hunting rifles. A little pistol shooting, but it's been a long time."

Hotel picked up the weapon, ejected the magazine, pulled the slide to the rear and locked it. He placed the cartridge from the chamber on the table.

"This is a Glock Model Twenty-Three, chambered in forty-caliber Smith and Wesson. The bullet is a jacketed hollow point. It mushrooms on impact and provides good stopping power. This magazine holds thirteen rounds, plus one in the chamber."

"Where's the safety?"

Hotel showed Nick the small secondary trigger built into the primary. "When your finger pulls to the rear, this is pressed first and releases the internal safety. All you have to do is point and fire, and that simplicity can save your life. You ready to bust some caps?"

Two hours later, paper targets stapled to a wooden frame showed evidence of improving proficiency until Nick transitioned to rapid fire and different shooting positions. By the time they were out of Hotel's hand-loaded practice ammo, Nick had improved a bit, with a sore arm and hand to show for it. Hotel handed him the factory hollow points. Nick loaded the weapon and slipped it inside his waistband. "Now what?"

Hotel turned toward the cabin and motioned for Nick to walk beside him. "I'm probably a fool for teaching you the fundamentals, but we can't ignore the potential danger. That said, don't even think about trying to hold your own in a gunfight with a professional."

"Then why bother?"

"As a last resort. If a confrontation is inevitable, I want you holding something more lethal than your dick."

"Well, actually, my—"

"I don't want to hear it."

They decided to leave the Explorer hidden in the forest near the ambush site and rode the bike to Hotel's residence on the outskirts of Cedar Valley to get the truck. At Nick's room, they found that the maids appeared to have obeyed the DO NOT DISTURB sign and followed his instructions about not cleaning the room without being asked. He tidied up, gathered the rest of his belongings, and they returned to Hotel's residence.

At the dining room table, they stared at each other for a moment before Hotel leaned back in his chair and crossed his arms. "The police may have a hard time understanding why we waited to tell them about a body down a mineshaft and a killer with a bullet in him roaming around armed, pissed off, and very dangerous."

"I don't doubt it. But I can be there and back in two days. Less than twenty-four hours has passed since the killing. The body is in cold storage and protected from animals down in that shaft. We have no other choice except to give up."

Hotel nodded. "Maybe I should go with you."

Nick considered that. "I don't need a bodyguard, because I'm not going into that house unless the housekeeper is alone. Stay here, write a follow-up article and hold on to it. You can add anything I learn and file after I get back."

CHAPTER TWENTY-FOUR

Nick arrived at the Tallahassee Regional Airport only two hours later than scheduled. Amazing. He reclaimed his luggage, picked up his reserved Camry, began entering Wilson's home address into the GPS, and paused. That would leave an evidence trail he might later regret. With directions he'd obtained online, he left the airport and drove to within a few blocks of Wilson's house.

A call to Mrs. Frazier confirmed that Mr. Wilson had not returned from his trip and it was still okay for Nick to wait for him at the house.

As required by federal law, he'd packed the Glock and ammunition in checked luggage and declared them to the airline. Transporting the weapon in the trunk was legal in Florida without a concealed-carry permit, but he felt as if the word *felon* were being carved into his forehead as he got out of the Camry.

With the temperature in the mid-sixties, wearing his heavy leather flight jacket might draw attention, so he took it off and tossed it in the trunk. He zipped open his duffel, removed the Glock in its case, the loaded magazine along with a single loose cartridge, and climbed back in the car. He locked back the slide on the Glock, slipped the single cartridge into the barrel, and released the slide. With a shove on the base of the magazine, he jammed it into the grip. then ran his fingers along the butt to ensure it was fully latched. He pulled out his shirttail and slipped the weapon inside his waistband. After a moment to reaffirm that, *Yes, I have to do this,* he took a few deep breaths and stepped into the bright Florida sunshine.

Tree-lined avenues and spacious homes on large lots in Wilson's neighborhood spoke of comfort and ancient money. Signs with peering eyeballs fastened to every light pole informed him he was in a "Neighborhood Watch Community." A little old lady peering out her kitchen window was probably reporting him to the cops at this very moment.

After a five-minute walk he reached a gated entrance, gave his fake name to the guard, and waited while the man called Wilson's home. When it became obvious from the conversation that Dorothy didn't remember him, Nick asked the guard for the phone and convinced her that she was expecting a business associate of Mr. Wilson's. Once inside the gate, it took another five minutes to reach a stone pillar mailbox with WILSON engraved on a brass plaque.

He took a deep breath, strolled up to the covered porch and rang the doorbell. Movement in his peripheral vision got his attention. A huge Siamese cat crouched under a potted plant, tail twitching. Nick stared at the ferocious-looking feline and whispered, "Don't even think about it. I'm packing."

After a few moments, the door opened. An elderly woman in a housedress with a flowered collar stared at him through the screen.

Nick smiled. "Mrs. Frazier?"

"Well hi there, Jody. I thought you were off at school."

"My name is Nathan Porter, Mrs. Frazier. We spoke on the phone a moment ago."

"Oh. Sorry. I left my glasses in the kitchen."

A pair of glasses hung from a beaded cord around the woman's neck. "Yes, ma'am. You said I could wait here for Mr. Wilson."

"I suppose I did, but I'm here by myself."

"I understand your concern, ma'am. Mr. Wilson asked me to give you this." Nick held out a letter of introduction he had typed on Hotel's computer. Wilson's forged signature was the best likeness they could make of the four examples left behind on Montana's driver's license, FBI identification, credit card, and the Explorer rental agreement.

Mrs. Frazier hesitated. She flipped up the latch on the screen door and opened it slightly.

Nick slid the letter through the thin opening and stepped back. As Mrs. Frazier unfolded the letter, he said, "I think you'll find that in order."

She took her time squinting at it. Finally she folded the paper and reached for the door. "Come on in, young man. I'd enjoy the company."

As she fumbled with the screen latch, Nick said, "That's a really big cat. Has he ever attacked your visitors?"

Mrs. Frazier opened the door. "Don't be ridiculous. He's just an old sweetie pie."

Nick accepted her invitation to have tea. While enjoying butter cookies and sipping Earl Grey, he thanked Mrs. Frazier for her trouble and said, "Dorothy—excuse me—may I call you Dorothy?"

"I don't know why not. We're having tea and cookies together."

"And they are both wonderful, thank you so much. I mentioned on the phone that Mr. Wilson and I have been involved in a business transaction and we've run into a little problem. He said I could wait here until he returned today for a meeting."

Dorothy's face clouded over. "Well . . . this is all kind of unusual, Nathan. I don't think I've ever had visitors here at the house while he was away."

Nick squirmed in his chair. "Yes, ma'am, I understand that. He told me how much he appreciated the way you took care of things. He said all I needed to do was show you the letter and I could wait in his office."

Dorothy hesitated for a moment and she nodded. "I suppose with this letter it'll be okay. Go upstairs, first door on the right. You want to take some cookies with you?"

Floor-to-ceiling bookshelves lined two walls of Wilson's home office. Afternoon sunlight streamed through the spotless glass of a bay window and reflected off the gleaming surface of a large executive desk. A beveled-glass-pane door by the window opened onto an elevated deck.

Nick set the plate of cookies on a lamp table and stared at the legs. Four vipers, each striking upward with fangs extended, supported the round top on their noses. He shook his head and approached the desk.

The side facing the room had been intricately carved with the image of Medusa. Her hair, a mass of serpents coiled around her skull, appeared to be writhing off the surface. Below her face, with eyes wide and mouth contorted in agony, the artist had carved a spray of blood from the ragged flesh of Medusa's severed neck.

Nick gazed around the room. All the furniture was made from the same dark wood, and each piece included a custom sculpture. He didn't care for Wilson's taste, but the man had spent some bucks.

On one corner of the desk rested a pedestal supporting a

scale model of a popular single-engine four-seater. Nick bent down for a closer look. The model was carved from a solid piece of wood, beautifully crafted and painted, including a tail number and other decals. If Wilson was a pilot, it gave even more credibility to the theory that he might have tampered with a navigation system to cause the crash.

Nick rolled a high-backed leather chair out of the kneehole. The center drawer had a lock, but when he pulled on the polished brass handle, the drawer slid open.

Although lax security probably meant there was nothing in the desk worth protecting, he sat down and began with the center and two smaller side drawers. Nothing there but standard office supplies. Two file-cabinet drawers, one on each side, contained manila folders in hanging files. He thumbed through them quickly to a folder marked BANKING. It held monthly statements from two banks, neither one located in the Cayman Islands. He leaned back into the soft leather of the chair.

No one living separate lives would leave evidence of one easily accessible within the other. But he might put it in a safe, and the four pairs of numbers hidden in the flashlight could be the combination.

He and Laurie had installed a home safe last year, bolted to the floor in a closet. He didn't see a closet in the room. A Persian rug covered the floor under his feet. He pushed back from the desk, knelt, lifted a corner, and found only waxed flooring.

A single large painting hung on either side of the door from the hallway. He checked behind both frames and discovered nothing more than wood paneling. Searching the bookshelves, he spent a quarter-hour pulling books out to examine the walls. No safe.

Among an impressive collection of hardbound classics, a group of four paperbacks stood out: *Techniques of Safecracking; Opening Combination Padlocks; Modern High-Security Padlocks: How To Open Them;* and *Lock Bypass Methods.* Reference books of use to a man capable of sabotaging airplanes and murder, maybe? Nick made a cursory examination of other titles, expecting to find the popular tome *Killing People for Fun and Profit.*

The safe could be anywhere in the house. A search of the entire residence would take too long and might push Dorothy's trusting nature to the breaking point.

But the rest of the upstairs deserved a look. He stepped into the hallway. To his left the stairs descended to the foyer. He turned right to the first of three doors off the hallway and found what appeared to be a guest bedroom. A quick search turned up nothing of interest. The second door opened into a home gym crammed with equipment. He didn't bother with it. A close scrutiny of the master bedroom proved only that Wilson was a clotheshorse. In a walk-in closet, more than twenty suits hung on a revolving rack, arranged by shades of gray and blue, pinstripes and solids. Wilson also had enough shirts, ties, belts, and shoes to go with each of the suits. The wardrobe suggested the man was a Fortune 500 CEO, or maybe a very successful assassin with better taste in clothes than furniture.

Nick returned to the study and stood by the desk. He'd been alert for photographs, but there weren't any. The house exuded a sterile quality; it seemed inhabited but not really lived in.

After a moment of contemplation convinced him this effort was a waste of time, he decided to leave. The nearest file drawer was open. He reached down to close it and paused when he saw that the first hanging file contained a thick folder labeled

RENOVATION. He'd scanned it earlier, maybe too quickly.

He put the folder on the desk and sat down. A lengthy contract detailed the work. He studied each page, and after ten minutes found an amendment that referred to the purchase of a security safe. He flipped to the specifications page, which listed the dimensions as 18"x18"x10". No installation location was given.

It had to be here, but he'd been wasting his time with the walls. The door jambs were no more than six inches thick. Where was the damn thing?

And then it hit him. The desk was the only place it would fit.

He stared at it. The top was at least thirty-six inches wide. A file drawer was pulled all the way out, about eighteen inches. He released the tabs on the guide rails, removed the drawer, and stuck his arm in until his fingers hit a solid wall. The edge of the desk came to a little past his elbow. He took out another drawer and found the same thing.

Walking around the desk, he looked for any indication of a sliding panel or door. The workmanship was superb. Even where he knew there had to be joints he couldn't see them. He removed every drawer. He didn't have a flashlight, so he hand-felt the interior of the desk for a button or switch.

Frustrated and nervous, even with the knowledge that Wilson usually called Dorothy from the airport, Nick decided to spend no more than ten additional minutes here. On his hands and knees, he crawled around the desk, peering at the undersurface of the desktop where it extended beyond the sides. He ended up sitting on the floor, staring at Medusa's severed head, her eyes glaring back.

The carving offered a way of concealing the straight lines of a door or panel. He scooted closer and examined it carefully.

Nothing on the entire surface was straight. The craftsman couldn't possibly have joined the edges of two pieces of wood within the coiled snakes so well that it was invisible to the naked eye.

He leaned back, rested his hands on the floor, and stared at Medusa, concentrating on the details. His gaze narrowed on her mouth, wide open, surrounding a dark cavity in the rich wood. It seemed to draw his hand as he leaned forward, extended his arm, stuck his forefinger into it, and pushed.

Click. The right side of Medusa shifted ever so slightly away from the desk. The outline of her snake hair appeared on the flat surface.

With a trembling hand, Nick rotated her open. A combination knob and metal handle glinted in the subdued light. From his shirt pocket he took the piece of notepaper from Hotel's cabin. He held the paper beside the knob as he spun it.

His hands wouldn't quit trembling. He couldn't read the numbers. With the paper flattened on the floor in front of him, he steadied his forearm on the desk and dialed in the combination. The handle wouldn't budge. Two more times he tried and failed.

He sat back on his haunches and took a few deep breaths. When the pounding in his temples eased, he peered at the fine lines on the dial, entered the combination once more, and gripped the handle.

It rotated ninety degrees with a solid double click.

He pulled the heavy door open. As he peered inside the dark interior, the doorbell rang. He jumped up, yanked the Glock out and dashed into the hallway.

Dorothy's voice carried up the stairs, muffled words he couldn't make out.

A door closed, then silence.

Nick listened for the sound of a man's footfalls.

Dorothy had said Wilson always called from the airport. And why would he ring his own doorbell? Nick went to the stairway and paused at the upper landing. Soft sounds. Somebody moving about, probably Dorothy, but he had to make sure. He slipped the Glock inside his belt above his left front pants pocket. With his right hand on the grip and covered by his shirttail, he descended the stairs.

Dorothy stood at the entrance to the utility room with a feather duster in her hand. "Are you looking for more cookies?"

Nick eased his hand off the Glock. "Yes, thank you. Do you perhaps have any more of that wonderful tea?"

Dorothy's face brightened. She nodded and walked past Nick toward the kitchen.

He glanced around the foyer. No luggage. "I heard the doorbell."

"A package for Mr. Wilson. You can put it on his desk and save me the trouble."

Ten minutes later, Nick climbed the stairs holding a cup of Earl Grey, a plate of cookies, and a padded mailer under his arm. He put the cookies and tea on the viper table, tossed the mailer on the desk, and sat down on the floor in front of the open safe.

Inside he found a folded bundle of papers stuffed in a manila envelope. One glance at the first page hinted at the importance of the find: documentation of phone conversations and meetings between Miles Larchmont and an unidentified person. And resting in the bottom of the envelope, a mini-cassette. Nick stared at it, wondering if maybe, just *maybe,* it provided a record of voices discussing seriously illegal matters. Like conspiracy to murder. If so, *gotcha!*

A single piece of paper remained in the safe. Handwritten on it were the same number sets he and Hotel had discovered in Montana's flashlight. The last set of numerals, previously unexplained, followed the phone number of the bank in the Caymans. He counted ten. The account number on Nick's checks contained ten numbers. Was that standard around the world? Probably not, but it didn't matter.

Below the ten-digit number: procedures and pass codes for depositing and withdrawing funds. And below that, a list of figures, numerically increasing, indicated a current balance of $15,273,000.00.

He stood, placed the papers on the desk, and stared at the mailer, no return address, postmarked in Denver. He slit it open with his pocket knife and peered inside at the single item lying on the bottom. Something with a faint sheen to it. He inverted the mailer over the desk and shook it.

Into the light fell the final piece of a truth puzzle, a Ziploc baggie with two database datacards, one of which he suspected had survived two recent plane crashes.

Nick stood motionless. In spite of the enormous difficulties that lay ahead, he felt as if he were floating, lifted by a balloon filled with euphoria.

Legal chain of evidence did not exist. Unless an official investigation produced additional proof, these pieces would have to sway public opinion enough to punish the conspirators at the ballot box. Far short of justice, but he'd take it.

Goddamn, it felt good. He remembered the words of a pro basketball player who had said after a big win, "It was like we went into their house and ate the food out of their refrigerator."

Nick smiled. He wanted to eat all the butter cookies and brew up every leaf of Earl Grey in the cupboard. Then the desk phone rang, and his whole body jerked. He rushed to the door and opened it slightly. The ringing stopped. Dorothy's voice drifted up the stairs with half a conversation.

After a moment, the shuffle of house shoes on tile. Dorothy called out. "Nathan?"

"Yes?"

"Mr. Wilson's home."

Nick's bowels threatened to dump their contents as he pulled out the Glock. "He's here?"

"No, silly boy. He always *calls* first so I can leave before he gets home. You won't have to wait long. Bye bye."

"Goodbye, Dorothy. Thanks for the tea and cookies." He closed the door and locked it, slipped the pistol inside his front pocket and hurried to the desk. He stuffed the datacards, papers, and mini-cassette in the envelope and shoved it inside his waistband at the small of his back, and paused. An idea seemed to appear before him in neon lights.

How about leaving a special calling card?

He grabbed a permanent marker out of a tray in the center drawer. On the blotter he scrawled a taunting message in bold letters, then opened the rear door and stepped onto the deck. A stone wall, had to be eight feet high, separated Wilson's back yard from a wooded greenbelt with dense shrubs and high grass. Except for a wrought-iron gate, the fence provided concealment and would give Nick cover as he made his way to the Camry.

He started down the stairs and jerked to a stop when he saw a dog—a pit bull—lying in the shade beside the house, eyes closed. Nick looked for a chain. He didn't see one.

Option one: back up the stairs and through the house. He probably had time. The airport was at least thirty minutes from the house, although Wilson could have flown into a closer airport or called Dorothy from his car.

Option two: continue down the stairs and try to make it—the dog moved, stretched its legs, yawned, its jaws filled with way too many sharp teeth. *I don't think so.*

He returned to the office, walked around the desk to the front door and opened it slightly. Nothing but quiet. He pulled the Glock and held it in both hands in a shooter's grip.

A gust of air ruffled his hair from behind. The rear office door slammed closed. Someone had just opened another door in the house.

Nick forced his legs into a backpedal. He scrambled down the stairs and hit the ground running, his hiking boots digging into manicured turf. He glanced over his shoulder. The dog was gaining.

Approaching the wall, Nick stuck the pistol in his front pants pocket and leapt, grabbed a thick layer of vines, hauled himself to the top and over. He hit the ground hard, felt a twinge in his right ankle as the dog found its voice.

Nick played a mind-tape of the map he'd downloaded with directions to Wilson's house and a Google Earth image of the neighborhood. The wall bordered the back property line of all the homes on Wilson's street. The rental car was parked less than a block from the far end of the greenbelt. He ignored his sore ankle and ran. When he got about thirty yards from the house, the dog stopped barking , as if responding to a command.

Nick took cover behind a fallen log. On the other side of the iron gate, the dog was looking over its shoulder. The gate began to open, triggering a replay of Hotel's warning about getting into a gunfight with a professional. Nick glanced around. Roof tops poked up through the foliage. Gunshots would bring the cops. Wilson wouldn't want that. Then Nick remembered the suppressor.

He stood up and ran, leapt a rocky, dry streambed, landed

on his bad ankle and fell headfirst to the ground.

Delilah quivered. Good dog. She was always eager. Wilson thought about letting her run, but he hadn't been able to spend enough time on training to control her. He snapped on the leash and wrapped it around his left wrist. With the suppressor extension on the pistol, he lifted the gate latch, pushed it open with his foot, lowered the pistol beside his right leg, and stepped into the greenbelt.

The dog leapt toward the woods and almost yanked him off his feet. He let her lead him. His side and leg hurt like hell. He'd feel a lot better when he found Phillips peering up at him, cringing, like Saddam Hussein cowering inside his spider hole in some godforsaken Iraqi village.

NICK LAY FACE DOWN on the forest floor, breathing deeply. He rolled over, pushed his upper body erect and peered over the low vegetation toward Wilson's house. His heart rate surged.

Fifty yards away, Wilson limped toward him. The dog lurched against a leash in his left hand. Nick knew what the killer held in his right hand. He'd seen the posture once before.

The Glock lay a few yards away. He snatched it up, got into a crouch and held the front sight on the center of Wilson's torso. At this distance, he ought to be hauling ass, especially with a crippled adversary, but the dog worried him.

He glanced around for an escape route. The stone wall, barely visible under a thick layer of ivy, paralleled Wilson's direction of movement. If Nick ran for it, the angle would complicate Wilson's aim. He peeked over the low vegetation one last time.

Wilson leaned over the dog, fumbled with the leash, stood erect and motioned with his hand.

Nick bolted.

DELILAH LEAPT INTO THE undergrowth and disappeared as Phillips popped up and ran to Wilson's right. He sidestepped, tracked Phillips with the pistol, fired twice, then a third time, muffled pops neighbors wouldn't even notice, low percentage shots but better than nothing.

Phillips made it to the wall just as Delilah intercepted him. An unsuppressed shot punched through the forest. She yelped and fell from sight. The fucker had killed his dog. Wilson fired once more as Phillips scrambled over the wall. A puff of white appeared where the bullet hit stone. Furious, deep-throated barking came from beyond the wall.

Wilson gritted his teeth and trotted toward the wall. Phillips had just challenged the turf of two Dobermans. The dogs were military trained for overseas duty, which meant they go for the crotch. Good. Save Wilson the trouble of castrating the bastard.

The Dobermans were still barking when he reached the wall. Phillips had probably made it into the front yard. If they'd caught him, they would have their mouths full. Wilson peered through a knothole in the wooden gate. Both dogs were frantically trying to vault the side wall where it joined the house.

He knew the owners of the next house were away on vacation and never locked their back gate. He slipped the pistol under his jacket and hobbled through their yard to the front of the house. Trying to appear as if he were out for a brisk walk, he searched the entire gated complex. His knee felt like it was going to self destruct.

Deed restrictions required owners to garage all personal vehicles. Overnight visitors could park in driveways, but only by permit. Wilson saw no cars parked anywhere. At the security gate, he tapped on the window of the guardhouse.

A guard Wilson had never seen before stood and opened the door. "May I help you, sir?"

"You screen everybody comes in here, right?"

"Of course."

"Visitors have to declare a destination?"

"And we call to confirm they are expected."

"Did Wilson have any visitors today?"

"May I ask who is—?"

"I'm Wilson, goddamn it." He pulled his wallet out and showed the guard his driver's license. "Sorry I snapped at you."

"That's quite all right, sir." The guard glanced at a computer screen and tapped a few keys. "Nathan Porter. Arrived at—"

"Excuse me, but has he left yet?"

"Five minutes ago, sir."

"Do you record the license plate numbers of visiting cars?"

"Yes, sir."

"Well?"

"Mr. Porter was walking, sir."

Wilson sighed, exasperated beyond measure, nodded his thanks and returned to the greenbelt. Delilah lay still in a pool of blood. He picked her up and walked back to his house. He placed her on the grass, climbed the stairs to the upper deck and approached his office. Sharp pain in his left knee punctuated every step. He stood in the doorway. His eyes lingered on each detail.

The empty mailer lying on the desk. Drawers removed and lying on floor. Something scrawled on the blotter. He limped over to the desk and read: I TOLD YOU TO HOLD THAT POSITION. On the other side of the desk, Medusa was rotated 180 degrees, the safe open, his secrets stolen. He looked toward the closed front office door.

Two plates of butter cookies and a teacup sat on the viper lamp table, one of the last snacks of a motherfucking NTSB investigator who had no more than a few days left to breathe.

CHAPTER TWENTY-FIVE

Tanner Osborne detested waiting for secure phone connections, especially when no one answered. The special operative using this number had no answering service, for the same reasons Tanner didn't on his private line. He slammed the handset down on the cradle and closed and locked the drawer. If the strange phone call yesterday meant his connection to the operative had been compromised, Tanner's ass could be hanging out in more ways than one.

Using a sterile cell phone, he punched in Nordstrom's number and discovered the customer was out of the area. He drained his second Scotch of the evening and poured another. Liquor usually helped him relax, but not tonight. The empty house, normally a refuge, pressed in upon him like a tomb. Sitting in the semi-darkness of his study felt appropriate. He might as well lie down on the floor and wait for the maggots.

A printout of Sweet's article lay on the desk. Tanner had read it twice, still didn't believe the reporter could have come up with enough evidence to get it by his editor. Unless the *Cedar Valley Gazette* had no journalistic standards, which was probably the case.

And why should Tanner expect anything else? The traditional journalistic guideline of *The Best Available Version of the Truth* had disappeared in the feeding frenzy for ratings. Sensationalism ruled, with talking heads yelling at each other and a brain-dead, self-serving anchor, immaculately manicured and coiffed, pretending to referee a word fight.

Tanner sighed and launched an Internet search to find a phone number for the *Gazette.* Even with the time change, he didn't expect an answer at this time of the evening, but maybe they offered a company directory. After wading through an interminable list of recorded choices, he finally heard, "For Harvey Sweet, press two four one."

Another no-answer convinced Tanner that everybody he wanted to talk to had left the planet. He called the *Gazette's* number for a second time and waited to the end of the message, which surprised him with, "Press zero for the operator."

"Cedar Valley Gazette, how may I direct your call?"

"Uh . . . hello, I'm surprised to find anyone there."

"We print seven days a week, sir, three-sixty-five a year. We got a hokey name, but we know how to play the game."

Lord, spare me from idiots, please. "I need to speak with Harvey Sweet."

"So do we. If you find him, tell him his editor's madder'n a woman missin' a shoe sale. He's got a column to write, and we got deadlines to meet."

"I tried his number from your directory, but he didn't answer. Do you have another?"

"Nope, and I've called every ten minutes for the past few hours. Hotel normally answers right off, doesn't want to miss a hot lead. Although until that Larchmont guy crashed, I can't say there's been anything even close to a lukewarm lead around here for years."

"What's that about a hotel?"

"It's his nickname, sir. Not too fond of Harvey, says it

reminds him of a rabbit."

"I'll bet it does. So the Larchmont story has been big news out there?"

"Biggest thing ever'd be my guess. Once the first body showed up in that plane, the idea caught on, know what I mean?"

Unfortunately, Tanner did. "Can I leave a message for Mr. Sweet?" After he did that, Tanner asked, "I need to send him something in the mail . . . and I'll need a physical address, not a PO box."

"The paper is at—"

"Excuse me, ma'am. I meant his home address."

"Can't give you that. They'd fire me for sure." She laid on the accent at the end. It came out, "fur shore."

Tanner had a nice trick that might work, especially with a frustrated comedian working as an operator at a small-town newspaper, bored out of her skull and hungry for conversation. He punched a button that controlled the blocking circuits on his very customized cell phone. "You have caller ID?"

"Of course. You called from a blocked number."

"Please look again."

"Oh. I don't know what happened, but—"

"Do you recognize the number?"

"Hardly. I can't recognize my own."

"Here's a hint. Look up the number for the White House."

"Sir, I don't—"

"Humor me, please."

After a few moments, the woman said, "So you're telling me I'm speaking with President Kilpatrick."

"Not quite. But the point is, I need to know where Harvey Sweet lives because someone way above my pay grade wants to know."

"This about Sweet's recent article?"

"Can't tell you that. He'd fire me *fur shore.*"

Tanner wrote down the address, thanked the receptionist, ended the call and dialed the emergency transportation number to arrange for a flight to Colorado.

ABOUT MIDNIGHT, TWO HUMORLESS characters with earpieces and coiled cords that disappeared beneath their coat collars arrived at Tanner's home in a black Suburban. They drove him to a small airport where a jet was waiting—pure white, no fancy stripes. He climbed aboard with the thought that he could get used to traveling like this, promptly fell asleep, and woke up four hours later to the thump of tires on asphalt and the roar of thrust reversers.

The left engine wound down during the short taxi. The copilot climbed out of the cockpit, opened the cabin door, and the screaming of the opposite-side fanjet filled the interior. He waved Tanner forward, handed him his coat and overnight bag, and motioned toward the stairs. Tanner had barely stepped onto the ramp when the door closed and the left engine began turning. It started up with a muffled whump. People could get sucked into jet engines. Tanner picked up his bag and backed away.

The jet moved forward a few feet, reversed course in a tight turn, and taxied toward the runway. Soon the engines increased to full power, and the little dart gracefully lifted off and climbed out of sight into a low overcast sky.

Tanner had neglected to arrange for ground transportation, so he looked around for a rental car sign. He didn't see one. A cluster of buildings sat at the far end of the tarmac. He buttoned his coat and trudged toward them. When he noticed light flowing from a window on the first floor of what looked like a terminal building, he made a beeline for it.

Above steps leading to a porch, an unlit neon café sign hung in a shuttered window. The aroma of coffee and doughnuts drifted by on a slight breeze. He postponed a recent resolution to avoid excess sugar and starchy carbohydrates and climbed the steps. A small bell above his head tinkled as he opened and shut the door. "Hello? Are you open?"

A shrill voice answered from the kitchen. "No. I get up hours 'fore dawn to come down here in the cold to make these here doughnuts and coffee so's I can stay closed."

"I wouldn't have asked if the sign had been lit."

One of Cedar Valley's more senior female citizens shuffled backwards through double swinging doors. She turned, set two handfuls of cups down and strode through the gap in the counter to the entrance. She flipped a switch and faced him, hands on her ample hips. "There. We're open. You satisfied?"

Tanner glanced at her nametag. "Not quite, Loretta. I could sure use some coffee and food."

She turned her back on him. "Have a seat, mister." By the time Tanner had put his bag on a stool and draped his coat over it, a cup of steaming coffee in a white mug sat waiting. He tried it, burned his lips, and decided he was going to like it here.

Loretta pointed to a hand-lettered menu on the wall. "I recommend the omelet, 'specially when you tell me to put in the works."

"Why's that?"

"Don't have to worry none 'bout choosin' the right stuff. Whatever I got goes in. No one ever complains."

Tanner nodded. "I bet they don't. How about a cinnamon-sugar doughnut for an appetizer, the works, then a chocolate doughnut for dessert?"

"Comin' right up."

Loretta moved like a whirlwind. She put a king-size oval plate on the counter in front of him before he finished his first doughnut. The omelet, had to be four eggs in it, chunks of "the works" poking out through a sheen of grease, covered only half the plate. The rest was loaded with grilled potatoes, onions, green peppers, a mound of buttered grits, and two biscuits.

Tanner wolfed down the breakfast and all but inhaled his second doughnut. He'd learned to be careful with the coffee by the time Loretta plopped down two stools away and poured herself a cup. She gulped a few swallows without so much as a grimace. "You must be one o' them investigator fellas."

"No, but I'm looking for one. A guy named Nordstrom?"

"Don't remember names too good. What's he look like?"

Tanner told her, and she nodded. "He was in here . . . would a been . . . a day or so ago, I reckon. Had two doughnuts, one plain, one cinnamon-sugar, no omelet, lots of coffee. Bought a paper, spent forever readin' an article most people finished in 'bout five minutes."

Tanner was impressed. Loretta might not recall names, but it was only because she didn't ask, or they didn't tell her. "Has he been in since then?"

"Nope. He met another fella, never seen him before neither. They left 'bout mid-mornin'."

"I imagine the article you mentioned was the one by Harvey Sweet?"

Loretta's head snapped toward Tanner. Her eyes glinted as she stared at him. "He writes for the local paper. I'm surprised you know 'bout that, not bein' from these parts."

"Sweet's article made it out my way pretty quick. You know where I might find him?"

Loretta gave him directions, including a detailed explanation of how to identify his turns with landmarks, many of which were no longer there, mind you. Tanner paid his bill, including a generous tip he had to lay on the counter three times before she'd accept it, and put on his coat. "Is there a rental car office close by?"

She stared at him. "You come in here on a jet and don't have no car waitin'?"

"It's a long story."

"I got time."

Tanner wished he did. "A car, Loretta?"

"Sorry, son. You might could hitch a ride. Folks 'round here are friendly 'nough. They see you walkin', they'll stop."

"What about a cab?"

"May take a while. That old coot never gets up 'fore nine."

"Okay, thanks. I need to walk off some of this breakfast anyway." Tanner left the café. Standing at the bottom of the steps, he glanced at the only vehicle in the parking lot, a Ford Taurus in a handicapped space. Tanner wondered if it was Loretta's car, but couldn't imagine her needing special accommodations, much less asking for them.

He buttoned his coat and turned up the collar against a freshening breeze. With the overnight bag slung over his shoulder, he turned toward the highway and stopped in his tracks. Below a temporary handicapped permit hanging from the rearview mirror of the Taurus lay an envelope with *Osborne* scrawled in black ink.

Tanner put his bag on the ground. He hadn't told anyone except the transportation service about his trip. They wouldn't have done anything he didn't ask for. Someone put this car here and arranged for him to notice it. Friend or foe? The way things were going, did he have any friends?

The thought of opening the door gave Tanner pause.

Turning the key might give him a lot more than that. And where were the keys?

He stood beside the car for a moment before deciding paranoia didn't suit him. If anyone wished him harm, they wouldn't have to go to all this trouble. The keys were probably in the car. He pulled on the driver's door handle. Locked. Okay. Somebody trying to take care of him screwed up.

He reached down to pick up his bag and noticed an open outside pocket. He carried an extra cell-phone battery there and was usually careful about keeping it zipped. Inside he found a set of car keys. The pilot who handled his bag must have put them there.

Tanner climbed in and started the engine. As he waited for the defroster to clear the windshield, he opened the envelope.

The handwritten note said: *Were you going to walk? Sudden, unannounced trips make me nervous. Call ASAP.*

Tanner tore up the note, stuffed it in his jacket pocket, and drove into the early-morning mist for his next starring role.

HOTEL YAWNED, LEANED AGAINST his kitchen counter, and watched the coffee brew. In spite of fatigue and drooping eyelids, trying to sleep would be futile. Missed deadlines and naps didn't mix.

At this moment the *Gazette* would be in turmoil, with his editor pacing the halls and asking everyone if they knew where Hotel was and why he had dropped out of sight without filing a follow-up article. And at some point in the last twenty-four hours, the editor had probably stood in the middle of the news room and shouted, "Will no one deliver to me this troublesome reporter who thinks deadlines are only suggestions?"

Hotel understood his editor's angst, but he wasn't ready

to reveal the events of the past thirty-six hours. Not only that, by reporting as a participant in the story, he had thrown the first pitch in a whole new ballgame. He didn't know how to do that objectively. Rather than show up at the *Gazette* with no excuses, he'd decided to stay missing-in-action until Nick returned.

In the meantime, his keyboard waited. He went to the study and sat down at his home workstation. His first installment had done far more than set the stage for a journalistic tour-de-force. It had changed the plot and triggered events that killed a man. With plenty of indirect confirmation at his fingertips, Hotel could breathe extended life into the story with a chronological sequence of events. Even without the complete answer as to why and how Larchmont was killed, it would be a riveting piece worthy of his finest efforts.

He also needed to be ready in case Nick returned with some hard evidence. An article in first draft could be revised and submitted quickly. Nothing silenced a shouting editor like finished copy.

As he scooted his chair up to the desk, someone knocked at the front door. Probably a gofer from the paper with a message of vitriolic rage from his boss. Hotel ignored the insistent pounding and tried to concentrate on his opening sentence.

But the pest wouldn't take a hint. Hotel went to a shuttered window and eased a slat up. A stranger wearing a long overcoat, gloved hands clapping, was doing a cold-weather shuffle on the wood porch. Hotel watched him for a moment, looking for bulges under the coat. He didn't see any, and a killer probably wouldn't walk up to the door and knock.

Then again, that's what Montana, or Wilson, whatever his name is, did.

Hotel rushed upstairs and got his Glock from the bedside

table. Thumb inside the trigger guard, first finger pressing just below the barrel, he eased back the slide to check that a hollow-point round rested "in the pipe." He released the magazine into his off hand, confirmed it was loaded with thirteen more rounds, rammed it back home and marched down the stairs and across the living room. Pistol in his hand, muzzle-down by his leg, he flung open the front door. "What do you want?"

The man stepped back from the door and raised his hands to shoulder height. "Whoa, there, sir. You won't need that. I'm just looking for Harvey Sweet, reporter for the *Gazette.*"

"Who are you and what do you want with him?"

"I'd prefer to tell him. Are you—?"

"What you prefer is of no concern to me. You're on my property. Answer me, or get your sorry ass off my porch."

"My name is Tanner Osborne."

Well I'll be goddamned. Hotel struggled to keep his face impassive. "And?"

"Can we talk inside? It's cold out here."

"I will ask you only one more time. What do you *want?*"

"To speak with Mr. Sweet about his latest article in the *Gazette.* I'm also looking for a colleague, Lars Nordstrom, and I thought Mr. Sweet might know where he is."

Hotel thought about asking for some ID, but this was far too bizarre to be anything other than what it seemed. He stepped away from the door. "Don't call me Harvey. Want some coffee?"

"I wouldn't think of it. Yes, thanks."

Hotel motioned toward the living room. "Have a seat on the couch." As the coffee brewed, he kept an eye on Osborne from the kitchen, then took the fresh pot into the living room, poured two cups, handed one to Osborne and sat down in the armchair. Exaggerating the movement, he adjusted the Glock, nestled inside his belt at the small of his back. "So, you came all the way out here to talk to me?"

Osborne tentatively sipped his coffee, as if concerned about the temperature. "That's part of it. Have you ever met Lars Nordstrom?"

"I know who he is."

"Do you know *where* he is?"

Hotel drank some coffee. "Yes." He shifted position and stared at the cold fireplace.

Osborne raised his eyebrows. "Are you going to tell me?"

"First I have to find out who I'm dealing with."

"I told you. I'm—"

"Tanner Osborne, close friend of and personal advisor to the President of the United States. But I don't know what *else* you are."

Osborne's eyes flashed with irritation. "Perhaps this was a bad idea."

Hopefully not. "You mentioned my article. What about it?"

"I'm surprised you ask. It performs a gross disservice to the President and America's security."

Hotel remembered his father's advice that the person doing most of the talking usually ended up losing. "Really. How's that?"

"Off the record?"

Hotel smiled. "I'd never betray a confidence."

Osborne leaned forward. "President John Kilpatrick has done more for the security of this country in the last three years than the previous five administrations combined. He stepped up after President Baker's death and told the American people what to expect. He promised to fight terror, and he made good on that pledge.

"Miles Larchmont was a patriot. He risked his life in the

service of his country. He was hounded to the very end by the nit-picking of ungrateful people who don't understand why we have to battle terrorists on their home turf."

Hotel scratched the stubble on his chin. "So . . . when he faces indictment for arms dealing and money laundering and whatever else is contained in those sealed documents, and says he won't go down alone, the public is supposed to turn a blind eye?"

Osborne pointed a finger in the air and gestured in emphasis. "*Assuming* there's any truth to the allegations, why the hell not? Americans turn away from unpleasant facts every day when it suits them. 'Keep the oil flowing, Mr. President, just don't tell me how you're doing it.' But look what happens when the isolationist anti-war crowd accuses us of violating the rights of the sons of bitches who send teenagers to blow up the innocent. Suddenly, Americans are ready to accuse the President of authorizing assassinations."

"So the public shouldn't question why and how Larchmont died in that jet?"

"The NTSB did that for them by conducting a complete investigation. For all Larchmont's strengths, he carried the expert syndrome with him into the cockpit, and it killed him. That crash was an unambiguous case of pilot error."

Hotel nodded. "Okay, I *might* be able to buy that. But don't the open door, the mysterious visitor, the datacards, and the collateral murders deserve additional scrutiny?"

Osborne shook his head and chuckled. "Your article was nothing more than rampant speculation about purely coincidental events. While I admire your honesty in admitting the lack of hard evidence, I despise the blatant sensationalism. You and the *Gazette* represent the worst in tabloid journalism at a time when the President needs support to win this election."

The time had come for what Nick in aviator lingo would call a "press-to-test." Hotel crossed his arms and relaxed into the soft cushions of the armchair. He looked up and scratched his chin, as if he were thinking about Osborne's argument and might be persuaded. It didn't take long before Osborne's intensity appeared to relax, as if he'd interpreted Hotel's silence as a victory in the debate. That made him vulnerable.

Hotel stared at him. "That's real interesting, Mr. Osborne, but my guess is you don't know the full body count."

Osborne frowned. "Sadly, I'm updated each morning on the toll in American dead. But don't give me that tired argument about how many innocent civilians have died. It's unavoidable in war. And if you believe figures published by our enemies, you're way too gullible for a reporter."

Hotel shook his head. "I'm not talking about the Middle East."

TANNER LISTENED TO SWEET'S description of the death of Nordstrom. He had to concentrate on each word for them to sink in, and he still didn't believe it. "He's where?"

"At the bottom of a mineshaft, thrown there by a guy we figure is good for a total of five bodies so far."

Tanner sat very still. It felt as if all the gravity had disappeared and he was about to float off the couch. Killing terrorists halfway around the world was so antiseptic, especially when he didn't have to deal with the details. Not all the casualties deserved it, but he understood the necessity of a shotgun approach to fighting an elusive enemy. Collateral damage on both sides was inevitable.

He'd lobbied hard against taking action to silence Larchmont's unpredictable mouth. The President had listened, as he always did, never interrupting, until Tanner's arguments ran out of steam. Then the President countered, point by point, and when it was all done, Tanner had reverted to the good soldier he had always been.

But four more dead? Including an NTSB division chief? That news hit much closer to the core of Tanner's beliefs in the difference between right and wrong. Not to mention that he had personally turned a killing machine loose in colorful Colorado and then refused to pay the man the rest of his money. In spite of secure phone lines, voice-modulation software, and never meeting face-to-face, Tanner knew he was exposed and vulnerable.

He picked at a piece of lint on his knee. "So, where is this murderer?"

"Hiding in the darkness. Waiting."

A shiver of fear climbed up Tanner's spine. He pointed behind Sweet's back. "Got another one of those?"

"I'm not sure I want a man like you around me with a weapon."

"He's on the loose and you're worried about *me?*"

"That's because I expect him to come at me head on. My guess is you work best from behind."

The words struck deep into Tanner's being, a knockdown punch.

So it all came down to this. Sitting in a beautiful home nestled in the foothills of the Rockies, he recoiled from the accusation that he was a coward, afraid to confront his enemies and look them in the eyes, afraid to make the hard choices and fight for what he believed was right, afraid that to resist involvement would be worse than to exercise control over a process he could not wholeheartedly endorse.

He tried to speak, but his dry throat choked off the words.

A sip of coffee didn't help much, but he managed to say, "In that case, I'd better be on my way."

Sweet nodded. "You might want to watch your back. Or you could get somebody to do that for you."

Tanner picked up his overcoat from the couch and set it in his lap. "And who might that be?"

"An ally. Go on the record and find out if you have any."

Tanner stared at Sweet for a moment. If only he could.

He pushed himself up from the couch, which felt as if it were trying to hold him captive, and put on his overcoat. "You look like a man who can take care of himself, Mr. Sweet. But if I may offer a word of advice?" When Sweet nodded, Tanner said, "People shift allegiances as it serves their interests. Take your own advice and watch *your* back."

Sweet stood up. "That's a good reason for choosing allies carefully, wouldn't you agree?"

Tanner knew it was way too late for that. He picked up his gloves and slipped them on as he walked to the door, then turned to Sweet and began buttoning his coat. "Off the record . . . don't give up, and don't *ever* get careless."

He drove away from the house with the image in the rearview mirror of Sweet standing on the porch. In every car he saw on the trip back to the airport, the occupants seemed to stare at him, point accusatory fingers, and mouth, *Murderer.*

LATER THAT AFTERNOON HOTEL woke with a start. His hand went for the Glock.

"Easy, buddy," said the voice of Nick Phillips. "You're lucky I'm not a bad guy. I can't believe it was this easy to sneak up on you."

Hotel shook off the lingering stupor of no sleep followed

by not nearly enough and struggled to focus on the hazy apparition standing beside the couch. "I knew you were there. Pretended sleep to draw you into the trap. What the hell time is it?"

"Show time," said Nick. "And I've got the tickets." He collapsed into the armchair and took off his jacket. From the inner breast pocket, he pulled out a manila envelope, removed a folded bundle of papers and held it up. "This is a Larchmont cover-his-ass insurance policy with names, places, and dates. It provides all the background we need." He laid the bundle on the table and lifted a mini-cassette tape out of the envelope. "This might document incriminating conversations. Where's the recorder you used to take my statement?"

Hotel eased himself into a sitting position and yawned. "It's digital. My old one is probably in a drawer around here somewhere. But we still can't *prove* any of it. *"*

Nick smiled. With slow, exaggerated movements, he reached into the envelope again and removed a Ziploc baggie held between his thumb and index finger. "And I'm betting that one of *these,"* as he wiggled the baggie, "will solve that problem."

Hotel blinked a few times, leaned forward, took the baggie and stared at it. Could less than an ounce of flash memory contain the power to bring down a jet? "From Wilson's house?"

Nick's eyes flashed with triumph. "We found the son of a bitch."

Hotel laughed. "Did you shoot him?"

"You told me not to trade shots with a professional." His face clouded over as he said, "But I had to shoot a dog."

"Justifiably, I trust."

"Under the circumstances, but it wasn't her fault."

Hotel pointed to the ripped cuff of Nick's shirt and a tear

in the leg of his jeans. "But in self-defense, it appears."

"The Dobermans that did this are alive and well." Nick related the story of his surprise when he hit the ground running and found that his dog worries had just doubled in size and number. "These guys were a tag team. I barely made it to the top of the fence when the faster one got hold of my jeans. I reached down to punch him and the second one clamped his jaws on my sleeve. Dobermans have very sharp teeth."

"Did you call the cops?"

Nick rolled his eyes. "I realize you're groggy and not thinking straight, but that's a stupid question."

"Careful, pilgrim."

"What would I have told them?"

Hotel laid the baggie on the coffee table. "Good point. You think the answer is in one of those datacards?"

"It's the only place left to look." He glanced around the room. "What the hell have you been doing?"

Hotel related the details of Osborne's visit. "Nick, this guy is as intense as any man I've ever known, and that's saying something. But when he learned about Nordstrom, it was like somebody stuck a pin in his balloon."

"I don't know. If he's been involved from the beginning, a sudden change of heart seems unlikely."

"I'm thinking reluctant warrior. A last-straw kind of thing."

"Maybe. How high does this go?"

"Nothing he said implied he was *ordered* to do anything. He could have made up his own mind to take care of the problem."

"But what do you *think?*"

"He's the President's go-to guy."

Nick nodded. "Where is Osborne now?"

"No idea. I considered keeping him here." When Nick raised his eyebrows, Hotel said, "In a nice, comfy mineshaft."

"I hear you." Nick glanced out the window. "You figure a couple hours to sunset?"

"Yeah, and it'll get dark fast once it starts. In the meantime, I should start writing."

"You know, I was beginning to like Nordstrom a little. He . . . I . . . god*damn* it. This pisses me off so much."

Hotel waited a moment. "I understand, Nick. The best we can do is to follow through."

Nick turned away and stared out the large front window. Hotel watched his friend in silence. Slanting rays of sun flooded the porch with golden light. Shadows from the support posts angled into the room. A shaft of sunlight slashed across Nick's face. His eyes glistened as he said, "I'm going to get these motherfuckers, Hotel. Swear to Christ I will."

"No."

Nick fixed Hotel with a hard glare. "What's that supposed to mean?"

"*We're* in this together."

Nick's expression softened. "I know that. What I don't know is how you're going to publish an article accusing the President of the United States of conspiracy to murder. Your editor—"

"Not a problem. Give him a good story to stir the journalistic pot, and he's one hell of a chef."

Nick smiled, in haunting contrast to the sadness in his eyes. "Well, okay then. Speaking of chefs, how about some food before we go?"

CHAPTER TWENTY-SIX

As sunset darkened the valley, Nick and Hotel left for the airport in Hotel's truck. The objective: find an airplane equipped with the same popular make of GPS navigation receiver used in the GoldenJet and Nick's aircraft.

The purring of a well-tuned engine and the hum of off-road tires filled the cab. Hotel glanced at Nick. "You wanted to stop along the way?"

"I need a good view of the airport."

"I know just the place."

Ten minutes later, Hotel parked on the side of the highway in a deserted rest area. They climbed over a metal barrier railing and scrambled down the embankment to a bare rock jutting out from the forest.

Nick scanned the airport with Hotel's night-vision binoculars. No airplanes were taxiing or being preflighted. Only a few cars sat on the ramp or in the visitor's parking lot. Dark windows in the line shack indicated the ramp workers had left. An NTSB security guard in the hangar with the wreckage had no jurisdiction anywhere else.

They climbed back to the truck in silence, drove to the airport and parked well away from the line shack. Hotel killed the engine. "How illegal is what we're about to do?

Nick stared out the windshield into the deepening night. "It doesn't matter. If we give the evidence we have to the authorities, we'll never see it again. The only way to prove tampering is to hold it up, cameras rolling, and announce that this final piece of the puzzle is the only navigation datacard in the world that could have caused Larchmont's death."

Hotel nodded. "To hell with prison. What do I do?"

"Wait here. I'll be right back."

"Where are you going?"

"To do a little breaking and entering." Nick got out of the truck.

Hotel said, "Hold up," reached under the seat and pulled out a Glock. "Protecting yourself with a handgun means you have to be ready all the time."

"Uh . . . I forgot it."

"I didn't."

Nick took the weapon, checked it, and stuck it in his jacket pocket. He trotted past two rows of hangars to the line shack. The key to the office lay hidden under the doormat where no one would think of looking. He unlocked the door and went inside, grabbed two handfuls of airplane keys off hooks in a wall cabinet and stuffed them in his other jacket pocket.

As they walked to the first hangar, Hotel said, "How many years are you setting me up for?"

"No more than twenty. Hold this." Nick gave Hotel the flashlight and pulled out a bunch of keys. Owners usually put a hangar key on the same ring they used for their airplanes. It took three tries before he found one that unlocked the deadbolt on the personnel door. He eased it open. Rusty hinges squealed in the quiet night. The sound reminded him of a hawk.

At the first airplane, Nick shined the flashlight beam through a side window and searched the instrument panel for the GPS navigation receiver. Different manufacturer. None of the remaining airplanes in the hangar had the equipment he was looking for.

They hit pay dirt at the third airplane in the next hangar. Nick dumped all the keys on the floor and found the set that matched the plane. He unlocked the door and settled into the pilot's seat. Hotel sat in the copilot's position.

With the battery switch on, Nick checked the instrument panel, interior, and exterior lighting switches off to minimize light spilling into the hangar. He flipped on the avionics master switch and turned off the GPS and all the radios. From the Ziploc baggie, he removed both datacards and gave one to Hotel. He already knew the information printed on both labels was identical, but maybe Wilson had marked the altered one in some way so *he* could identify it.

In the beam of the flashlight, Nick studied the label on the datacard he held, then Hotel's. "I can't see any difference. We'll have to examine the data on both."

Hotel smiled. "Maybe not." Out of his pocket he pulled a set of car keys, which Nick instantly recognized as those to the Explorer, with the mini-flashlight and the magnifying glass attached on a removable ring. Hotel gave Nick the keys, took the flashlight and shined it down into Nick's lap. "Give them both a closer look."

On the second datacard, Nick found a tiny mark on the corner of the label. "This could be mean nothing, but we've got to start somewhere. He gave Hotel the flashlight. "Shine it on this panel." Then he replaced the installed unit's datacard with what he hoped was the altered one. When he turned the power knob back on, the screen displayed the self-test procedures.

Hotel tapped Nick on the shoulder. "What are you looking for?"

"I'm not sure."

"That's terrific. We could end up in prison and you don't know why we're here."

"Quit complaining and help me figure this out." Nick tapped the face of the GPS. "The answer is in the navigation information."

"You mean like . . . something to fool the pilot about where he is?"

"Exactly."

"Do GPS navigation receivers in airplanes work the same as the one I carry with me in the mountains?"

"Yes."

"What about messing with the GPS signal?"

"That would require very sophisticated equipment. I'm not sure it's even possible."

"I bet the military knows. They rely on it for targeting and weapons guidance. They must have vulnerability studies."

Nick shook his head. "It has to be something simpler. The question is how could you introduce a positional error that wouldn't announce itself?"

"What do you mean?"

Nick explained that pilots are taught to use all available information to confirm their position, and the best way to do that is to crosscheck one navigation source against another. "If they don't correlate, you have a problem."

"What do you do then?"

"Immediately climb if there's any doubt about safe separation from the ground."

"How do pilots crosscheck position when flying into Cedar Valley?"

"Good question, especially from a dumb-ass reporter. You have to use onboard systems."

"Call me 'dumb-ass' again and I'll get my rifle. What does that mean?"

"Since Cedar Valley has no ground-based navigation aids, you'd need two independent GPS receivers in the airplane. The GoldenJet was using its one and only GPS to fly the approach."

Hotel nodded. "Okay. So Larchmont didn't have a backup. Let's say the GPS is steering him wrong. If he can look out the window and see the ground, that's as good as any instrument, right?"

"Better. Pilots have a saying: 'One peek is worth a thousand cross-checks.' In the fall and winter the chance for clouds over the airport is greater, but Wilson couldn't control when Larchmont would be coming here."

Hotel stared out the windscreen for a moment. "Maybe his plan didn't rely on control. Larchmont flew in here a lot. Wilson was confident in the sabotage and content to wait until the conditions were right for it to produce results."

"But after the datacard is altered, what if Larchmont flies into Cedar Valley on a nice day? The GPS is leading him off course and he notices it. The whole plan falls on its ass."

"Why would he fly the approach when he didn't have to?"

Nick stared at Hotel and grinned. "You're a lot smarter than I thought. He probably wouldn't. Most pilots make a visual approach whenever possible because it saves time and fuel. But there's another possibility. If Larchmont was flying an approach in the weather and the clouds weren't real low, he might break out in time to see the ground and notice he was off course."

"I can't believe Wilson wouldn't know that and plan for it. And wouldn't landing after dark make the altered database even more likely to cause a crash?"

"Absolutely."

"How often did Larchmont fly in here at night?"

Nick shrugged. "Most aircraft flight logs don't indicate takeoff and landing times. A pilot's personal logbook wouldn't either, but it will show how often he logged night time. It's a moot question, because we don't have access to—wait a minute. I just remembered something."

"What?"

"The facilities report indicated the runway lights were inoperative."

Hotel shook his head. "I drive right by the airport to and from the hunting cabin. You can see the runway from the highway, and it's usually dark."

"Yeah, but the lights aren't on all the time. There's a pilot-controlled lighting system. It's tied in with the common radio frequency. Pilots click the mike button a specified number of times to turn the lights on. The system didn't work."

"What was wrong with it?"

"Popped circuit breaker. Maybe Wilson was waiting nearby. He knew Larchmont was on the way. It's nighttime, the weather requires an instrument approach, and he takes care of that last detail."

"But he'd plan to fix it and cover his tracks, wouldn't he?"

"Sure, but no one is perfect. If criminals were, they'd never get caught. And circuit breakers pop. Nothing unusual about that."

"Then how do we catch these bastards?"

Nick turned his attention to the GPS. "Find out what they did to this database." He cycled through the navigation screens, looking for any indication that someone had tampered with the data. The bright green text and numerals began to blur with the effort as his eyes grew tired. He leaned back in the seat, stretched, and yawned. "It's got to be here somewhere."

"Forget that for a minute. You're the pilot. Think about the approach, what the dangers are, how it's designed to provide safe separation from the ground."

Nick closed his eyes and pictured the GPS screen as he flew into Cedar Valley. He worked through the steps and got to the fix with the altitude restriction above the ridge where both planes had crashed.

Memories of the last few seconds prior to impact with the trees suddenly came vividly alive. His heart pounded. He began to tremble.

A kind hand touched his shoulder. "Easy, Nick. Take a deep breath, man."

Nick inhaled and exhaled slowly a few times until he calmed down. "I've been so wrapped up with all this that I haven't had time to face it. I really fucked up."

"And if that had been the end of it, you'd have nothing to show for the mistake. But we're close, Nick. Can't you feel it?"

"Not really. I keep coming up with nothing."

"Then keep trying. Talk through it."

"Okay." Nick leaned back in the seat and stared at the headliner as he put himself in the cockpit of Larchmont's airplane on the night of the crash and let his mind wrap around the situation.

"The GPS receiver was using satellite signals to fix Larchmont's exact position in three-dimensional space. The GPS has two complete databases. One is for terrain, with all the information you'd expect to see on a map. The other is for aerial navigation, with all the fixes, or waypoints, that define the highways in the sky that pilots use.

"When he crashed, Larchmont was in what we call the 'terminal phase.' Not a comforting term, but it means the GPS guidance was extremely precise. And I'm talking down to a few feet."

"Then how the hell did he get so far off course?"

Nick stared at Hotel. "In case this has escaped you, that's what we're here to find out."

"Please continue, professor."

"Larchmont was flying a non-precision GPS approach. That—"

"But you just said it was very precise."

"Hotel? Shut up and let me do this. I know it's hard, but you can do better."

"Sorry."

"The lateral part of an instrument approach, the ability of the GPS to guide a pilot to the centerline of the runway, is *very* precise. It creates a course line on the moving map and sends signals to other instruments." He pointed to the course deviation indicator. "When this airplane symbol is superimposed on this vertical needle and kept there, either by the pilot hand-flying or by the autopilot, the airplane is exactly where it needs to be."

Then he described the vertical part of the approach, and that the term "non-precision" meant the procedure didn't provide a glide path reference. "This horizontal needle on the instrument was automatically driven out of view, so it couldn't guide Larchmont on a constant descent angle to the runway. That's why pilots like precision approaches. Keep that needle superimposed on the airplane symbol, and you're guaranteed safe separation from the terrain."

Hotel settled deeper into the seat. "Okay. He's not receiving vertical guidance. How does he land safely without it?"

Nick explained that each of the navigation fixes on final approach had an associated minimum altitude. In profile, the approach looked like steps. "We call it a 'step-down.' Larchmont had to adjust altitudes according to the minimums printed on the approach chart. He'd have to be in level flight until reaching the next fix on the approach, at which point he'd descend to the next altitude and level off, and so on."

Hotel shook his head. "I'm still confused about the lateral part. The GoldenJet was right of course. The radar track indicated that Larchmont turned right to intercept. The *wrong* way. That seems extremely imprecise."

"No shit. Dickson and I never found an explanation."

Hotel shrugged "Well, there you have it."

Nick stared at him. "What am I missing?"

"If the pilot controls altitude during the approach, but trusts course guidance to the GPS, and we start with the premise that Larchmont didn't screw up, the only question is how somebody could alter the guidance. If you say messing with the GPS signal is unlikely, and evidence points to alteration of the database, then what is the most logical explanation for an airplane hitting an obstacle to the right of course when the pilot thinks he's on the centerline of the approach?"

Nick pondered that a moment. "Meaconing."

"What?"

"Bending a ground-based navigation signal to lure airplanes off course."

"But you said GPSs aren't ground-based, and the signal can't be messed with."

"I don't mean meaconing in the original sense. This might be modernization of an old concept. Move the course, and it has to be done within the GPS system."

"How would you do that?"

"I don't know, but the answer is in here someplace."

Nick began cycling through the screens for the third time. Within the navigation group, he examined the moving map and terrain displays. In the waypoint group, he concentrated on airport location, runway, approach, and user waypoint data.

When his eyes began to blur, he leaned back and yawned. "I cannot even begin to think about trying this again with the other datacard."

Hotel glanced around the cockpit. "Where's the written information pilots use at for the approach?"

"The charts are in those brown binders. Look in the section for Colorado, then in the Cs."

Hotel found the binder and laid it in his lap. He began flipping pages, then paused as he studied a chart in the beam of a flashlight.

Nick glanced over to see if Hotel had the correct approach. The binder lay open to the GPS Runway 35 to Cedar Valley, Colorado. He returned his attention to the airport data screen.

"They aren't the same, Nick."

"Yes they are. You found the only approach chart for Cedar Valley."

"Listen to me. The coordinates shown for the airport aren't the same as the ones on that screen."

Nick's whole body tingled. He looked at the beam of Hotel's flashlight and read the map coordinates for the Cedar Valley Airport. Feeling as if he were moving in slow motion, he opened the rings in the binder and removed the page. He held it up next to the GPS screen, shined the beam of his flashlight on the chart page, and compared it with the airport data page on the GPS. It took him a moment to comprehend what he was seeing.

"I'll be goddamned."

"Did we find it?"

Nick heard the question but it didn't register as the words flowed out. "Pilots don't use geographic coordinates directly. We dial in the identifier for a location and tell the GPS to take us there. The system always requires an extra step to confirm the identifier and coordinates. We typically indicate a 'yes' answer with one push of the ENTER button and never think twice about it."

Hotel turned from the screen. "Answer my question."

Nick nodded. "I think Wilson's a pilot. If so, he knows from personal experience exactly how pilots enter waypoints.

"When Larchmont selected the GPS approach for Cedar Valley from this database, he put the GoldenJet on a final approach one mile to the right of the charted course and directly into the ridge."

CHAPTER TWENTY-SEVEN

Tanner Osborne closed the door and dropped his bag on the terrazzo tile of the foyer. The 4500-square-foot home he'd inherited from his parents embraced countless memories and only a few ghosts of times past. Contentment usually came with the territory, such that he seldom ventured out except for work-related demands. But as he returned from his latest foray into the harsh world of reality, the ghosts seemed to have taken over.

He marched directly to his father's study, slightly aromatic with Cherry Blend pipe tobacco even after all these years. From the beveled-glass antique liquor cabinet, he took a cut-crystal decanter and poured three fingers of Old Weller Antique bourbon. He collapsed into the executive desk chair, drank a full swallow, savored the burn and tried to absorb his surroundings into his soul and possess them. Pale yellow light from the rising moon cast long, thin shadows into the room. Bare trees outside the window created a stark pattern of approaching winter on the walls, ceiling, and floor.

Tanner lived physically alone most of the time, and mentally on a continuous basis. He and his wife of twenty-seven years co-existed in a marriage of mutual convenience, and neither of them was eager to alter the arrangement. In her case, scads of social acquaintances and an occasional hard-bodied lover met her needs well enough so long as the bank account remained bottomless. For Tanner, solitude was fine. He'd never met anyone he liked better than himself.

Most of the important decisions in his life had been made right here. The wisdom to choose the best of less-than-perfect options seemed to permeate the room and guide his thoughts. Tonight he needed all the assistance he could get.

The chime of the side-entrance doorbell by the garage brought him upright in the chair. Only a few people knew the door existed. Casual visitors used the front. No one up to any good would use either in the middle of the night. He doubted that danger would ring the doorbell, but recent events suggested caution.

From a side drawer he removed his Colt .45 Model 1911 pistol, cocked the hammer and flipped on the safety. His father's cautions about carrying the pistol "cocked and locked" echoed in his mind as he descended the stairs to the first floor.

The doorbell chimed again.

Thankful for the darkness—he never left lights on in unoccupied living space, a legacy of his father's frugality—Tanner followed the hall to the kitchen and peered out of the bay window by the breakfast nook.

A dark figure stood on the walkway leading up to the side door. Big guy wearing a long, unbuttoned overcoat, hands hanging loose by his sides. His arm extended and the doorbell chimed for a third time.

Tanner studied the shadowed figure. Was that a communications cord? He leaned closer to the window, noted movement to his left. He swiveled and trained the Colt on the far edge of the bay window. A second man raised his arms and displayed empty, gloved hands in the moonlight.

Tanner exhaled in a rush. His legs trembled, so weak he almost fell. He leaned forward and put his hand on the breakfast table. After a moment he checked the safety on the pistol.

Damn. He'd forgotten to flip it off with his thumb. He lowered the weapon to his side, silently cursing his mistake. More of his father's remembered words repeated the lesson that pointing a safetied pistol at someone was a damn good way to get shot.

Tanner opened the door. The familiar face of a Secret Service agent appeared to glow in the moonlight.

The agent stepped forward. "I'm glad you didn't shoot my partner."

"You guys ever hear of using the front door?"

"This time we didn't. He wants to see you. You'll need your coat, but leave that." He pointed at the Colt.

Ten minutes later, Tanner sat in the back seat of a bulletproof Suburban and wondered what it would be like to know that the security modifications were meant to protect *him*. Would it be worth it? To have all that power, and in using it create all those enemies? Or was it better to stay in the background, exercise the muscle through others, and let them take the heat? He thought about that for a moment and decided he didn't want to know the answer.

After a trip of about twenty minutes, most of it with Tanner's brain in idle, the driver turned onto a deserted park drive, continued a half-mile and stopped. The headlights went out. Another black Suburban squatted like a monstrous bug in the middle of the one-lane asphalt road.

The agent riding shotgun jumped out and opened the door. Tanner stepped into the damp chill. A brisk on-shore breeze tickled his nostrils with a hint of salt as he walked toward a meeting with his boss.

FROM THE BACK SEAT of the Suburban, President John Kilpatrick peered through the windshield at the silhouette of his best friend marching along the cracked asphalt ribbon toward him. He lowered the fogged-up side window and flipped the glowing stub of a very expensive Cuban cigar in a gentle red arc over the bridge railing. Out on his own, minus the entourage and the prying cameras of the media, and free of the First Lady's inevitable griping about the smell, this was a rare opportunity to enjoy a good smoke.

Osborne's face registered instant revulsion as he got in. "Goddamn it, Jack. You send your goons to scare the piss out of me, drag me out to a deserted park, and then you poison my lungs with your cancerous expulsions."

"Quit your bitching. If they'd been goons, they'd have brought you here sporting some spiffy concrete footwear."

Osborne lowered his window and waved his hands in front of his face. "I cannot tell you how much I hate that smell."

Kilpatrick opened his door. "Then let's take a stroll." He climbed out and buttoned his overcoat as Osborne fell in step beside him. They walked along the park road, accompanied by the sound of their shoe soles scraping softly on asphalt and trailed by streams of condensed breath. Shadowy figures kept pace in the distance.

Osborne walked in step to Kilpatrick's right and slightly to the rear. The President had never seen his friend do that. Walking on his left side was a habit from Osborne's years in the military, descended from a long-standing tradition with practical roots.

Knights wielded swords with their right hands and defended themselves with shields strapped to their left arms. A subordinate, considered easily susceptible to the lure of reward for betrayal, could disable his sovereign with one thrust of a dirk to the sword arm and render him defenseless.

"You don't own a dirk, do you, Tanner?"

A slight smile played over Osborne's lips. "No, but there are times in my life I could have used one."

Kilpatrick chuckled. "Just so this isn't one of those occasions." He slowed his pace. "Aren't you cold?"

Osborne shrugged. "Not really."

Kilpatrick had become used to subordinates, even those as highly placed as Osborne, mimicking his actions. A tie adjustment would send a ripple of hands to cravats all the way around a conference table. Coat buttoning would as well, even to the number of buttons and in what order.

He laughed softly as he remembered a story from the early twentieth century about a multi-millionaire, most-eligible bachelor who set the standards for fashionable attire in social circles far and wide. He loved to sail, and following a mishap aboard that injured a foot and caused it to swell, he appeared in formal attire wearing one white slipper. The next evening, a large percentage of males about town did the same. Since taking up residence in the White House, Kilpatrick had dreamed of trying something like that with one of his wife's slippers.

"What are you smiling about?" from Osborne brought Kilpatrick back to the moment.

"Your overcoat."

"What?"

"Never mind. Where have you been?"

"Colorado."

Kilpatrick waited a moment. "You know goddamn well I meant that as a two-part question."

"Yes sir, and the rest is a two-part answer. I wanted to

talk to the new lead investigator and see if I could get that local reporter to understand and appreciate the harmful consequences of driving the media bandwagon. Maybe get him to back off. Give the report time to prove it was an accident."

"From your demeanor, the trip appears to have been less than successful."

Osborne sighed, a sound heavy with fatigue. "It's going to get worse, and it may never get better. That reporter has got his shit together."

"Tanner, if this is nothing more than the same media—"

"No, sir. It's different. And he's in league with the previous lead investigator."

"But they don't have any proof, right?"

"I don't know. Nor do I know if there's a smoking gun. But he seemed confident, like he couldn't wait to haul something out of a hat."

Kilpatrick shook his head. "All reporters want you to think they know more than they do. He was just fishing. Any luck with the lead investigator?"

Osborne hesitated for an instant, like a mental hiccup. "I never got to meet him."

Kilpatrick climbed the gentle slope of an arched bridge that spanned a curving, black ribbon of water flowing toward the ocean. He leaned his forearms on the cap railing and stared into the darkness. As Osborne joined him, shoulder-to-shoulder, Kilpatrick said, "How long have we known each other?"

"I don't often do the math, but my body tells me it's been a long time since high school."

Kilpatrick's mind ran a quick scan of memories, beginning with the first time he had talked with Osborne at a student council meeting, through hours of debate in college over serious issues about careers, entry into political life, helping to save the world from the growing evils of terrorism, and right up to the present moment, a president and his most trusted friend standing on a bridge. "And you've supported me, despite our many differences, through tough times."

Osborne nodded. "From your vision of a superior high school to creating a new America and a safer world, I've always believed in you."

"Then why is it so hard to wrestle your agreement on everything?"

"All great men need challenges from inside the fold. It hardens them for what happens out there." Osborne waved his arm at the black void surrounding them. "The most useful adversity begins at home."

"Maybe, but we've got way too much of the troublesome kind camped in the Rose Garden. I'm hoping you can continue to believe in the basic good of our mission." Kilpatrick turned around. With his back against the railing, he looked to his right and made eye contact with Osborne. "If I get tossed out come next November, everything we've worked for is lost. In spite of your objections to the road we chose, it's time to be aggressively proactive."

Osborne returned Kilpatrick's gaze, then stared into the deepening night, facing a sodden breeze carrying the threat of rain. "I don't like the sound of this."

"I know you don't, but hear me out."

"I always do. It's what you say that gives me ulcers."

Kilpatrick pivoted to face Tanner, a presidential move designed to bring the full force of his persuasive skill to bear. "With Larchmont's flapping gums silenced we don't have to worry about him verifying his part of the story. If his mouth had only come equipped with a zipper . . . but that's history. Hopefully you can put the lid on this investigation, and the sooner the better. That still leaves us with a problem."

"Only one?"

"Okay, the *biggest* one. We can't let this complication deter us from the course we've set, and you're just the man for the job."

"I *really* don't like the sound of this. What job?"

"We've been following Larchmont's blueprint, built on the principles of compartmentalization and containment. The time has come for a change in tactics. I want you to be the commanding general of the new war."

Osborne looked at Kilpatrick as if he couldn't believe what he was hearing. "I can't fill Larchmont's shoes."

"I'm not asking you to. I said *new* war, one that will be fought in the hearts and minds of the American people. The isolationist rabble have been winning because we've been in a hunker-down mode, waiting for the storm to abate. It's time to attack. I want you to come out of the shadows and into the spotlight."

Osborne shook his head. "I'm not the man you want."

"The hell you aren't. Trust me on this. You'll get over being uncomfortable in front of the cameras."

"That's not what I mean. It's . . . it's not . . ." Osborne seemed to leave the bridge for a moment and travel to a personal place. Then he looked at Kilpatrick, but his eyes were still far away. "Do you *ever* doubt that we chose the right course?"

"Never. Those bastards changed the rules. We run a free country, so we let them in and train them to fly big airplanes into buildings? Every bozo knew our airports had Swiss-cheese security. I've never understood why that doesn't make you as mad as it does me."

Osborne took a deep breath and let it out with a long sigh. "Our relative emotional reaction to the horror of terrorism isn't the issue. You know as well as I do there are reasons for these things. What we did—"

"Are you saying—?"

"Let me finish, goddamn it!"

The power of Kilpatrick's office flowed into his clenched fists. He repressed the urge and glowered at Osborne. After a moment, his temper retreated just enough. He nodded.

Osborne continued, "It's easy to define the enemy in terms that justify whatever we do against him. You don't have to ask yourself what you might have done to contribute to his hatred. It's taboo to think about, much less admit, that he might hate us not for what we stand for but for actions we took against his interests and beliefs."

Kilpatrick leaned forward and locked eyes with Osborne. "This gets right to the core, doesn't it? You think that somehow we deserve what has happened."

Osborne returned the glare. "That is fucking bullshit. I'm just asking why anyone thinks we can apply all our enormous clout against the rest of the world and claim we're doing it because it's best for *them*. When you try to reshape the world in your image, there are consequences."

Kilpatrick crossed his arms to keep from pounding sense into Osborne's head. "You helped me plan the campaign, Tanner, including the decision to keep secret our real plan for fighting terror. Even if I agreed with you, I can't rewrite history or redress wrongs of the past. All I can do is go after these sons of bitches with all the power at my disposal. Taking it to them is the only answer. That's what *we* were doing, whether it sits well with you or not."

Osborne stuck his hands in his pockets and shivered. "Would you *ever* acknowledge that the price is too high?"

Osborne's voice had softened. Kilpatrick leaned closer to

press the point home. "No. And you knew it might come down to this. Larchmont was a casualty of war. Call it friendly fire if it makes you feel any better. He knew what he was getting into, and he was a goddamned traitor in my book. Should've kept his mouth shut and let them prove something without throwing chum in the water."

"So it's his fault?"

"And maybe yours. I'm assuming you had no direct involvement in the details, but maybe you did."

"Don't question my methods in supporting what you wanted, or how I tried to clean up your mess."

"My mess?"

"What else would you call it? Or have you forgotten my resistance to using him?"

"I haven't forgotten how you thought the whole plan was crazy, never mind who ran it. You've never acknowledged how wrong you were, and you didn't predict that Larchmont would yank the lid off by becoming personally involved."

"That's old news. The current mess is a result of how quickly you pounced on the option to terminate him and tried to cover it up when a bulldog investigator found evidence that doesn't correlate with an accident."

"How the hell is that *my* mess, Tanner? Getting it done was your job. I didn't suggest leaving evidence at the scene. And for the record, if I'd thought there was any other way to shut that loudmouth up, I would have tried it. Leadership takes bold, decisive actions, and I'd do the same thing again in a heartbeat." Kilpatrick paused, a calculated move to let his friend work it out and come around, as he always did.

Osborne nodded and gazed into the darkness. He buttoned his overcoat, flipped up the collar, dug his gloves out of his pockets, and put them on.

Kilpatrick punched him lightly on the arm, a gesture he used to signal the end of a conversation, decisions made, ready to press ahead. "Now that you have your wardrobe arranged, what's next?"

Osborne drew in a deep breath, held it, and expelled a cloud of condensed vapor, pale white in the dim moonlight. "I'm through, Jack."

"How can you possibly be through? We've still got work to do."

"I can't do this anymore."

"What the hell are you talking about? We're in this together. In spite of our differences, we made America safer, and you're as committed as I am to the final result."

Osborne nodded. "I want the same things you do, but there comes a point at which I can't ignore the cost of getting them."

Kilpatrick rested his forearms on the railing and gazed into the distance. "Okay. Something happened out there. We can work through it, just like we always have."

"You can, but it'll have to be without me."

Kilpatrick bolted upright and pointed a finger at Osborne. "Fine. Quit if you want to, that's always been your prerogative. But before we break up a partnership of over thirty years, you owe me an explanation. You went to Colorado without telling me. What the hell happened?"

Osborne looked down at his shoes and scuffed them on the rough pavement. "I may have unleashed a black apparition into the night who doesn't understand the term 'collateral damage.'"

Kilpatrick laughed. "Is *that* all? Not to worry. Do you have any idea how easy it is to—?"

"Oh yeah. Don't forget I've done this a few times myself."

"Then take care of it."

Osborne shook his head. "You just don't see it. With each one, it becomes easier. Pretty soon it's like snapping your fingers and a man dies. But that's not the problem."

"Wait a minute. You just said—"

"This guy has killed *five* people, Jack, and one of them was the Director of the Aviation Division of the NTSB, for Christ's sake. We can't shove that under the rug."

"The hell we can't. Let's just ride it out."

"It won't work. I can't do any damage control on this."

Kilpatrick raised his arms and waved both his hands. "Okay, okay. Run off and hide with your precious conscience. The rest of us will press on and do what has to be done. I'm sorry to see you go, but we'll manage without you."

"There's something else you need to know."

Kilpatrick glared at Osborne. "I can't wait to hear this."

"There'll be an article. Don't know when, but soon. The world deserves it, and so do we."

The ground under Kilpatrick's feet seemed to tremble, like the pre-shock to an earthquake. "What have you done?"

"Nothing. Yet. But I've looked into the eyes of the future." Tanner began walking down the road deeper into the park.

"Where are you going? The car's this way."

Over his shoulder Osborne said, "I'll walk."

"What's wrong? Afraid to get in a car with my goons?"

"It wouldn't matter what they did. Goodbye."

"Hey, Tanner?"

Osborne turned. "Yes?"

"Remember me asking if you owned a dirk?"

Osborne nodded.

"Tonight you walked on my right side . . . where traitors strike."

Osborne nodded again and marched into the darkness.

CHAPTER TWENTY-EIGHT

Nick laid the last page of Larchmont's written record documenting conspiracy to murder on Hotel's dining room table. He stood and walked into the living room. A blustery north wind howled outside after last night's arrival of a cold front. He stared at the dead fireplace and shivered. Too much caffeine, the elation of success, and too little sleep had put him in a strange mood, tired, agitated, anxious. He looked over his shoulder. "We need a fire."

Hotel was listening to the Larchmont tape. He turned off his mini-cassette recorder and removed the earpieces. "Then build one."

Nick wouldn't admit it to anyone, but he'd never been any good at starting fires without a gas flame. Smug confidence soon replaced the fear of failure as old copies of the *Gazette* and a pyramid of split-pine starters popped and crackled under oak. Admiring the result of his efforts, he sat and watched flames beginning to char the dense logs.

He and Laurie could sit in their family room and enjoy a fire without so much as a spoken word between them because all the significant communication occurred without either of them thinking about it. Being on the same wavelength was so comfortable that he couldn't imagine living without it.

Hopefully, he wouldn't have to.

He'd called home every day since his argument with Laurie. She seemed cool, but at least she never mentioned lawyers. Promise of a late-model Beemer ensured that Brad shed no tears over loss of the Mustang. Nick wished his son had gotten to see the damned thing, but photos would have to do.

Conversations with Stephanie had been the most difficult. Following the home invasion, his ferociously independent daughter had suddenly become eager to have Nick home. Although she remained uncommunicative about any details of that night, Nick had no doubt that Wilson had been the messenger. Without revealing any of his own details, he convinced her that the threat had been taken care of.

Continued presence of Walter Thorpe's cop buddies also helped. According to Laurie, Stephanie had taken an interest in the youngest of the group. Quite a stud, apparently. Nick didn't particularly like that, but he knew better than to say a word to anybody.

He tossed two more chunks of oak on the fire, stood and stretched his back. Wonderful aromas from the kitchen and the occasional clanking of pots and pans augured a fine evening meal. Maudie had taken a rare day off from the diner to prepare something special, her famous Spaghetti Bolognese. Though tinged with bittersweet tragedy, the day deserved a celebration.

"Nice fire."

Nick turned. Maudie stood in the doorway to the kitchen. He shrugged. "Miracles never cease. I usually just fill the house with smoke."

"It always helps to open the flue," said Hotel. "You through looking at the memos?"

"Yes." Nick walked back to the dining room and sat down.

Maudie joined them. "It's time to tell me about it."

Nick and Hotel collaborated to relate the short version. Maudie listened with rapt attention. When Hotel described the final discovery and how it proved sabotage, she nodded and patted the table with both hands. "Sounds to me like you guys have more work to do. What's the plan?"

Nick clipped the memos together. "I'd put four things at the top of the list."

"Great minds think alike," said Hotel. "Get the authorities involved with recovering Nordstrom's body, shut my editor up with an article, figure out how to present the crucial evidence while maintaining control of the datacard, and put that murdering son of a bitch Wilson in the ground."

Nick stared at Hotel. "We'll let the law handle it, right?"

"What are the cops going to find to tie him to anything? All the evidence is compromised."

Against a background of wind and a branch scraping on the metal roof, Maudie said, "That doesn't sound like self-defense to me."

Nick shook his head. "I don't think—"

"It's the only way," said Hotel. "He knows who we are. We fucked him up good. Stole his stuff. He'll be back. I'd rather not wait."

Maudie put her hand on Hotel's. "You can't just haul your past out of storage and start hunting humans again."

Hotel glanced from Nick to Maudie and back again, his eyebrows raised. "What would you two suggest?"

A PEACEFUL SCENE GREETED Wilson as he peered from behind an evergreen. Nice log home, tucked into the edge of dense forest. Smoke rising from the chimney, whisked away in gusts of frigid air. Three people waiting inside: two enemies and the foxy diner owner. The perfect weapon to keep them at bay, nice and docile, until he retrieved his property.

His rented Explorer was parked deep in the forest on an old logging road. He'd stayed in the woods and reconnoitered the homesite and surrounding area. The nearest neighbor lived about a mile away. Earlier that day, he had paid a visit and entered through an unlocked back door, dialed 911, left the handset off the hook, and watched from the forest. Thirty-two minutes later a Sheriff showed up, sans lights and siren. Within another half-hour the owner arrived, an acquaintance, apparently, with all the handshaking and backslapping. Out here in the boonies, security was a joke. The cat probably did it, yuk, yuk. A bunch of idiots.

Wilson glanced at his watch. Three hours to sunset. He'd wait for the ally of darkness unless a better opportunity came along. It usually did. In his line of work, with Joe Citizen as a target, the predator needed only to keep a watchful eye.

HOTEL DIDN'T LIKE PROPOSING vigilante justice any more than Nick and Maudie appeared fond of hearing about it. He also couldn't imagine living the rest of his life wondering when Wilson would pay a visit. The only way to defend against the threat was not to defend at all. Let Wilson do that.

During a period of silence in the heated discussion, Maudie announced that she needed to bake the rolls for dinner and ordered Hotel and Nick into the living room. "Figure this thing out without taking the law into your own hands. There has to be a way."

Fresh logs drew flames from the glowing embers. They sat quietly staring at the fire until Nick said, "The animal part of me agrees with you. So does the practical human part. What

I'm having trouble with is the morality."

Hotel nodded. "Taking a life presents that dilemma for any normal person. The only way to deal with it is through societal justification. War and self-defense are prime examples. I consider our situation as covered by one or both."

"Self-defense I understand. But you're talking about hunting him down. You've obviously been trained to kill, maybe done some of it. That takes something I'm not sure I have."

"Then let me take care of it."

Nick sat up straighter. "I didn't say I couldn't do it."

"Wrong attitude. You need to believe you can. Period."

They sat again in silence. Logs popped, wind howled, and the aroma of baking bread drifted into the room.

WILSON WAITED PATIENTLY FOR the opportunity he knew was coming. Human behavior, so predictable, dominated by habit and repetition, would show the way. Through the kitchen window the woman's face and upper body appeared. Her shoulders and arms moved like a scullery maid's. Washing dishes. After a moment she disappeared from view. A light came on in the utility room.

He dashed across the open space between the woods and the house, drew the knife, and pressed his body against the wall behind a tool shed. A deadbolt snapped. His heart rate accelerated. The door opened. The screen door swung outward, taken by the wind, and banged against the house.

She stepped onto the landing. Holding the door open with one hand, she reached back with the other and hauled out a heavy garbage sack.

Wilson glanced at three trash containers standing on a concrete slab. Perfect.

THE FIRE FLARED AS a gust of cold air rushed past the couch. Hotel sat up in the armchair and looked over his shoulder. "Hey, Maudie?"

No answer.

"Hey, Maudie!"

"What?"

"You got a door open?"

After a moment, Maudie strode into the living room. Hands on her hips, she scowled at Hotel. "You know I don't like to be hollered at."

"Sorry. I felt the cold air. Have you been outside?"

"I'm trying to put out the trash, if you'll let me."

Hotel stood. "I'll do it."

"Sit your ass down, buster. I can handle it." She turned on a heel and walked toward the utility room.

Hotel rolled his eyes at Nick. "She's getting really bossy."

Nick laughed. "They'll do that. Does she have her own keys?"

Hotel stared at Nick. "Of course."

"That's when it really starts. And speaking of keys, I've still got the ones to the airplane we were in last night. I stuck them in my pocket and forgot to put them back in the line shack." He stood and snatched his jacket off the chair.

Hotel shrugged. "It can wait until tomorrow."

"Nah. Better when it's deserted." Toward the kitchen he said, "How soon until we eat?"

Maudie appeared in the doorway and glanced at her watch. "I'm planning an early dinner. Say an hour?"

Nick put on the jacket and zipped it up. "You won't have to wait on me."

DAMN IT! **WILSON HAD** just missed the perfect opportunity when the woman turned, let the screen door close against the garbage bag, and disappeared into the utility room. He considered waiting for her to come back out, but couldn't think of a good reason not to get this over with. As he approached the stairs, advancing footsteps, heavier than those of the woman, stopped him. He backed into the garage, turned the corner, flattened himself against an inside wall and pulled out his pistol.

Somebody came out of the house and clumped down the stairs to the driveway. Wilson aimed the pistol at the garage door opening and at the level of a man's head. The sound of boots on gravel grew softer. After a moment, a car started. He peeked around the garage wall. The investigator's Jeep backed out of the driveway.

Okay, then. One adversary was always better than two. He stepped out from the garage and heard more footsteps. The woman's. Crouched behind the tool shed, he waited.

Once again she emerged, grabbed the top of the sack, easily hefted it over her shoulder—watch out with this one—stepped off the landing and walked to the bear-proof trash container. She opened it, checked one of the cans inside, put the top back on. Opened a second, put the sack down on the ground, leaned over the edge of the container and shoved down hard on the contents.

Wilson slipped his hand into his jacket pocket for the sap. He'd win any struggle without it, but he needed her silent. He glanced toward the door. No threats from behind. Three long strides brought him close, arm cocked. Her head turned toward him just as he thudded the sap against her skull. She went down hard, a rag-doll of arms and legs.

He hauled her into the garage. She moaned. Her arm moved. He cable-tied her wrists in front of her body and unsnapped the shotgun from the sling over his shoulder. He duct-taped the short, double barrels to her neck so the muzzles rested at the base of her skull, and put a strip over her mouth. Kneeling by her side, he whispered in her ear. "Wake up. I need you mobile."

HOTEL PUT THE ENVELOPE with Larchmont's memos, the mini-cassette tape, and the baggie with the datacards into his office safe and spun the dial. As he sat down at his computer to continue drafting the next article, a draft of cold air rustled the papers on his desk. Maudie and doors.

She'd been staying over more often during the past few months, and they both were dealing with the inevitable petty irritations of meshing the lives of two independent adults. Hotel never left doors open. He didn't know why, that's just the way it was. Maudie would go outside and leave a door open for however long it took to come back in the house. Hotel would chide her about it, and she'd respond by telling him to shut up and get used to it.

Another gust of cold air. Hotel went into the kitchen and peered out the window. The trash container was open. A garbage sack lay on the wet ground. The screen door banged against the house as the north wind filled the utility room.

He stepped onto the landing and stared at the scene of a chore interrupted. Frosty, bitter wind enveloped him, nothing compared to the chill flowing outward from his gut.

A shouted, "Maudie!" carried away with the gusts. He called for her repeatedly as he hurried into the open garage. The sight halted him: muddy footprints on concrete led to the rear of the utility room. A thin stream of light spilled from the open door.

He reached for the Glock at his hip and felt nothing but an empty nylon holster. *Goddamn it.* He'd put it on the end table beside the couch so it wouldn't dig into his back while he transcribed Larchmont's recordings. A rookie move, one of the hazards of a ten-year holiday from the business of hunting humans.

His heartbeat accelerated as he rolled the dirt bike out of the way, opened a storage closet and pulled a baseball bat from an equipment bag. He eased the door into the utility room open farther and peered in. Bits of mud on the floor led toward the kitchen. He stepped past the washer and dryer, stopped at the entrance to the kitchen, and peeked around the wall. At the doorway into the dining room, an undulating shadow from the firelight lay across the floor. Someone stood just beyond.

Slowly he stepped into the kitchen far enough to see into the living room. A man dressed head to toe in black clothing stood by the front door. In his left hand he held a shotgun, the barrels taped to the back of Maudie's neck. He was staring toward the fireplace.

Hotel clamped down on the urge to attack. Back away. Get the Glock. He took a step to the rear. The man's head turned.

Hotel froze. The eyes of a predator glared out of the only two holes in the mask. The man, it had to be Wilson, shifted position and pulled Maudie around to face Hotel. Tape covered her mouth. A red welt swelled on her forehead. Tears filled her eyes, glistening with reflected light from the fire. The man's right hand held a pistol.

Wilson's voice reached out to Hotel with palpable malice. "Uh oh. Looks like you brought a bat to a gunfight. How unfortunate."

Hotel gripped the bat so hard his hand hurt. He tried to keep his voice from cracking. "What do you want?"

Wilson chuckled. "I'll give you three guesses."

Hotel took a step forward.

"Oh no no no no. That would not be a smart thing to do."

Hotel again fought down the urge to kill. Hold on and wait for an opportunity. Wilson had to get the evidence before killing him. Nick was due back soon. Professional or not, controlling the actions of three people was tough.

Hotel decided to volley. "Let's make a deal."

"No deals. I want the datacards, the papers, and the audio tape."

"Okay. But she has nothing to do with it."

"Of course she doesn't."

"We can trade."

Wilson laughed. "Or, I can take. Before I do, I'm curious about why you think you have anything to deal with."

"How are you at safe-cracking?"

"Under the circumstances, I'm an expert." Wilson slipped the pistol into a holster strapped to his thigh, pulled a combat knife from a scabbard inside the top of his boot, and laid the gleaming point on Maudie's cheek. "This face won't be so pretty when I get through."

Hotel's knees weakened. He almost fell. "Don't hurt her."

"It's all up to you. Where is this un-crackable safe, anyway?"

CHAPTER TWENTY-NINE

Nick rolled to a stop by the line shack and crawled out of the Jeep. Two airplanes sat in the transient parking area, one a standard single-engine piston four-seater he thought he might have seen before, the other a heavily modified version of Nick's wrecked airplane. He couldn't resist taking a moment to look her over.

The owner had spared no expense: full instrument panel with the latest electronic displays, leather interior, custom paint job with an eagle's head on the cowling, and a turboprop engine conversion, all of which spoke of uncompromising attention to detail and mind-boggling speed. A parachute lay in the front seat, attesting to the owner's frequent participation in aerobatics.

Nick sighed and went into the line shack. Only one ramp attendant was on duty, if you could call it that. He lay sprawled on a tattered couch, mouth open, alert to nothing other than his dreams.

Nick quietly opened the door to the locker and replaced the keys on the hook labeled with the airplane's tail number. On the ramp, he gazed at the sleek little rocket ship and said a silent goodbye to owning and flying his own airplane. When the system got through with him, he'd be lucky to retain even the memory of his pilot's license.

Did I used to be a pilot? Oh, yeah. Before I turned monumentally stupid.

With one more glance in the rearview mirror and a wave, he bid a final adieu to aviation.

WILSON STOOD IN THE doorway of Sweet's home office. The woman trembled, her shudders passing down the barrels of the shotgun to his left hand. In his right he held the pistol on Sweet and watched him open the safe and bring out the manila envelope. "Show me."

Sweet dumped the contents on the floor: the memos, mini-cassette tape, and baggie with the datacards.

Wilson motioned to his small duffel. "Put them in there."

Sweet did that, zipped it closed and held it out.

"Don't be an idiot. Set it on the table and step back."

As Sweet complied, the woman twisted her body, slammed her elbow into Wilson's face. The sudden movement almost yanked his hand off the shotgun as Sweet dove at him, arms outstretched. Two hands closed around his own gripping the shotgun, an antique Sicilian Lupara.

The collision took all three of them to the floor in a tangle of arms and legs. Wilson's fingers lost some control, but he managed to pull both triggers. The hammers snapped down, but the weapon misfired.

Wilson jerked his hand free and dug his fingers into Sweet's eyes.

Sweet ducked.

Wilson smashed the pistol into the woman's face, then shoved the suppressor against the reporter's side and pulled the trigger.

A muffled pop. Sweet's body jerked, went slack.

Wilson cursed, pushed himself away from the two bodies and stood. Sweet lay in a fetal position, groaning. Blood pooled under his body. The hammers of the Lupara dug into his right hand, which insulated them from the firing pins.

Wilson stared at the crumpled form. How about that? A matter of luck? Doubtful. This guy was especially observant and well trained in something other than journalism.

He knelt beside the woman. With his knife he slit the tape and retrieved the shotgun, his special companion over the years. If gunfighters still notched their weapons, it would have more than a few. He looked at Sweet, then the woman, back to Sweet, and considered his options.

His life as Wilson was over, the Florida sanctuary compromised. In spite of all the bullshit of this assignment, he had accepted a contract, and he had everything he needed to collect final payment. The airplane and a new identity gave him the freedom to implement the final stage of his career. Retirement in luxury waited, tempting.

Still, living witnesses were like a cancerous prostate. You could reject surgery, endure radiation therapy, be declared cancer-free, and end up back in the oncologist's office. All you really knew was that if they cut the damned thing out, it could never betray you again.

On the other hand, the best bait was live. Squirming and thrashing, like a worm on a hook. If Phillips saw a chance to save the lives of one or both of his friends, he'd do something really stupid. Probably instinctively. Okay, then. Kill them later.

He stood. Three place settings sat on the dining table. Dinner bubbled on the stove. He glanced at his watch. The investigator might be on his way back.

Wilson holstered the pistol, which he'd abandon along with

the shotgun before crossing international borders, grabbed the duffel and went into the kitchen. He found water in the pantry, stuffed three bottles in the duffel along with a handful of granola bars, and put it in the utility room beside the door. From a laundry basket he took a sheet and draped it over the duffel. It looked like a pile of dirty linens.

He returned to the home office. Avoiding the blood pool, he pulled the woman away from Sweet's inert form. She'd been hit hard twice, but he needed her conscious . . . or maybe not. He played the tape in his mind of what Phillips would see when he walked into the house. After a moment of considering *what if,* he knew it could work.

Prior to his initial move on the house, he'd cut the phone lines. Now he searched every room, found two cell phones and smashed them. In what appeared to be a guest bedroom, he emptied onto the floor the contents of two duffel bags with tags identifying the owner as Nick Phillips. No cell phone. Okay, he probably had it with him. But with unreliable cellular service once he left the main highway on the road to Sweet's house, it wouldn't do him any good.

Wilson found a purse on the kitchen counter and got her keys. He hurried to her truck, started it, turned on the headlights and walked around to check the tires, registration, inspection sticker, turn signals. He pressed on the brake pedal and noted the faint red glow against the wall of the house.

He thought about pointing the truck toward the road. No. Too obvious a change since Phillips left. He killed the engine, released the parking brake, put the headlights on AUTO and pulled the keys partially out of the ignition. With the door open, he searched for the switch and turned off the dome light.

Another truck sat in a carport attached to the garage, which had been converted into a workshop. He walked to the side out of view from the driveway and knelt beside the rear tire. With the point of his knife against the sidewall, he paused. A truck leaning on a flat tire might draw attention. Find the reporter's keys and hide them? No. Take too long. He popped the hood and with his multi-tool removed the positive battery cable.

He closed the hood. A dirt bike sat in the garage, the key in the ignition. He snipped the wire to the coil.

In the front yard, he stared at the house for a moment and noticed the trash bag and the open can. With that taken care of to create an exterior scene of undisturbed domestic tranquility, he went inside and found a cozy closet to wait for the little mouse to find the cheese.

NICK PULLED INTO THE Quik-Stop parking lot and called to see if Maudie needed anything for dinner, but the house phone didn't seem to be working. A call to Hotel's cell phone went directly to voice mail. He didn't have Maudie's cell number, so he gave up on the idea and continued driving.

Ten minutes later he turned off the highway onto the road leading to Hotel's property. He drove about a mile, and without warning his whole body went cold like the inside of the Jeep had just turned into a freezer. He let off the gas and coasted to a stop.

Why didn't I connect the dots?

That first airplane in the transient parking area. He *had* seen it before, in the form of a model on Wilson's desk. Same tail numbers and paint job. Nick pulled off the road, grabbed his cell phone out and called 911—damn it! No service. Turn around? No time. He turned off the ignition, got out, locked the Jeep, and trotted into the woods.

Five minutes later he knelt breathlessly at the edge of the

clearing around Hotel's home. It appeared peaceful, sitting amid long shadows of evergreens blocking the golden rays of a retreating sun. Was there something wrong, or was he being paranoid? After a moment he noticed it.

No smoke drifted up from the chimney. Hotel and Maudie both loved fires, and the day was perfect for one, cold and blustery. They'd tend it if they could. Nick pulled out the Glock and scrambled around to the rear of the house. Deeper shadows covered the open space between the forest and the back wall. He waited for a few moments, saw nothing unusual. They'd probably be laughing about this soon, but he wanted to make absolutely sure. He crouched down and scurried up to the house below a window.

With the top of his head just below the sill, he paused, then took a quick peek into the master bedroom: four-poster bed, neatly made; two bedside tables with lamps; two dressers, a messy man's and a tidy woman's; one large closet, door partially open. No sign of an intruder or a struggle.

He low-crept to the next window, which he figured was Hotel's home office. After another quick peek, he crouched low and breathed deeply to calm his racing heart.

Beside Hotel's computer desk sat a safe, door wide open, papers on the floor and a lockbox turned on its side. A stack of magazines that used to be neatly splayed out on top of a coffee table in front of a couch lay scattered about. Over the top of the table, a rounded object, barely visible in the doorway. Nick couldn't make out what it was.

He resisted the temptation to take another look and crept to the next window, which opened into the hallway with a view into the living room and part of the dining room. He quick-peeked and saw nothing to confirm his fears that Wilson had paid a visit and might still be lurking about.

The solid back and side walls of the carport allowed Nick to stand and work his way to a view into the carport, garage, and along the driveway. Both trucks were where he'd seen them last. With the exception of the dirt bike moved from its usual location and an open door to a locker, nothing appeared disturbed.

He entered the garage and walked toward the door into the utility room. As he passed the dirt bike, he touched the exhaust pipe. Cold. He checked the Glock again and stepped to the utility-room door. With the pistol held close to his body at the waist and pointed at the door, he opened it just enough to see through the utility room into the kitchen.

The faint glow of a digital display on the dryer illuminated the utility room in pale green. A brighter light fell on the kitchen floor. Probably from the stovetop. The aroma of Maudie's Spaghetti Bolognese and fresh bread lingered.

He eased into the utility room and toward the kitchen. A beep sounded, startled him. He glanced at the dryer. The clothes were ready. Hotel had told him Maudie hated wrinkled clothes.

At the door into the kitchen he paused and sniffed. Within the tempting cooking aromas loitered a slight odor, not unpleasant, just . . . something burning? Or close to it?

He peered around the door jamb at the stovetop. A large, covered pot sat over a medium-low flame, the top rattling as the sauce bubbled within. Eyes trained into the dining room, Nick side-stepped to the stovetop, lifted the lid, and glanced inside. The sauce had thickened into a gooey mass turned black around the edges. He turned off the burner and approached the entryway into the dining room.

The wind rattled windows, whistled in the eaves, and shoved branches against the metal roof. Inside, the house was way too quiet. He slipped into the dining room, the Glock held ready. Details jumped out at him: the table set for dinner, a bottle of Chianti in a wicker basket, two candles, cloth napkins rolled and stuffed into holes in intricately carved and painted wooden ducks.

He paused at the entrance to the living room. The fire didn't have one glowing ember. Eyes fixed on the hallway, then the stairs and back in a repeating sequence, he advanced until he could see over a free-standing bookcase between the living room and the hallway.

On the floor, just past the wall dividing the hallway from the staircase, a lower leg and booted foot: one of Maudie's High-Country Hikers, gray with teal and purple accents. The urge to rush forward and the craving for shelter held him motionless. What next, Phillips?

Wilson could have gotten what he came for and crawled off into his black hole. Or he could be waiting for the right moment to strike. Where would the killer hide?

Between Nick and the utility room? No. His back was covered. But to his front, closets, walls, rooms, blind corners, and the whole upstairs waited. Even well-trained professionals didn't advance without backup under these conditions.

Nick stared at the leg and booted foot. If he saw movement, even a twitch, he'd know that exposing himself any more might be worth the risk. But the silent, still atmosphere in the home seemed devoid of life and filled with danger.

Maybe he could retreat and find another way in. Hotel's father had built this log home and included hand- and foot-holds in the exterior walls below all the second-floor windows for escape in the event fire blocked the stairs. The windows were probably locked, but Nick had to try.

He took the first step backward, froze. The forest. Suddenly

Nick's back didn't feel quite so covered. Head moving, he slowly retreated into the dining room, kitchen, and utility room. Approaching the door into the garage, the full effect of his vulnerability hit him. He'd walked into a deadly maze. Wilson could be watching him leave. Crossing thirty yards of open ground between the house and the trees would be suicide. But waiting solved nothing.

Nick crept up to the door. His foot hit something. He looked down. The toe of his boot rested against a pile of dirty linen. He stepped over it, paused, glanced around the utility room. Fresh clothes in the dryer. A hamper filled with folded bed linens sat on top of the washer. Fresh creases lined the top sheet on the pile on the floor.

He knelt and lifted the sheet. An unzipped duffel sat underneath with a SWEETWATER SPRINGS water bottle poking out. One quick glance inside noted a familiar envelope.

WILSON THOUGHT HE HEARD a voice, but it could have been the wind swirling around the chimney. The agitated branch of an overhanging tree scraped against the metal roof. He listened for a moment longer. The wind seemed to become even more furious. It bent more branches, sounded like fingernails on slate. He opened the closet door and stepped into the hallway.

And heard it again—definitely a voice—somebody calling his name. So much for an ambush. With the pistol in one hand and the shotgun in the other, he eased past Sweet, stepped over the woman and looked into the dining room. Nothing. The kitchen and utility room. Empty.

Then he noticed the duffel was missing.

"That goddamned asshole." Wilson had dealt with a whole truckload of bad characters in his life, some of whom had come close to fouling up an assignment, but nothing like this. Phillips was the mother of all bubble gum on his shoe.

"Wilson!" drifted in on a gust through the open door leading to the garage.

No mistaking that. He stepped to the door, pressed his face against the jamb. "I want my stuff!"

From the forest, "If they're still alive, we can trade. If not, you're mine. Take a look at the truck in the driveway."

Wilson crept into the kitchen and peered through the window over the sink. The duffel lay on the hood. He returned to the utility-room door. "How do I know it's in there?"

"How do I know they're alive?"

"You can take my word for it."

"Likewise."

"Looks like a stalemate."

"Not quite. I've got all night."

Enough of this crap! Wilson charged out the door, hit the ground running, and zigzagged into a shoulder roll to the passenger side of the truck. From a kneeling position, he snatched the duffel off the hood.

His stuff was still inside. Phillips really cared about his friends. What a fool. But a lucky one. And still dangerous.

Wilson opened the passenger door and crawled into the woman's truck, head low, lying on the bench seat. He pushed the key in, tried to turn it. Jammed. He yanked the key out, shoved it back in and tried again. No.

Was this the door key? He pulled it out, stared at it.

What an idiot. Cars don't have separate keys anymore.

Then it dawned on him. He thrust the key back in the ignition, leaned across the console, pressed the brake pedal down with his left hand and turned the key with his right. The engine cranked up on the first try. He slammed the pedestal-mounted gearshift into reverse, peered through the rear window and shoved down on the gas pedal with one hand as he steered with the other.

The passenger door swung away from his legs. The cab filled with the roar of an over-speeding engine and the whining of gears.

Something rattled and bumped against his feet.

He glanced inside. The duffel and his pistol lay on the floor under the glove compartment, but the Lupara was gone.

CHAPTER THIRTY

Nick dashed from the woods as Maudie's truck lurched backward toward the road. He dropped to one knee and put the front sight of the Glock on the windshield. Too much distance, but he fired until the slide locked back. He released the magazine, groped for the spare inside his waistband, fumbled it.

Damn it! He snatched it up, rammed it home, released the slide and raised the pistol.

Too late. Wilson was hauling ass down the road toward the highway.

He ran into the house, knelt beside Hotel and Maudie, pressed his fingers to carotid arteries and held his breath.

Yes! He ripped the tape from her mouth, checked her airway and breathing, then Hotel's. *Call for help.*

The phone on the desk had no dial tone. Cell-phone service didn't extend this far into the canyon.

Blood glistened on the floor. Whose?

He probed Maudie's matted hair. Scalp wound but no skull damage. No torso wounds.

Hotel lay in a fetal position. Nick leaned over him. A starburst pattern of powder burns surrounded a hole in his shirt. Close contact gunshot.

Nick looked at Hotel's back. No exit wound. That bullet should have—wait a minute. He pressed Hotel's chest, felt something hard, ripped open the shirt. Blood seeped from a hole in a protective vest. Wilson probably used hollow points. The slug would have expanded and lost energy punching through the vest.

No artery damage, praise be to Kevlar. Pressure. But he couldn't just sit there doing that. Maudie had no obvious signs of spinal injury. He had to take the chance.

With his knife he cut the cable tie binding her wrists. A page with diagrams and the proper steps seemed to float before him, a first-aid hologram from long-ago training: roll her to one side; bend the top leg with both hip and knee at right angles; tilt her head back; keep her warm; monitor her condition.

Strike that last one. From the kitchen he brought two towels, one soaked in tap water. He mopped her face. "Hey, Maudie. It's Nick. Wake up. Hotel needs you."

She moaned. A leg twitched, then an arm. Not good enough.

Never slap an unconscious person. What about shouting? "Maudie!"

Her body jerked, arms flailing.

He wrapped his arms gently around her and continued talking until she seemed to wind down. Confusion and disorientation indicated a mild concussion. He helped her sit up, put the dry towel in her hands and pressed them against Hotel's wound. "You've got to push down while I go for help."

Her eyes shifted from Nick's face to the floor, followed the blood trail, opened wide. She gasped. Her arms went slack.

Nick gripped her hands and reapplied pressure. "He's alive, but you've got to keep pushing. Understand? Push down like this and hold it. Can you do that?"

After a moment, she nodded.

"They'll be here soon." He stood. "Okay?"

Tears filled her eyes, slid down her cheeks. "Nick?"

He knelt beside her. "Maudie, I have to—"

"Don't leave me."

"Wilson's gone. You've got to take care of Hotel. I'll send help as soon as I can."

"Where are you going?"

"Unfinished business."

She stared into Nick's eyes and set her jaw. "Good."

He ran from the house and skidded to a stop in the driveway. His Jeep was too far away. He trotted to Hotel's truck. The keys fell from the visor where he'd seen Hotel put them, but the engine failed to start. He flipped on the headlights. Nothing.

Hotel's motorcycle. Nick scrambled out of the truck and climbed on it. After a minute of furious kicking and not so much as a sputter, he collapsed into the seat. A backpack was strapped to the seat. He glanced inside. Three water bottles, a couple of energy bars, other stuff he couldn't see. He unhooked the pack and ran down the driveway.

About halfway to the road, he jerked to a stop beside a short, double-barreled shotgun lying on the ground. He grabbed it and opened the breech. Two fresh shells rested in the barrels. With a fingertip he eased one out. Twelve gauge double-ought buck. Designed to overkill. Had to be Wilson's. Good. The asshole might want his property back.

And Nick would say, *Here it is . . .*

He snapped it closed, shoved it in the backpack, and began running. Time to ignore pain, suck it up, and do this.

After a few minutes the reality set in. Gasping for breath he slowed to a trot, then a walk, his boots scraping the gravel with each lungful.

But he had to get to the main highway and find some goddamned cell phone service. Call 911 and get a BOLO out. But what if Wilson had another vehicle stashed close by? He'd dump Maudie's truck, and the cops wouldn't know what kind of vehicle to be on the lookout for.

Suck it up and run!

His legs turned to lead before he'd gone a half mile. Between ragged breaths he heard something. A rhythmic thunking. He turned toward the sound. A wisp of smoke drifted skyward from the forest about a hundred yards ahead. He trotted toward it and began yelling when he saw a pickup nosed into the trees. "Hello the truck!"

A man appeared from the forest carrying an axe in both hands, like he was ready to use it.

Nick thought about the shotgun, decided against it. "I'm FBI! I need your help!"

That didn't seem to have much effect. Nick slowed to a walk and tried to smile between each rasping lungful of air.

The man cocked his head. "Did you say FBI?"

Nick stopped outside what he figured was maximum axe range. "Yes, sir. Nathan Porter, Special Agent-in-Charge of the Anti-Terrorism Task Force, attached to the Department of Homeland Security in an undercover capacity. I really need your truck. It's a national emergency."

"No shit."

"None whatsoever."

"And I suppose 'undercover capacity' explains why you didn't show me any ID and you're carrying that sawed-off."

Oops. Forgot that zipper. "You could say that."

"I just did."

"Yes, sir." Nick stood very still. He knew that police officers had this . . . rule . . . or whatever, about getting any closer than

. . . ten feet? . . . to anyone holding a cutting weapon without having the person at gunpoint. He could get the Glock in play way before the shotgun, but—what was he thinking? Shoot a man who's out minding his own business cutting wood? *Get a grip, Phillips.*

Nick held his hands out to his sides, palms up. "Have you been following the Larchmont controversy?"

"Who hasn't?"

"The shotgun in my backpack belongs to the asshole who killed him and four others we know of. I'd like to see that he gets it back."

After a long moment, the man lowered the axe. "You promise to return the truck?"

"Without a scratch."

The man glanced behind him at the dented and rusty pickup. "Got your work cut out for you. Keys are in it."

Nick backed the pickup away from a pile of cut timber alongside a burn pile, pulled up to the man, and extended his arm out the window. "Nick Phillips."

The man shook hands. "That I might believe."

Passing his Jeep sitting by the side of the road, Nick noticed that all four tires were flat. Another Wilson calling card. Nick turned onto the highway in a four-wheel drift with one hand steering and the other punching in 911. The voice was familiar, the same operator who had answered when Nick sent Deputy Thornton to look for Wilson. And to Thornton's death. After she dispatched EMS, Nick asked her to send all available units to the airport.

"It'll be a while, sir. There's a big accident north of town with a tanker truck, a train, and spilled fuel. It's a real mess. By the way. Aren't you the one—?"

No time for this crap. Nick ended the call, stuffed the phone in his jacket pocket, then took it out and turned it off. No GPS tracking today, thank you. Not with what he was planning to do.

Ten minutes later, he rounded the last curve and caught a glimpse of the airport transient parking ramp. Deserted, except for Maudie's truck. He raced through the entrance and braked to a screeching halt by the line shack. Hotel's backpack in hand, he jumped out of the pickup and heard the sound of an engine at takeoff power. He ran to the end of the ramp and looked around a hangar at the runway. Wilson's airplane lifted off and turned to the southeast.

Nick tasted the hatred, like baking powder on his tongue. He ran back to the line shack. The attendant sat on the floor, blood dripping down his face. Nick knelt beside him. "What happened?"

The attendant touched his split upper lip, turned his head and spit blood. "Dude that came in this morning in that blue four-seater wanted keys to that eagle's-head ship. Asked him why he needed two airplanes. He clubbed me with a big-assed pistol. Long-barreled thing. Ugly."

"Did you give—?"

"That little rocket don't need a key. I gave him ones to an old junker. Hasn't turned a wheel in years."

"Where's the experimental?"

The attendant looked at his bloody fingers. "Owner wanted it hangared. I put it in Two." He grinned, winced. "Fooled that fucker with the gun."

"Good for you. Know how much fuel is in it?"

"Haven't a clue."

There'd either be enough, or there wouldn't. "I'm sorry I don't have time to explain, but I'm taking it."

The attendant looked up at Nick, peering through strands

of blond hair. "The hell, you say."

"I'm one of the good guys. Trust me." Nick set the backpack on the floor between them, the twin shotgun barrels peeking out with dead eyes. "Can you get yourself medical attention, or should I call?"

The attendant's eyes flicked down, up. "Have a nice flight."

CHAPTER THIRTY-ONE

Nick felt like he'd paced a trench in the ramp by the time the immense bi-fold hangar door finally opened to reveal the eagle's head, sharp beak, and fierce eye pointed toward the four-bladed prop, ready and waiting to claw some air.

The experimental airplane's relatively light weight maneuvered easily from the hangar onto the ramp with a manual tow bar. He slid the canopy to the rear, locked it half open and climbed in. The front contour seat with a parachute gripped him from thighs to upper back. A four-point shoulder harness cinched down tight around him ensured he'd stay there. The backpack barely fit between his legs in a soft-sided storage pouch.

He donned the headset and studied the cockpit. He'd never flown a turboprop, but this beast had wings like any other airplane. It couldn't be that difficult.

The essentials: battery—on, ignition—armed, fuel pump—normal, prop—forward, throttle—idle, mixture—cutoff, and the avionics master . . . where is it? . . . right there . . . should light up the displays after engine start. Figure the rest out later. Time to rock.

Hit the start button . . . rpm to 15% looks about right,

mixture—ground idle . . . watch the temperature . . . light off—*oh crap! Is it supposed to climb that fast?*

He stared at the gauge. It peaked out with no red lights showing anywhere. Must be okay. What's next? Oh yeah, disengage the starter.

Wow. Smooth engine. Avionics master—on.

Three glass displays lit up the panel, completed their self-tests, and presented a familiar suite of instruments. The fuel gauges both indicated half capacity. It would have to do. He released brakes and eased the throttle forward. The airplane felt like a filly anticipating the starting bell, eager to run and hard to control. Following the yellow stripe out to the runway, he decided the taxiway had plenty of width and length for takeoff. He slid the canopy closed and locked it, reminding himself to be careful of the torque from this big engine.

Control stick held full aft, he inched the throttle forward, added right rudder to keep the nose straight. A *lot* of right rudder. The thrust and acceleration reminded him of a fighter pilot's description of "having your eyelids peeled back."

After rolling about two-hundred feet, she began skipping. He eased the stick forward. The tail wheel lost contact with the asphalt and the mains lifted off. He pulled back on the stick to enter a climb. Gear handle up.

Sweet Mary. The airspeed increased so fast that Nick couldn't read the numerical readout beside the tape.

He pulled back more, lost visual with the horizon under the nose. The vertical speed tape pegged out. He couldn't see the airport or surrounding terrain.

Safe to turn? You betcha. He'd be into orbit soon. Which direction?

He settled on southeast. Maybe Wilson hadn't abandoned his Florida digs yet, figuring that Nick would leave the law out of it. Without the evidence, there'd be no proof of anything illegal. Tie him to a Cedar Valley crime scene? After what Wilson had done with a little datacard? The bastard's DNA had probably been camouflaged.

When high enough to communicate with Denver Center, he glanced at the call-sign placard on the instrument panel, checked in with the controller, and asked if he had radar contact with an airplane off Cedar Valley Airport within the last five to ten minutes.

"November Six Five Echo Delta, Denver Center, that's affirmative."

"Is he in radio contact with you, Denver?"

"No, sir."

"Where is he in relation to me, please?"

"Five Echo Delta, he's in your three o'clock, heading one seven five degrees, twelve miles."

Nick turned south. "Do you have an altitude on him?"

"His transponder is reporting eight thousand two hundred, Five Echo Delta, and climbing."

Okay. Nick took stock: Wilson's using visual flight rules, he hasn't activated a flight plan, he isn't talking to Center, he took off ten minutes ago and hasn't reached his cruise altitude, probably an odd altitude plus five-hundred feet for his direction of flight.

He's not in a hurry and he's not trying to avoid being seen on radar.

Seemed strange for someone running away, unless . . . of course.

More stock-taking: Hotel keeps everything he owns in top condition, especially his transportation. Yet, neither his truck nor cycle would start. Wilson sabotaged both just like your truck. He also knows you owned a piston version of the eagle's-head ship. Hard to fly it without keys.

He thinks you're stranded and he's home free. Bad assumption.

Last problem: How high can Wilson fly? Neither airplane is pressurized. Both are limited to a cruise altitude of 12,500 feet. Unless . . .

Nick glanced around the cockpit. At his elbow beside a green knob, a leather pouch sewn into the sidewall. He yanked open the Velcro closure and peered inside. A cannula for supplying 100% oxygen directly into the nostrils. Nick smiled and offered a mental *thank you* to the builder. The killer had no refuge in the sky today. Time to find the son of a bitch.

"Denver, Five Echo Delta, could you provide assistance for a rendezvous?"

After a pause with no answer, Nick said, "He was supposed to wait for me so we could fly in formation." After another pause, he added, "Together."

"Uh . . . Five Echo Delta . . . how about I give him a call on guard and bring him up this frequency? I'll ask him to turn and expedite the join up."

Bad idea. Aircraft usually monitored the International Air Distress channel. Any pilot within radio range would know what was going on. Including Wilson. Nick declined the offer and asked for his speed differential.

"About a hundred and fifty knots, Five Echo Delta. What kind of airplane are you flying?"

"A fast one." Nick knew Wilson's airplane had a normal cruise speed of about 150, and this little rocket was doing close to 300, which meant about five minutes to merge.

"Five Echo Delta, Denver Center."

"Go ahead."

"I can't put you that close unless he's on the same frequency. I'll also need his concurrence."

"I understand, sir. I'll level off a thousand feet below his altitude and take it from there when I have visual contact."

Another pause. "Take what from there, Five Echo Delta?"

"It's a surprise. Uh . . . I mean . . . not to *you*, sir. To him."

"Copy that, Five November Delta, you *will* maintain one thousand feet vertical separation until visual contact. At that time, radar services will be terminated and you will leave my frequency. Understood?"

The controller obviously didn't want any part of this, which was fine by Nick. "Roger that."

He hadn't reduced the throttle since takeoff. He didn't know the limits on this airplane and engine, but he didn't have to. Green arcs on gauges were good, yellow not so good, red very bad. The only instrument reading near the red was the airspeed indicator. He ignored it. All airplanes were designed with a generous safety factor. The fuel gauges, however, refused to be ignored. It felt as if they had little eye magnets in them, demanding attention to needles approaching one-quarter capacity.

Heading south under a retreating sun, Nick followed minor corrections from the controller and soon noted a tiny speck on the horizon at his twelve o'clock. Wilson had leveled at 11,500 feet. Nick held 1000 feet low, not right for his direction of travel, but Denver Center would keep other aircraft clear. The controller's frequent position reports indicated rapidly decreasing range and confirmed Nick's suspicion that he would soon be climbing up Wilson's ass. *Speed, thou art my savior.*

"Five Echo Delta, Denver Center."

"Go ahead."

"I am directing you to reverse course and return to Cedar Valley. This order comes from the Sheriff's Department. Do you copy?"

Yes, but to hell with that. Nick switched his transponder to standby, which removed any enhancements from his radar return and made his airplane all but invisible to the controller. But Wilson had no idea he was being stalked. He'd left his transponder on, as any pilot normally would even when not in radio contact with Air Traffic Control. They could see him and provide separation from other airplanes on their frequency.

Eyes on the speck, Nick watched it grow into the tail-on view of a low-wing, single-engine piston four-seater.

Gotcha, you bastard. Now what are you going to do?

Nick's question suddenly became his own to answer when the unfamiliar speed differential, combined with the tail-on approach aspect, caught him gloating. Wilson's airplane appeared to balloon in size and fill the windscreen.

He yanked the throttle to idle and snatched back on the stick.

G-loads drove him into the seat. His vision dimmed. He was in a black universe with a million tiny spots dancing before his eyes, spinning, whirling, pretty little things . . . and deadly.

He kept the stick neutral. And waited.

After what felt like an eternity, his vision returned. All he could see was sky. He locked his eyes onto the attitude indicator. All blue. Airspeed, zero. *Power up goddamn it!* He shoved the throttle full forward.

The prop, driven by more horsepower than Nick had ever known, yawed the airplane violently to the left. The nose plunged through the horizon, wings in a ninety-degree bank.

One problem solved, replaced by another.

He snapped the throttle to idle, rolled the wings level, *eased* the stick aft to recover from the dive and slowly added power. His whole body tingled like an extremity waking up.

Sweet ever-loving Jesus.

He searched the sky. Empty. Check heading. Turn south and climb. He leveled at Wilson's last cruise altitude and scanned the horizon.

The next few minutes filled with anxious, futile visual hunting. Too much sky out there. But he couldn't give up. Maybe he could—hold it. Nick glanced into the cockpit. *Is that a . . . ?*

Yes! Embedded among all the goodies the builder had stuffed into the avionics suite was a traffic collision and avoidance system. Nick had never used one and hadn't noticed it.

He found the dimmer switch set for night flight, switched to day mode. The screen brightened. Running the tapes of what he knew about the system as an investigator, he selected ten-mile scope and peered at the display for an indication that it detected a transponder signal in the reception cone.

Nobody home. He turned left forty-five degrees, held that for a moment. Nothing. Right ninety degrees and search. More nothing. He turned back south. No specks or sun glints, just vacant sky. *Son of a bitch. I—*

Hold on a minute. What search is this? Above.

That shifted the cone to look from slightly below Nick's altitude to much higher. Wilson probably wouldn't have climbed. Nick pressed the button that controlled the elevation search and changed it to level.

Bada bing! A target at one o'clock. Was it Wilson? Other than being in the right sector, Nick had no way to tell for sure. *Go find out.*

A thirty-degree right turn put the target at twelve o'clock on the screen. He kept it there with the throttle shoved to the forward stop and scanned the horizon so hard his eyeballs ached.

Then, a sun flash directly ahead. Probably off a window.

Watch out, Phillips. Don't play dummy again.

Eyes locked on the spot, he pulled the throttle back and slowed. The faint silhouette of an airplane in rear profile grew out of the horizon. As the distance closed, he eased to the right to get a good look at the fuselage.

Nick's heart tried to pound its way out of his chest. The paint job and tail number matched the model on Wilson's office desk. Unable to resist the urge to look into the killer's dead eyes, Nick moved farther right and closer for a better view into the cabin.

Wilson's upper body moved rhythmically in time with the snapping fingers of both hands. He must have the autopilot on. Listening to a CD. Enjoying himself.

Nick wanted to reach out and tap the bastard on the shoulder. *Hi there. Remember me?*

Wilson's head jerked around as if he'd heard Nick's taunt. His eyes appeared to widen.

Nick flashed him the one-finger salute.

Wilson snap-rolled his airplane into a ninety-degree bank, turned hard into Nick and filled his windscreen with fuselage, wings, and a flashing propeller arc.

Nick yanked back on the stick.

Wilson's airplane flashed by underneath.

Nick rolled inverted and waited until his prey was at the top of the canopy, then pulled the nose down to point at Wilson's airplane as it plunged for the dirt. With the throttle shoved forward, Nick locked his eyes on his target.

Try all that shit you want, fella. You're mine.

CHAPTER THIRTY-TWO

Wilson kept the nose pointed in a steep dive, throttle at idle to avoid exceeding max airspeed. He was shock-cooling the engine, but he had no choice.

That lucky-ass-NTSB pit bull had avoided death at the bottom of a mineshaft by having a reporter-sniper checking his six. Lied his way into Wilson's house. Stole his stuff. Escaped his trap. And here he was, dogging him like a goddamned gnat.

Nose forty degrees low, in a shallow turn, Wilson peered over his shoulder. He couldn't see worth a damn behind him. Might as well quit trying—

Nothing but green rushing up, the windscreen filled with it. His sphincter felt like going on holiday. He closed his eyes and pulled, expecting the end.

One second. Two seconds. Reprieve? He forced his eyelids open. Trees rushing by looked like they were tickling the exhaust stack. Throttle shoved full forward, he fixed his eyes on the horizon directly in front of the airplane. Another ten minutes, he'd be joined with the darkness and home free.

Tree-Top Airways, here I come.

NICK SHOOK HIS HEAD. Wilson was proving to be either a damn

good pilot or one committed to using all of his allotted nine lives in one day. To maintain visual contact and keep from hitting the trees, Nick settled into a "shadow" position, high and slightly offset from Wilson's six o'clock. In the civilian world, rearward visibility seldom crossed the designers' minds. Not being able to keep track of Nick was probably driving the killer crazy. Good.

Down "in the weeds" with the low sun angle, especially in this rugged terrain of ridges and canyons among the lengthening shadows, Nick's speed advantage was becoming irrelevant. When he finally lost sight of Wilson, that would be the end of it . . . unless his engine flamed out first. Fuel starvation threatened to turn his sexy little ride into a glider.

Pilots who survived aviation nightmares often referred to the slow-motion effect. Nick had read accounts, and a calmness settled on him as he experienced one of his own.

Crisp sensations: the smell of the leather interior combined with the inevitable tinge of petroleum, the persistent feeling that the fuel gauges had hijacked his eyes, the smooth whine of the engine through the noise-attenuating headset, the rushing slipstream over the canopy, the comfort of the steed beneath him, fitting like a favorite pair of jeans, part of him, and each gentle caress of the flight controls instantly reflected in the ship's response. The world's finest video game.

If he didn't do something, Wilson would disappear with the only physical evidence proving sabotage. Nick could scream his heart out and no one would listen. The egregious abuse of power, conspiracy to murder, and cover-up would go unpunished.

Then, as Wilson climbed to cross a tree-shrouded ridge, Nick's attention shifted when the retreating sun bathed the only answer in burnt orange: the four-bladed circular saw hauling him through the air.

It all came down to this. He could remain helpless and impotent, let evil win, or smash it into the dirt where it belonged. The parachute on his back gave him better than a suicidal chance.

Wilson had turned off his position lights and anti-collision beacon. His airplane's outline against the shadowed terrain had dimmed to almost nothing.

With only minutes to spare, the calm of the past became the tranquility of the present as Nick pulled the backpack out of the storage pouch, wrapped one of the straps through those of the parachute, and cinched it down. He rolled into a steep bank, let the nose fall to point at his target, and adjusted the power to close the distance.

Level with Wilson at his six o'clock, Nick reduced his range until Wilson's tail section filled the propeller arc. The vertical and horizontal tails and the elevator appeared close enough to touch. He ducked his head and shoved the power up.

His world came apart: hard jolts, shudders, the screech of metal on metal, thunks against the airframe. The airplane rolled violently left and put him on his back.

Elevator work? *Push the stick forward and climb.*

Ailerons work? *Level the wings.*

Through the top of the canopy, he saw Wilson's airplane below him plunge nose first into the trees. It had no tail.

Most of Nick's prop was gone. The engine over-speeded, but some thrust remained.

Keep the nose up and trade airspeed for altitude.

At the split second he lost pitch control and the nose fell toward the horizon, he eased the stick back to neutral elevator and added aileron to roll upright. The engine was trying to shake itself loose from the mounts. He snapped the throttle back, feathered the prop to reduce any remaining drag, killed the fuel and ignition. The airplane approached stall and shuddered. He eased forward on the stick to maintain glide speed and searched for a place to put her down.

There's a bare spot. Too small. That one? No. He banked into a gentle turn to check behind him. Nothing better. What about in the trees? If he could take most of the impact in the wings and keep the fuselage intact, he had a chance.

One spiraling turn answered the question: too rugged.

He yanked the canopy lever to OPEN. The slipstream took it. Windblast ripped off his headset. Cold air watered his eyes. He couldn't see anything. He lowered his head below the windscreen and glanced down at the four-point harness release in his lap. The backpack blocked his view.

He released the stick, pulled the backpack up with one hand and felt for the release with the other. The airplane rolled to the right. The nose dropped. Unforgiving earth rushed up. He punched at his lap belt with the fury born of a last-ditch effort. The buckle released and he floated free.

He fumbled for the ripcord, pulled it with all his strength.

The parachute straps dug into his crotch and thighs and hauled him upright.

With a carpet of trees below and no time to steer the chute, he clamped his legs together, crossed his arms, ducked his head and closed his eyes.

Branches tugged and ripped at his body, clawed his face. He jerked to a stop, swaying in the harness. Silence.

He opened his eyes, tested his arms and legs, surprised they still worked. Below, the lower branches of an evergreen swayed in the wind, about ten feet above the rocks and dirt of terra firma. He took a few deep breaths of the sweetest air he had ever tasted.

"Thank you, patron saint of aviators, whoever you are."

WILSON WOKE UP HANGING from the seatbelt and shoulder harness. He peered out the windscreen and side window. His airplane was suspended vertically in the trees, nose down. The fuselage remained intact, the wings sheared off.

Blood dripped from his forehead into a puddle on the glare shield and instrument panel. He probed the wound with his fingers. Shallow. Take care of it later. He flipped off the master switch and fuel selector, looked about him, planned his exit.

Knees against his chest, he rested them on the instrument panel and supported his body with one hand. A hard pull on the lap belt released it and the shoulder harness. He rotated toward the door on the copilot's side, turned both latches, shoved. Jammed.

He raised his good leg. Pain filled his bad knee. He'd probably always walk witha limp. That goddamned Phillips, lying helpless by the mineshaft, had lashed out like a dying animal with one last act of defiance and maimed him for life.

Wilson kicked the door until it popped open. The duffel from Sweet's house lay on the copilot's rudder pedals where it had fallen from the seat. He shoved it out of the airplane. It fell to the ground with a swish of nylon on pine needles. He squeezed through the door and climbed down.

Unsteady legs quivered under him. His stomach churned. He bent over and vomited. Dry heaves racked his body. He pulled one of the water bottles from the duffel, rinsed out his mouth, chugged the bottle dry and looked up at the airplane.

The tail section was almost completely gone. Corkscrew slices along the fuselage extended about halfway to the passenger compartment.

Holy motherfucking shit. Phillips had rammed him.

Wilson had faced some seriously bad boys during years of dealing out violence, but nothing like this. How do you fight crazy? He didn't know, and he didn't want to try. Would he have to?

The forest reduced his world to a circle of no more than fifty yards in diameter. He scanned the dark trees for another crash site, hoping for the flickering glow of a nice fire. Lead him to a barbeque pit filled with charred Phillips. No such luck. Maybe Phillips hadn't crashed—wait a minute.

A column of smoke, invisible against the shadowed background, had just risen above the ridge and caught the last few rays of sun. How far away? Wilson stared at it, trying to determine the color. Black meant a petroleum fire. He couldn't tell for sure. Best to assume the worst: Phillips had survived the collision and didn't know the meaning of the word "quit."

Wilson pulled out the pistol, removed the suppressor, checked the magazine and chamber, and slipped the weapon inside his waistband. With his arms through the straps of the duffel, he limped down the slope. A reminder of his hatred punctuated every other step.

NICK'S HEART POUNDED. Gulping air helped calm him. He unbuckled the parachute harness, let the backpack fall, and used a branch to pull himself closer to the trunk. Hanging onto limbs, he slipped out of the harness, lowered himself to the forest floor and looked around him.

The tree-covered rise where Wilson's airplane had crashed poked into the horizon. Nick couldn't tell how far away it was, but it didn't matter. He would get there and find Wilson in pieces or on the run. Either way, the son of a bitch was his.

A column of black smoke rose above the trees nearby. Nick saluted the final resting place of the little rocket, pulled the Glock out of his backpack, slipped his arms through the straps and jogged toward a final confrontation with evil personified.

After about twenty minutes of breathless effort, the wreckage appeared through the trees. He trained his pistol on the open door and darted from one tree to the next until he could see inside.

No Wilson but lots of blood. He couldn't be hurt bad if he had climbed out of there. Scalp wound, maybe. That asshole had way too many lives. He could be hiding, watching, waiting. Nick knelt beside a tree and thought about that.

The killer's escape plan had to provide for contingencies . . . lots of them . . . except maybe for getting the tail of his airplane chewed off. He'd lost his ride, needed another. A recent bullet wound, a bad knee, and now a bleeding crash injury, combined with rugged terrain, limited his options to the path of least resistance. Which meant following the canyon down. Any way to confirm that?

Nick found a flashlight in the backpack. It had a rubber shield around a removable red lens, just like the one he carried in the airplane. Better for preserving night vision. He crouched low to the ground, found a puddle of vomit, drops of blood, black in the red light, and an empty water bottle with a SWEETWATER SPRINGS label. He stuffed it in the backpack. No need to leave a signpost to Hotel's hunting cabin.

In an outside pocket of the backpack Nick found a compass. Woodsy Hotel to the rescue again. Nick put his back to the wreckage, took a bearing on the blood trail and advanced into the forest. More blood drops, still moist, soon confirmed Wilson's most likely escape route.

Escape, my ass. I'm coming for you . . .

WILSON HAD NEVER SPENT a single moment running for his life, but this seemed like the perfect time to start. After a quarter-hour of stumbling down the canyon, he stopped to catch his breath and looked behind him. He'd seen no sign of Phillips, but—what's that? A flash of red light blinked through the trees.

A laser sighting device? Goddamn it.

He turned and shuffle-ran, scrambling over rocks, dead limbs, his knee screaming at him. After a few minutes, the terrain began to close around him as the canyon narrowed. A dead end? Moonlight cast enough shadows to pick out variations in the ground and backlight the ridges on either side. The knee felt better going uphill. High ground had the defensive tactical advantage if it came to that. Start climbing.

Fifteen minutes of scrambling up the rocky incline gained the crest. Below him stretched a wider canyon. Breathing deeply, he scanned the terrain and in the distance spotted a small opening in the forest with a faint light and plume of smoke rising above the tree tops. Behind him, no sign of pursuit. Easy decision. He lined up the smoke with a distinctive rock formation on the far slope and set out to see what might be down there to help him shed the attentions of an accident investigator turned man hunter.

TIME HAD BECOME MEANINGLESS for Nick, along with direction, purpose, and very nearly the will to proceed. With no other reason than refusing to give up, he pressed ahead until the terrain became too rough as the canyon narrowed.

Wilson probably wouldn't try to bushwhack through this. To the left, a steep ascent to a high ridge. Nick chose the gentler slope to the right and climbed to the top. Gasping for breath, he stared at the forest-covered valley below him.

People tend to settle near roads and reliable flowing water. That meant closer to the valley floor. Nick scanned the basin. After a moment, he spotted a thin column of smoke, bathed in moonlight, silvery against the darker trees. If he were Wilson, that's damn sure where he'd go. Then, against the background of wind in the branches, he heard two distant, quick pops, followed by a third. A pistol? Sure sounded like it. And where there's gunfire . . .

Nick took a compass bearing on the smoke and scrambled down the slope as fast as he dared. After a rough ten minutes, a flicker of light appeared in the trees. He paused to catch his breath, then crept closer until the forest opened up to reveal the vague outlines of a cabin. Soon a broad clearing came into view. A rectangle of yellow light from a window angled onto a wood porch. Behind the cabin, a lean-to sat within a corral framed by cedar posts. A mule stood as still as a sculpture. Hogs lay in another fenced rectangle, and beside that, a chicken coop.

Walking up unannounced seemed like the worst choice. This might no longer be the Wild West, but what if the occupants didn't know that? He cupped his hands around his mouth. "Hello the cabin!" After a moment, he repeated the call, then twice more. He was about to give up and approach when a twig snapped behind him.

Nick stood motionless. "Hello?"

"You said that already." From behind him, the voice rumbled like a locomotive.

Nick began to turn around.

"Uh-uh, partner. You just keep looking at that cabin. What's that in your hand?"

"A shotgun."

"Drop it and take a couple steps forward."

Nick did as told. "I'm not here to cause any trouble. I just—"

"Doesn't matter why you're here, son. There won't be any more trouble unless I start it. You hold still. I mean it."

Nick waited, curious why the man said *more* trouble. In spite of the cold air, trickles of sweat crept down his sides. Footsteps on dry leaves and twigs approached from behind. Silence, then a distinctive snick of the Lupara's breech opening. After a pause, "Real slow, walk on ahead to that porch."

"Uh, mister? I've got a pistol. I don't want you thinking I was hiding it from you."

"Where?"

"In my waistband."

Nick followed instructions to remove the weapon, drop it on the ground, and take another two steps forward.

"What other weapons are you hiding on that skinny body?"

"Other than a lock-blade pocket knife, none."

"You sure?"

"I've got no reason to lie."

"We'll see about that. Watch yourself on those steps. The second one's a bit loose."

Nick entered the cabin. The single room was clean and neat, with shelves for canned goods, dishes, utensils and large canisters for bulk flour, sugar, salt, and cornmeal; a wood-burning cook stove with split firewood stacked on each side; a fold-down cot; a writing desk with an oil lamp, chair, and bookshelves; a wardrobe; and in the center, a picnic-style table with attached benches.

The man limped past him. "Welcome to my home, sweet home. Have a seat."

Suddenly tired to his bones, Nick plopped down on a bench, wanting nothing more than for this all to be done.

The man lowered the cot and placed the shotgun and Nick's pistol on a green Army blanket stretched tight over a thin mattress. He turned around.

Nick stared at a pummeled face. Blood stained the man's shirtfront. A strip of cloth encircled his right thigh. Blood had seeped through and left a glistening trail down his leg. The butt and receiver of a Colt .45 single-action revolver protruded from his waistband.

The man crossed his arms and locked eyes with Nick. "I live out here by myself because that's the way I like it. One of the reasons I like it is because I never get visitors. And in less than thirty minutes, two strangers show up. Based on how that first asshole looked and how he greeted me, I'm guessing I don't need to put you at gunpoint any more than I already have."

"Your presumption is correct. I don't mean to be rude, but I'm in a hurry."

"To do what?"

"Settle a score."

The man nodded, touched his swollen, bloody lips. "Maybe I can help with that."

CHAPTER THIRTY-THREE

Wilson had never spent enough time around horses to form an opinion about them one way or the other. But in the last hour, he'd accumulated all the reasons he needed to despise the miserable creatures.

This beast must have been trained specifically to frustrate him. Or maybe that mountain man had whispered something while putting on the bridle. Told the beast to go left when Wilson wanted to go right. Or to stop every couple of minutes, jerk the reins out of Wilson's hands, and chomp something growing beside the path. What a pain in the ass. Literally.

During his mount's current rest stop, Wilson unzipped the duffel and pulled out the quadrangle map from the cabin. He shined his flashlight on the route drawn in black marker across the contours of a canyon.

"Don't worry," the man had said. "It only looks like a dead end. I know these mountains. You can cross the ridge right here, bushwhack across this draw, and follow this stream into the valley."

Wilson had thought about ignoring the instructions. But he had to go somewhere, if for no other reason than to put some distance between him and that wily mountain man. Must have had that big cowboy .45 stashed in the hay shed.

With the horse between them, the old fart had snatched it up and taken off. Running. Wilson would have never guessed the guy could move that fast. Hopefully, Wilson's third shot had hit him. Slowed the bastard up.

He put away the map. "Okay, Seabiscuit, or whatever your name is, giddyfuckingup!" He jammed his heels into the horse's flanks.

The world turned upside down. He landed on his side, pain shooting through him like electricity.

Goddamn it. Something's broken.

He moved, felt a grinding in his bad leg. The other seemed to be okay. He crawled to the nearest tree and pulled himself erect.

The horse had disappeared. Traitor.

Oh crap. The duffel. If that nag took it—is that it?

He pulled out the flashlight and focused the beam on a dark shape on the forest floor.

Maybe there was a god. Wilson hobbled over, picked it up, slipped his arms through the straps.

Okay. If he had to crawl all the way to civilization, that's what he'd do. But after a few excruciating minutes, he stopped and leaned against a tree. He'd never make it without a crutch or a splint. With the flashlight he searched the ground and found a likely branch. He whittled away the smaller limbs with his knife and tried it for a few steps. Then he cut it to length and duct-taped it to his leg.

He'd limped a few hundred yards when something snapped behind him. He turned.

The silhouette of a man, barely visible against the black forest, stood on a boulder with something in both hands.

That fucking Phillips. Wilson reached for his pistol.

A brilliant flash of light and sledgehammer blow to the

chest. He blinked, tried to raise his head. He sensed a presence above him and blinked again.

Phillips straddled him, looking down. Breath flowed in misty vapor from his mouth and rose around the outline of his head.

Wilson coughed up a gob of blood. "How'd you find me?"

Phillips dropped a pistol from his right hand. It hit the ground with a metallic thunk. He put the stock of the Lupara between his body and right forearm, cocked the hammers, each with an ominous click, brought the wicked little Sicilian shotgun up and rested his cheek on the stock.

Just below the two dark muzzles, night vision binoculars hung on a strap around his neck, silent answer to Wilson's question.

He coughed again, spewed blood. "Thanks for bringing my shotgun."

"Don't mention it."

He laughed through the coppery foam in his throat. "What's next, you son of a bitch?"

"Give me a reason."

"Gladly." Wilson raised the pistol.

FAINT LIGHT IN THE eastern sky proclaimed the end of the longest night of Nick's life. Shivering, his body aching, his mind numb, he stood and tucked his hands into his armpits.

As darkness retreated, details of the surrounding forest emerged in shades of black and gray. Wilson's inert form lay in a depression within a circle of boulders, silent testament to the final act of the Larchmont saga.

After so many hours filled with unwavering purpose and immediate goals, a strange emptiness settled over Nick.

Exhaustion left him without motivation. But he couldn't ignore the unforgiving reality that confronted him like a persistent, nagging pressure on his brain.

Standing immobile in the near silence, with the whish of wind in the evergreens and the chirping of birds greeting the dawn, he closed his eyes, let his mind run the instant replay of tragedy and death at the hands of a stone-cold killer.

It was like a DVD with alternate endings. The only constant: he had taken the law into his own hands. No one else need be implicated. How best could he alone finish it? Could he find something decent among all the filth of Wilson and his handlers?

Nick stared at the corpse of a man who didn't exist. When Wilson had donned that black combat clothing and entered the sewer of his professional life, he became something non-human. An anonymous creature of the darkness. There he died. And there he would remain, a fitting end to his time on this earth.

Nick put on the backpack, picked up the duffel, and backtracked his route from the cabin. He stopped at the edge of the clearing. A horse had joined the mule in the corral.

Rather than hailing the owner, Nick stood quietly. After a few moments, footsteps approached from the forest behind him. Nick stared straight ahead.

The owner hobbled past. "Hungry?"

After a silent breakfast of coffee, eggs, flapjacks and bacon, Nick sat across from the man at the table and stirred his coffee. He drank it black, but the simple act gave him something to do. It also helped avoid the man's gaze. It seemed to bore into him, probing below the surface, mining for secrets.

Nick fiddled with his spoon some more, finally gave up. "You probably have some questions."

"I won't ask them. None of my concern. Just like me living out here is none of yours."

"Works for me. I need another favor."

"Figured as much."

"How about me using that horse? Or the mule?"

"For riding or packing?"

Nick thought about his answer. He didn't believe the man would take advantage of anything he knew about what had occurred, but why reveal any more than necessary?

Before he could reply, the man snatched both coffee cups off the table and carried them to the sink. "Let's get you fixed up."

Ten minutes later, the man handed Nick a halter with the mule on the other end. "Know where you're going?"

Nick scuffed his boots in the dirt. "Any abandoned mineshafts around?"

"What the hell you think I've been doing up here all these years?" He reached out and touched the bloody front of Nick's jacket, then looked him straight in the eyes. "How deep you need?"

"Halfway to China would be good."

"Wait here." The man went into the cabin and returned a few minutes later with a hand-drawn map. He explained the route and cautioned Nick about a couple of washouts in the trail. "Better get moving. You don't want to be up there in the dark."

Nick slipped the map in his jacket pocket. "I'll keep you out of this as best I can."

The man's brow furrowed. "Out of what?"

NICK WAS NO MULE skinner, but he managed to approach the

boulder-strewn clearing with the animal under control. He half expected to find Wilson's body missing, off on some new assignment dishing out mayhem and murder.

The mule turned skittish, hard to handle. Nick heard them. Coyotes? Or maybe wolves? Sightings were up in many western states. But a pack? He hung on to the halter with all his strength and tied it to a tree. Heart pounding, he trotted toward the snarling sounds of fierce competition.

The first glimpse stopped him in his tracks. A gray wolf stood between two trees, staring in his direction. In the background, movement, glimpses of legs and tails. Not a casual wildlife gathering.

He had no idea whether a pack would attack a lone human, and he didn't want to find out. Three shots in the air from the Glock scattered them. He ran back to the mule and led it to Wilson's body without losing his grip.

The wolves had not been kind.

For a moment, Nick considered walking away. Nature would clean up the mess within a few days. Rugged terrain, miles from the crash sites, what's the chance of anyone finding the remains?

But somehow that seemed . . . *too* vicious. Killing this asshole had been hard enough to deal with. Letting wolves reduce a human being, even one so despicable as Wilson, to a scattering of bones and excrement in a Colorado forest stepped past a self-imposed limit beyond which Nick was not prepared to go.

He used his jacket to blindfold the mule and spent a half-hour maneuvering Wilson's body onto the pack frame and lashing it down. With the map and Hotel's compass, he picked out landmarks, found a narrow pack trail, and followed it into a rugged area of steep canyons and rushing streams.

His destination: a mine abandoned years before, but which had produced enough gold dust and tiny nuggets from the tailings to support a simple life off the grid in the wilderness for many years. Played completely out, it sat forgotten by all but one man, and now two, both of whom wished it to remain so forever.

Leading the mule up a narrow defile, Nick turned a corner and reached a dead end. The scene was a snapshot of mining history, frozen in time. Men tougher than the granite cliffs had carved a flat space from the mountainside large enough to support the heavy equipment they needed. Three horizontal shafts extended into the mountain. The miner had recommended the center one. Nick dropped the halter, walked to the entrance, and peered inside.

Pitch-black darkness triggered a frightful memory, of being hauled to the edge of a shadowy hole to face his own death at the hands of the man draped over the mule not twenty feet away.

Nick stepped back and breathed deeply to settle his nerves. With his flashlight he entered the cavern and made his way toward the first vertical shaft.

Inching closer, he fought the panic he'd never understood enough to conquer: the urge to jump, to surrender himself to the gravity he defied in airplanes.

An eternity passed. Gray dirt became a black void a foot from his boot. The depths swallowed the flashlight beam, mocked it for the insignificant probe it was.

What kind of man would go down there by choice?

Nick shuddered. Time to end this.

He returned to the mule, unstrapped Wilson's body from the pack frame and lowered it to the ground. With his flashlight stuck into his belt at his side and pointed behind him, he dragged the killer by the arms into the tunnel following a jittery circle of yellow light. When the shaft came into view, he very slowly rolled the body to the brink of eternal darkness.

After a moment of reflection, his thoughts and emotions an untidy heap of life's experience, he nodded to himself, put his hiking boot against Wilson's back, and shoved.

CHAPTER THIRTY-FOUR

Nick took a taxi from the airport to a neighborhood park near his home and directed the cabbie to stop by the children's playground. A cold, late-afternoon drizzle, turned dirty white in the glow of a streetlight overhead, coated the equipment in a glistening sheen.

The cabbie unloaded his bags, thanked Nick for the tip, and paused at the driver's door. "You don't appear to be homeless."

"Excuse me?"

"Hop in. I'll put you on your doorstep. No extra charge."

Nick made eye contact. "Thanks, but I need some time right here. It's not far."

The cabbie nodded and smiled. "Good luck with your homecoming."

Nick carried his bags to a bench and sat down. Jacket collar pulled close around his ears, he stared into the deserted park. The earthy smell of damp vegetation rose from the soaked ground and brought back memories of countless, precious hours with his kids. Being a dad. The laughter. The inevitable tears from a bump or scrape, quickly dried with a kiss and a diversion in the form of a new activity. He thought of the saying: It's a good thing kids are built low to the ground and bounce so well.

Ah, yes. Another consequence of growing up. You have to lift yourself up and find your own Band-Aids. Nick leaned back, crossed his legs, closed his eyes and took a deep breath of home. As if on cue, his mind began the replay of an investigation gone haywire and its aftermath.

Hotel had survived a gunshot wound, thanks to a protective vest, Maudie's first aid, and prompt EMS response. Other than bruises and lingering nightmares, Maudie came through the ordeal unharmed. Nick spent the better part of a day recounting to the authorities the events of the past three weeks. He held nothing back except the truth of what occurred in the woods that terrible night.

The mid-air collision occurred "accidentally" when Wilson turned hard into Nick to force him off his tail. The cockpit was empty when Nick got to the wreckage, and he found no sign of Wilson. Another professional criminal slipped the noose. Happened all the time.

Once the altered story had been told, the legal system responded. Hotel's actions in saving Nick's life were considered to be a case of justifiable defense of a third party. The consequences of failure to promptly report the murder of Lars Nordstrom, Nick's removal of evidence from the GoldenJet wreckage, and the unlawful commandeering of a private airplane remained unresolved. For the time being. He fully expected fallout of the nuclear variety before it was all over.

When asked why he didn't shadow the airplane and stay in contact with Air Traffic Control, Nick reminded them that he had been ordered to return to Cedar Valley and land.

"Why didn't you explain to the controller what you were trying to do and why?"

"I would have, but I lost contact with Denver Center when my radio quit."

The NTSB, working under FBI direction, couldn't verify or dispute Nick's version of events because the stolen airplane burned on impact. According to rumor, they didn't try very hard.

Regardless of the final legal outcome, Nick's career had suffered a fatal blow. The NTSB wouldn't ask him to stay, and he had his own reasons for calling it quits. The FAA had seized his pilot's license. Although regulations didn't address the legality of removing a suspected GPS database and using it to fly into a mountain, the catch-all "gotcha" of "unsafe operation" applied well enough. In addition, law enforcement can commandeer transportation in hot pursuit of a suspect. NTSB investigators cannot.

As for the question of conspiracy, Nick handed the reins to Hotel, newly famous reporter for the *Cedar Valley Gazette*. From his recovery room, Hotel wrote a series of articles in the glow of the national spotlight.

Tanner Osborne denied knowledge of government complicity in running a secret war on terror and accused the media of a slander campaign to sabotage the President's reelection campaign. He challenged anyone to produce a shred of proof connecting him to the death of Larchmont.

Following disclosure of evidence to the contrary in the form of a navigation datacard, memos, and an audio tape, Osborne was still protesting his innocence the evening before the morning his wife found him in his study. A bullet to the brain from his father's Colt .45, quickly ruled a suicide, rid him forever of the embarrassment and shame of taking matters into his own hands in a misguided attempt to protect the President.

Fighting for his political life, John Kilpatrick publicly mourned the loss of his best friend and advisor and put his case directly to the American people. He disavowed all knowledge of shadow armies stalking terrorists in violation of US and international law. But he praised the results, claiming admiration for warriors of freedom and democracy no matter where they might be found, and irrespective of their harsh methods. "We owe them our thanks and best wishes for success in eradicating the most abhorrent blight the world community has ever experienced. I wish I'd had the guts to do it."

Specialized spelunkers, for whom descent hundreds of feet into the cold, damp murk of an abandoned Colorado mineshaft held no terrors, recovered the body of Lars Nordstrom.

Nick kept silent about one other detail. He had anonymous access to $15 million in US funds. Blood tainted the bills, but he couldn't do anything about it. Wilson had no past, no trail leading to his previous employers, no family to discover. He was the ultimate missing person, a testament to his professional skill at staying in the shadows.

One decision didn't take much thought and brought Nick immense pleasure. He contacted the president of the bank Wilson used in Florida, opened an account, and deposited a substantial amount in the name of Dorothy Frazier. The donor was to remain anonymous.

He took similar steps for the families of Larry, the NTSB security guard, mechanic P. J. Knowles, and Deputy Sheriff Barry Thornton. Lars Nordstrom's wife was wealthy enough and appeared to be enjoying the role of widow. Through these actions, the satisfying glow of poetic justice illuminated Nick's way. Innocent lives shattered by the arrogance of power implemented by inhuman machines like Wilson deserved some compensation. Not as a replacement for loved ones, but to provide a ray of sunshine on the horizon of life.

While making financial arrangements for the victims, Nick agonized over what he should do with the bulk of Wilson's ill-gotten fortune. For the present, his only decision remained in the negative: not a dime would make it into the hands of a government he could no longer trust as being run by honorable men. Who knew what and when did they know it would never be answered, but the fact that it could happen justified keeping this final secret to himself.

Of all the consequences Nick faced, only one had arrived with nightmares. How do you face a pilot whose airplane you destroyed, never mind the reasons? He dreaded the encounter, fully expecting to be pounded senseless. They agreed to meet at Maudie's Diner. Nick picked the booth farthest from the entrance. He'd drunk so much coffee that his hands were trembling when a man came in. The call letters N65ED were embroidered on his baseball cap.

Nick stood on unsteady legs. Maudie, her face still marred with purple and black bruises, turned from the griddle and without a word pointed toward Nick. The pilot marched up and stopped. Nick introduced himself but didn't offer his hand, worried the guy might rip his arm off.

After an awkward moment of silence, the man said, "Don't I deserve a handshake?"

"I figured I didn't."

"Bullshit." The man gripped Nick's hand, pulled him close, and whispered, "I spent twenty years in military fighters, two combat tours, and what you did amazes me. Did that sumbitch really get what he deserved?"

Nick fought back a smile, or any indication that he was answering the question, and stared the man in the eyes. They stood like that for a long moment.

The man nodded. "Well, then. Guess I'll be going. I've got another airplane to build." He turned and walked toward the door.

Nick said, "Excuse me, sir?"

The man opened the door and looked back. "Yes?"

"Put a nice paint job on it this time, will you?"

With a grin and a nod, the man stepped out of the diner.

A week later, Nick mailed a package to the man filled with enough cash to do the job right, and it felt really good.

He pulled back the left wrist closure of his jacket. The hairless, un-tanned outline of his father's watch, worn constantly for so many years only to be smashed into junk in an airplane crash, brought thoughts of home and family.

He stared into the dreary mist and counted off the shafts of illuminated drizzle receding into the gloom. The fifth streetlight marked the turn onto his street. Laurie, Stephanie, and Brad were probably home. All he had to do was walk down there and try his best to re-enter their lives as a husband and father. It was time to get—

Faint ringing of a cell phone startled him. He looked around. The playground was as desolate as when he arrived. Then he realized it was his own, a new one with an unfamiliar ring, buried under layers of clothing. He managed to dig it out in time.

"You're a hard man to find these days," said the voice of James Dickson.

"Uh . . . yeah . . . it's a new number. How'd you get it?"

"Wasn't easy. I had to twist Harvey Sweet's arm."

Nick doubted that. Hotel would probably break Dickson in half for just touching him. "What can I do for you?"

A long pause made Nick think he'd been cut off, but Dickson finally said, "They promoted me to the Director's slot."

"Congratulations."

"And I convinced them we need you back."

If Nick hadn't been sitting down, he would have fallen on

his ass. "That's the most ridiculous thing I've ever heard. I'm still under investigation."

"Don't worry about that. Before you cut me off, just listen. Are you listening?"

"I thought you resigned."

"No need to after Nordstrom—it's a long story, but that's not why I called. Everyone agrees that while you went too far, the truth would have never been uncovered if you hadn't . . . well . . . been Nick Phillips. Anyone else would have given up and gone home."

Dickson's words seemed to hang in Nick's ear, resonating with the power of persuasion.

"You still with me, Nick?"

"I'm here."

"Don't you still want to do this job?"

"Yes, but . . ."

"What?"

Nick sat very still, unable to answer, until a peaceful calm settled on him like the fine mist falling from the low clouds hanging in the tree tops. "I really appreciate this, James, but I have to decline the offer."

"You what?"

"You'll do a great job, and with my blessings, by the way. Thanks for calling."

Nick flipped the phone closed and stuffed it in a jacket pocket. His butt was sore from the hard park bench, his ears and hands were cold, and his legs didn't want to work. He stood, shook off the chill, slipped the strap of his large duffel over his shoulder and picked up the two smaller bags.

Misty signposts of light illuminated the way. Nick reached the intersection with his street and counted down to the fourth mailbox in a line beside the glistening sidewalk, barely visible in the insipid light of gathering dusk. The Phillips family lived there.

Cold dread seemed to flow out of the fog, pass effortlessly through his jacket, and settle in his heart.

No lawyer had called. No stranger had appeared with papers in his hand, sign here, please. Phone conversations with the family, reserved, impersonal, had never strayed far from the question of legal proceedings, what's happening today, like news reports. The future had remained a mutually ignored topic, a blind corner just ahead.

He hiked to the curved brick pathway leading to his house and stopped to absorb the view, to enjoy this delicious moment of anticipation. At least for him.

Smoke, tinged with the fragrance of piñon, drifted up from the chimney and hung low in the heavy air. He and Laurie had spent their honeymoon in Santa Fe. The wood was widely used in fireplaces there. Limited supply made it impossible to get here, but every winter Laurie ordered processed logs infused with the scent. They burned slowly like incense, and the aroma reminded Nick of a past time with bright futures ahead, new love blossoming, and nothing beyond their reach.

The soft glow of yellow light from the front windows spread over the lawn in slanting rectangles. He stood motionless, his feet heavy, as if glued to the sidewalk.

Then a change, slowly at first, building, filled him with the overpowering sense of freedom from his past and the ghost of his father's death. He smiled. It's going to be okay. It has to be. He strode to the front door and rang the bell. After a few muffled shouts from the interior, the door opened.

Laurie stood in the doorway, large cooking spoon in hand, smudged apron protecting her work clothes. The tantalizing aroma of beef stroganoff wafted past Nick's nose. Laurie's face softened as she opened her mouth to speak. She paused, and tears slid down her cheeks. After a moment she stepped back from the door.

Nick entered the foyer, set down his two smaller bags and lowered the big duffel to the floor. Laurie closed the door, turned to her husband, and moved in close for a hug. She rested her head on his shoulder and whispered, "Nice to have you back."

They held each other for a long time.

The sound of footfalls on the upstairs hallway interrupted the moment. Nick and Laurie looked up as Stephanie and Brad appeared at the upper landing.

In the silence Nick could hear his own heart beating in counterpoint to the ticking of the grandfather clock.

Laurie stared at him with glistening eyes and said, "Hey you two, your father's home."

About the author:

Following graduation from the University of Washington in Seattle with Bachelor of Science degree in Psychology, Tosh entered the Air Force with the intention of serving a four-year commitment as a pilot before deciding what he really wanted to do with the remainder of his professional life. One ride in a jet trainer consigned that plan to the scrap heap.

Twenty years of flying jet fighters (including two combat tours) remain the highlight of his aviation career. Another twenty years as a commercial airline and corporate pilot and current enjoyment of sport aviation in light aircraft have embedded within him a passion for sharing with others his unique perspective of what it means to be an aviator.

Pilot Error is his first novel in a series that will interweave a life-long fascination with writing and thousands of flight hours in pursuit of one goal: to create stories that entertain and put readers up close and personal within his world of the cockpit.

Red Line continues the adventures of Nick Phillips as he hunts for the elusive clues to solve another case of airborne murder shrouded in a smokescreen of pilot error.

Connect with Tosh online:

http://toshmcintosh.com/

21361909R00228

Made in the USA
Columbia, SC
16 July 2018